TO DO
OR DIE

Mike Shepherd

ACE BOOKS, NEW YORK

THE BERKLEY PUBLISHING GROUP
Published by the Penguin Group
Penguin Group (USA) LLC
375 Hudson Street, New York, New York 10014

USA • Canada • UK • Ireland • Australia • New Zealand • India • South Africa • China

penguin.com

A Penguin Random House Company

TO DO OR DIE

An Ace Book / published by arrangement with the author

Ace Books are published by The Berkley Publishing Group.
ACE and the "A" design are trademarks of Penguin Group (USA) LLC.

For information, address: The Berkley Publishing Group,
a division of Penguin Group (USA) LLC,
375 Hudson Street, New York, New York 10014.

ISBN: 978-0-425-26252-8

PUBLISHING HISTORY
Ace mass-market edition / March 2014

PRINTED IN THE UNITED STATES OF AMERICA

10 9 8 7 6 5 4 3 2 1

Cover art by Scott Grimando.
Cover design by Diana Kolsky.

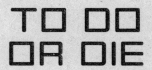

TO DO
OR DIE

ONE

IT WAS A port dive like any other humanity had built since some lucky bastard brought the first log *back* to shore. And the topic today was no different from when the Phoenicians sailed the middle sea—pirates and slavers.

Only this dive stood in the shadow of the New Birmingham bean pole. The shops and heavy-fabrication barns that gave a thirst to this bar's customers sent their goods and gear up the elevator to starships in the orbital yards of High Birmingham.

Today was different for Captain Terrence Tordon. Trouble to his enemies, Trouble to his friends, and more often than not, just plain Trouble, he'd come to accept the label for all it meant. Born, raised, and commissioned in the Society of Humanity Marine Corps, he had passed many a happy hour in dives such as this.

Today, however, was the first time he followed his wife into one.

Commander Uxbridge led them through the bar's door with its flashing beer ads. It was he who suggested the sun was below the yardarm and their business might better be completed in informal surroundings with a drink at hand. Uxbridge was finishing up his forty years with the Navy at the disappointing rank of commander, so no one would be surprised if he put in less than a full day.

Trouble and his wife, Ruth, followed because she had questions about the source of funds now flowing into Uxbridge's numbered Swiss accounts on Old Earth.

Officially, Uxbridge was the czar of Navy scrap on New Birmingham. He sold off surplus gear, battle-shattered hulks—and defeated Unity ships from the recent unpleasantness. They weren't supposed to be in working condition.

So why were said ships showing up in the hands of pirates and slavers? Trouble had had the unfortunate experience of accepting said slavers' hospitality not once but twice a few months ago.

It was a major source of embarrassment for a combat Marine.

Trouble glanced around the bar as he settled into a chair next to his wife. This early, the booths lining the walls and the tables scattered around the floor were empty except for two men in one booth. They seemed lost in haggling. Given the time and place, it likely had something to do with recreational pharmaceuticals.

The front entrance was balanced by a rear exit. The lights were up, throwing in harsh relief dilapidation that went unnoticed in the smoky shadows at night. Behind the bar, a mirror ran the length of the room. It exhibited dents and dings that proved it metal, not glass.

Trouble fingered the table. Painted to look like wood, it was heavy metal.

That's one way to avoid replacing the furniture every time the customers get rambunctious, he thought with a smile.

Then he went back to splitting his time between Ruth's conversation with Uxbridge and the rest of the bar. He was, after all, the guard dog here.

Ruth, a farmer born and bred, even looked the stereotype today. Her long black hair was braided into two pigtails, and she wore a calico dress with full skirt.

How much she looked the part of the contract farmer for a light cruiser, providing fresh fruit and vegetables from hydroponic gardens between the ship's ice armor and main hull, had been a hot topic between husband and wife that morning. However, since the Navy Department had only just started this crazy farm program, no one was too sure what the proper appearance of a ship-based farmer was.

Ruth had dressed as she wanted.

Trouble, who'd never lost a firefight, was getting used to losing to his bride.

Whatever her appearance, Ruth could talk farming. And she was talking Uxbridge's ears off about hydroponic agribusiness and her need for additional tubing, tubs, and pumps.

She was laying it on thick. So thick, no one would mistake her for an Alcohol, Drug, and Explosives Enforcement Agent.

Even a part-time one.

At least that was what Trouble and Ruth fervently hoped.

A waitress showed up. Ruth interrupted her monologue long enough to order a beer; both men followed her lead.

Trouble noted that the conversation between the two men in the booth seemed to be getting more heated, but they kept their words too low for him to make them out over Ruth's voice. He rested a hand on her knee under the table, hoping she'd take it for a request for a pause.

She brushed his hand off.

Did she really think he'd make a pass at her right now? Still, this was her show. Captain Umboto had made that clear as they left the *Patton* this morning.

Ruth leads; Trouble follows.

But Ruth, love, do you have any idea where we're going?

The drinks arrived. As Trouble reached for his, he noted that the booth's conversation was on pause as one of them answered a phone. Was there a twitch of a nod in their direction?

Uxbridge was seated with his back to the booth. Was he looking at Ruth, or beyond her to something in the mirror? Trouble started to turn, to check the mirror out, but Uxbridge was lifting his glass in some kind of informal toast.

Trouble raised his mug, glancing at Ruth, who was smiling as if she had good sense. The commander was smiling, too, kind of smugly.

Movement at the corner of his eye drew Trouble's attention.

"Honey, I think we got a problem," he muttered.

His bride ignored him . . . a habit developed since saying "I do."

She missed the pistols coming out across the room.

"Down," Trouble growled—and upended the table.

Their drinks went flying, adding little to the heavy aroma of yesterday's brew, smoke, sweat, and more exotic odors.

"What are you doing?" Ruth screeched, and made to follow Commander Uxbridge as he headed for the back door.

Trouble kicked the chair out from under Ruth, unbalancing her enough that he could pull her down beside him—just as two rounds from across the room filled the air where her head had been.

"Huh?" Ruth came out of her fixation on Uxbridge to glance around. "What's going on?"

"A friendly exchange of joy dust for cash seems to have gone wrong," Trouble offered as he edged his head above the upended table and ducked fast as the two people across the room squeezed off more incoming in his general direction.

"Assuming it was what it looked like, and not cover for your friend's withdrawal."

Ruth's automatic was out of hiding from its rather nice place that Trouble enjoyed roaming in quieter times. Set for sleepy darts, she squeezed off two rounds at Uxbridge as he disappeared out the back door.

"Darn," she muttered as she only added more chips to the bar's battered motif.

Trouble edged his own service automatic around the tabletop and sent a few of Colt-Pfizer's best toward the erstwhile entrepreneur and client. He glanced around for the bartender, but she had made herself scarce.

To call the local constabulary?

Not likely. Trouble had noted a distinct lack of New Birmingham's uniformed finest as he and Ruth approached the "friendly watering hole" the commander had suggested.

Trouble ducked as another couple of rounds shoved the table against his shoulder and showered plaster from the wall above him. He tapped his commlink.

"Gunny, I could use some help here. Where are you?"

The pause that followed was decidedly longer than Trouble expected.

"Stuck in traffic, sir," finally came back.

Marine NCOs are people of few words—but they pack a lot of meaning into what they do say, just as the Corps packed a lot of power into its chosen few. What Trouble heard was straight information underlain with rock-solid determination, overlain with more embarrassment than he believed possible for a Gunnery Sergeant.

"You wouldn't believe the traffic here, sir."

Trouble would. Raised by the Corps at bases around the rim of human space, this was his first venture deep into the overpopulated heart of humanity. From orbit, New Birmingham was one glowing orb, whether in daylight or darkness.

"We're fifteen blocks from you, sir. Should I get the crew moving on foot?"

The image of four combat-loaded Marines double-timing through this industrial area, even in the camouflage they'd dummied up for today, made Trouble cringe worse than the next burst from across the room.

He glanced around the lower corner of the table.

The two were running—one for the front door, the other for the back.

"They're bugging out," he shouted to Ruth. He snapped off a three-round burst at the back of the one headed for the front door. Ruth tried for the other.

Both got solid hits.

And the rounds just stuck there like darts on a dartboard.

"Body armor," Trouble spat as he stood, dusting plaster from his one set of civilian clothes. But he was talking to himself.

Ruth was up and headed for the back door.

Trouble caught her elbow and swung her back around. "You're not sticking your pretty head out that door until all concerned have had a few minutes to reflect upon their evil ways."

"But Uxbridge is getting away."

"He's gotten away, Ruth. Diamonds to donuts, there was a car waiting for him out there. And *his* driver knows how to get around this damnable local traffic. All that's out there now is a buddy of our gun-toting trader from across the room."

Trouble waved at the now-vacant table.

"Oh! Yeah, I guess that's how I'd do it." Ruth looked around, probably taking in the pub's decor for the first time.

Imitation wood paneled the walls in dark swirls. Blinking signs for local brews and sports teams paled in the full light of day. *Now* the bartender wandered out from the bathroom.

She noted the situation with an unconcerned eye and asked if they wanted fresh drinks. Trouble declined, righted the table and chairs, settled their tab, and led Ruth cautiously out the front door.

A half dozen people in working overalls passed them going

in. It was as if an OPEN FOR BUSINESS sign had been turned on. A dozen more in pairs and trios followed.

A moment later, a cab drove up.

Gunny piled out to report as the other three Marines took point, covering 360 degrees around them.

The idea was for them to be inconspicuous today, since New Birmingham had its own police force . . . however invisible . . . and strong gun-control laws . . . that now seemed less than perfect in their application.

The Marines' body armor was covered by their new, multicolored sweat suits, making them look for all the world like children's crew-cut, hard-eyed teddy bears. Their guns were hidden in bags, making them only slightly less conspicuous.

"Sorry about the delay, sir. Next time I do this, we use one of our own drivers."

"I agree, Gunny. Let's get out of here."

The cabby had no trouble delivering them quickly to the space elevator. An hour later, they were up the bean pole and reporting to Captain Umboto in her day cabin on the *Patton*.

"He got away, Izzy," Ruth blurted out.

Trouble gritted his teeth at his wife's familiarity. He'd spent much of his two months of married bliss trying to introduce Ruth to the Navy Way.

He hadn't been all that successful.

She had finally acquired the ability to identify rates and rank. The wardroom still chuckled at Ruth's initial effort.

Standing in line at the Navy exchange at High Woolamurra, Ruth had proudly told Trouble, "That one's a captain, 'cause he has four stripes. But what's five stripes?"

"Five stripes?" Trouble asked, puzzled as he followed Ruth's gaze . . . to two chiefs. One, with over sixteen years in the Navy, sported four gold hash marks. The other, with twenty-plus years, had five.

Trouble spent the rest of the wait in line trying to stop laughing as he explained the difference between officer rank stripes, that encircled the sleeve, and enlisted service hash marks that angled up to cover part of the sleeve. Undaunted, Ruth shared with the entire wardroom over supper that night how she'd made her latest discovery.

Half of the officers had almost laughed up their chow.

The skipper surprised him; she'd nodded understandingly at Ruth. "Learning all the secret handshakes of this bunch is a bitch," she muttered encouragingly.

The skipper surprised Trouble again today. She just nodded at the announcement that the bird had flown the nest and changed the subject. "Better get the farm ready for fluctuating gravity, Ruth. We're clearing the pier in two hours."

"Orders, Skipper?" Trouble asked.

"The yard at Wardhaven finally thinks they've figured out the spaghetti that passes for wiring in our main system. We've got a week's reduced availability there."

Trouble and Ruth both knew the truth behind those words. The *Patton* was one of many hasty war conversions from merchant vessel to light cruiser. The yards had rushed the ships into commission, paying attention only to what would make them fit to fight . . . and wasting little time on minor things like system standardization.

Thanks to that haste, the *Patton* had damn near ended up a permanent fixture at the end of a pier. Trouble wouldn't have minded that, except he and Ruth were in slavers' hands about then, growing drugs on a stinking, hot planet named Riddle.

The work was bad; the supervision was worse.

Slave drivers stalked around with whips in their hands and rape on their minds.

Ruth and he had risked their necks to help an invasion fleet show up.

But those were yesterday's problems. Today, the *Patton* was in the best shape she'd ever been, and the skipper had a tiger grin on her face.

The call to Wardhaven came from the people who made planets shake.

When they talked, people died.

Hopefully, it wouldn't be anyone Trouble knew personally. With a salute and a shrug, the Marine officer went to prepare his detachment to get underway.

TWO

A WEEK LATER, Ruth galloped up to the captain's gig. Trouble was waiting for her, his face the mask it became when he was busy being Marine. Catching her breath, Ruth glanced around. Good, Izzy wasn't there yet.

She flashed her husband a proud grin, which he ignored as he always did when he was in Marine mode. Still, she had a right to be proud.

She'd heard Trouble grouse, and other naval officers, too, that every civilian considered themselves a brevet admiral . . . and acted accordingly. Ruth was doing her darnedest to be their obedient servant . . . and act accordingly. Although it was none too easy to meet their expectations. Take this situation, for example.

All Ruth's life, she'd been taught to defer to her betters, to let her elders enter a room first and take their preferred seat before she and the other kids started squabbling over who got what was left.

Always, age before beauty.

But not now, not the Navy Way, as her husband had done his best to make clear. Here, the junior entered a vehicle like the captain's gig first and God help her if she didn't guess what seat the senior wanted and avoid taking it.

"It's madness," she insisted.

"No," her new husband would remind her, "it is neither the right way nor the wrong way. It is the Navy Way."

Movement caught Ruth's eye. Izzy and the new exec were entering the docking bay. She flashed Trouble a quick grin and entered the captain's gig first. Taking the measure of the eight seats available to her, she picked a middle one on the right. That left seven free for the three officers to squabble over.

Her husband entered right behind her, took the seat across from her and began belting himself in. The XO entered, took a quick sidestep, and let Izzy pick her seat.

Smart man, he'd go far in any Navy Ruth ran. She shrugged internally, doubting any Navy operated that way.

Izzy settled down in the seat ahead of Ruth. "How's it going, Ruth?" the captain asked as her hands automatically belted herself in.

Ruth was still trying to figure out the five-point harness the Navy used and didn't look up until she heard her name. "Oh fine, Izzy," Ruth said and watched both Trouble and the exec blink at the familiarity.

Well, darn it, I'm a civilian. There have to be a few advantages to that disability, Ruth did not say.

"How are the farmhands working out?" Izzy asked, settling back in her seat, all harnessed in.

Ruth was still struggling. Trouble popped his one-point release and reached over to help. Another time, his hands' feathery touch on her breasts and inner thighs would have been a turn-on. Today, it just added to her frustration as he inserted tab A into slot B with an ease that eluded her.

Then again, he was always good at getting his tab A into her slot B. Trying not to blush, Ruth concentrated on Izzy and let her husband strap her in.

"They're catching on fine," Ruth assured Izzy. "Chief Yellin and Petty Officer Dora grew up on farms. They're fast learners, and they pass it along to the rest very quickly."

Actually, *retired* chief and petty officer, but you don't tell captains what they already knew. At least that was what Trouble insisted.

"You've been eating our produce for the last week," Ruth pointed out.

"I know. I signed the pay chit before we docked. I mean the other hands."

Trouble flashed Ruth just a hair of a raised eyebrow. He'd warned her that nothing happened aboard ship without the captain's knowing.

"We were expanding the tanks," Ruth began as methodically as she could while the gig went zero gee and pulled away from the *Patton*. "We were back at High Woolamurra station, and where I grew up, a farm wasn't a farm without the farmer's wife."

"So you hired on Chief Yellin's wife," Izzy finished.

Ruth nodded.

"And kids?" the XO asked.

"No, sir," Ruth shot back. "They're all grown and on their own."

"Although if this experiment of yours works out," Izzy went on, quoting almost verbatim from what Ruth was thinking, "the youngsters on your farm will want to bring along their wives, and they will want to have kids."

"I'm housing them in the farm area, between the ice armor and the main hull, and I'm paying for their rations, same as any other of my contract labor force."

"And if we have to fight?" the XO led on.

"The ex-crewmembers will report to their battle stations. Chief Yellin has identified a very safe area near the ship's core for me *and* the wives to report to."

The exec turned to Izzy for The Word. If Ruth's eyes weren't deceiving her, the skipper was sporting a sliver of a grin.

"Someone with too much time and too little brains back at the Navy Department decided it was cheaper to lose a ship or two rather than keep full crews aboard in peacetime," Izzy said. "Some other dunderhead decided the planet-bound farmers were charging too much to provide certified bug- and fungus-free fresh fruits and vegetables for the ships. I figured I could combine both directives and give the *Patton* a farmful of willing hands only too ready to down tools and race back to battle stations."

Izzy stroked her chin as entry gees built up. "Should have realized I wasn't the only one with an imagination. Whose idea was it, yours or Chief Yellin's?"

"Mine," Ruth said.

One thing she'd learned fast from Trouble . . . and his troubles . . . was that when higher-ups asked who was responsible, the only answer was the senior officer present.

At the farm, that was Ruth.

Izzy's grin was pulled down at the ends. Ruth hoped it was by the extra gees they were under. "Hope you're just as creative for what we're getting into."

After that, the captain lapsed into thoughtful silence. The others followed suit.

Ruth raised an eyebrow to Trouble. *What* are *we getting into?*

His almost imperceptible nod added nothing to her growing sense of apprehension. *What kind of nut farm have I signed on with?*

Until a few months ago, Ruth had never been off Hurtford Corner, the planet of her birth. Since being drugged and dragged into the filthy hole of a slave ship, she was up to five planets now . . . four in the last month alone.

It was nice seeing new places with Trouble's arm comfortably around her. How pleasant Wardhaven could be would have to wait for a time when Trouble wasn't being so darn Marine.

Once the gig landed, a government limo was waiting for them. Ruth quickly entered and took a jump seat, Trouble right beside her. A civilian had attached himself to their group sometime during the walk from gig to limo. Izzy actually broke into a wide smile at the sight of him and made a point of entering ahead of him.

"Woman, I'm a civilian now."

"And a deputy minister, if I'm not mistaken," Izzy shot back. "This is your get about, isn't it?"

"Rita refuses to have anyone assigned a limo. Good woman. Trying to be as tight a skinflint on the nonessentials as her husband would want."

"How is she?"

"More pregnant every day. And the happiest woman on ten planets since her husband made it back." The civilian reached a hand across to Ruth's husband. "Trouble, isn't it? I see you've got your captain's bars back."

"Yes, Captain Anderson," Trouble answered quickly.

And Ruth did a quick reassessment. The old guy was retired Navy. That raised his stature in the strange game these folks played. If this was *the* Captain Andy, skipper of the 97th Defense Brigade in the recent war, he was darn near a god to Izzy and Trouble.

"And this must be your bride," the old fellow beamed.

Ruth beamed back, unsure if she should nod her head,

offer her hand, try to curtsy where she was seated, or salute. Flustered, she just sat there and blushed.

"I read the report on what you and your husband did on Riddle," Captain Anderson continued. "A fine bit of action. Well done. Very well done."

Ruth might be new to the Navy, but she knew that to be the highest praise available to these tight-lipped, unexpressive people. Now she was blushing red-hot, but for a civilian in the presence of a god of war, it seemed like the best response.

"What are we headed for this time out?" Izzy asked.

"I have no idea. The spy has been keeping busy and offering no tidbits for the rest of us to gnaw on. I, myself, have been fully occupied trying to restore one lost bridegroom to the side of his lady-in-waiting. Shall we just go along, my feline friend, and enjoy the ride?"

"This tiger says why bloody not," Izzy said.

The rest of the drive was quiet enough to give Ruth plenty of time to wonder what a farm girl was doing among the likes of these hardheaded fighters. When she'd signed herself up to be Izzy's part-time ADEE Agent, she'd figured it for a minor thing.

Apparently, there was a lot more to saying "Yes" to the likes of Trouble and Izzy than she'd ever dreamed of.

Their destination was an imposing building of gray stone pierced by row upon row of windows. The limo drove into a basement garage and dropped them off next to an elevator, which disgorged them onto a thickly carpeted, high-ceilinged hallway, lined at long intervals by dark, wooden doors.

This is definitely not the poor side of town.

The empty conference room that Captain Anderson led them to smelled of wax and wood. A thick slab off a huge tree dominated the center of the room. Trouble took Ruth's elbow and edged her toward one of the high-backed wooden chairs lining the wall. Izzy and Andy seated themselves at the table. Ruth tried not to look like she was gawking as she surveyed the room.

Two chandeliers provided a gentle light. The walls were a rouge-and-cream paper, marred by empty hangers. Ruth would have bet paintings once hung there. Why keep the empty hangers?

She doubted it was an accident.

Nothing in the room spoke of carelessness to detail. Except the hangers . . . and the two large screens at the front and back of the room. They must be recent additions; their cables were neat but showed in stark, modern contrast to the carefully contrived ancient elegance of the rest of the room.

Interesting, very interesting. Turning to Trouble, she opened her mouth . . . and was immediately shushed by a curt shake of his head.

She followed his gaze to an opening door. Quickly, the room filled with purposeful people, talking quietly among themselves, juggling armfuls of readers, looking for seats. Several seemed to know her husband.

One gorgeous blonde flashed him a brilliant smile. "How's it going?" she gushed.

"Great," Ruth answered Trudy Seyd.

They'd met on Riddle. Tru had not only been Ruth's bridesmaid, but had gotten the planet's records center back up so that it could issue Trouble and Ruth a marriage license.

"What are *we* up to?" she shot back.

Tru's grin got even bigger. "Can't spoil the boss's announcement, but I think Trouble here is gonna love it."

The Marine beside Ruth groaned. "They don't pay me enough for what you get me into."

"Hey, you never would have met Ruth except for the last mess I got you into," Tru protested, which wasn't exactly correct but was close enough not to argue over.

"Oops, here comes the boss." Tru turned to take a place near the head of the table.

The announcement was ambiguous since three entered the room.

A rotund man in a rumpled white suit easily could have deserved the title; clearly he was used to dominating any room he entered.

Then Ruth caught a hint of the steel in the other man's eyes. Back ramrod straight, the taller man took the room in with a commanding glance, nodded at whatever the other was saying, then turned a loving smile to the woman that seemed surgically joined to him at the elbow.

The woman was clearly pregnant. The smile she shared

with the man was warm enough to make comfortable any long winter night.

Ruth remembered such glances between Ma and Pa, and sighed in hope that she and Trouble might one day share the same.

Then the woman spared a quick, appraising glance for the room, and Ruth ditched her first impression. The steely eyes and the assessing look were a startling contrast to the loving wife.

"Everyone is here," the woman announced, taking the chair at the head of the table. The men moved smoothly to fill the empty seats at either side of her.

"Hopefully, this is the last ministerial meeting I'll be chairing, now that my long-lost husband has wandered back from where*ever* it was he strayed off to."

That drew a chuckle from the room.

"Captain Umboto, I'm glad you could make it. I see you've brought your key staff." Which came as another shock to Ruth, piled so quickly upon the last one.

Since when was I promoted to key staff?

Then the woman turned to the big man. "Well, Mr. Spy, what have you and yours been up to?"

THREE

CAPTAIN IZZY UMBOTO leaned forward in her seat, hungry for action, for anything to sink her teeth into. As far as she was concerned, most meetings were a waste of time. Not with this bunch.

While the minions around the walls would have readers overstuffed with the raw feed, the discussion at the head of the table would be lean, mean, and with a bit of luck, something worth fighting for.

Andy patted her hand gently. "Down, tiger. Overeager people in our trade get the wrong people killed." Under the Buddha-like gaze of her old master, the captain of the cruiser *Patton* leaned back in her chair, took a deep breath, and waited.

Fortunately, the spy did not make her wait long. "My technicians have been sifting through the scraps you enthusiastic field folks left us on Riddle. Fortunately, it was enough. Although I suspect it does not take a genius for intelligence analysis to glean the essentials from the debris." The spy fixed Izzy with wide, inviting eyes, tempting her into his realm.

"The station above Riddle was too small and its capacity too limited to maintain a fleet of pirate cruisers," Izzy said quickly. "It lacked the yards to refurbish the pirated ships or to file the serial numbers off them so that they could appear again on regular shipping lanes." Izzy continued with growing confidence and a touch of disappointment.

It had felt good to grab a space station, capture three pirate raiders and bring down a planetary government of drug lords and slavers. Still, in the back of her mind, even then she'd known the fish was too small for the damage it did.

She needed to look further for the bastards that gave her niece Franny the drugs that killed her.

Okay, spy, point me at something I can blow up.

"A very accurate assessment," the spy said, rewarding her with a smile, a most strange rearrangement of his face. "We winged the buggers, but we missed the heart."

"So where is the bankroll for those bastards?" said the other man. Izzy liked the sound of the question. She studied the man for a moment, then blinked in surprise.

This was Colonel Ray Longknife, the man who killed Unity's President Urm and ended the war. But in all the videos, he hobbled around with a cane or two, the results of a chunk of iron her brigade had put up his backside.

Izzy frowned her own question at Andy.

"A long story," he whispered back. "Later."

"A good question," the spy answered. "And one that gets straight to the heart of matters like these. In military operations, you follow the flow of energy and munitions. In matters like these, you follow the money, and it leads you to the source."

"And?" the woman cut in.

"We lost the trail," the spy said bluntly. "Which says something in and of itself. Only old money can hide that well. Old money from Earth. Fortunately, while money can hide, what it does often leaves telltales behind. For example, Colonel Longknife, we have taken apart the little present left behind in the *Second Chance*'s main network. A delightful bit of code, created by a sterling programming boutique back on Old Earth."

The colonel looked very interested in the spy's work.

"They serve a very select clientele, very discreet. Only recently has their conscience been pricked about the use certain of their customers have put their code to in the recent war. But they have come forward and made a clean confession of it."

Why did Izzy doubt that guilt and absolution had anything to do with this sudden turn of affairs? She grinned, for once enjoying the chase.

"There is also the recent bit of luck that Mrs. Tordon gave us, putting the fear of God in her Commander Uxbridge and allowing him to take flight."

Izzy swiveled in her chair to observe the spy's high praise turn Ruth beet red. Still, she did a decent imitation of the

Marine seated next to her, saying not a word to deflect the kudos or correct the spy's misconception . . . if indeed he did not already know she had meant to bag the commander that day.

"Uxbridge's sudden withdrawal of all funds in certain numbered Swiss bank accounts allowed us to trace not only where he went, but also where the funds came from."

"Where does the trail lead?" The woman leading the meeting rushed the spy; a glance her husband's way made it clear she had better uses for her time.

"Forward, to a certain planet misnamed Savannah. While we on Wardhaven were successful sending our Unity thugs and politicos packing, their President Milassi managed to hang on, pointing to an election he won before Unity took over five years back. He has to face elections in a few months. Interest in the outcome of those elections goes far beyond Savannah."

"Savannah was settled before Wardhaven," Colonel Ray Longknife mused. "Industrialized from the get-go. I never had to fight them. Glad of that. Anything else we need to know about Savannah?"

"The Humanity ambassador to Savannah has requested additional Marines to bolster his small guard. Milassi seems to be having trouble maintaining order. The Senate also has a fact-finding committee due there soon. They want a cruiser in orbit for their stay."

The spy turned to Izzy. "You will shortly receive orders to the Savannah system."

"Nice of you to tell me about them. Did that trail you're sniffing after lead anywhere else?"

"Yes. Forward the trail led to Savannah. Backward, and not as a total surprise, it led to this gentleman."

The screen behind the spy came alive as Tru Seyd tapped her reader right on cue. A face smiled out at them blandly, the kind of pictures that the business section of papers featured under the headers of "promoted" or "heading the mega-mergered stellar corporation."

Izzy found such pictures lacking in conviction.

This one was no exception. If the years had lined that face, given it any wisdom or character, computer processing of the negative or surgery on the original had removed any evidence.

The face was bland, blank, uninformative.

Still, Izzy memorized it, as she might the electromagnetic fingerprint of a new enemy's flagship. This was the target. This empty face had retailed the drugs that killed Franny and too many others.

Deep within Izzy a question formed. *Why would anyone as outwardly clean and straight as this man mess with poison?*

Izzy waved off the question; the odds of her getting an answer were not worth betting on. Then again, the odds of her getting such a man in her gun sights were pretty slim, too.

If it came, Izzy didn't want to miss.

"Mr. Henry Smythe-Peterwald's money was mature when old money was just being minted. His family has been buying and selling politicians since before graft had a bad name." The spy examined his notes. "I believe one or two popes are in his direct lineage, though that was before the pope gave up his army.

"The family's money went from obscene to merely plentiful until a few generations back. Henry's grandfather got in on the ground floor of the interstellar net. He got a lock on the hardware and managed to buy up all the software. He also invested quite heavily in several planets just opening up."

"Was Savannah one of them?" Izzy asked.

"Yes."

Izzy made a gun with her finger. "Bang," she said to the picture.

"Were it only that easy," the spy fairly moaned. "Money and power build walls that keep investigators out more thoroughly than prisons keep ordinary people in. The trap that captures Mr. Peterwald must be carefully baited and cautiously sprung."

"He wouldn't be going to Savannah anytime soon?" Izzy asked.

"He has never set foot off Earth in his life. No one in his family has."

Izzy had never even seen Old Earth.

She sighed. Sailors didn't get to pick their battles. They fought where and when they were told. She did have orders to take the *Patton* to Savannah and offer all assistance. She might just have a chance to bring some well-deserved pain and discomfort into Mr. Peterwald's life.

Others, way above her pay grade, would be the ones to bring down such a gold-encrusted scumbag as little Henry there.

FOUR

HENRY SMYTHE-PETERWALD X paced his father's room. Twenty paces took him to the windows that looked out over a thousand pristine acres of woodlands.

The old man had nurtured the waste just to impress lesser beings. Henry never knew his father to actually walk among those trees. In his youth, Henry had tried to hide there, to find some special place that was his alone.

Father's guards always found him.

Today, Henry ignored the view and whirled to cover the twenty paces back to the white wall, bare except for the myriad of medical gear that kept the old man alive.

His father had bragged, "I will live forever. I'm buying the rejuvenation treatments other people are dying for."

The old man would laugh at his joke, enjoying it immensely.

"You stupid, old bastard," Henry snarled. "You warned me never to trust a beta version. 'Wait until the second or third upgrade to risk your own system to the new damn code.' But you had to have the first rejuv the labs came up with. Now your brain has turned to snot?"

Remembering what his father could not, Henry laughed. He laughed in the old man's face.

It was safe to laugh now.

The old man couldn't call his guards.

The eyes that had made Henry cringe now stared blankly at the ceiling, blinking rarely. Breath flowed in and out as the ventilator pushed and pulled. The body could easily pass for a healthy thirty-year-old's, a good twenty years younger than Henry.

"Now live with what it's got you, old fool," the son snarled at the blank face.

The beeps and weaving patterns on the monitors quickened. Henry stepped away from the bed, put several paces between him and his father before the nurse passed through the self-opening door.

"Mr. Peterwald, your father seems to be having a distress episode," the woman said as she hurried to the bed.

"I'll leave him to you," Henry said, avoiding even a glance at the nurse. Ms. Upton was probably the ugliest woman to pass the Nursing Boards in the last fifty years. Several others on his father's support team rivaled her for that accolade, but Upton brought a second factor to her credit.

Her voice made stripping gears sound melodic.

His father had always kept the beautiful and graceful at his beck and call. Now, if the old man actually could hear, could understand what was going on around him, he'd be hating every moment of his immortality.

Served the bastard right.

Henry smiled as he left the room.

An elevator took him down to his office area. The wide space it disgorged him into presented a view of plants, trees, and a waterfall.

Hidden behind the façade, dozens of people in this room labored to fulfill his slightest whim.

More waited patiently, hopefully, for him to permit them a moment of his time.

He was distracted by none of them as he walked to his office. A word from him, and the waterfall would have disappeared, giving him a view to his primary secretary.

Henry walked, breathing the aroma of the woods, listening to the chirp of birds. Almost, he was in his hiding place, his special place.

Only now, no guards would dare disturb him. Today, no father could yank him in to put on a senseless display for lesser petitioners.

Someday, he might go back to the woods, the real woods, to see what his secret place had become. Not today.

Not now. There were things to do. Grandfather had remade the family fortune. Father had added to it, reaching new heights until presidents and prime ministers sweated as waiting petitioners in this very room.

Now that Henry had finished paying off the courts and been formally appointed the old man's guardian and master of the family fortune, Henry would show him who was the better.

But he'd have to do it quickly, before the old man's brain was totally mush.

The drug money had offered him a quick way to the heart of Unity. Grandma Smythe may have razored out the bootleggers from the family tree but that didn't mean Henry was ignorant of the many ways the family made its fortune.

The Unity propagandists were right. Henry and other powerful men *were* jacking up the price for finished goods, and offering cutthroat prices for the raw materials the outer rim could offer for payment.

Why shouldn't the rim send Earth the drugs its teeming masses demanded for their distraction?

It had been an easy alliance for Henry. He had the ships; he knew which of his captains weren't obsessive about following every little law. The profits hadn't been all that great. Unity middlemen and the skippers had robbed Henry blind.

But he'd gotten the connections he needed with President Urm.

And Urm had happily promised Henry a war, with all its chances for war profiteering. And when it was done, he'd be in the prefect position to buy up losers for pennies on the dollar.

Yes, the war could have doubled or even tripled the family's fortune. If there was a brain cell left in the old man, he'd have had to admit that his son had beat both him and Granddad.

But the war ended too soon.

"Is Whitebred waiting?"

"Yes, Mr. Peterwald," his secretary immediately answered.

"How long has he been waiting?"

"Two days, Mr. Peterwald."

"Good. Send him in. And, Milly, change my office to one most intimidating for his personality profile."

"Yes, Mr. Peterwald." There was a brief pause. "Done, Mr. Peterwald."

Around Henry, the room wavered, then solidified. Patterned after the Hall of Mirrors at Versailles, this was one routine you couldn't download from every site on the Web. Just keeping the mirrors synchronized took more computing power than a large city.

Henry loved it. He relished what happened to others when he surrounded himself with these ancient trappings of power.

Yes, it would be fun working Whitebred over in the Hall of Mirrors.

A short, dark-haired man entered.

He wore the buttonless gray suit that was *de rigueur* this month for high-powered business executives. Molded into the shoulders and arms was probably enough computing power to work a small starship.

In Henry's view, numbers appeared beside Whitebred, showing his respiration, heartbeat, and blood pressure, probably stripped right off his own coat's confidential medical monitors. When Whitebred opened his mouth, Henry would get an immediate stress analysis, matched against Whitebred's nominal stress in his last couple of corporate meetings.

Henry kept such data on file for all his people. Good information on your subject made meetings like this easy.

He checked the make and model of Whitebred's own office software and suppressed a snort. Henry would know everything about Whitebred. He, in turn, would know nothing about Henry, or be in worse shape still if the poor man actually trusted the readouts that his own system fed him about Henry.

Yes, Henry would enjoy this meeting.

"Thank you for seeing me, Mr. Peterwald," the supplicant said.

"Hope I didn't keep you waiting too long," Henry lied.

"No, no sir. No wait at all," the man lied in return.

"Are you enjoying your work with us?"

"Yes, very much," he lied again. "I think I have a lot to offer the corporation." That was not a lie, at least as Whitebred saw it.

"Well, we have to look out for our returning war heroes."

The man winced visibly.

"I liked your idea. The way you were running that fleet, you could have ended the war in a day."

The man preened.

Henry abstained from pointing out that his bottom line was

predicated on the war's going for another six months. Whitebred did not have permission to end the war so suddenly. Then
again, his actions hadn't mattered one whit.

"I really could have if those mutineers hadn't ruined
everything."

"Apparently, yours weren't the only mutinous hands around.
It was one of his own men that killed Urm." *And ruined all my
profitable plans.*

"Yes," Whitebred hissed.

"I understand that you were able to leave a bit of a present
behind for your mutineers."

"Yes, Mr. Peterwald."

"Well, I have a surprise for you. That Colonel Longknife
who killed Urm also bought your cruiser off the scrap heap.
Even hired what was left of its crew, most of your mutineers,
I understand."

"Have they attempted a jump?" The man was hardly
breathing.

"As I understand it, Longknife, Abeeb, and the Marine
captain went tooling off to a meeting several jumps from
Wardhaven. Never got there," Henry announced dolefully.

Whitebred beamed from ear to ear.

"Yes, I think you have taken care of all our problem people." Henry chuckled.

The other man laughed out loud.

This was going rather pleasantly. The man was Henry's
kind of fellow.

"How would you like to be an admiral again?"

"I don't think the Navy would have me, Mr. Peterwald.
But, if you can arrange it, sir, and that's where you want me,
I'm your man," he quickly corrected what another man might
mistake for a rejection.

Henry smiled his understanding.

"No. There's nothing in the Humanity Navy that interests
me. However, Savannah is in need of a new fleet commander.
The station there is doing double duty for me. The Navy shores
up a government I find very convenient, and its yards will
work on ships other places are squeamish about handling, if
you know what I mean," Henry said with a raised eyebrow.

"Definitely, sir," Whitebred said, no question even hinted at.

"Good. I want a man there in charge of all that. President Milassi of Savannah owes me several favors already. What with an election coming up, Milassi will want to owe me many more."

Henry snickered at the malleability of politicians.

Whitebred joined him in the laugh.

"Having my own man on the scene is just what I need. You'll command not only the ships and yards but several battalions of Marines. Think you can handle that?"

Whitebred had the good sense to say nothing at this reference to his recent inability to command his own fleet.

"I might add, that unlike the fools you had to put up with in the war, most of these officers know where their money comes from. The real money, not that pittance they draw from Savannah."

With it clear that all the important officers were in Henry's pocket, Whitebred leaned back in his chair. "When do you want me to start?"

"Right now would be good. I want to update you on the history of Savannah. Not the crap the media would feed you."

Henry stood, walked around his desk, and put an arm around Whitebred's shoulders as the man scrambled to his feet. "My grandfather started that colony. I think of it like a plantation that's been in the family for generations. Can't let it be tossed around like a ball among strangers, can we?"

"No, Mr. Peterwald, we can't let that happen."

"Good, how would you like to do dinner?"

Henry beamed happily as the man nodded.

"We can talk more over food. Milly, have security scrounge up my son from wherever he's hiding. It will be an education for him to hear how the family runs things."

FIVE

WHERE RUTH GREW up, they had words for how she felt: useless as tits on a boar hog. Worthless as a fifth wheel.

None of those were as useless as an officer's wife while he was busy moving his detachment. Trouble was prowling around his green-clad troops, talking with his Gunny, busy as a man could be . . . and impervious to Ruth's presence.

Older Marine officer wives had warned Ruth about this. She understood it . . . in her head. But living through it . . . that was another thing entirely.

Maybe she should have stayed on the *Patton*, or come down on another shuttle.

But she had work of her own to do.

And it would help if she was introduced to the embassy staff by Trouble so that they would connect her with him.

After all, if she got in trouble and had to run for the safety of the legation, it would help if the Marine at the embassy gate knew to let the captain's woman in.

And Ruth was busy getting herself in trouble.

Or at least not doing what a simple space-based farmer or officer's wife should do.

Izzy and Trouble covered this during the time the *Patton* was in transit.

Those idiots back on Riddle had hardly known how to grow the drug plants. Surely, they hadn't done the bioengineering that turned common Earth-based plants into forget-the-world dust. No, someone else had created the stuff.

Ruth's job was to find that someone and do something about them.

Right! Easy! Just land on a strange planet and wander around asking any stranger, "You know where the illegal-drug research station is?"

I wouldn't survive a day.

Izzy and Trouble had looked at her dumbly, and said, "That sounds like a plan," and left her to stew over a real one.

As Trouble got his Marines and their duffel bags loaded aboard a bus sent by the embassy for his company, Ruth rented a car from a counter in the spaceport.

Now she understood why Izzy had been so insistent that Ruth get a credit card with her corporate name on it.

Pa never borrowed anything. If he and Ma couldn't pay for it, they went without.

Here, Ruth needed borrowed wheels, and no one rented without a credit card for collateral. The Navy wasn't the only place that took some getting used to.

Ruth completed her rental agreement and pulled her tiny car up behind the bus to wait. The fellow who rented her the car had assured her that its map screen would show her how to get anywhere in town.

Yeah, right. Ruth would follow the bus.

While she waited for Trouble to get moving, she asked the computer to show her the best way to the Society of Humanity Embassy.

The computer told her there was no embassy, "Glorious Unity forces being at war with Earth's running dogs."

Someone hadn't updated their database.

Trouble seemed in no hurry, so Ruth expanded her research. "Where's the illegal-drug research center?"

"I know of no such business," came back at her.

"Chemical research center?" she tried.

"I know of no . . ."

"Farm or plant research center?"

"I know of . . ."

"What do you know?" Ruth snapped in exasperation.

That was a mistake. The computer began an unstoppable exposition on all the bars and bordellos in town, some with quite graphic descriptions of the services offered.

And it wouldn't shut off. Ruth tried punching buttons. If anything, it got louder.

"Hey, woman, want your windows washed?" a young voice piped.

"What?" Ruth asked, glancing around for the voice's source.

"Want your windows washed? They're dirty."

"What? Where are you? I can't hear you very well. This thing won't cut off."

In answer to her first question, a squeegee started waving outside the passenger side of the car.

Ruth rolled the window down.

The squeegee reached in and rapped the dashboard. "Shut up, you machine mouth," the young voice snapped.

The silence was delicious.

"That's better. Woman, you want your windows washed? I do a good job. Only one dinar."

Ruth checked her purse. "I don't have any Savannah money yet."

A face, very dirty and horribly thin rose on tiptoes to smile at her from the passenger window. "That's fine. I can do your windows for one Earth dollar."

Ruth wasn't sure what the exchange rate was, but she was pretty positive it wasn't one for one. She glanced at her windows. They were clean.

She studied the kid; his hopeful smile was hard to deny. Ruth held up an Earth quarter.

"You drive a hard bargain, woman, but you win." And the kid quickly went to work smearing her front windows.

"Where you want to go?" the kid asked as he came around to her side of the car, giving Ruth her first good look at him.

The rest of the boy was as thin as the face had promised. He looked maybe six or eight, but allowing for a tough street life, he might be twelve. His clothes were dirty, torn, and way too big for him. What passed for shoes were held together by string with used newspaper for soles.

Following behind him was a girl, maybe a year or two younger.

"Are you his sister?"

"No, he's my brother," the girl piped back.

"Tiny gets confused easy," the boy explained, not slowing down his work. "Where you going?" he asked again.

"To the Society of Humanity Embassy," Ruth answered this time.

"The old one or the new one?"

"The one with the ambassador, I hope."

"Oh. The traffic's bad through town. You could get lost real easy, ma'am. I'll show you a shortcut. Get you there real fast. Only cost a dollar."

"I'm planning on following that bus."

The boy studied the big vehicle ahead of them. "You could lose it at a stoplight. I can make sure you get there. Only a dollar."

Ruth looked down into the pleading eyes of the girl . . . and weighed the chances that these two kids could hit her over the head and leave her body in a ditch somewhere.

Concluding that neither one nor both together could hurt her, Ruth nodded. "You make sure I get to the embassy, and I'll pay you two quarters."

"You drive a hard bargain, lady," the boy answered.

But his sister was nodding yes.

"Okay, we do it. Just for you."

Sis let out a squeak of joy and clapped her hands. A moment later, Big Brother opened the passenger door and helped Sis into the backseat. She ignored the seat belt and stood, leaning on the front seat. Brother then settled himself down beside Ruth.

"I can take you there now. Why you want to follow stinky bus?"

"Because my husband's on it."

"He one of the jarheads?"

"Marines," Ruth automatically corrected the epithet she now knew to smile when she said, and better yet, knew not to say. "And since he may have to loan me an extra quarter for your tip, it's Mr. Marine to you."

"Yes, ma'am, boss lady. Whatever you say."

The bus rumbled into life, and Ruth discovered why the kid called it stinky. The engine let off a blue cloud of poorly burned hydrocarbons that made Ruth want to cough.

Sis held her nose and made a "Pee Euw" sound.

Brother gave Ruth his "Whatever you say, woman, you're paying for this," shrug. Thankfully, the bus quickly got in gear.

Ruth followed it out of the port.

"It's gonna turn left at this light," Brother told her. It was a good thing Ruth had been warned; the bus did a quick left at the light without even slowing and nary a signal.

Ruth hit her turn light and followed.

"I told you so." The boy grinned.

"That's worth an extra quarter," Ruth assured him, keeping her eyes on the road, the traffic, and the bus.

"It'll take this on-ramp to the expressway," the boy offered.

"Expressway?" Ruth cringed inside. On Hurtford Corner, she'd never driven over forty, fifty kilometers an hour.

She'd since learned that speeds on expressways . . . unless clogged with rush-hour traffic . . . could be a hundred or more. Swallowing her fear, Ruth followed the bus up the ramp. Again, no turn signal.

She listened for her own turn signal; it made happy clicks. Yes, turn signals weren't outlawed on this planet.

But they did seem distressingly optional.

At least for large buses.

And trucks and anyone else who wanted in her lane.

Everyone behind the wheel on this planet seemed possessed by some urgent death wish. Cars and trucks rocketed along at speeds that must have exceeded the *Patton*'s best, changing lanes with only inches to spare.

The bus, not to be outdone, aimed itself for the far left lane as soon as it entered the highway and dared anything smaller to get in its way.

Ruth started to follow.

"I know the way to the embassy," the kid assured her, "if you want to go slower."

The boy huddled on the seat beside her. Sis was no longer hanging over the front seat; a quick glance behind Ruth didn't show Sis on the backseat.

She must be cowering on the floor.

Ruth started to ask if the two of them had ever been on an expressway before. Then swallowed the question, unwilling to strip the boy of his man-of-the-world airs.

Ruth stayed in the slower right lane and let the bus disappear in traffic ahead.

"Where is the embassy?" she asked her guide.

"Near the river, a couple of blocks from Government Center," he said through clenched teeth.

"Computer, show me the way to Government Center," Ruth ordered. A map appeared on the dash in front of her, showing the expressway in red. The fifth or six exit ahead showed as yellow and a trail led off it to the right.

"Thank you, young man," Ruth said as cheerfully as she could manage with a huge truck riding her bumper, eager to push her along.

"Ah, you are welcome," the boy said, the words seemingly strangers to his mouth.

How often was the poor kid thanked for what he did?

As Ruth motored along at a stately speed . . . and cars whizzed by her on the left . . . the children regained their confidence. Apparently, they'd never experienced the view the expressway offered. As they came over a rise and began the descent into the river valley, their excitement returned.

"Oh, there's the river," the girl squealed.

"Those tall buildings near the river are Government Center," the boy offered.

Ruth risked a glance. Several skyscrapers shot up in the center of town. Whether all of them were Government Center or just a few, Ruth didn't know or ask.

Not doubt, she would find out soon enough.

SIX

FIFTEEN ADRENALINE-FILLED MINUTES later, the kid pointed out the Society of Humanity's new embassy, and Ruth pulled up behind the now-parked bus.

Marines had formed loose ranks, with their kits in front of them, rifles slung. Trouble wanted the rifles in full view, though only he and Gunny's sidearms were loaded. That was one of several hints that Ruth had picked up that this was not going to be just a case of the Marines showing up in fancy dress blues and saluting smartly.

The kids seemed reluctant to leave the car, so Ruth pocketed the keys and headed for Trouble.

He stood beside a young lieutenant in undress greens, observing as Gunnies did the work, a strange way of doing things, but apparently much required by the Navy Way.

Ruth came to a halt several paces from her husband and waited to be recognized. It took only a moment for Trouble to turn a smile her way, reminding her why she loved the big galoot.

"Lieutenant Tubby Vu," Trouble said by way of introduction to the rail-thin officer, "I'd like you to meet my wife, Ruth."

"The infamous Trouble has a ball and chain?" The young man laughed as he offered Ruth his hand.

She replied with a firm handshake, solid enough to show that she worked for a living, but not so tight as to challenge the man to a test of grips.

He responded with a broadening grin.

"My *wife*"—Trouble corrected Ruth's official status—"is the ship farmer for the *Patton*. She'll be nosing about town for equipment and supplies, so she may occasionally need some semiofficial help."

There, that provided Ruth with enough cover to hide a multitude of sins.

"I'll be glad to be of any service that I can. I'll advise my Gunny to make sure the troops get The Word."

Was there a wink and a nod involved in the lieutenant's communication with his newly arrived captain?

As Izzy said, learning all the unofficial handshakes was a challenge.

"Hon, do you have a couple of dollars? I need to pay off my native guides."

"Doesn't your car have a map?" Trouble asked, with just a hint that if she didn't know how to make it work, he'd explain it all to her later.

"Oh, yes it does," she answered sweetly. "Do you know that Savannah has no Society of Humanity Embassy on account of Unity being at war with Earth's running dogs?"

"Someone hasn't updated their database?" Trouble said.

"I think I said the same thing myself a few miles back," Ruth said, smiling sunnily.

"I have some Savannah dinars if you haven't had a chance to get any local currency," the lieutenant offered helpfully.

"I promised them Earth dollars," Ruth pointed out.

"The official exchange rate is over eight to one." The lieutenant frowned. "I've seen local cops break a street kid's arm for overcharging a tourist."

"They wouldn't . . ." Ruth started, then realized that was only one example of the kind of world she'd landed in. With a swallow, she changed her answer. "I promised them Earth dollars, and I always pay my debts. Captain?"

Trouble reached in his pocket and came up with two one-dollar coins. "This ought to do it."

The kids had stayed in the car, their heads below window level. *Gosh, they were short.* In the few steps to the car, a plan came together in Ruth's mind. She opened the passenger-side door and went down on one knee, level with the boy's eyes.

"I'm going to be doing a lot of traveling around town in the next couple of days. You seem to know your way around, and when you don't, you have the right words to get the computer to answer my questions. Would you like to hire on with me?"

Sis's face lit up like a Lander's Day fireworks display. Brother tried to look thoughtful, but failed when he saw the two coins in Ruth's hand. "Two dollars a day, Earth?" he yelped.

"Two dollars, each day, every day. You meet me across the street tomorrow morning, under that tree beside the bridge at eight."

It hit Ruth that the kids might very well sleep under the bridge that night to make sure they didn't miss their date with her. No watch was in evidence.

The boy seemed to read her mind. He scowled. "I know how to tell time. Eight it will be." With that, he grabbed the coins, and he and his sister scooted off.

"What was that all about?" Trouble asked, as Ruth rejoined him and the lieutenant.

"I think I just hired some native guides for our port stay." She laughed.

The lieutenant seemed dubious. "You could do better than kids. For Earth dollars, half the cabbies in this town would sell you their cars."

"And other things," Trouble added with a raised eyebrow.

"Well, sir, yes, but she's your wife."

"She's the *Patton*'s contract farm manager," Trouble corrected. "Get used to it, Tubby, the worlds are changing."

"So I've noticed. And here comes one of those changes. Your new boss, oh captain mine, and no longer my problem."

Ruth turned to see a tall woman striding toward them. Her beige suit highlighted her green eyes and blond hair. She offered Trouble her hand; as he shook it, she introduced herself.

"I'm Becky Graven, the embassy's first political officer. Think of me as the senior person inside that works for a living," she said with just the hint of a smile.

"I'm Captain Tordon. Most of my friends call me Trouble."

"So I'm told. For good reason?"

"Maybe. Sometimes."

"All the time," Ruth drawled, one woman to another.

"And you are?" Ms. Graven said, turning to Ruth.

"Ruth Tordon, contract farmer on the *Patton*. It's a new

business, and I'm still trying to get the right mix of gear, seed, and chemicals."

"Tordon," Graven said, looking at Ruth, then at Trouble, "Tordon. No family resemblance."

"We've only been married two months, so it may not show that much," Ruth quipped.

Graven snorted. "A Marine officer's wife. You poor sucker."

"A ship's farmer," Ruth repeated.

"If you say so, dearie. A year from now, I'll love to hear how it's working out."

She turned to Vu. "Lieutenant, we've rented the building behind the embassy to quarter this new detachment as well as your own. Several of the Foreign Service Officers are moving off the economy and into the embassy. They'll be taking your old quarters.

"Wasn't that building a prison?" Vu asked.

"It's presently office space. Before that, it was a prison, and before that, it was an apartment building. One thing you'll learn about Savannah, things change fast around here. Occasionally for the good. Captain, will you walk with me for a few moments? Ruth, you might as well get the standard briefing from me now rather than secondhand from your husband."

Dismissing the lieutenant to his housekeeping chores, Graven turned and began to walk toward the river. Ruth hurried after her.

Trouble delayed to order the young officer to "Carry on" and return a salute before he marched briskly to catch up.

Marine officers did not run.

Ruth had seen Trouble run. She squelched that memory of fire and explosions.

At the river, Graven paused to glance up and down the empty promenade, "This ought to be secure if we keep walking and talk softly."

"It's that bad?" Trouble observed.

"Yes and no," Graven answered quickly. "Unlike the ambassador, I don't think we have to worry about anything so crass as peasants storming the legation. Unity made its play, fell flat, and most of its thugs and hoodlums are busy running for cover." She paused to frown.

"That may not be the case on Savannah. My intelligence

officer swears that a load of fingerprint files were dumped in the river during the last days of the war. Now, some of the worst thugs and hard cases are employed by Milassi's police force and secret police."

"Secret police aren't allowed under the Society of Humanity's constitution," Ruth observed.

"Right, but if you name it after the Central Bureau of Investigations back on Earth and use their table of organizations, it takes the civil rights watchdogs a while to spot how differently it works. I've signed off on the initial report. In a few years, they'll get a task force out here to investigate."

"But not before the coming election," Trouble concluded.

"Smart for a Marine."

"Some of us are. What is this Senate committee looking into?"

Graven gave them a sideways look. "Don't be too smart, soldier. But if I've been informed correctly, the two of you are some kind of a team and you, Marine, are here to see to more than keeping the ambassador's flower garden from being trampled."

Ruth and Trouble answered that with a slight nod.

"You notice the industrial park on the drive in from the port?"

"That bus driver was pulling more gees than I've had on some combat drops. I was busy just hanging on," Trouble drawled.

"Lots of factories," Ruth observed. "Savannah's supposed to be highly industrialized. Why did it go with Unity? I would think it would be selling its finished goods at as high a price as anything from the hub of humanity. It doesn't match the usual profile for a rebel Unity planet."

"For a farm girl, you know an awful lot about high finance," Graven frowned.

"Just because we didn't want all the expensive doodads doesn't mean we're ignorant. And I've had good reason to study Savannah for the last week. Some things just don't add up."

"They do when you have all the pieces," Graven told them. "What they built on Savannah did sell for top dollar, just like Earth stuff. But that didn't mean a lot of the money stayed here. Take a big fusion generator, for example. Certain high-value parts, like gears and turbines aren't made here. They have to be imported from one of Earth's big orbital plants. And strangely enough, most of the profits in the generator's construction get sucked right back to Earth to pay for those parts."

"Wouldn't that close them down when the war started?" Ruth asked.

"Should have. Absent a large inventory of critical parts, Savannah's factories should have become ghost towns in a few days, weeks at the most."

"How many Daring class cruisers did Savannah contribute to the Unity effort?" Trouble asked, then answered his own question. "Thirty, forty?"

"Thirty-seven," Graven corrected. "Each with three generators. General Fusion only has local warehousing capacity for a dozen of the Earth-supplied critical parts."

"So somebody was shipping them turbines from Earth during the war."

"It seems that way."

"Is that what the committee is here to find out?" Ruth asked.

Graven chuckled wickedly. "Hay is showing in your hair, darling. I've seen the list. I know their backgrounds. Three or four of them might be here to dig. Trust me, the others are here to bury it as fast as those four uncover it."

"Where does that leave us?" Trouble asked.

"Doing the job we came here to do. That's all any of us can do. The job we hired on for. Sometimes, we get to do a thing or two before anyone up there knows what's happening. As I understand it, that's what you two did on Riddle. Must have been fun."

Ruth and Trouble looked at each other and shook their heads at the same moment.

"No, trust *me* on this one," Ruth said, "it wasn't fun at all."

SEVEN

COLONEL RAY LONGKNIFE watched his wife ready herself for bed. For two long months, he'd held himself together with memories like these. He took a deep breath of her scent, content to just refresh the recollection . . . for the moment.

As she brushed out her long hair, it fell over her bare shoulders. In the mirror, Ray watched as her diaphanous gown flowed over and around the gentle swell of her belly. Thin straps struggled to hold her now-enlarged breasts and frequently failed, as darkening areolas played peekaboo with him.

Ray thoroughly enjoyed the view.

Quickly, he finished undressing so Rita could see how much he enjoyed the view. She smiled wickedly at him, settled the last hair in place, and turned to gasp in mock surprise. "Soldier, you must have been gone a long time, to find an old married hag like me so . . ."

"Not long enough for you to become an old married hag, young woman, now get over here, and I'll show you how long I've been gone."

"But you've been back ten whole days." She sighed as she came to stand above him.

"It's not the days, woman, but the nights."

"And such nights." She laid herself down beside him in one languid motion. "Baby's enjoying the visits. He'd been about to put out a sign on the front lawn, baby available for rent, apply within."

"The only thing getting within is me, woman," Ray growled, but his fingers were gentle as he explored the silken flesh of her breasts and made widening circles toward her thighs.

"Oh yes," she murmured.

Ray was home from the wars. Home from the stars. And

now he had legs, real legs. He didn't have to just lie there, waiting for her to do something.

Damn it was good to have his legs back underneath him. Or in this case, above her.

President Steffo Milassi signed the commission with a tired flourish. Horatio Whitebred was now a full admiral in the Savannah Navy.

Which ought to keep that idiot Peterwald happy for a whole five minutes. Didn't the man know that navies did not win elections!

Then again, if the stories he'd heard about Riddle were right, navies certainly could lose elections.

Milassi sighed. It had been a long day, full of meetings with lamebrained henchmen who had plenty of muscle. Unfortunately, they were clueless as the pavement they stumbled over when it came to using the power Milassi gave them in order to keep it.

Fortunately, he wasn't the only one who couldn't get good help.

Take that whimpering Society of Humanity ambassador. He now had fifty more Marines to guard his door. Did the fool really think he was in any danger?

Hell, nothing happened in Petrograd, nothing happened on Savannah without Milassi's writ.

And Steffo wasn't about to get Earth any more involved on Savannah than it already was. He made a marginal notation, adding an extra block to the no-violence zone around the damn embassy.

Best not to risk the ambassador's even seeing a head being bashed in.

Steffo was about to go on to the next report when his eyes fell on the last paragraph.

A woman had landed with the Marines . . . a ship's farmer. What in the name of hell was a "ship's farmer"?

That forced him to turn another page. Even Earth couldn't be dumb enough to put farms on warships! He made a notation to his flatfoots to follow that woman.

There had to be more to this story.

Then, again, maybe it *was* just part of Earth's effort to prevent local farmers from getting their hands on hard Earth currency.

Steffo started to scratch through his order, then chose to leave it in place for a few days. It wouldn't hurt his hounds to follow her around a bit.

Intelligence hounds couldn't be used for the more blunt bits of election campaigning. If the ones asking questions also broke heads, people began to avoid them.

Milassi had learned the benefit of keeping the two apart.

Milassi rubbed his eyes, letting them wander for a few moments over the trappings of money and power that surrounded him. He snorted; they were nothing but a prison.

He laughed as he turned to the next report, a list of troublemakers who needed to be rounded up before the senators arrived. This prison was much to be preferred to the ones he sent these problems off to.

He scribbled his initials on that report and went to the next.

Ray lay spooned around his wife, his chest to Rita's back. His hand measuring the slowing race of her heart. He had brought exquisite pleasure to the woman he loved, and now it had given way to tranquil sleep.

He felt like he could leap any mountain in the worlds.

His hand moved lower, coming to rest on the bulge of her belly. Rita said she could feel the baby moving. Ray held his hand lightly there, but that miracle of budding life eluded him.

"I'm here, little one. I'm back."

And I'll be leaving again soon, came to him, unbidden.

Ray sighed. Yes, he would be going out again. But not for long.

I'll be back real soon, little one. Real soon.

Ray rolled over on his back, slowed his own breathing, and prepared for sleep. A fast run to Savannah couldn't cause all that much trouble, could it?

In his head, a quick course for Savannah played out. Just three jumps using the ones only he knew about now, after Santa Maria.

Unbidden, a second route superimposed itself on the first.

This one was six jumps. And deep in the system of the fourth one . . .

Sleep came to Ray . . . and dreams.

Morning light played on the ceiling as Ray slowly came awake to the gentle touch of fingers playing in the hair on his chest.

He smiled.

"Make us late for work," Rita breathed throatily.

He reached for her, kissed her. For a long time, nothing else mattered.

As he lay beside her, catching his breath, her grip on his hand tightened. "You're dreaming more now."

"Yes." He nodded, not taking his eyes from the ceiling, from the unseen stars that still haunted his vision. "I kind of had to learn to trust my dreams."

Rita rolled over on her side, rested a hand against his cheek. "You have all those star charts locked in your skull. You have to let us get them out. I'm converting the three pirate ships we captured at Riddle into scout cruisers like the *Second Chance*. The Wild Goose class, we're calling them. They can spread out, using your charts. Think of what they'll find for our baby!"

Her other hand went to rest on the bulge below her heart.

Ray smiled. His wife was a dreamer, a tiger, all those and more. She had been enthusiastic about exploration before the baby.

Now she was a fanatic.

"I'm meeting with a group of astronomers who have some ideas about how to match what I know with what they have in their databases," Ray said. "In a day or two, they should have enough to keep our ships busy for the next year."

"In a day or two?" she echoed, both hands now on her tummy.

Ray rolled into a sitting position, pulled Rita into his arms. "A day or two will be enough."

"I want you to stay here until the baby comes."

"I'll be here when the baby comes."

Rita pulled away from him. In a flash of flying pillows, blankets, and sheets, she was on her feet. "You want to go out again? Last time almost killed you! For God sakes, man, haven't you done enough for any ten men?"

Ray took a deep breath. It was going to be a long morning. The ministry would just have to manage on its own while the two of them had it out.

EIGHT

RUTH HEADED OUT the front door of the embassy, flashing a sunny smile at the young Marines on guard duty in reply to their salutes. She was at the curb before she noticed that there was no one waiting for her under the tree across the way by the river. As she came to a halt to consider what might have happened to the kids, a cab rolled up.

"Need a ride, lady?" the bewhiskered man behind the wheel called through the open window.

"Not at the moment," Ruth answered automatically, still scanning the rolling green of the riverbank for any sign of two kids.

"I know Petrograd. I can find you anything you want. Anything. Nothing goes on around here I don't know about." He smiled with absolute confidence.

"Thanks." Ruth innocently smiled back. "I'm just starting my day off with a walk. My husband's a Marine, and he's already done a three-mile run," she added by way of explanation.

Trouble had had the gall to wake her up at "oh dark early" with a grin and a suggestion she join him.

She'd hit him with the only thing handy—a pillow. Tonight, she'd arrange to have something heavier at hand. Like the combat rations they'd had for breakfast.

Even split four ways, that thing was still heavy in her stomach.

"Have it your way," the cabby said and gunned away, leaving Ruth in a shower of gravel from the worn road and fumes from his tailpipe.

Can't anyone around here tune a motor?

Ruth headed for a wooden bench looking out over the

wide, cobbled promenade facing the river. As she suspected, the kids were hiding in it, huddled behind its high back.

"What are you two doing?"

"Don't talk to us. Just sit on the bench. Is the Bear gone?" the boy whispered quickly.

Ruth sat down beside the boy and looked out on the river rather than at the kids. "The Bear?"

"The fuzzy-faced cabdriver," he said. "He works for the crushers."

"Crushers?"

"Blues. Black boots," the boy hurried on, frustrated at the failure to communicate.

"You mean the police," Ruth offered.

"Police," the boy echoed, frowning in puzzlement at his sister.

Both the kids looked much better today than they had the day before. They had washed off a couple of pounds of dirt. Both sported new, if badly worn, shoes.

Ruth decided to try another approach. "What do the crushers, ah, black boots do?"

"They keep us out of this part of town," Sister offered. "Rat's still seeing double from the kick the Bear gave him in the head."

"They twist the bigger girls, make them pay rent for their corners. Break our arms if they find us sleeping around parks. Crushers," he said, as if the word said it all.

Ruth decided it did. She'd had no idea the risks she was asking the kids to take when she told them to meet her here. "You two stay put. I'll bring the car around and honk for you. You come running then."

The kids nodded with understanding.

Ruth stood, stretching lazily as she took in the river-park area. No one was walking along the promenade. Some traffic roared across the bridge into the government center, but none looked interested in two kids huddled on a park bench. She checked traffic along the road in front of the embassy.

Bear and his cab were gone.

Casually, Ruth sauntered back to the embassy. The Marines saluted; she smiled.

On her way to the car, she did a quick detour to their quarters for her sidearm.

Izzy had warned Ruth that Savannah had strict laws against civilian weapons. Since Ruth was a civilian, her military automatic was anathema and could easily land her so deep in the local jail that they'd never dig her out.

Ruth checked the weapon, made sure she had plenty of both nonlethal and lethal rounds, checked again to make sure her bra had the locator beacon Trouble had insisted she sew into its lining.

Only then did she trot out to the car.

Why, oh why, did I ever leave Hurtford Corner? Trouble, you better come home early tonight. And horny, too.

Ray drove them to the ministry building. As Rita had asked, they were late.

The ride, however, was silent. Rita sat like a stone Madonna on her side of the car. As the elevator carried them up, she said to the door in front of her, "You meet with your stargazers and shrinks. I'll keep the paperwork moving. Can't let the ministry collapse around our heads."

"Thank you, dear," he said.

"Don't thank me," she snapped. "I'm doing it for me and my baby. Not for you."

"I still appreciate it."

"You might show some of that appreciation around here a bit more often."

"I won't be gone long."

"That's what you said last time."

"Damn it, woman, they've fixed the ship."

"And what will go wrong next?" she fired back at him, as the elevator door opened onto four people waiting for a ride.

They took one look at Ray and Rita and took several steps back.

After a moment, the doors closed on Rita's silent anger, returning them to the appearance of intimacy.

"Rita, I could get killed crossing the street. This damn elevator could fall. Hell, wife, you knew I was a soldier when you married me."

Rita slapped the STOP button. "Yes. I knew you were a soldier. Damn it, I carried you out there to die. I brought you back and put the pieces together, then took you off to kill Urm and yourself. I did all the things a good soldier's wife should do. And you got discharged, remember? Check that ID card you carry. R-E-T-I-R-E-D. The war's over. Baby and I have paid our dues. So when are you going to quit chasing after a new place to die?"

The tears were streaming down her face now.

He took two steps to her, folded his arms around her. She was stiff as a board. He caressed her hair.

"Honey, I'm not going out to war. I'm just going to a business meeting. Your dad has gone to a million of them. I'll spend my days with people in gray and brown business suits. No uniforms this time. These are politicians from Earth I need to talk to. Just a few days. Then I'll be headed right back here. I promise. This time is different. I'm not a soldier anymore."

She seemed to relax. "You're not a soldier anymore."

"Yes, honey, no uniform. Just look at me." Ray stepped away.

Her eyes flitted up and down the conservative gray suit he'd put on today. "You're back's too damn straight for a businessman."

Ray hunched his shoulders and stooped over. She laughed through her tears. "Why do you have to go now?"

"The senators are visiting Savannah."

"Savannah. Why does it have to be Savannah?"

Ray straightened himself back up, then shrugged his shoulders. "Why is it any place? It just is."

"Mr. Raymond Longknife, civilian, once this baby is born, we will fit out a lead-lined room on the *Second Chance* for you, me, and a nursery. Next time you go gallivanting, we all gallivant."

"Most certainly, Senior Pilot Nuu," he said as he bent to kiss his wife.

"Discharged," she mumbled around his kiss.

"Definitely," he agreed.

NINE

RUTH DROVE WHERE the kids directed. They were showing her the sights, and in not a few cases, probably seeing them for the first time themselves.

Her "native guides" had a lot of holes in their knowledge. The computer helped. It presented Ruth with an official sightseeing list.

For this morning, Ruth followed it as she struggled to get her bearings in a town a hundred times larger than any on Hurtford Corner. At least, it seemed that way.

Initially, somebody had put some thought into planning this city. Wide boulevards quartered the city, north, south, east, west, with trolleys providing easy public transport.

The Anna River flowed in from the northwest and out to the southeast. A wide expressway drew a circle around the city center three mile out from Government Center.

There should have been additional circles six, nine, and twelve miles out, but urban sprawl had gotten ahead of planning.

Beyond the planned zone was a hodgepodge of roads, at different angles, with different widths and at different levels of upkeep ranging from poor to nonexistent. That was where the industry and its workers lived. That was where the kids guided Ruth after she took them through a drive-through and fed them lunch.

Twice.

"Don't eat so much you make yourself sick," Ruth said in her mother's voice, startling herself and the kids . . . for different reasons.

"You can eat too much?" the boy said, raw disbelief competing for room on his face with dripping ketchup, which he'd been delighted to learn came at no extra charge.

"Yes," Ruth said, checking the tone of her voice and wondering why she was being the mommy to these kids.

The two kids exchanged looks, silent communication that Ruth suspected was nine-tenths disbelief and one-tenth dismay.

Before they could say anything further, Ruth asked the computer to show them where the General Fusion Inc. plant was located. The boy helped her follow the directions. In fifteen minutes, after only three wrong turns, Ruth was slowly driving by the front gate.

There were a dozen lunch trucks parked on the dusty field in front of the factory. A profusion of smells wafted from them, mixed into an eclectic potpourri that reminded Ruth of a Saturday afternoon at the annual farmer's fair as the women competed with each other for the ribbons.

Ruth smiled at the pleasant memories.

Then a fight broke out on the hard-packed dirt field.

There were shouts in languages that Ruth didn't understand. A circle formed as two men threw spirited, if wild, punches at each other.

Guards in blue uniforms sauntered from the factory gate toward the fight with no urgency until several people along the periphery started swinging at each other.

Then, whistles blowing, the blues trotted forward, clubs up to wail on any and all, irrespective of their belligerence.

Brother eagerly watched. "Fights don't usually break out until quitting time. Us kids will hang around the factories, seeing if anyone needs help home. You can make a nickel if your guy is really beat-up."

The kid swallowed his excitement, aware he'd given away the local going rate of help.

Ruth continued her slow drive by the plant, turning left to follow its northern side. The fight broke up, and men headed back to work in ragged clumps. There were shouts between groups, and hand gestures that Ruth expected were obscene but she was unfamiliar with.

When one of the blues took an interest in Ruth's slow-moving car, she accelerated, took the first right away from the plant, and asked for directions from the computer to Consolidated Electric LLC's plant.

It had the same dusty foreyard. Peeling paint and broken windows were the only break in the large, dreary factory walls.

"People come to work there day after day," Ruth breathed, appalled.

"Only if your old man has a job there. You got to have family ties to get a good job," Brother informed her with bleak innocence.

"Can you get fired for fighting?"

"You can," Brother said.

"But the one you kept helping home, last year," Sister piped in. "He's a foreman now, isn't he?"

"Yeah," Brother agreed. "Omar did get the foreman's job. He doesn't fight anymore," the kid said, probably mourning his lost nickels.

"Why were they fighting?" Ruth muttered, half to herself.

"Maybe one of the right-handers said something about a left-hander's wife or daughter. Maybe one of the scrapers crossed the line that morning. Who knows? They fight, the blues watch, then they break it up," Brother said with a shrug.

Ruth had more questions but doubted that her diminutive informants had the knowledge or the wherewithal to answer them. Drives by several more dilapidated factories showed her nothing new.

The kids knew of no place with green stuff growing around it. Ruth could easily believe that. She'd never seen a place so gray, dreary, and drab. Admittedly, Savannah was only her sixth planet, but she had to wonder what it was like when the rainy season came, and the dirt turned to mud.

When she asked, the kids just shivered.

About midafternoon, Ruth noticed definite signs of the fidgets in the kids. "Is there a problem?" she asked.

"If we don't get in line early, we won't get a bed at the mission," Brother explained, then rushed on. "It's okay if we don't. It's nice, and we can sleep outside. It's just, if we're sleeping someplace and the big kids find us, they'll twist us for most of what you pay us. That's all," he finished with resignation.

Ruth tried to flash Brother an understanding smile even as her heart felt ripped in half.

"I've seen about all I need for today. Where's the mission?

I can drop you off there and pick you up tomorrow. No need for you two to dodge the Bear again."

Brother stared at her in wide-eyed amazement.

Sister hopped up and down on the backseat. "Would you? Could you?"

"Shush, Tiny," Brother said, trying to draw himself up to man height. "I'd really like that a lot," he said studiously. "You don't have to. We can walk there from here."

"Not before dark," Sis corrected, but in a whisper.

Brother threw her a quick scowl, and she fell silent.

"Consider it part of your pay," Ruth said, then realized the kids might think they were losing today's two dollars. She added, "Along with the eight quarters I've got for you."

The children's faces lit up like a morning sunrise. Tiny even managed a smile.

Brother, of course, was too much the man to let himself go that far.

No surprise, the mission was not in the computer's memory.

The kids told her the nearest factory, then guided her along a twisting maze of streets and alleys that left Ruth praying her car's GPS unit was in good shape.

She'd hate to have to activate her emergency beacon.

The thought of sitting here in an alley while people squeezed around her car, of her talking into her bra, asking Trouble to locate her and give her a heading for the embassy, was too embarrassing to contemplate.

Brother finally pointed her up a middling narrow street bordered by a mix of multistoried stone, stucco, and wooden buildings that would have been the dismay of even Hurtford Corner's libertarian zoning codes. Only one building among them showed any attention to its paint in the recent eon, a brown-painted three-story whose green metal roof seemed to have been appended as an afterthought. It angled off to the right as if it might slide in that direction at any moment.

Then again, none of the buildings on the street looked any too secure on their foundations.

However, while the rest huddled alone where they had been shoehorned into the block, unnoticed by passing humans, the brown one had a line of about a dozen people crouching in front of its door.

"Good," Sis cried. "We're early."

"I'm sorry," Brother apologized, "you never know when the line will start. If you want, Sis can hold our place, and I can show you around some more."

"I've seen enough for today," Ruth assured him, slipping eight Earth quarters across to him, keeping them out of sight of anyone passing by. It would be a shame to have the poor kid murdered for a dollar or two. "Who runs this place?"

"Major Barbara," Brother answered, getting out and helping Sis from the backseat.

"I'd like to meet her," Ruth said, getting out herself.

The heat, dust, and stink assaulted her immediately.

Ruth had slopped pigs on hot summer days. Those were honest smells. This was . . . the stink of poverty and squalor and hopelessness. It bowled Ruth over with a power that sapped her, leaving her in its malaise by the second breath.

"I think Major wants to see you," Brother said. "Here she comes."

Ruth turned toward the brown building. A woman in a blue blouse and skirt, red piping along its edges, advanced toward Ruth. In the last month, she'd been marched on by Marines, Navy, and the best of Wardhaven's Guard. There was none of the military pacing in "Major" Barbara's walk . . . just the power.

Unconsciously, Ruth stiffened her back as she would to face Trouble in full kit or Izzy at full sail.

"I want to talk to you," the woman said. "Will you walk with me?"

"Yes," came immediately to Ruth's lips.

"Someone will have to watch her car," Brother piped up.

"Mouse, get Alice Blue Bonnet," the woman snapped without looking back. Brother . . . no, Mouse . . . ran off.

The woman strode right by Ruth without slowing.

Ruth whirled on her heel and followed her quickly down the street until it rounded a block. Only then did the woman turn to face Ruth.

"I am known around here as Major Barbara. You're flashing a lot of money at Mouse and Tiny. What are you setting them up for?"

"Two dollars is not a lot of money," Ruth defended her charity.

"It is for those poor kids. If virgins are what you're after, it's too late. Neither of those kids are. Tiny's rapist didn't leave much of her behind, but if you intend to use her, I will resist you with all the power at my disposal."

Ruth had watched one evening when Pa and the boys found a rat's nest in the barn. The mother had fought for her young with a blind courage that left Pa shaking his head and Brother almost willing to let them run loose. This was what Ruth saw in Major Barbara's eyes—defiance in the face of sure defeat.

Ruth took a deep breath. She swallowed, trying to rid herself of the sick taste Major Barbara's accusations left in her mouth. She rolled her shoulder, as if to slough off hopelessness bad as any that had sapped her during her marriage to her first husband, Mordy.

"Major, I am what I told the kids. I manage a farm aboard a Humanity cruiser in orbit. I'm looking for better tanks, piping, seed, and software. I'm married to a Marine at the embassy, and he's all I ever dreamed of coming home to. Mouse and Tiny are as safe with me as I hope my own kids will be when I have them."

Ruth studied the woman's reaction. Barbara's face was lined with care, her brown hair just starting to show gray. She wore no makeup. The face was honest, plain, and, as determination marched off it, a kind of open optimism seemed to come to the fore.

"Now, if you've got a second, that café across the way seems to have just brewed up a new pot of coffee. Can I buy you a cup?"

"You work on a Navy cruiser, growing food?"

"The best fruits and vegetables," Ruth said, pointing the way to the café. Barbara took up the offer and started across the street.

"Why put a farm on a warship?"

"Some Navy reg about assuring the fruits and vegetables are disease-free. Or so I'm told."

"Or to keep hard Earth currency away from the poor local farmers," Barbara breathed. "They have it tough enough as it is, getting hard money to pay their debts. Now it will be tougher."

Ruth had no answer to that. She took a table well into the

shadows of the café's open room. Here, she had a good view of other customers and anyone walking by; she ordered two cups of coffee. The waiter recognized Barbara and seemed happy to serve her.

"Was your ship one of the first to get a farm?"

"Yes," Ruth said. "The captain figured if I was fool enough to fall in love with a Marine, I was fool enough to run a farm on her ship."

"Yes." Barbara nodded. "You said you were married to a Marine. And now you are on Savannah, a few weeks before the coming elections and asking street kids to show you around. Madame farmer, Marine's wife, what are you up to?"

That knocked Ruth back. Was her cover that thin? Or did this woman, dedicated to the poor, have eyes that saw more than most and a brain that did a better analysis than most of the intel types Ruth had met?

Ruth weighed all the possibilities and tossed the dice.

"I'm like lots of people, just trying to figure out how things work. Like today, passing by the General Fusion plant at lunch, I saw two men start slugging it out. Mouse told me it might be because a right-hander said something a left-hander didn't like, or maybe a scraper. What was Mouse telling me?"

Barbara glanced down the street at her mission. "The line's getting long early. I'll need to get back to oversee supper. That's what we offer them: a meal, a half hour of chapel, and a bed for the night. If I'm there, some of the more distressed folks stay calmer."

Ruth held her coffee cup with both hands, took a small sip, and spoke from behind it. "I imagine they find you a mothering influence. Soothing."

"Many of the worst cases hate their mothers, and for good cause."

"And you are dodging my question," Ruth pointed out.

"You've got the entire embassy staff to answer your questions. Why me?"

"I've asked them. What they can, they answer. Like the senior political officer has signed off on a request to have the civil rights people investigate how the Central Bureau of Investigations works on Savannah." There, Ruth provided some trading stock. She waited to see what the other would offer in return.

Major Barbara snorted. "This election, probably the next one, too, will be long gone before anything comes of that."

"Probably. Meanwhile, I'm trying to figure out what I can, and I doubt the embassy staff speaks the same language as the kids. To the staff, they're police out here. To the kids, they're black boots or blues or crushers."

Ruth shrugged. "I doubt anyone in the embassy knows what a left-hander is."

"They know what they are. They just don't know them the way the kids do. The view from the sewer is quite different. Left-handers are usually Croats, though they could be French Catholics as well. Those that make the sign of the cross going to the left shoulder first. Not like the Orthodox, who go to the right shoulder first. Like a Serb. Scrapers are those of the Islamic faith among us who bow toward Mecca when they pray." Barbara shook her head.

"Not an easy thing when you consider that as our planet rotates, the direction to Mecca changes. Praise the Lord that someone came up with a single direction for those poor people." Barbara shook herself. "But you aren't interested in the fine points of religion."

Ruth frowned. "On Hurtford Corner, we had Moslems, Jews, and several flavors of Christian. Even Wiccan. They weren't killing each other. There wasn't much Earth history in my education, but I seem to recall that even back in the Balkans, they've quit killing each other. Bad for the tourist business or something."

"But it's good for business, here," Barbara snapped, then went on more slowly.

"In a plant, you have different shops doing different things. You have different line gangs doing their work, but not actually having to talk to each other . . . to get the job done. Back on Earth, when these different shops and line crews started talking, they discovered they had a lot in common. That's what workers need if they're going to organize and face managers with a united front. You've never been around unions, have you?"

"My pa was a farmer. I never heard of unions until one of my ex-Navy farmhands asked if he could organize the farm two weeks ago. 'Nothing against you and what you're doing, ma'am,' he told me, but his dad was a union man and he feels safer with a union rep talking to management. Me, a manager," Ruth squeaked.

"My father was the last union organizer anyone dared send to Savannah," Barbara said. "When he disappeared, I asked the Salvation Army to send me here. Savannah is not a sought-after assignment even in the Army of the Lord. I found my dad's notes in a locker at the spaceport. He'd sent me the key.

"A hundred years ago, when they set up this planet, they hired on folks who couldn't speak the same languages. Who hated each other's guts and had been killing each other for five hundred years. Back on Earth, they put an end to the killing. Here, it's company policy to keep it going. If the chain gang hate the line crew, they're not going to listen to anyone from there tell them they need to unite against management thugs. If the craftsmen look down on the shop-floor crews, they're going to go home to their tiny houses and not worry about what's going on in the slums across town. Back in the early twentieth century, they played that game on Earth."

Ruth sat back, trying to absorb what she'd been told. "I don't see how . . ." she started slowly. But Major Barbara was coming out of her chair.

"I'm sorry, but I can't agree with you. The kids at my mission would not make good space farmers. They'd be upchucking their toenails, and I wouldn't put it past you to just toss them out an air lock if they caused you too much trouble."

Ruth followed the major's glance; a wizened man made his way slowly into the café. His twisted wooden cane made tapping noises on the tiles. The man wore sandals, but Ruth would bet the kids would call him a black boot.

"I'm sorry you feel that way," Ruth shot back, as if continuing an argument. "Where I come from, a farm isn't a farm without kids to do the small stuff. Why should I pay a man a full wage to do what a kid can do just 'cause my farm is on a starship?"

Barbara stomped out of the café. Ruth tossed down a few coins and ran after her. "We aren't finished! Your kids need jobs! They aren't going to get any here. Scut work on my farm is the best they can hope for. You ought to be promising me the best you have."

"Enough," Barbara said, raising her voice, and her hand. Together they walked around the corner and out of view from the café.

"You're a quick learner," the church worker whispered.

"That's what kept me alive raising drugs on a Riddle slave plantation," Ruth said, all cover story aside.

Which caused Barbara to miss a step. "I heard about Riddle. I was asked to take lead in a new mission starting up there. I chose to stay here. What do you want?"

"The idiots growing drugs on Riddle didn't know which end of the seed to put in the ground. They didn't develop it. Some friends of mine say it was developed here. Do you know anyplace that might be a research center for something like that?"

"You definitely aren't what you appear to be, are you, ship farmer?"

"And if I'm found out, my body will be floating down the river tomorrow."

"Like so many each morning." Barbara gazed ahead. "The line is long at the mission. I better get back. Alice Blue Bonnet is watching your car. Sometimes, she sells drugs. She used to sell her body, whatever it took to get by. She taught herself to read. I'm giving her time on my terminal for schooling. She'll be with Mouse and Tiny tomorrow. I think she'll have something interesting to show you."

"Can I trust her?"

"Probably," was all the answer Ruth got, as Major Barbara made a straight line for her mission's front door.

Sitting on the hood of Ruth's car was a girl of maybe fifteen. Her shirt and pants were worn black Unity fatigues. On her head perched a small blue pillbox hat. Hardly the bonnet Ruth had worn to work in the fields. Then again, where she grew up, police were safety volunteers, not crushers.

Different human worlds took a lot of getting used to.

"I kept your car safe, lady," Alice drawled, sliding off the hood.

"Looks that way. Thanks," Ruth said, fishing in her pocket for more quarters.

"You don't owe me nothin'," the youth said. "Major said do it. I done it."

Ruth recognized the sound of pride, when pride was all you had, and almost she pulled her hand from her pocket, empty. Almost.

This poor kid had done a lot worse to keep body and soul together. And when her money ran out, she'd do it again. A few quarters might delay that time. Ruth caught one of the young woman's hands with one of her own, then forced four quarters in it.

"You don't owe me," Alice insisted.

"I pay the people who work for me," Ruth insisted back. "Ask Mouse and Tiny."

"They're just free ridin'. Havin' more fun than workin' for you."

"They've shown me a few things I needed to see, and gotten me out of a few places I didn't want to be. Major says you can help me, too. Tomorrow."

"She did?" Eyes that had been distant, almost dull, lit up. A smile almost creased the disinterested, undemanding face. Almost.

"What she want me to do?"

"She'll tell you. I'm not sure, yet."

"Some boss. You don't know what you want?" The challenge lacked force. Still, the young woman had found enough of herself to make it.

"Sometimes, not knowing what you want is where you discover what you need." Ruth smiled back. "I'm going to enjoy working with you."

"I got to hurry, or all the food will be gone," Alice said. "See you," she tossed over her shoulder as she rushed for the mission.

TEN

COLONEL RAY LONGKNIFE was frustrated. When frustrated, he was used to giving orders that ended said frustration . . . often with loud booms.

In the 2nd Guard, it worked.

It wasn't working this morning.

The three astronomers, a dozen technicians, and the two psychologists assigned to help them fumble around in his memories had succeeded in tracking eight jumps all morning. Just eight!

On Santa Maria, Ray, Matt, and his jump master, Sandy, had done two in a few minutes!

"This is not working," Ray growled as lunchtime approached. He pushed himself back from a conference table with its heavy load of star projectors, star charts, and data records. At least this conference room was less ornate that most in his ministry.

"We're getting the hang of it," the senior astronomer assured Ray. "Things will go faster this afternoon."

The senior shrink looked ready to say something unctuous, again. If Ray heard another soothing comment about how stressed out he was and what he could do to better control his stress, he was going to show these people just how stressed *they* could be.

Instead, he gritted his teeth and tapped his commlink. "Get me the skipper of the *Second Chance*. It's at the Nuu docks in orbit."

There was a brief pause as connections were made. The professionals around him fidgeted, flipped through their readers, and otherwise showed clear disapproval of this interruption.

"Captain Abeeb here, what can I do for you, Ray?"

"Send down Lek. I'm going to scare up the stone we

brought back from Santa Maria, and I want him to do that hookup he did there. Folks here want to know the star charts in my head, and we're going way too slow to keep me happy."

Rita maybe, but not me.

"You sure you want to go fast on that stuff?" Matt answered with the wise diplomacy Ray had come to expect from a merchant skipper who'd been haggling over cargo prices for more years than Ray could contemplate.

"Whose side are you on?"

"I'll have Lek down there in two hours," Matt quickly said.

"Where's the stone from Santa Maria?" Ray asked the astronomers.

"It's being evaluated," told Ray little.

"By whom?"

"Interested parties," added nothing.

"You tell those interested parties I want to borrow that rock for a day or two. They'll learn more watching me and Lek put it through its paces than they will navel gazing at it for a year."

"It not rated for human use," the counselor said, as if looking for a door to escape out.

"I used it, Matt and his jump master used it. That's man rating enough for me."

"We're still assessing its potential impact on you," the research neurologist said, eyeing Ray as he might a pinned insect in someone's collection.

"Doc, there's no better place to study something than from inside it. Now, let's go visit some 'interested parties.' Oh, and you better have someone deliver lunch there, or I'm going to start biting off heads."

Wherever they'd set up the artifact from Santa Maria, no one was in a hurry to show Ray. Still, nobody refused to take the man who killed President Urm where he wanted to go. They just did it slowly—and after a sit-down lunch.

Ray's patience lasted an hour before the irresistible force took over. "Enough. Where's the rock?" he said, wadding up his linen napkin and tossing it onto the plate with its half-eaten steak and potatoes.

When they reported to Rita how they'd tried to delay him, they should at least report that he'd eaten all his vegetables.

A young woman in a lab coat showed up at his elbow at the same split second. He remembered her. "Trudy Seyd, isn't it? You run infowar for him," which was as good a way of naming the nameless spy as Ray could think of.

"Yes, Colonel. If you will follow me."

He did. She led him up, down, around, and through a maze of corridors, elevators, and halls. His legs were just starting to protest, this being the longest walk he'd attempted since giving up his canes, when she stopped at an elevator door.

"What has us stopped dead is that the damn thing doesn't do anything. It just sits there. Nothing we do activates anything."

"I got it going," Ray said.

"I know, Colonel. How?"

Ray tapped his head. At last check, the tumor that he'd suddenly grown on Santa Maria was still there. God knows, the dreams were still there. And, as this long walk had proven again, his war-battered back was still fixed, and his legs were no longer half-dead.

"You think it will only work for someone who has the . . . ah, additional communication port?" the woman said, not sounding at all convinced.

"What do you say we put it to the test? By the way, Lek, the tech who put the comm package together for me on Santa Maria, is headed down. Make sure some rat shows him through this maze of yours."

"Lek," Trudy said, nonplussed. "Isn't he that self-taught electrical technician?"

"Child," Ray said, letting just a whiff of his temper loose, "that self-taught tech got that gear working when my life and a whole damn planet depended on it, and he did it a hell of a lot faster than you have."

"Yes, sir." The woman started talking into her commlink.

The elevator door opened, and Ray walked into a pristine lab.

Brightly lit, it was windowless. The air tasted of crisp, sanitary security. Ray doubted an electron got out without showing ID.

The astronomers had lost their technicians, Ray's team was down to just him, three stargazers, and, for some reason, the two shrinks.

Their persistence did not hint of good sense, but that was their problem.

Ray's stone stood on an elevated platform in the center of the lab. It, and other stones cut from Santa Maria, were the only things in the lab that didn't gleam, whirl, or blink.

Ray approached it slowly. One of the four sides of the obelisk seemed to summon him. He avoided that side and would until Lek checked it out. Just because Ray had used the technology of the Three, the races that built the jump highway between the stars when humans were struggling to maintain fire or utter their first words, didn't mean he understood it any better than the next guy.

The Three had vanished a million or two years ago, leaving behind their jump points—and a half-mad something on the world humans named Santa Maria.

The elevator behind them whirred again; this time the door disgorged a thin, bald man of ancient age in a wrinkled and smudged shipsuit. He took in the lab with one glance.

"Fancy place you got here, Colonel. Can it do anything?"

"So far they haven't gotten the rig up, Lek. You want to check it out with Ms. Seyd and her team?"

"No problem, sir." The man whipped out a tech reader from his breast pocket and opened it. A holo picture appeared above, showing the jury-rigged contraption as it had existed on Santa Maria.

Ms. Seyd signaled three of her specialists. "Let's go over the layout with this man."

Ray settled into a desk chair, put his feet up on the nearest flat surface, and prepared for what he expected would be a short wait.

The astronomers collected as far from him as they seemed able to in the spacious lab.

The research neurologist joined them. The counselor sidled up to Ray.

"You figure that man can get it working when those other specialists haven't?"

"Yep," Ray said, getting comfortable.

"What makes you feel that way?"

"Doc, I'm a combat trooper. If my informed grasp of the

situation, aided by any intuition I trust, is right, I win. If I'm wrong, I'll need a surgeon, not a shrink."

"You were wrong, once. You lost most of your command and barely got out with a broken back."

"Yep," Ray swung around to face this magpie, dropping his legs firmly on to the floor. "I served my time with the surgeons."

"How does it feel to be walking again?"

"Great. Any other answer, and I would be crazy. Now, if you'll excuse me, Doc, I got a . . . some planning to do. I need to think."

Clearly stonewalled, the doctor joined his comrade, saving Ray from having to answer his next question. Saving him from admitting that he'd almost said he had a battle to plan.

Saving him from admitting that the battle was with his wife.

Ray drove Rita and himself home as dusk settled over the capital of Wardhaven.

"I understand you got the stone working," Rita finally said to break the long silence.

"Yes," Ray admitted to the cool evening air. "We plotted eight jump points that will take you from here to Santa Maria without the wild ride we had." He felt mighty proud of that.

"We would have gotten even more done, but that Spy's infowar specialist wants us to wring some kind of weapon out of that rock. I think she's chasing up the wrong tree. Lek needed the help of a part of Santa Maria's world computer to make it do what it's doing for us. We can no more reprogram it than a caveman could program a course into a starship. We're going to have to settle for what it does."

"And what does it do?"

"I suspect you know. They got several hundred jump points debriefed out of me. We're concentrating on those in known human space and working out from them."

"So I heard."

Ray reached across, let his finger brush her stomach. "Honey, I'll be back before this little butterfly that you feel fluttering around within you is stomping around enough for me to feel him, her, whomever. You haven't told me if it's a boy or girl."

"I haven't asked," Rita answered. "I don't intend to."

Ray accepted that with a shrug. He was doing what he felt he had to do. That didn't leave him much room for telling her what to do. "I'll be back quickly."

Rita turned away to look out her own window. In her reflection, Ray saw a tear work its way down her cheek.

ELEUEN

RUTH NEEDED TO talk, to Trouble, to Becky, to lots of people.

She got out of the warren of slums fairly easily but found her way back to the embassy blocked by a long line of tanks and troop carriers slowly making their way up the main avenue that led past the embassy's front door.

Ruth used side roads, now unusually busy, to find an underpass and her way to the parking lot beside their quarters. As she expected, Trouble was not at home.

On a hunch, Ruth headed for the tanks. Sure enough, her Marine captain was happy as any kid at Christmas, inspecting the hardware inventory lumbering by.

"Not worth shit," Gunny grumbled beside Trouble.

"Looks that way." Trouble nodded.

"Looks pretty impressive to me," Becky Graven, the senior Foreign Service Officer, said, joining them.

"Not to infantry swine what hunt tanks for fun," Gunny growled.

"Enlighten me," the woman from the embassy said.

"To start with, notice the paint," Trouble offered.

"Fresh and shiny," Becky observed.

"And put on nice, thick, and in all the wrong places," Gunny said, butter melting in his mouth.

"For Christ sakes"—his good humor vanished—"some five-thumbed nitwit painted over the laser range finder on that one. Those ladies don't know shit from Shinola."

All Ruth saw was a big, lumbering, thoroughly painted mass of heavy metal. Apparently, Becky was just as unenlightened.

"I don't get it."

Gunny started to point, but Trouble cleared his throat, and

the sergeant turned the gesture into an ear scratch, then let his hand fall back to his side.

Trouble turned to Becky, and in a voice that carried just barely above the rumble of the tanks said, "We're watching them. They're watching us watching them. I don't want to tell them anything I don't have to, but notice where the turret meets the hull of the tanks."

"Yes," Becky and Ruth said.

"There should be a black gasket showing there. They've painted over it. Not good for the gasket, not good for the tank. It leads cynical folks like me and Gunny to suspect that tank hasn't moved its turret for quite some time."

He paused to take in more of the parade, then went on.

"Notice the mantle on the next three tanks coming up. That's the big blocky thing where the gun joins the turret. Solid paint. That gun hasn't gone out of battery since it was painted. All the guns in this battalion are at the same angle. I don't think they've used 'em since Christ was a boot. I don't think they know how to use 'em."

"What's it tell you, Marine?" the diplomat asked.

"These tanks might be able to hold their own in a fight—with unarmed civilians. Then again, if the civilians knew how to concoct Molotov cocktails, maybe not so much."

"Captain, new battalion coming up," Gunny noted.

There was no break in the three-abreast parade of metal monsters, not to the untrained eye. Under Gunny and Trouble's tutelage, Ruth now knew what to look for.

These guns were pointed up, but at slightly different angles. The tanks had been painted recently, but unlike the ones before, they didn't look like they'd been dipped in the paint bucket.

Places had been missed. Places that Ruth now knew shouldn't be painted.

Becky nodded beside the two Marines. "Then again, some do know shit from Shinola."

"Looks that way, ma'am," Gunny agreed. "Looks that way."

Ruth took the pause in the conversation that followed to run through her day.

As she described the side of Petrograd she'd visited, a scowl grew on Trouble's face. When she finished, he turned to Gunny.

"I want a load out from the *Patton*. Three units of fire of nonlethal area suppressants for a platoon. Include both personal and squad-size canisters."

"Yes, sir," Gunny answered.

"Ruth, you don't leave here tomorrow without a couple of those personal canisters. Gunny will see that you get trained in them."

Ruth refused to answer yes, sir. "If you say so, love." Neither Gunny nor Becky attempted to hide their smirks.

"Yes, I do say so, Mrs. Captain, love."

Ruth refused to let the blush rising on her cheeks fluster her. "Becky, what do you make of this story about the plant managers keeping the different nationalities fighting?"

"Interesting," Becky said slowly. "I've wondered about that. I don't have any good answers. We don't have any intel from inside the plants, either, until now. We should have, but before the war, this planet was handled by the commerce side of galactic affairs, not political. Might explain a lot of missing holes in my model of this place's operation. Ruth, will you debrief with one of my people on everything you're finding?"

"I'd prefer she debriefed with you," Trouble cut in. "This building leaks like a sieve."

Ruth would have rather said that herself. She elbowed her husband.

"I have to agree with you." Becky laughed. "Too many holdovers from the old regime inside as well as outside. And I'll take that nudge to be agreement in content if not the process of delivery, Ruth."

"Yes," she said, with a defiant frown at the now-blank-faced Marine beside her.

"I suspect we all have things to do," the political officer said, and left.

President Milassi worked his way through his nightly reading. Most of it bored him to tears, but he left tears to those who displeased him. Knowledge was power, and power was something Steffo Milassi liked very well.

Eyes glazing over from one too many reports from fools who couldn't tell a rebellious citizen from a tired worker just having a bad day, Steffo called up the Bear's report. It usually was enjoyable reading.

So the woman had just smiled like an empty-headed mannequin and walked away. He highlighted her name and had his database check her history. Born and raised where? Hurtford Corner. What kind of name was that? Another data call.

Did country-bumpkin places like that still exist? Apparently so!

Steffo read the rest of Bear's report and started to go on to the next one.

Then he paused.

This Ruth was married to a Marine officer. Lots of Milassi's henchmen had quiet women to come home to, to raise the children, show up at formal parties . . . and make no waves about what happened elsewhere.

Had the Marine chosen such a zed?

This woman was not staying home. Raising crops on a warship! Again, Steffo shook his head. The worlds of men were strange. He tapped the Marine's name.

The database started immediately providing him with news clippings, published and private reports that the man figured prominently in. It took a long time for the database to complete its report to him . . . an unusually long time.

So this was the man who had cause Peterwald so much trouble on Riddle. Steffo allowed himself a belly laugh at the thought of how Henry would have taken the news of yet another failure.

Steffo's laugh died quickly. He had that man here. Now!

His minions had reported on this man. Trouble he called himself. His agents said he was just another little boy who liked to play soldier. Just another time server.

Hadn't they checked him out? Milassi noted that the Riddle material had just been added to the database. He had the database search those files for Ruth's name.

Nothing.

"Where were they married?" he asked.

The database promptly answered Riddle.

"Search the files of slaves on the farm that owned Trouble." Yes, there was a Ruth. Different last name. He didn't bother checking her maiden name.

He already knew enough. That woman was no innocent child on a strange planet.

"Bear, tell me everything about this woman," Steffo growled at the report. "If you need more men, get them. This Marine and his woman are up to something. Hunt until you find it."

TWELVE

RAY LONGKNIFE SETTLED his back firmly against his seat, tightened his straps, and rested his hand where his thumb could flip on his seat's high-gee switch in a split second.

The *Second Chance* was about to make its fourth jump this voyage; everything was working perfectly. But the memory of a bad, a very bad jump, just three months ago still burned.

Now, Ray entered each jump cautiously. Probably would for the rest of his life. Caution, a strange word for an old warhorse. Still, he was alive, and caution seemed a good watchword for him and the baby Rita was carrying.

"Coming up on the jump," the *Second Chance*'s jump master announced.

"This puppy's got more wiggle than I expected," she added in a low mutter.

Ray frowned; Sandy had drained Ray's head of all the information about this particular point. She knew it orbited eight different solar systems. She'd seemed confident that she now knew all there was to know and that she'd have no problems plotting the strange meanderings of this jump point as it orbited this one star.

Interesting.

The stars on the main screen flickered, went out, and came back—different.

Ray took his usual deep breath and waited while experts on the ship's bridge did their job.

"Star matches expectations," sensors reported first. Ray let out his breath and took another.

"No electronic emissions on the usual communications frequencies," came from the radio shack.

That was usual, but for this system, it puzzled Ray.

"We've identified ten planets. Do you want a close-up of the fourth on main screen?" the helm asked.

"Do it," Captain Mattim Abeeb, beside Ray, ordered.

The fourth planet in this system haunted Ray's dreams. It should have been a nice Earth-like orb, blue-green with water and life, orbited by one large moon.

The picture that came on screen showed a yellow-brown planet with a halo of dust.

"Enhance," Matt ordered.

Ray watched as the computer remapped the picture two, three, four times. The color resolved itself into patches of red, yellow, brown, blue, and black. There was none of the fuzziness around the edge that planets with atmospheres had. Splotching the patches, adding to them and dividing them, were craters.

"Some of those holes must be hundreds of miles across," someone breathed.

The skipper glanced at Ray with a raised, questioning eyebrow.

Right, what next?

Ray was just as puzzled. This was supposed to be a quick duck in, take a few pictures, and run.

If the system were still teeming with the people who'd built the jump points, one or two million years ago, Ray would have reported back to Humanity that it was time to make a first contact.

Now?

"Sandy"—Matt turned to his jump master—"could the orbit of the fourth planet's moon have decayed in a million years?"

The woman shook her head, short, red curls flying in their low-gee acceleration.

"I've been looking that over. It was good for a billion years or more. Don't know anything about its interior, though," she added, answering the next question. "No idea what could have cracked it like that." She nodded toward the screen.

"Captain, this is real interesting," a diminutive woman in midshipman grays muttered.

Ray suppressed a groan; Matt was less successful.

When this tiny member of Matt's brain trust found

something "interesting," it usually meant the next month was blown.

Kat turned to them. "Captain, you really ought to see this. Can I put it on the main screen?"

"Do it," the skipper said with a sigh.

The main screen changed; a gas giant filled it with a wild kaleidoscope of colors.

The screen began to zoom. A tiny dot grew and took on form.

"It looks like a space station. It's orbiting the nearest gas giant to this jump. Just a hop, skip, and jump away," the middie explained. "But look at what it's trailing!"

The whole bridge took a careful look.

"It can't be dragging that through the upper atmosphere of that gas giant?" The helmsman said, shaking his head.

"I think it is," Sandy said from beside Kat. "That station has an electromagnetic field. It's strong enough to protect it from that giant's radiation, and solar noise, too."

"Still?" Matt said.

Kat started to shoot an answer back, but Sandy elbowed her young assistant in the ribs as the jump master rubbed her eyes with both hands.

In the following silence, the two women went over their board again, fingers flitting from one readout to the next.

"Yes." Sandy finally answered. "Assuming a million years has passed since the data in Ray's skull was updated, that planet down there has been rocked to hell by its fractured moon, but this station is still electronically active."

Sandy frowned. "And it's still towing something through a gravity well that sucks to beat Sol's old Jupiter."

"How long to get there?" Matt asked.

"Nineteen hours at one gee," the helm answered. "Less at one point five."

"You good for one point five gees, Colonel?" Matt asked.

Ray nodded.

This mystery was too much to walk away from. His arrival at Savannah would have to wait.

Later, the *Second Chance* settled into an orbit well above the . . . something.

While that something might be protected from the radiation

coming off the gas giant below, the exploration ship was most definitely not. Exploration of the . . . something . . . would have to start with remotes.

Probes were launched, and while most held back, one slowly made an approach to what began quickly to look like a space station, complete with docks and other paraphernalia that you'd expect on a transit base.

And since any such place in human space would have a good selection of defensive gear, the lead probe was very expendable.

But nothing happened.

Nothing continued to happen while the probe approached and actually parked itself a bare fifty meters from the longest dock.

The station was not turning.

"Folks were either weightless on that thing, or they've got or had controllable gravity," the middie seated beside the jump navigator whispered.

"So it seems," Mattim agreed, but softly, not wanting to disturb anything or feed Kat's voracious mind.

Still, the middie preened at the praise.

"Well," Ray said, "do we sit back here, or do we go in and see what they left for us?"

"What we, *sir*?" the captain said.

"I've got a good pair of legs under me. If there's gravity aboard that station, I can walk. And if there is not gravity, I can float as good as anyone."

"Mr. Minister," Mattim began.

"Don't give me any of that Mr. Minister stuff. You think I'm getting the taxpayers of Wardhaven to pay for all this exploration just so you folks can have all the fun. I get some of the fun, or you can find yourself another sugar daddy."

"You get yourself killed, and our sugar *mommy* is going to string us all up by our balls."

"Even those of us who don't have any," Sandy added.

"I'm going over there," Ray said, brooking no opposition.

The captain and the colonel stared at each other for several seconds.

"Mary, report to the bridge," announced Mattim, leaving the question hanging.

Mary, the chief of security was formerly a captain in the Society of Humanity Marine Corps. Her platoon of Marines had defeated the colonel's proud 2nd Guard Brigade in the recent unpleasantness.

So, would Captain Mattim order her to pump the colonel full of sleepy darts or escort him off to be outfitted with a space suit?

THIRTEEN

DESPITE THE SCOWL on Captain Abeeb's ebony face, the space suit won. Though later he would claim it was a close call, only settled on points.

A very few points.

However it was, Ray found himself suiting up and surrounded by a big chunk of the crew that had defeated his proud 2nd Guard Brigade. Mary had called in the miners from the *Second Chance*'s security detachment.

"Du, you better come, too," Mary said. "I've got to have someone from the street kids or they'll think I'm dissing them. You want anyone else?"

"Bruno, report to the drop bay."

"Why Bruno?" Mary asked. "If you don't mind me asking?"

"He reads a lot of that science-fiction shit. I figure he'll love the chance to see some of it up close. And if not, he deserves it for bending our ears all the time."

Bruno arrived, with a tiny slip of a woman right behind him.

"Kat, what are you doing here?" Mary demanded.

"I'm going, too," she said, and if there had been any gravity, she would have put her foot down. "Me and Bruno are a team. He's got the imagination, and I got the book learning." Kat seemed a bit taken aback by what she'd just said. "At least that's what he says."

"Did you ask Captain Abeeb's permission?" Ray asked as he settled his suit around him.

"I figured I'd ask forgiveness later. That seems to work best around here," she said with a most angelic smile.

"Do we even have a suit that will fit you?" Mary asked.

"You think I'd head out to explore the galaxy and not have a space suit?" the scientist said. "It wasn't easy, but I found a place that máde suits in any size. They even had a can for babies."

Kat headed for a locker and began pulling on a suit that was perfect for her diminutive frame.

Shuttle 3 had been rigged with a compartment that could be opened to space without dunking the pilots in vacuum. It took them over to the longest dock projecting from the station and waited patiently as they disembarked.

Mary went first and used her experience in the mines to jet over to the dock's hatch with a tether line. In a few moments, she had it attached to a metal loop that looked like it had been put there just for the purpose.

Lek went hand over hand across and joined her, staring at the hatch. There was a pressure plate that looked like it would have opened it if it had power.

Being Lek, he pressed it.

Nothing happened.

However, as he felt around it, a small door opened and the two of them found themselves looking at a lever. He and Mary discussed it, but not for long.

Lek worked the lever up and down several times . . . and the door opened a crack.

"Keep it up, Lek. It's working," Mary said.

The hatch gaped more and more inviting.

"I'm the first in," Ray said, and found he'd fallen into his command voice.

"Like hell you are, sir," Mary shot back. "I broke your back once already, Colonel. Don't make me break your head. Du, you're my best shot. You go first. How good a shot is Bruno?"

"Better than him," came back fast.

"Not yet, Little Brother, but you come second."

"I'm third," piped Kat. "If it's a bug-eyed monster, you shoot it. If not, I'll identify it and figure out what we can do with it."

"Okay," Mary said, sounding exasperated to Ray.

How did this bunch beat the 2nd Guard with this kind of a command lash-up?

"Lek, you go in right behind me, and, Colonel, then you can come in. Okay?"

"How come you make me follow orders when the rest of this mob doesn't?" Ray demanded of Mary.

"Because you, sir, know what an order is when it bites you, and you, *sir*, have a loving wife and baby waiting for you. Enough said?" Mary said, as she waved her first trigger puller through the hole.

Ray sat back to wait his turn, assuming no bug-eyed monster tried to gobble down the first two through the hatch. No bloodcurdling screams came on net, and Kat's tiny form wiggled her way inside.

Lek kept pumping, and the hatch gaped wider. Now it was Mary's turn. Rifle at the ready in one hand, the other on the side of the portal, she moved herself slowly through the opening.

"Lek, it looks okay in here. Come on in, and, Colonel, you come, too. It's a sight to see."

Ray waited patently while the old electronic wizard made his way in, then pushed off from the wire and glided through the hatch.

Mary was right. It was a sight to see.

The corridor, or whatever it was meant to be, was wide and high. Along what Ray took for the ceiling was something that glowed softly.

"Did someone turn on the lights?" Ray asked.

"I don't think so," Du answered him. "We just flashed our own lights around, and those things started glowing when our lights touched them. The more we put light on them, the more they glow, and the farther down this hall the light goes. Ain't that something?"

"Not as interesting as the way there ain't no hatch here," Lek said. "What do these folks do, drain the station every time someone goes outside?"

"Will you look at that?" Bruno marveled on net. "If you ask me, they had something that started here and kind of kept in the air as you walked out to the hatch."

"What kind of crazy are you, Dude?" Du said. "You read too much shit."

"No," Kat said. "It makes sense. There's all this writing on the wall, and a big line here on the floor. At least I think it's the floor. If those really are lights, that would make them the ceiling, right. I read about some ideas like this."

"That's crazy," Lek said. "They've got to have an air lock."

"But they don't," Mary said. "Maybe the kids have it right."

"Old lady, you going crazy on us, too?" Du asked.

"No, Du, I'm not crazy, just fitting what we're seeing to what the kids think it might be. Lek, there is no air lock, but there is a hatch. Either they had something here to keep the air in when they opened that bugger, or they drained the air out of this place every time they opened the door. Colonel, how dumb do you think these people were?"

"Not dumb at all. Let's assume for the moment that the kids have the better explanation of this than we've heard so far. Whatever it was, it clearly isn't working now, so let's move along. There's a whole lot of stuff left to see. Let's see it."

"You heard the colonel," Mary said in a straw-boss voice. "Let's move."

In a loose formation, with gunners out front, they drifted along the huge corridor. As they got close to the station, it got really strange.

"They definitely had artificial gravity," Ray said as the entire passageway did a twist and the ceiling with the lights switched over to where a wall had been.

The new floor was where the other wall used to be.

With that rearrangement, they found themselves moving into the main station.

On a human station, the A deck was the outer wall of the station. As the station spun, people walked on the outer hull. Occasionally, a window in the floor would let them look down and see the stars.

On this station, down was where you'd expect it, and the windows with the stars were on the walls, where they belonged.

"Nice," Mary said. "I wonder how they did it?"

"Your guess is as good as mine," Ray said.

The floor here was wide open and huge, except for a small spindle at the center of the station, and several ramps up and down to the next decks. As they approached the nearest one, Mary asked, "Colonel, up or down?"

"How about up. I'd like to find the control center. I'm kind of curious as to what it looks like."

"Me too," said Lek.

"Then the control center it is."

Still, Mary told off two of her miners to hang in the general area of the ramp. They still had radio contact with the

Second Chance, but the static was getting worse the farther they went.

Bruno made another discovery, or guess. One side of the ramp had a different-color floor and some sort of writing on the wall. "I bet that section has less gravity so people can walk up it easier."

Ray shrugged, as much as his suit let him. One guess was as good as any. His guess was that they were for directing traffic. Folks going up were to stay on one side, those going down the other.

Of course, his explanation limped a bit. Why was there signage on only one side?

He was glad he kept his mouth shut. Let the young jabber on like magpies; it hurt them less when they fell.

The next deck was much like the one below it although there seemed to be shops and other places of business spreading out from the spindle. At least that was what Bruno and Kat named them.

Ray let them guess and headed for the next ramp.

There things got interesting.

The spindle reached out to cover half the deck. There was still plenty of room for the promenading customer to look out the windows or head for the next ramp up. But to the inward side was a lot of blank wall.

No art. No signs. Just blank wall.

Interesting.

Mary sent Du with several of her miners to the right. She and Ray, with Lek and the kids, went left around the spindle.

For the first time since they'd entered the station, the science-fiction pair were quiet.

They were halfway around when they found doors. Discreet doors with small signs that, no doubt, said, FOR AUTHORIZED PERSONNEL ONLY. KEEP OUT! THIS MEANS YOU! WHAT PART OF KEEP OUT DON'T YOU UNDERSTAND!

The kids provided the commentary. Apparently, they had vivid imaginations and a lot of experience with not keeping out of what they had been told to keep out of.

Ray smiled and asked Lek to figure out a way in.

That took more time than he expected. Du and his team of

explorers were just coming up on them when Lek said, "Well, bless my soul. It's that easy."

"How easy?" Mary asked.

"Well, likely it wouldn't be this easy if the station were still under power, but if I just slip a thin blade of metal where the lock is, I can push the thing back in its socket, and bingo! The door opens."

It didn't.

"Okay, let's see if there are more locks," the old miner said.

There were. The three species that built the space jumps used three locks to secure important doors.

Lek applied three thin blades of metal, and those three locks were defeated.

The doors opened wide. Mary assigned a miner to see that they didn't close. He wedged them open, and they all moved into a dark space that began to light up as its overhead reflected back to them the light of their own lamps.

Clearly, this was a vestibule. Three doors led out, one to the right and left, and one deeper in.

Ray didn't even have to tell the rest of them; they headed for the inner door. It resisted them for a few minutes until one of the kids asked if it might not open inward but maybe sideways.

Lek pried it open with a simple crowbar, then strong backs went to work pushing the doors back into the wall.

"Just like in the movies," Kat said.

Inside was one big circular room. Above was the usual glow stuff that took up their light and gave it back a hundredfold.

Along the walls were blank spaces that took in the light and gave back nothing.

"Monitors. Computer displays," Kat guessed before Ray could even open his mouth. There were "things" beneath the so-called monitors, but whether they were readouts or their type of keyboards was anyone's guess and, for once, the kids weren't guessing.

It was what stood in the middle of the room that drew them in.

It was an even-sided obelisk. At first glance, it looked like the stone from Santa Maria. But only at first glance.

This one was as different from the stone one as a plastic mock-up is from a real rocket ship.

One glance at it, and Ray was filled with a thousand questions as to why a mere stone had been made to do what it did when something like this was so much more. So much . . .

Looking at it, Ray didn't know what "more" he was trying to describe. What he did know was what the stone had been carved to look like. That the stone had done anything left Ray with so many questions that he couldn't begin to order them.

"What is that thing?" Kat asked.

"The main control of the station," Ray said without the slightest doubt in his mind.

"How does it work?" Mary asked.

"I haven't the foggiest idea," Ray said.

"Is it working?" Mary asked.

"Matt," Ray called on net. "What do things look like from your end?"

"We moved the *Second Chance* in close to the station," came through clear as a bell. "The ship was building up an electrical charge. As soon as we got within ten klicks of the station, it drained away, and we're doing fine."

"Is the station showing any activity?" Ray asked.

"Nothing that it hadn't previously. Which wasn't a lot."

"Fine. Let us know if anything changes."

"You'll be the second to know, right after me," was the skipper's reply.

"It feels like soap," Kat said.

While Ray was talking, the two kids, clearly showing a deep and sincere lack of good sense, had been messing with the obelisk.

"Feel it. Your gloves just slips off it like it was a bar of soap," the young scientist said.

"Be glad it didn't eat your hand," Du, ever the pessimist, growled.

"Don't be silly," Kat said.

"Does it reflect light?" Ray asked.

"Hard to tell," Lek said. "Too much light in here."

"Everyone, douse your lights," Ray ordered.

"How come?" one of the miners demanded.

"What's the matter, you afraid of the dark?"

"No, but being in the dark in a weird place like this don't strike me as the best idea ever."

"Please douse your lights," Ray said, having a hard time believing that he was asking *these* Marines, even these *former* Marines, to please do something.

"You heard the colonel. Lights out," Mary growled. "If any of you get eaten by monsters in the dark, I'll apologize and put you on light duty for the rest of the month."

"It's the twenty-eighth already," someone shot back, but the lights went out.

It took a long minute for the room to darken, but when it did, it was darker than any place Ray had ever been.

"I guess this is what dark really is," Kat said.

"It gives me the willies," someone said.

"Colonel, what do you want to do?" Mary asked.

Ray leaned close to the obelisk. He'd coasted around it before the lights went out. This particular side seemed to call to him. If anyone asked, he'd never be able to say just what he meant by that. Still, as the dark got darker, he'd waited at this particular side.

Leaning against it, he felt nothing he hadn't felt walking around it. There was some kind of weird, minimal greeting for him, but nothing more.

He leaned as close to it as the laws of physics allowed, two items not being able to occupy the same space, and switched on the three lights of his suit.

The obelisk reflected nothing back. It took the light in and kept it.

None of Ray's light made it up to the overhead. Those . . . whatevers . . . stayed dark.

"That's interesting," Mary said.

"Very interesting," Lek echoed. "Colonel, would you mind if I shined a laser into this thing? All my instruments haven't been able to give me any kind of analysis of it. My eyes tell me it's sitting right here in front of me. My best stuff for field testing minerals don't tell me a thing. It's as if the damn thing isn't there."

"Go ahead, Lek. It seems to like the light. Let's see what it thinks of a small laser. It is a *small*, low-power laser, isn't it?"

"I couldn't lug around anything else. All I'm looking for is a reflection. Something that tells me what it's made of. I'm going to beam it at one of the edges. With luck, some of the light will get through to the other side, and we can tell something from what it lets out.

Ray waited for half a minute while nothing happened.

"Lek, turn on the laser."

"Colonel, it's been on since you told me to turn it on."

"I don't see any light."

"Neither do I, sir. It's taking in the laser and not giving anything back."

"Folks," came Captain Mattim's voice from the *Second Chance*, "we're seeing changes in the station. We're getting readouts from the station where before, we weren't getting anything."

Ray beamed his lights up at the overhead. The blackest black went to gray, then almost decent illumination.

It was just enough for him to see the door roll closed behind them.

FOURTEEN

"THAT'S INTERESTING," WAS Kat's only reaction.

Mary ordered Lek back to reopen the door. He went as fast as he could drift.

"I think we're getting some gravity," he said as he hit the wall next to the doors.

Bruno held out his rifle and let go of it. It didn't stay suspended in space but began a slow, lazy descent to the floor.

Bruno grabbed his gun and spun around, looking for what monster had made it fall. He, of course, saw nothing but his fellow humans.

Kat held up her box of sensors. "Maybe a hundredth of a gee. No air, though. It's still vacuum."

"That would depend on where they kept their air and how much of the life support system is still working," Mary said with the calm that Ray expected in a good leader.

"Lek, how's that door coming?" she next asked.

"Not so good, ma'am. What I used to get in here isn't working to get us out. This door is sincerely locked."

"Matt, what are you getting?" Ray called on net.

"Folks, things are happening on that station. Not a lot, but my people tell me that some thing or things are powering up. One makes noises like a big defensive laser, but we don't see anything like a laser anywhere on the station. It's kind of like the lack of readouts on that Vanishing Box on Santa Maria."

"That got you worried, Matt?"

"This whole thing has me worried. Could you folks hotfoot it back here?"

"No can do, Matt. It seems we're now locked in, and the door won't open for us anymore."

"Damn. Ray, I'm going to have to back the *Second Chance* off a few thousand klicks. Maybe more."

"I understand. Could you leave the shuttle for us?"

"Sorry, Ray, but the crew already docked back with us. I'm not sure if I ordered them back that they'd go."

"Not everyone loves me like Rita," Ray said, remembering how one pilot had held on the deck against orders so his crippled body could be lugged aboard.

"When we get out of here, we'll signal for you to come in and pick us up."

"We'll be waiting for your call," Abeeb answered.

Mary leaned close to touch helmets with Ray. "Which begs the question, how do we get out of here?"

"Or how do we get this station to go back to sleep?" he added.

"Was it asleep?"

"That's the impression I got."

"You're feeling things about this place?"

"Sort of."

"You want to lean against this thing and see if it will talk to you?"

"That's what we do next."

Mary stepped away, then had two of her miners rig a line around the obelisk and attach it to Ray so he was held in close to it. He pressed his hands firmly against the surface of what he had come to think of as the command mechanism.

Nothing.

He rearranged the gloves on his hands to bring more of his palms and fingers to the place of contact.

More nothing.

Now he kept his hands there, but pushed his helmet against the obelisk.

Again, nothing.

"Mary, could you help me? I need to get my forehead up against the faceplate of this helmet."

"They aren't designed for that. I think they're designed to prevent that."

"Yeah, that's what I'm finding. Could you and Lek hold it in place and pull back on my collar? Do whatever you think will help me get my head up against the surface."

They worked at it for a minutes before Ray was satisfied.

"You think maybe we ought to blow the doors? We got some C-14. We could do it," Du suggested while they struggled with the helmet.

"And if it doesn't blow out the door, where's the pressure going to go?" Mary asked back.

"I don't know. You miners blow a lot of things."

"Not in an enclosed space, we don't. You want smashed miner, you might try that."

"How strong are these walls?" the street-smart kid demanded.

"You take two of my miners over there and try to drill a hole in one of them," Mary said, then leaned her helmet against Ray's. "I hope this works, 'cause I don't know how long I can keep these folks from trying damn-fool stunts like that one."

"I hear you," Ray said. "I think I've got it the way I want it," he said on net.

He leaned hard against the obelisk, hands and forehead separate from it only by the thin film of his gloves and the few millimeters of faceplate.

Hello. Everything is fine. Sleep now. Go back to sleep.

He might as well have been talking to himself.

He leaned back.

"Anything?" Mary asked, helmet to helmet.

"Not a damn thing."

"Any more ideas, Colonel?"

"Yeah, but you and Rita ain't going to like it."

"What ain't I gonna like?"

"Help me take the gloves and helmet off."

"Bad idea," Mary said.

"You got one better?"

"No," she admitted.

"You and Lek help me get the gloves and helmet off. I make contact and as soon as I sing it a lullaby and put it back to sleep, you lock me back in my suit."

"The idea stinks, sir."

"It's the only idea any of us have."

"Du, how you doing drilling that hole?" Mary asked on net.

"Not. We ain't even marred the surface."

"So we're not likely to blow our way out of here. Okay, listen up. The colonel thinks if he goes naked with this thing, he can maybe talk it out of what it's doing and put it back to sleep."

"Don't space kill a guy?" Du asked.

"It does, Du, but it takes time," Mary said. "Not a lot of time, but a few minutes. Okay, listen up, folks. Here's what we're going to do. Du, you got fast hands. You work on his right glove. Kat, you're small. Do you think you could handle his left glove?"

"I'll try," had more tremble in it than Ray liked hearing when his life depended on it, but Mary was right. It was going to get awfully crowded around him, and a small set of hands might be just what he needed.

Without a word, several of Mary's miners began rigging more cables around the obelisk and attaching Du, Kat, and Mary firmly in place around Ray.

"Ray, have you ever considered anything as crazy as this before in your life?" Mary asked.

"Can't remember ever."

"Well, the old-timers in the mines like to tell every nugget about what they did back in the day. No doubt, none of them ever did the naked-to-space thing, but it makes for a scary tale.

"When you're naked to vacuum, you let everything out of your system. Your lungs, your gut, your whatever. You try to hold any of that inside, and you're likely to pop your guts like a balloon. Even after we put you back together, you'll be bleeding out internally, so Colonel, if you got any problem with farting or maybe pissing your pants or pooping in them, get that silly shit out of your head. If it wants out, you let it. And yes, you'll be having a hell of a time getting air back into you when you're done with this stupid idea, but we'll worry about that later. Assuming there's enough of us left later to worry about you."

"Thank you for your loving advice," Ray said, wondering just how bad this was going to get.

"And if you think I'm making this worse than it has to be, Colonel," said Mary, as if reading his mind, "it's going to be a whole lot worse than I'm telling you. Just pray that once all the pain starts, you can remember why you are doing this. Okay?"

"Okay," Ray said. "This will hurt more than I've ever hurt in my life, and I've got to remember through the agony that I'm here to talk nice things to this rock, or whatever it is."

"That's the way it is. You still want to go through with this?"

"Anybody come up with a better idea while you were scaring the shit out of me?"

That brought a big silence.

"Now, before we start, you get as much oxygen as you can in your blood."

Ray took deep breaths, all the time wondering what that would do to his bloodstream and trying not to think about the bends, not that he knew a lot about them.

A minute later, he said, "Okay, folks. On three, start taking the gloves off. Helmet, too, Mary."

"One, two, you still want to do this?" Mary asked. He didn't say anything.

"Three."

Immediately, he began feeling his life-giving air leak from his hands and neck.

Don't hold anything in, he remembered to tell himself. *Let it all out.*

And it was fast going out. Air spewed from his mouth and ass. He found himself pissing and not all the stuff heading out his rear was gas.

My suit's going to be a mess.

But now was no time to be squeamish. His hands were free, and Mary was holding his helmet over his head. He touched the obelisk.

Damn that thing is cold. It was, but not so cold that it froze his hands to it.

He rested his head on the thing.

Immediately, he got the worst brain freeze of his life.

Everything is fine, he thought. *There is no threat to you. Go back to sleep.*

Over and over he repeated the same message.

At first, he felt agitation. It was hard to separate what he was feeling from the obelisk from the agony that was starting to sweep through his own flesh and blood.

It was a struggle to keep the pain out of his thoughts, but

that was what he had to do. Years of hard discipline bent his flesh to his will.

Slowly, the agitation from the station settled down. Almost, Ray could hear a lullaby in the back of his brain.

And Mary was bringing the helmet down on his head and dogging it down fast. His hands were wrapped in gloves again and precious oxygen was flowing into his mask. His suit was taking on pressure, pressing all sorts of squishy stuff against his skin.

Oh, joy.

But the real joy was the fresh air on his face.

He opened his mouth wide and let it flow freely in. He could feel it coming in the other end as well. What a mess he'd be.

"You did it," Mary shouted on net. "You did something. Matt says the station cut off like someone had hit a light switch. One minute there was stuff causing his board to show red, the next minute it was back to being dead air. Now, we need to get out of here fast. Whatever was protecting this place from the magnetic storm around it is not there anymore."

Du and Mary unstrapped Ray from the obelisk and aimed him at the door Lek already had pried open. They basically flew Ray out of the control center, down the two ramps and out the long dock, touching down on surfaces only long enough to push off again.

That was mighty kind of them, because Ray was starting to feel pain in every inch of his body. It didn't matter what it was, it felt full-on agony.

The shuttle was there waiting for them. The *Second Chance* had pulled back in close. But it was boosting out of the gas giant's orbit at 1.5 gees even as they dragged Ray from the shuttle.

They shucked him out of his suit. Not all the mess in there was brown. He'd bled as well from several embarrassing orifices. The medics bundled him up, and, as he expected, put him in a chamber to slowly bring him up to the proper pressure.

Mattim called him from the bridge.

"You okay?" was his first question.

"As good as any soldier has a right to expect after he does a damn-fool stunt like that."

"That saved us all," Matt added.

"We headed for Savannah?" was Ray's response to the praise.

"We sure ain't hanging around here, old man. Yes, Savannah will be our next stop."

"Okay, but Matt, digging around stuff left by the Three is going to be dangerous."

"You noticed."

"Yes, even an old soldier can notice that. We need those three kids from Santa Maria who worked with me out here. It's too risky to go into this kind of stuff without someone with their commlink."

"How do you think their parents will take to the idea of their having to do something like you just did?"

"Not well," Ray admitted. "Still, we need to ask. If I hadn't been there, your entire exploration team would be dead."

"Not to mention my ship if that thing had decided to vanish my engines or my bridge."

"Exactly."

"Maybe we humans need to stay home in bed?" the starship captain said.

"What are the chances of that?" answered the retired soldier, now politician.

"Slim to none. I'll advise your wife of what just happened and send along your suggestion that exploration ships that intend to mess with the stuff left by the Three need to have either you or one of the kids."

"Could you go easy on how close we came to almost getting killed?"

"You want your smart bride to read it, or read it between the lines?"

Ray made a face. "She is smart, isn't she?"

"Which begs the question why she married you."

"Too true. Okay, report it as it came down and I'll batten down the hatches for the blowback I deserve, and maybe she can get us some reinforcements."

"I'll see what I can do."

Ray lay back in the chamber, breathing in the nice air, and thought about how Rita would take to his latest stunt. They must have given him something because he fell asleep mulling that unpleasantness.

FIFTEEN

RUTH STUDIED THE farm reflected in the glasses she wore.

The picture came from a gossamer and tiny observation vehicle she had launched an hour ago by simply waving her hand out the window of the car as she sped down the expressway.

It had fit in her hand, weighing maybe twenty grams. In the sunlight, it had powered up and flown right out of her palm. Neat. Like some invisible bee.

Ruth could get to like this job.

Her "bee" had checked out the other two possibilities Alice had shown her a few days back. As expected, they were legitimate research centers, supporting the French-Catholic or Palestinian-Moslem farmers who kept the produce flowing into Petrograd.

Someone, about a hundred years back, had gotten together quite a collection of Earth's refuse and unwanted. Ruth scowled; no doubt they'd done it at cut-rate prices, too.

She was developing a distinct dislike for the folks running this place.

Take that fellow the kids called the Bear. He'd been all over her the last couple of days. She'd had to pick the kids up at a different place every day, taking a new route to lose him and his cab.

Becky had put Ruth in touch with the embassy's chauffeurs; they'd offered her tips on how to lose a tail. The kids, however, had been her best advice.

Ruth now knew paths and alleys that the chauffeurs just shook their heads at.

And to help the kids in juggling different pickup sites,

Ruth had gotten Alice a commlink of her own. The girl had almost cried.

"But now Major Barbara won't let me use hers."

"You've got your own," Ruth had answered, missing the point entirely.

"But if I don't have to go to her to use her link, she won't . . . I won't . . ."

Ruth began to see the problem. "I bet if you ask the Major if you can teach the other kids how to use a link, and tell her you'll sit with them to make sure they use it right, that you can use this link and other kids can use hers."

It had worked. At night now, Alice spent as much time as she wanted reading, listening, and learning.

And three other kids were taking turns where before it had been only Alice.

A small victory, but even small ones were worth celebrating on a place like Savannah.

Ruth glanced to the right, blinked three times. The picture on her glasses zoomed in on "The Farm," as Alice called it.

Unlike the other areas that had row upon row of crops that were familiar to Ruth, this place had a lot of different crops. None of them were familiar from her growing up on Hurtford Corner. A few looked familiar . . . from her time as a slave growing drugs on Riddle.

But there were so many. Some stood tall. Other were low to the ground. Some were bushy. Still others were spindly.

Ruth had her computer compare the crops to any that existed in a normal agribusiness database.

None came up.

She switched to her Drug Enforcement database.

Several plants came up immediately. Others might be related to known plants.

Ruth smiled. She'd found the experimental station she was hunting for.

Now, what to do about it?

She pulled off the expressway three exits down; she needed to refuel. She gave the kids money to buy food from the station. The kids looked wide-eyed at what was offered and timidly selected burgers and chips.

Ruth had them add a drink and paid for all using cash.

She had her credit chit, but this close to a hot site, she wasn't leaving any tracks.

As it turned out, that didn't matter.

A cab rolled into the station. The Bear glanced around from behind the wheel. When he saw her, he smiled.

The Bear's smile was downright nasty.

Ruth turned away.

That was a big mistake.

She heard the squeal of brakes and tires before she turned back to spot the two black police cars that had just charged in. Four men were out of the cars in a second and racing for her.

"What's the matter?" she said.

They didn't answer, just hit her, knocked her to the ground and started kicking.

The security team at the embassy made sure she had seen the video on self-protection. When she was knocked down, she went down on her butt. Once down, she did her best to cover her face with her arms and to roll with the kicks.

When a boot slammed into her stomach, she rolled with the boot. If she spotted a boot heading for her, she started rolling away from it. That even worked out well for the unseen boots slamming into her back. As often as not, she was rolling away from them before they could build up a good hit.

It still hurt like hell.

Thank the heavens Trouble had brought something new home last night.

An armored corset.

It wasn't very sexy, but it was supposed to stop a bullet.

It did seem to soften the force of the kicks.

Ruth rolled and thanked all that was good and holy for the new armor.

And punched the locator beacon and panic button between her breasts.

How long will it take a Marine reaction team to get here or wherever they intend to take me?

One roll let her glance at the children.

Tiny had dropped her drink and stuffed her fist in her mouth even as tears rolled down her cheeks. Alice Blue Bonnet had one hand on Tiny's arm, the other wrapped around Mouse, and was dragging them back around the corner toward the restrooms.

They'd stepped away to go to the bathroom, thank God, and been there when the Bear drove up.

Tiny was right to force her fist in her mouth. Now was no time for the kids to be seen or heard.

The kicks kept coming.

Is that all they're here for? Just to kick me to death?

Ruth had done what she was supposed to do, but it wasn't enough, not with four strong men doing everything they could to kick the stuffing out of her.

Her mouth was bleeding; she could taste the blood. Blood from somewhere on her forehead was flowing down into her eyes. She wished she could just pass out, but to lose consciousness would be to leave herself helpless under those boots.

What did the kids call them? Crushers.

They had that right.

Another car gunned into the station and came to a squealing halt.

Did these four guys need reinforcements to beat up one lone woman?

I'm a Marine's wife, not a Marine, fellows.

Suddenly, one of her assailants was on the deck beside her, holding his arm and screaming.

On second glance, and Ruth had to admit, her vision wasn't all that clear, the fellow's arm was twisted all wrong.

Since she hadn't been kicked for a second or three, Ruth risked rolling over. One of her attackers was backed up against the gas pump. Someone familiar was pummeling the black-clad thug.

That someone was familiar, but wrong. Oh, he was out of uniform.

Ruth could now spot a Marine a mile away. It must be the strange way her eyes were working that she needed three blinks to recognize this one.

Bear was out of his car now. No, the door hadn't been opened; Gunny had hauled him out through the window and was doing really horrible things to his face.

Ruth would have smiled at that, but it hurt to move any muscle.

The two other black boots had been turned into a pretzel by a woman Marine. They'd made the mistake of swinging on her. She'd used their swings to wrap them up and tie them in a knot.

Almost, Ruth laughed at that.

Almost. It hurt to even breathe, much less laugh.

Now the woman Marine was bending over Ruth. "They get you too bad?"

"They got me good," Ruth admitted.

"We'll get you back to the embassy, dearie."

"First, the kids. You got to get them out of here. We can't let the crushers see them, or they'll kill them."

"I hear you, dearie. None of these shits are looking at anything just now. Gunny, she's got the kids with her. Can I drive her car and the kids back where they belong?"

"You do that, Debbie. I think our job here is done. We'll take her back to the infirmary."

And a moment later, Gunny and the other Marine gently lifted Ruth into the backseat of a large sedan. Debbie corralled the kids and got them into Ruth's rental, and all of them were driving away before any of the local toughs finished their beauty sleep.

Gunny drove, leaving the other Marine to begin first aid on Ruth. He had her take a painkiller, then gingerly began cleaning the blood away.

"I'm seeing funny," Ruth told him.

"Concussions is way above my pay grade, ma'am. You'll have to talk to the doc about that."

"How did you get here so fast, Gunny?"

"Your husband, ma'am. The captain, he's been worried about you getting in over your head. He kind of gently suggested that we might want to take a drive in the country. He said you wouldn't much like it if you spotted us, so we hung well back. Maybe too far back, ma'am. Sorry we took so long to get here after you hit your panic button."

"I'm alive, Gunny, and very grateful to you for that privilege. I don't think those guys intended for me to be alive when they finished. I expected to be hauled in when they started, but they just kept kicking and never stopped."

"Yeah, we kind of noticed that, ma'am."

"You won't be in any trouble, will you?"

"Not if they know what's good for them," had an evil grin

in it. Ruth really regretted not being able to see Gunny's evil grin, but the pain meds were taking over. Her eyes were drooping, and she felt so sleepy. The pain was getting further and further away, so she let herself float on the relief as it came in.

SIXTEEN

MARY RODRIGO, CHIEF of Security for the Wardhaven explorer ship *Second Chance*, stepped from the shuttle into the bright Savannah sunshine.

A quick glance around showed her that no one had come out to greet the arriving dignitary. She considered that strange. Ray Longknife had killed President Urm and ended the Unity War. Mary figured everyone would want to turn out and give the man a cheer.

She'd been warned Savannah was different. It was already showing its colors.

Ray exited the shuttle now that she'd cleared him to. He did his own look around. Except for the usual workers on the landing field, it was pretty much empty.

"I guess arriving a day late helped us miss the party," Ray said as he nodded to Mary and her team of former Marines, now guards and whatever an explorer ship needed dirtside.

Mary shrugged. As soon as the *Second Chance* finished this job of running Ray out to Savannah and back to Wardhaven, they'd be off to the great unknown, opening up space and planets for humanity.

Mary liked that.

A black limo arrived, flanked by two big black SUVs fore and aft. Mary ushered Ray to the limo. She intended to ride shotgun. Du would take the lead SUV.

Then the trouble started.

Two more SUVs drove up and disgorged a dozen heavy-weight uglies. All sported machine pistols slung over their shoulders with their hands near the triggers.

The one that sported a pair of silver captain's bars strutted up to Mary. "We got laws here. No guns. Youse guys got guns. Youse got to turn them over to us."

Before Mary could say a word, Ray stepped up. "These people are my honor guard. They are all members of the Wardhaven Marine Corps and as such, have every right to bear arms."

Mary was, indeed, an officer in the Wardhaven Marine Corps Reserve. Apparently, Ray was activating her commission.

Would that solve this little problem?

Apparently it didn't for the big police captain. He said, "I don't see them in no uniforms."

"They've been seconded to the Wardhaven Explorer Corps to provide security for space exploration," the colonel said evenly.

Mary was wearing a merchant marine gray shipsuit. She pointed at the captain's bars on her collar. She'd thought they were just a way to show her seniority among the troops. Now she saw the wisdom of it.

"We'll see about that," the big ugly with rank said, but he didn't move to disarm Mary's security team.

Smart move on his part.

A second later, another pair of big black SUVs drove up and disgorged a dozen fully armed Marines in dress blue and reds. The Marines deployed in a tactical circle, not at all like candy-assed toy soldiers. Their captain reported to Ray.

"Sir, I'm Captain Tordon," the officer said as he saluted. "The embassy sent me to, ah, reinforce your own security team."

Whoever this dude was, he was a quick study. Mary liked that in a guy.

He also looked familiar.

He was eyeing her as much as he could without ignoring the visiting dignitary.

Recognition came to both of them at the same second.

"Trouble?" Mary said.

"Mary!" Trouble replied through his usual mischievous grin.

"You two know each other?" Ray asked.

"We were both on the same worthless rock in the recent unpleasantness," Trouble provided.

"Then all three of us were," Ray added. "Unfortunately for me and my brigade, I was on the opposite side."

"Well, we can't all be perfect, sir," Trouble said.

"Trouble?" Ray said, quizzically.

"Yes, sir. I got the nickname 'cause I was always trouble to the enemy. Usually trouble to my superiors, and, in general, all-around trouble, or so my friends say. Even I've come to admit to myself, at this hardening-of-the-artery age, that I'm just plain trouble. So Trouble it is."

"I see," Ray said, glancing around at the trouble that had arrived before Trouble. "Well, I'm glad to have you with us. Will you kindly join me in my limo?"

"Gunny, prepare to mount up the troops. Captain, ah, Mary, I've kind of forgotten your last name?"

"You proposed to me, and you didn't even get my last name?" Mary growled through a smile.

"Well, you had all that cool entrenching stuff and mine-laying gear. It did kind of distract me. And oh, about that marriage proposal. I've kind of gotten really married to this wonderful farm girl. We'll have to do lunch sometime. You'll love Ruth."

"I'd love to meet her, too," Ray said.

"Captain Trouble, I'm Mary Rodrigo," Mary provided to get them back on track.

"Yes, Captain Rodrigo, where do you intend to deploy your troops?"

"I intended to put one rig of guards fore and aft of the limo. I didn't give any thought to whether or not I'd be first or second in line.

"My Marine drivers have gotten to know the lay of the land here. If you don't mind, I'll lead out and provide the rear guard."

"Then I will have my troops closest to the limo, Captain."

"Very well. Gunny, mount up the troops as soon as we get Colonel Longknife safely in his ride."

That didn't take long. Soon they were headed out of the port, with a load of thugs trailing behind them.

"Head for the embassy, right, sir?" Mary said, as the convoy approached the first turn from the port.

"No," Ray said, eyeing his computer assistant. "It seems that President Milassi has just invited me to tea. I think I'd better see the big man first."

"I know the way," the driver said. Mary got busy telling her two rigs' worth of guards about the change. Trouble did the same.

Twenty minutes later, they pulled into a large circle in front of a white house with tall colonnades. It reminded Mary of something she's seen on the educational channel.

She held the door open for the colonel, and he stepped from the limo to be greeted by the great man himself.

With a hearty handshake and a smile that looked like it might be worth two cents, the planet's dictator took Ray off to some meeting, leaving his honor guards, both Explorer Corps and Marine Corps, to cool their heels.

The goons in the two following SUVs got out and made themselves comfortable, laughing and telling jokes with the guards from the president-for-life's inner circle.

Mary had heard that the so-called president-for-life was up for reelection. Politics must be an interesting pastime. What it said and what it meant didn't seem to connect very well.

She joined Trouble where he stood with his Marines, stationed around the vehicles with their M-6s at parade rest. "You think those 'police' are going to cause us any trouble?"

"Your guess is as good as mine. The local word on the street is that the difference between street toughs and cops is only a question of what they're wearing at the moment. How good are your crew at holding on to their tempers?"

"Some better than others. Maybe I better do a walk around."

"Please do."

Mary checked in with Du. He was sporting the gold bar of a second lieutenant, but his street origins were always there, close to the surface.

"Get a load of those duds," he said as Mary joined him. "They're trying to bad-mouth us into something."

"They doing a good job of it?" Mary asked.

"I've heard five-year-olds trash-talk better than these guys. You want maybe we give them a lesson?"

"No," Mary said. "Odds are that they're looking for an excuse to take a swing at you. Word from the local Marines is that these guys are just street thugs jumped up and put in uniforms."

"That don't sound good for this place."

"Yeah. They got problems. I don't know if Ray is here to do something about them or if he's just passing through. If he gives us the word, fists are free. You and your folks can have some fun. Right now, we hold it tight."

"Got the word, old lady, hold it high and tight. Wait until we get the word to go out and play with these babies. We can do that."

"Then pass the word."

"On my way, boss gal," he said, and threw her a kind of salute.

"By the way, Du. The only reason we've still got our guns is because we got reserve commissions. I'd suggest that we start acting like we were still Marines."

"Mary, we didn't act like candy-ass dudes when we *were* Marines. You know, we killed stuff. We didn't salute stuff."

"We better clean up our act, Du. They don't want us to kill nobody, but they do want us to look smart."

"You're no fun, old lady."

"Old Lady Captain, to you today."

Du snapped to attention and threw Mary a smart salute. "Yes, ma'am. I will get on it right away, ma'am."

He did a by-the-book about-face and marched off to talk to his former street kids.

Mary had a quick talk with one of her old miner friends who wore three stripes, and he marched off to carry The Word to that half of the detail.

Even after all this time, Mary's command was still split down the middle. Half were like Mary, asteroid miners who'd kept their noses clean while they built up seniority in the union, only to get their downsizing pink slip and their draft notice in the same pay envelope. The other half were street kids who woke up, stoned and hung over, to discover they'd signed themselves into the Corps.

Even those who couldn't write their name or anything else.

How this mismatched bunch had made it through the war and into the peace with their skins still in one piece was either a God's honest miracle or a violation of the laws of probability.

Mary wasn't sure which she'd credit with her still breathing.

At the moment, the captain was coming up on her elbow. "You got a problem?" he asked.

"None at all, Captain. My folks may not be into spit and polish, but then, we aren't actually a military unit at the moment."

"You sure saved my neck, and a lot of others like me, back on that rock. We're here with Captain Izzy Umboto from the old unit. She's got a ship now. The *Patton*."

"I guess that makes her happy," Mary said. "I'm with Captain Mattim Abeeb, skipper of the *Second Chance*. At least that's what they're calling her now. She was the *Sheffield* back in the war."

"*Sheffield*, wasn't she the one that almost rocked Wardhaven?"

"That was our orders. I heard them straight from the mouth of some shit-for-brains admiral. Whitebred was his name. After things calmed down, and we didn't rock nobody, they hauled him off in cuffs. Nicest perp walk I ever did see."

"You'll have to tell me about it over a beer. Excuse me. I've got a call coming in."

The Marine officer stepped away from Mary, but she could still hear him.

Suddenly, all color drained from his face.

"What?" came out loud and clear. Even Du turned to see what was up.

The captain exchanged a few more words. Most sounded like questions, but Mary couldn't follow them word for word. He looked intently at the local thugs-for-cops as he got answers.

Trouble's face was deadly grim when he rung off and walked back to Mary.

"Trouble?" she asked.

"Some police thugs just beat up my wife."

"Huh," Mary said. She'd heard the words, but she found she couldn't really believe them. And if she did believe them, then there was a whole lot of trouble headed for someone.

And while her uniform might be gray today, not blue and red, she and her crew would not leave all the bloody knuckles to them with the gold buttons.

Face a cold, angry mask, the Marine expanded on his few words. "I just got a call from my Gunny. Some thugs in police uniforms cut off my wife at a filling station and beat the crap out of her. He and his returned the favor, but she's in bad shape, possibly concussed. They're rushing her to the embassy's sick bay."

"You want to take off?" Mary asked, expecting she knew the answer but making the offer nonetheless.

"No. No, here is my station, and here I stay. I just hope the president doesn't bend your colonel's ear too long."

"He ain't my colonel, though I think he *is* the minister of exploration in the Wardhaven government. Mostly his wife handles the job. He does a lot of gallivanting. We just got back from a sour jump. It's a long story. We'll need a couple of beers for that one."

The look on Trouble's face was pure pain. Mary had seen people torn between a hard duty and their heart's desire. Here was a man caught between them. A real hard rock and a really hard place.

It might have gotten worse, but the double doors of the mansion flew open and the colonel marched out. He made a beeline for his limo. Sergeants for both the blue and red and the grays shouted orders and doors opened and people recovered their places.

Only when the doors were closed and the cars moving did the colonel let loose with a string of epithets that would have made a DI blush. "That . . . That . . . shit for brains had the gall to tell me that I better keep a tight hand on my people. *My* people, as if anyone that isn't one of his poor beat-up and cowed citizens belongs to me.

"Who does he think he is and who does he think I am?" Ray exploded.

"The guy who killed President Urm," Mary said softly. "Colonel, I think you need to ask the Marine sitting next to you what just happened to his wife. I think that political shit was giving you the second warning of the day."

"Second warning, Captain?" he said, turning to Trouble.

"Just a moment, sir. Mary, tell the drivers to step on it. The embassy and fast."

"The word's out," Mary said a second later. "Du's in the lead car. He likes fast."

"Thank you, Mary. Sorry, sir. While you were in there being warned, I got word that a bunch of local police thugs caught my wife alone and beat her up badly."

"Good God, man, how badly?"

"Not as badly as it could have been. My wife has a larger job than her official one. We'll talk about that later, but she was going out farther and farther, taking the measure of this hell, and I asked my Gunnery Sergeant if he'd mind taking a drive in the country kind of where Ruth was going, if you catch my drift."

"I catch it, and I'd do the same myself."

"So when she pushed the panic button on the new armored corset I gave her yesterday, they were less than five minutes out. Still, in those five minutes, Milassi's thugs beat her up pretty badly."

The colonel leaned back in his seat, his face going to stone. "Is the underside of this place as bad as I've heard?"

"Sir, from the looks of it, I'd say it's worse."

"I'm beginning to get that impression. We've got a Senate investigation team headed this way."

"Word is that most of the team is more interested in burying what the others find," the Marine officer said.

"Yes, that's the story I got. It seems to me that we're going to have to do some digging ourselves. What say you that we get all this shit out in the open so no one, no matter how big their shovels, can bury it."

Which left Mary wondering exactly what was the job of a security team on an exploration ship when it came to digging up the muck on a bloodthirsty, vicious dictator.

No doubt, she'd find out soon enough.

SEVENTEEN

RAY WATCHED THE hubbub going on around him as he arrived at the embassy. This must be what it's like to have a new queen bee arrive at the hive and make the old pecking order obsolete.

He'd hated such shows when he was a junior officer and didn't like them any better now that he was an elephant himself.

At least as soon as the limo stopped, he'd been able to dismiss the Marine captain to race to the side of his wife.

Meanwhile, the ambassador had come to shake his hand and promise the help of his embassy in anything he needed during his stay.

"How long will you be with us, Colonel?" had been far too early a question. It was as if the ambassador found Ray just another of his many problems to rush out the door as quickly as possible.

Ray did notice a tall blonde holding back, hardly in the shadow of the ambassador. She was the embassy's first political officer, if Ray had caught the title right.

Was she the real power in the place? He'd have to find out, and find out fast.

He'd come to attend a meeting. He was rapidly growing his agenda, and little of it had to do with meeting some zeds from Earth's Senate.

Correction, it was now the Senate for the entire Society of Humanity. At least it would be soon. That Senate was supposed to grow with representatives from 150 planets. They'd join a much-reduced number from Earth and her first fifty colonies.

But the new kids weren't there yet.

Things were changing. And, no doubt, there would be those eager to see that they stayed the same.

Ray intended to toss a few rocks into their machinery of sameness.

Assuming he could.

Back with the 2nd Guard Brigade, he issued an order, and things happened. Now that he wore civilian clothes to work . . . not so much.

He waited while the falderal died down. The ambassador left, insisting he was a very busy man and had things to do.

He failed to mention what any of those things might be.

Finally, Ray found himself alone with the first political officer.

"I didn't get your name," he said.

"I'm Becky Graven. Will you walk with me?"

Without waiting for a reply, she headed for the door. He followed. He followed her down a hall, then down a flight of stairs into what must be the basement.

Along another hallway, uncarpeted and with bare cinder-block walls, she led him to a large room, spartan to the maximum.

Still, without a word spoken, a man stood and went over Ray with a device that looked like something between a lint brush and a remote control.

Wordlessly, the man signaled Ray to remove his jacket. When Ray handed it over, he took it to another device that might have once been a clothespress, but now had a lot more bells and whistles attached. Quickly, he ran the coat through it.

"I got it, ma'am. We can talk now."

"Check it out," the Foreign Service Officer ordered. "I want to know if they're still using the old design, or if they've got something new.

"Will do, Becky."

"I take it that you're not with the Foreign Service," Ray said.

"Actually, I am. The spooks have to have someone to report to. I just happen to be her. I'm sure the idea of a woman running the intelligence and counterintel operations against his bullyboys has Milassi bent totally out of shape. Now, please step into my web, said the spider to the fly."

And Ray was invited into a utilitarian room with a raised

floor and lowered ceiling. Its walls were merely cinder blocks. They looked rather roughly put together.

Becky pointed him at a comfortable chair as she took one across from him. "Yes, we built it ourselves, Colonel. We've done what we can to remove the bugs from the walls, floors, ceilings, and whatever else in our new embassy. Still, this place leaks like a sieve. We know this room is clean because we put every damn brick in it ourselves. And yes, I helped mix the mortar and laid a few bricks."

"What I just went through. Are you telling me that I was bugged?"

"Very likely while you were in Milassi's own office."

"That bastard!"

"Certifiably. Murderous bastard most definitely. Our problem is to make sure that president-for-life is not at all that long a job for him."

"With or without killing him?" Ray asked.

"Spoken like a soldier. I'm in a more peaceful line of business. If we have our way, he will get to run off with all his girlfriends and his ill-gotten gain to someplace pleasant and live to a ripe old age."

"Any chance the next government will recover some of that loot?"

"That is up to the succeeding government," the FSO said evenly.

"So, tell me, what can I do to make sure all that happens?"

"I was told you were just a visiting fireman. We should wine you, dine you, and see that you were sent home quickly and happily to your expectant wife."

Ray winced. "So I've already been ratted out, huh?"

"I have express orders from the Prime Minister of Wardhaven to get you home as quickly as possible, or he's going to have your wife and your father-in-law raising hell."

"So, assuming I can keep them off your back, I ask again. What can I do to help? I understand the wife of the Marine skipper was beat up today. What happened?"

"I made a mistake," the Foreign Service Officer said, folding her hands in her lap. "She had a good cover. As a matter of fact, a real cover. By right of some dimwit back at BuFinance, warships have been ordered to load themselves down with hydroponic gardens. She's the contract farmer for the Society of Humanity cruiser *Patton* now in orbit. She needs to expand her tanks and is down here looking for cheap gear. She and I thought that such an actual requirement could be used to cover some snooping."

Here, the FSO paused to frown at her hands. "What you have to understand is that just about none of us can get very far from our tails here in Savannah. What that translates to is that we can read the official news accounts and attend the official government briefings and parties."

"I get the picture," Ray said. "You're kept in a fishbowl. A very small fishbowl, and you get only what they chose to drop into the bowl."

"Exactly. Ruth was the first chance we had to have someone out and about, talking with the locals and eyeballing reality more than three blocks from this building."

Becky shook her head ruefully. "The stuff she got from three street kids was gold. We knew it was bad out there. Those kids filled in the assumptions with real facts."

"So she, this Ruth, got beat up?"

"Badly."

"Do you know who did it?"

"Aside from the fact that the guys were in State Security Force uniforms, jumped out of State Security Force cruisers and had the gall to plant one of their listening bugs on her while they were beating her up, no, I can't be at all sure who did it," Becky finished, with sarcasm in full rage.

"That's pretty flagrant."

The FSO snorted. "Flagrant? I'll give you flagrant. Milassi's telling you to have us pull in our horns within a half hour of his guys beating up Ruth. That's flagrant."

"I forgot to tell you that. Where'd you hear it?"

"You shot off your mouth at the White House. Besides everyone else, your limo's chauffeur heard it. He's one of mine."

"Sorry. I should have told you that immediately."

"How could you know whom to tell? Thank goodness you didn't say something to the ambassador. If you had, all of us would be on lockdown for the next month. That guy's a nervous Nellie in long hoop skirts."

"How is the woman they beat up?"

"Thanks to the Marines arriving in the nick of time, she'll live. I suspect that was not what her attackers intended."

"So they planted a bug on what they intended to make a dead body? I'm not tracking this."

"No doubt, they wanted to hear what her husband said over her dead body, and maybe me. Anything is worth a try for these types."

"I'm taking a strong dislike to 'these types,'" Ray said. "May I meet her?"

"Certainly. I don't know what you can do."

"Neither do I, but I'm getting ideas," Ray said. He didn't have an idea yet. But he had some of the parts that might make up a good one.

He tapped his commlink. "Mary, could you and Du meet me in the embassy's infirmary in five minutes?"

"Of course, Colonel."

"Who's Mary?"

"She damn near killed me, her and her miners who were drafted by the Society of Humanity to fight their last war. She's good, and, at the moment, she happens to work for me as the chief of security on the exploration ship that brought me here."

"And?" the FSO asked.

"And she may be just the beginning of an idea for what could make this woman a whole lot safer."

"Then let's go see Ruth."

EIGHTEEN

MARY DIDN'T MUCH care for the smell of hospitals. She really didn't much care for what she saw. Trouble sat beside a bed. In it, a woman was covered in bandages.

Looking more vulnerable and hopeless than Mary had ever seen a Marine, Trouble held a hand, gingerly, as if to even caress it was to inflict more pain on the woman he loved more than the entire universe.

Mary approached him. "I'm sorry, Trouble."

"It's not your fault. It's not my fault. She was doing the job she wanted to do. I gave her all the protection I could manage. At least, that's what I keep telling myself. Who would have thought that the local thugs would take on someone from outside?"

"And a Marine officer's wife," Mary added.

"Yeah, that, too."

Mary turned as Ray entered with a lovely, tall blonde at his elbow. If she didn't know how married Ray was to Rita, she'd be worried.

But both of them only had eyes for the woman in the bed.

The doc arrived with the visiting elephants.

"How is she doing?" Ray asked.

"Better than she has any right to," the doc said. "That new protective corset did better than advertised. I know the bully-boys couldn't have stinted on what they were trying to do to her. I've patched up Marines who were in a lot worse shape after bar fights that didn't look all that coincidental."

"I find that hard to believe," Ray said.

Becky made a sour face. "Believe him. I've seen them after the doc got done wrapping them in so many bandages that they could pass for an Egyptian mummy. Several we had to disability retire."

The Marine captain turned from his wife. "They haven't done any of that shit since we arrived," he said.

"Maybe having a lot of Marines handy has crimped their style," the FSO said.

"Well, I intend to have even more troops standing to here," the colonel said. "Mary, as of now, you and your guards are back in uniform. I know you do not fit the usual expectations for the Corps, but please work with Captain Trouble and his crew to fit in and add to the strength of this embassy's Marine presence. Also, when this woman is fit to return to her duties, I expect her to have one of your crew in civilian clothes at her elbow whenever she sets foot outside the embassy."

"Can we shoot, sir?" Mary asked, maybe a bit too enthusiastically. Well, if she sent Dumont with the woman, he'd go with guns ready.

The colonel winced at the question. So did the Foreign Service Officer. She answered, "Dead thugs in State Security Force uniforms will be a major embarrassment. I'd prefer we avoid that outcome."

"So would I," the colonel added. "However, if it's a choice between a dead Marine, or Marine's wife, and a few dead thugs, I want the Marines alive. Understood?"

Mary came to attention. "Yes, sir. We are under weapons lock unless things get mortal, and we should use smarts to avoid a confrontation. However, if it comes to it, we win, they lose."

"That sounds fine by me," the colonel said, eyeing the diplomat.

She scowled but nodded. "Yes. I've had enough of shipping broken Marines back to their folks. Be careful, but do what you have to."

"Then pardon me, sir, I think I'd better do the escorting myself," Mary said. "I'll take along a few folks for distant overwatch, but I think me and this nice woman should become the best of friends."

Ray nodded. "Let's do that."

"If you will excuse me, I need to pass The Word to my team. Captain, with your permission, I'll start working with your second-in-command to merge our two teams."

Mary paused for one moment. "Did I understand it right?

Trouble's Gunny and his team beat up the thugs who were beating up this woman. Will there be repercussions?"

The woman diplomat smiled. "I doubt it. There were five of them. There were only three Marines, and one of them was a young woman. I understand she took out two of the thugs. How many brave boys want to tell everyone that they were beat up by a woman, let alone a woman who beat the stuffing out of two of them?"

The FSO laughed. "No, I doubt we'll hear any more of this."

NINETEEN

THREE DAYS LATER, after breakfast, Mary found herself called to Captain Trouble's office. The captain and his wife were there. The woman still looked like she'd been through a meat grinder, but under the bandages was solid determination.

If Mary had any skills at reading couples, they were just finishing a fight.

"Ruth wants to go out today," Trouble growled.

"And I understand that you intend to go with me," his wife said, not rising from the chair beside her husband's desk.

"It's Colonel Ray Longknife's orders, ma'am," Mary answered. "I can be out of this uniform and into civvies in a few minutes. I'm told you want to keep a low profile, ma'am."

"Yes. *I* want to keep a low profile. That means *me* and no one else."

"I understand your meaning, ma'am," Mary said, casting a glance at Trouble and getting a worried look back, but a look that said this was the final phase in a battle he hadn't done at all well in.

"I understand that I am to do what you want," Mary continued, "exactly the way you want, ma'am."

"Then what *I* want is to be left alone to work on this *myself*," shot right back at Mary. But it was a retort the Marine expected.

"Sorry, ma'am, I've got my orders from the colonel. Once upon a time, I could shoot the damn bastard, but now he's my boss, and I got to do what he tells me."

"You could shoot the colonel?" Ruth said.

"Ma'am, I *did* shoot the colonel. Busted up his back real good, but now he's signing my paychecks, so I can't shoot him, and I got to do what he says. He says I'm to be your new best friend for at least as long as you're on this mud ball. We can figure out a way for me to fit right in, or you can make my job miserable, but I'm gonna be joined at your hip."

"You're a stubborn old cuss," Ruth said.

Mary smiled. She tried to make it as pleasant a one as possible. "Yes, ma'am. My boss at the mines said I was. The Marine officers I worked for said I was. Come to think of it, I can't think of anyone I've met who didn't say that about me."

The Marine wife laughed, but only for a moment. She winced. "We need to avoid humor. It hurts too much."

Her husband was out of his chair and at her side. "It hurts too much for you to go out. You need more time to heal. The doc said a week or two more."

"The kids are out there. They must be worried to tears. And I won't let those bastards who did this keep laughing in their beer. I'm going out, Terry. I'm going out."

The Marine looked up at Mary, helpless in the face of his wife's determination. "Can you do anything?"

"Yeah, Trouble. I'll go get into civvies."

And she did.

Fifteen minutes later, Mary was arguing with one determined woman over who got the car keys.

Mary had picked them up from the motor pool. True, this car was a local rental, but when a Marine returned it after the dustup, it had been parked in the back of the motor pool, with its keys locked up.

A young woman Marine had intercepted Mary on the way out and told her where to get both keys and car.

So Ruth stood, her hand out, demanding the keys, and Mary stood, with her hands in her pockets, refusing to give them up.

"You don't know the streets like I do," Ruth said.

"You can tell me where to go," Mary countered.

"Don't tempt me," Ruth said, then went on. "I can get us there faster."

"You've still got ribs healing, ma'am. You could end up busting that cute car into some tree or building if you can't turn the wheel fast enough."

"I'm fine."

"I'm driving."

Possession being nine-tenths of the game, Mary won.

But she hadn't driven three blocks when she muttered, "We seem to have developed a tail this morning."

Ruth adjusted the mirror on the passenger side, and growled, "Yeah, that's the Bear. He's the guy that arranged for me to be beat up."

"Then I suggest we lose him," Mary said.

"Turn right next chance you get."

"Is that my next chance?" Mary said, nodding toward an alley.

"That's what I meant. Now you know why I wanted to drive."

Mary took a hard right turn into an alley, giving no warning, and no turn signal. The alley was not only narrow, but cluttered with cans, boxes, and other refuse. Fortunately, clotheslines were strung from second-floor windows, and few items fell to the level of their small car.

Mary dodged as best she could, but some cans got knocked over, and a few boxes got flattened.

"Turn left at the next alley," Ruth ordered.

Mary did just as the Bear's taxi turned into the alley behind them.

The second alley was no different from the last.

"Turn left at the next one," Ruth said.

"That will take us back to the road."

"Where you can make some time before you duck down the first alley on your left."

Mary did. By the second turn, she'd lost the Bear. She'd caught nothing of him in her rearview before she made the left-hand turn into the next alley.

"Go straight ahead until you get to the next main street, then hook a right."

"Back to the embassy already?"

"No. Make a right the first chance you get. That should take us out of this area fast."

It did. There was no sign of the Bear, or any other tail, as Mary settled down at the speed limit and headed down the road. Knowing how buggy this place tended to get, Mary set one of Lek's jammers on the dashboard and pushed its button.

"That ought to keep us safe," she told the civilian.

Ruth was on her phone. "Alice, I'm traveling today. Can

you and the kids meet me at the three trees by the river? You can. Good. See all of you in thirty minutes."

Ruth hung up, then told Mary, "Turn right at the next light."

Fifteen minutes later, they parked beside the river, just a few meters from three lovely old elms.

"That wasn't too hard," Ruth said, pausing to catch her breath. "I never have figured out how the Bear knew where I was. I was sure I lost him."

"Your car was bugged," Mary said.

"But the embassy motor-pool staff said they'd cleaned it."

"Yes. They washed it down real good while you were in sick bay and found nothing. You'll excuse me if I say I don't trust the local hires here. I had a buddy of mine, Lek, go over the car just before we took it out today."

"He find anything?"

"Two. Good ones. The standard-issue debugger at the motor pool missed 'em."

"How'd *he* find them?"

"Lek makes his own gear, and upgrades it when the spirit moves him, which is a whole lot sooner than the stuff you buy. Anyway, he found the bugs, and he's dissecting them with a couple of the Marines. Between his debugging and his jammer, you can count on us not being disturbed today."

Ruth made a pained face. "But if we head back to the Farm, they'll be waiting for us."

"The Farm?" Mary echoed.

"An experimental station for growing new illegal drugs. At least that's what I saw before I got kicked into next week. My handheld got smashed so I don't have the records of what I found that day."

"Did the thugs get your handheld?"

"They probably would have if the Marines hadn't wrecked their little show. No, Gunny policed up my gear, but it was too wrecked to make out anything. I'll have to do the recon all over again."

"But not today," Mary said with determination.

"Not today," Ruth agreed without enthusiasm. "That would be too obvious."

The kids arrived then, and Mary lost her heart to them.

There was a little girl who started crying the moment she

set eyes on Ruth. The woman opened the car door and took the little girl in her lap, speaking soothing words to calm the urchin.

"I'm fine, Tiny. My friends stopped the crushers. I'm fine."

A wisp of a boy stood at the door, his wide eyes taking this all in. He looked to Mary like he'd like to climb into the woman's lap, too, but felt his extra year or two precluded such mothering.

Behind them, a girl in a tiny blue bonnet who might be a teenager stood, looking both ways nervously.

Mary rolled the rear window down and spoke to her. "We lost the Bear. He won't be finding us today."

"If you say so, ma'am, but we kids still can't be seen in River Park. It's for gentry, you know."

"Then get in, and we'll be off," Mary said.

The youth got the small boy into the backseat. Ruth held the youngest, and Mary drove. She had no orders on where to go, so she just drove along the river. It was nice. Raised in space, lucky enough to have a job when she graduated from the orphanage herself, Mary had rarely seen so much water.

Yes, on Santa Maria she'd discovered the ocean, but rivers, lakes, and oceans were still new enough to Mary that she had yet to get enough of them.

And this river had trees along it. Lots of green things growing out in the open for everyone to see.

Unless, of course, they were kids like these whom the authorities didn't want messing up the view.

Mary's opinion of the local authorities was bad and getting worse.

It was edging toward lunchtime, and Mary could hear empty stomachs rumbling. If not her own, then definitely the kids'. None of them had so much as a spare bit of flesh on them. Tiny, what passed for a name for the small girl, was curled up in Ruth's lap, no longer crying, but sucking her thumb.

The boy in the back was now busy looking around, as was the teen.

Apparently, they didn't trust Mary that they weren't being followed.

They came upon a factory where several lunch wagons were setting up, but the lunch whistle hadn't blown yet. Mary pulled in.

"I'll get you kids something. What do you want?"

That got blank stares.

"Get them three sandwiches," Ruth said, "milk if they have any, and fries."

The kids' eyes lit up, but they didn't risk a word. Mary suspected they wouldn't believe the food was for them until they had it in their own empty bellies.

It hadn't been easy, growing up in the orphanage. But at least Mary had friends and the promise of two meals a day. They were told that they were the lucky ones, kids whose folks died in the mines and the companies were paying for.

Mary had a hard time seeing the luck.

Then her friend Cassie took Mary outside the mining consortium into town to help one of her church groups care for the street kids. Kids with no mom, no pop, and no loving company to tuck them in at night.

Mary discovered that things could be worse.

Now she was seeing it again.

She bought sandwiches meant for workingmen, heaped with ham and cheese on thick black bread. She got the fries; thick slabs of potatoes cooked to golden crisps. And she got three large cartons of milk.

Loaded down, she returned to the car and doled the food out to the kids.

It was as if they'd won the lottery.

The older girl asked if she might take half of her lunch back to Major Barbara's. "I'm studying with three other girls at night. It's not easy, studying when you're hungry."

"You eat that, Alice," Ruth said. "Mary will get two more sandwiches for us, and your friends can have half of ours."

Mary headed back, getting in line just before the whistle blew. She had the two sandwiches cut in thirds. She smiled at Ruth as she, too, ate the smallest part of her sandwich and left most of the fries untouched.

After lunch, they drove around some more. The kids in the backseat rattled on about the factories and what their fish-eye view of the place told them. Mary hit RECORD on her wrist unit and let it run as the kids rambled.

To them, it was just the way life was.

To the specialists back at the embassy, it was the truth about a lot of things that puzzled them.

Mary had fought her battles, both in the war and after. She knew the value of intelligence. What she was hearing from the backseat wasn't anything that pertained to troop movements or gun emplacement. Still, Mary had learned a lot by keeping her ears open in the mines and in the Corps.

What she heard said a lot was rotten here, past rotten to gangrenous. Below the surface, rage seethed. And when that rage came out, it could be all hell, or it might bring hope.

Mary had seen Marines bring hope where there was none. Hope that she and her friends could survive. Hope that a planet or two would not be demolished down to bedrock, with all its people smashed or worse.

Mary finished the drive with her trigger finger twitching. There were targets out there, and she was finding out what she needed to draw a good sight picture on them.

TWENTY

TROUBLE WAS RELIEVED beyond words to see Ruth and Mary drive back into the motor pool. Losing battles was something that didn't happen to him.

Losing arguments with his wife was something he was getting used to.

He still didn't like it.

He'd taken out some of his frustration on the motor-pool manager. When Lek brought him the results of his bug dissection he'd taken the evidence straight to the boss who was supposed to keep the cars running . . . and clean.

The manager insisted his cars were clean of bugs. Their little talk had gotten hot and loud.

Before too long, Becky hustled in to calm things down.

Hand firmly on Trouble's elbow, she'd half dragged him out of the pool manager's office.

"Marine, he's a local hire. We need local hires. And while that guy may not *now* be working for anyone besides us, you keep that up, and he'll go *looking* for someone to talk to, and we won't like the results."

"But he got my wife damn near beat to death."

"It wasn't him," she said calmly into his rage.

Trouble swallowed what he was about to scream. "It wasn't?" he whispered.

"No. I've had my own bugs drifting around the motor pool. He's not the man. But I know who is."

"Point me at him."

"Down, devil dog. We're playing a long game here. Your wife got out bug-free today, and we'll make sure she does every day. The guy that's cashing two paychecks is mine, and I'll play him the way I want to."

"What game, exactly, are we playing?"

"Follow me," she said, and quickly led him to the secure room. Once the door was shut, she did not sit down. "Marine, you're asking too many questions. I like you. I think you'll do a better job for me if you know something about what we're doing, but do not expect to have all the answers handed to you on a platter. You don't tell your wife what you're doing, do you?"

"Not as often as she'd like," Trouble admitted.

"Well, don't expect her to tell you a lot about what she's involved in either."

Trouble waited. This was the diplomat's game. She said she'd deal him in. He stood in front of her, waiting to see what cards she'd allow him.

"What keeps Milassi in power?" she finally said.

"His thugs?" Trouble answered weakly. He strongly suspected his answer was wrong. The problem was, he didn't know another one.

"Not even close. Not that bunch of brutes and perverts. There aren't enough smarts in the lot to add up two and two."

Trouble waited.

"Ever heard 'follow the money'? It was good advice years ago. It's the best advice right here and now."

"Where is the money for Milassi coming from?" Trouble asked.

The FSO shrugged. "You tell me, Marine."

"I don't do accounting," he said.

"You were on Riddle. Tell me what you saw."

Trouble took a step back. "Riddle?"

"Yes, Riddle."

"I lived a nightmare, and I saw a lot of drugs growing," Trouble said.

"You know anything about the drug you were growing? Anything about where it came from or where it went?"

"Nope," Trouble said, "and I doubt many of the people on Riddle did either."

"Finally, a smart answer, Marine. Yes. Lots of stuff growing but not a lot of know-how."

"Ruth said the folks running the plantations didn't know how to grow anything."

"Yes, I read that in her report. Very observant."

"So, we're dealing in drugs, huh?" Trouble said, and waited for the next card.

"We've done the numbers on Savannah. None of it adds up. These plants could be a lot more productive and profitable, but the way they're running, it's a miracle they even break even. No, a whole lot of what's putting money in Milassi's pockets and what he's using to pay the thugs is coming from off world."

"And that money is drug money," Trouble said.

"But why is he getting drug money to run this place?" the Foreign Service Officer asked, as much to herself as Trouble. "There are no drug plantations in the backcountry. One of the reasons we asked for the *Patton* was to do a full and exhaustive survey of the planet from orbit. It's not being grown here. It's not being shipped out of here."

"Drug lords are not known for paying for anything that doesn't put money in their pockets," Trouble said.

"So, your wife stumbled onto something, and they beat her up for it."

"What was it?" Trouble asked.

"Officially, she found nothing," the diplomat said. "Her hand-held was busted up real good by her attackers, and she remembers nothing about the attack or before it. Sad that, but it's the word around the embassy, and it's the word on the street."

"But?" Trouble said. He'd held his wife. He'd heard her talk about the attack. He knew she remembered every kick.

Becky grinned. "Ruth told me what she found and the boys and girls at the workstations outside pulled that off her ruined unit."

"A drug plantation?"

"No, a drug-research center. Fields and fields of the next street plague and the poison after that."

"So we go in and burn it out," Trouble said. There were times when it was good to be a Marine, and this looked like one he'd really enjoy.

"In your dreams, old boy. In your dreams."

Trouble eyed the woman.

She shrugged. "The research center is owned and licensed by a major pharmaceutical research group. I've seen its reports. They are all clean and in order. No illegal drugs here. Oh, and the corporation that owns the corporation that runs the research labs. It's untouchable. Roots all the way back to Earth."

"Oh shit!" Trouble said.

"Or something like that."

"Are you going to let them get away with it?" the Marine demanded.

"That's not my intention, but charging in there with a flamethrower is not one of the options open to us, so down, boy. Down and heel."

"Growl," Trouble said, then added, "What are you going to do about it?"

"That is above your pay grade, Captain. What you are going to do about it is take your wife to dinner tomorrow evening. You'll pick a place in the hills above town, and you two will have a fine dinner. You may take your field glasses with you, if you wish, and you may even study the research farm from twenty klicks away, but you will not go near it. You understand me?"

"Orders received and understood," Trouble said, finding himself coming to attention. "I'm a diversion. A demonstration to draw them away from the main effort."

"Something like that. Just do what I want and, come the right time, you'll get to do what you want to do."

Trouble scowled. "I'm not used to being the diversion."

"No, I don't imagine you are. Trust me, you won't be for long if we get our way."

"Yes, ma'am," Trouble said, and turned to go. As he was closing the door, he glanced back. Becky had settled into one of the chairs. She was eyeing the wall, an expression on her face that Trouble had seen before.

Some of his senior officers wore that look, just before battle. Some of his subordinates had worn it, too. No doubt, Trouble had put it on a few times himself.

A hell of a fight was coming fast. He and his Marines would be in it up to their ears. And they would not be on the losing side.

TWENTY-ONE

MARY GOT RUTH back safely to the embassy, but that wasn't the end of her job today.

First, she checked in on her tiny company. Dumont had done good work with the embassy Marine detachment's first lieutenant in sharing out the duties of this mixed command.

Some of the Marines were from the original embassy detachment. Most were from the ship's company that Captain Trouble had brought down from the *Patton*. Now her team from the *Second Chance* was being attached to the rest.

It was a crazy lash-up, but no Marines had been cornered in any bar and beat to a pulp. Not for the last couple of weeks.

Mary grinned at the thought of someone who wasn't used to being scared of anything now learning to fear Marines.

That done, she turned to what she'd accomplished this day.

She'd reported to Trouble's office that morning with only the shortest of briefs. She was to protect the man's wife. Ruth was doing more than it looked like on the surface. Exactly what that was remained unspecified.

Mary's job was simple. See that Ruth wasn't beat up again.

Mary had driven out of the embassy compound with no idea of where she was going or what she would do when she got there.

That was no way to run a successful operation.

Mary settled into her chair in her tiny office and ordered up a map of Petrograd. One glance at the available map, and Mary saw a problem. The map in the screen had none of the alleys she'd driven today. "Computer, can you access a better map?"

"This is the only map available," her computer told her.

"Do you have any orthophotos, aerial photos of Petrograd?"

"There are none available."

Mary pushed her chair back from her desk, which about put her in the hall. This wasn't right. Every major city was supposed to have regular overhead photos taken, for pollution studies if for no other reason.

She was about to order the computer to do a further and more in-depth search when there was a soft knock at the door. The knock came as a surprise. Her office was little more than a broom closet, and Mary couldn't close the door when she sat at her desk. Most Marines who wanted her attention just hollered, "Captain."

Standing in the open door was the tall woman diplomat. She was practically leaning over Mary's shoulders.

"May I help you, ma'am?" Mary said.

"More likely, I can help you," the woman said, and motioned Mary to follow her.

Mary followed down the hall, down some stairs and up another hall. The door they came to was quite substantial, and it took a swipe of the card around the woman's neck and the keying in of a long access code to open it.

Inside, Mary was treated to something she'd seen in videos but never expected to walk into in real life—an honest-to-God war room.

Men and women huddled over workstations. One wall was a huge screen with a map that changed as Mary watched.

It was Petrograd. And it showed the alleys Mary had driven today.

The Marine smiled her happy smile. The woman smiled with her.

"See anything you want?" she asked.

"All of it, I think," Mary said.

"Let's not be a glutton. Pete, check her over."

A man ran a device that Mary suspected was a bug hunter. It was a lot smaller than the one Lek used and looked store-bought. It passed her.

"I could have told you there weren't any bugs on me," Mary said. "I had Lek check me when I came back this afternoon. Somewhere along the line, I picked up two, none of special interest, not that they reported anything through his jammer."

"Well, we like to make sure of things ourselves," the

woman said, then led Mary into a room in the center of the bigger room. She closed the door behind them; it locked with a solid click. "Would you take a seat?"

Mary did.

"I'm told you want a good map."

"That was what I was hunting for," Mary admitted. "Is there a law against it?"

"Here on Savannah, I think there is," the woman said, with a pained expression. "How can they keep the people in the dark if they let them see things? They do a lot to keep the locals from knowing what's really happening. Our level of ignorance about the situation is only a blowback from their main effort."

"So I can't have a decent map," Mary said.

"I didn't say that. One of the nice things about having a Society warship in our sky is that it can take pictures from orbit. Pictures like you saw on the main screen. I'll see that you get a copy of it before you leave here."

"Thank you, ma'am," Mary said. Then remembered a question.

"Those kids, what they say when they get to talking. Is that good intel?"

"Some of the best we're getting from this place," the FSO admitted.

"That drug farm that Ruth got beat up for discovering," Mary went on slowly. "What do the kids know about it?"

"Not a lot. It was mainly Ruth and her farm experience that led her to it. That and our orbital analysis that it's growing crops that didn't match any in our Ag database."

"But you didn't have me and Ruth go near it today."

"Or tomorrow or the next day for quite a few days to come. It's too hot."

Mary made a face. "That's not good. When are those visiting senators supposed to be here?"

"How do you know about them?" The diplomat didn't look happy that Mary did.

"Ma'am, my job is to protect the colonel. And the only reason he's here is for that bunch. I have to know why we're here."

"Yes, I imagine you do. Yes, I'd like to blow the cover on that drug lair before they get here, but I'm not seeing how I can. Not without us running a very big risk of getting a mob charging through this embassy and ransacking everything."

"What about the kids, ma'am? They could get close to the Farm."

"I asked Ruth about them. She doesn't think they could."

Now it was Mary's time to wince. "Ma'am, Ruth is kind of a mother to those kids. You can't expect her to go along with putting them out on the pointy end of the spear. But, from what I saw today, they are pretty much invisible, at least when they aren't around the river park. Anyway, they could check out the neighborhood. They know stuff we don't, and they can go places we don't dare. I think they are just what you need."

"A Baker Street Irregulars kind of thing, huh."

"Baker Street Irregulars?" Mary echoed.

The FSO chuckled. "You haven't read much Sherlock Holmes, have you?"

"There weren't many books where I grew up, ma'am, but yes, I've heard of him, now that you mention it. He was a smart detective, wasn't he?"

"And he had a smart bunch of street kids who helped him find out things that respectable grown-ups couldn't."

"Like Alice and Mouse," Mary said.

"We'll need to talk to Ruth about this in the morning."

"She can be a very stubborn woman," Mary said.

The woman chuckled. "Yes, so Trouble tells me. We'll see how this goes in the morning. Now, let's get you that map and get us all to bed. Today's been a tough one, and I don't see any days ahead being any easier."

Mary hated it when boss types made predictions like that. Too often, they came true.

TWENTY-TWO

RUTH DIDN'T LIKE being summoned to the basement with her husband as an escort. She really didn't like the soft smile on his face.

A certain Marine captain knew something she didn't.

But when they met the diplomat Becky Graven at the door to some tight security room, Trouble was left behind without so much as a growl from him.

They passed through a glistening room full of people with their heads down over computers into some sort of super-secret room with three chairs. Mary, Ruth's so-called new best friend forever, was in one. Ruth settled herself into another and waited to see what the head woman was up to.

A minute later, Ruth was back on her feet. "No. No. No! You can't use Mouse and Alice as spies. They've got it tough enough just staying alive! You can't gamble with their necks!"

When the FSO's lack of concern didn't change, Ruth tried a different tack. "You saw how they beat me up. Those crushers would *enjoy* beating Mouse to a dead pulp or hauling Alice off to one of their brothels."

When she still saw no reaction from the woman, Ruth turned to Mary. "You've seen what it's like out there, even for one day. You've heard what those kids said. You can't believe we should *use* them?"

"She suggested it," Becky said.

"Mary!" Ruth screamed.

"We need to break this local game wide open," the Marine said as calm as any woman waiting for a bus. "I grew up in an orphanage. Those kids are tougher than you think. They also are street-smart, and right now, street-smart is what we need."

Ruth looked from Becky to Mary and found only a wall of

determination. Ruth threw herself back into her chair and scowled at the wall for a moment.

Then she smiled. "You're missing two points. These kids are street-smart on *this* side of town. You're talking about sending them all the way to the other side. To you it may look like just a couple of kilometers, but to them, it might as well be on another planet. And even if that wasn't the deal breaker I see, you got to get around Major Barbara. No way will she let us put her kids in harm's way."

To Ruth's great joy, the FSO blinked several times, then nodded. "I guess we will have to get this 'Major' Barbara's permission."

"You'll never get it," Ruth said bluntly.

"She runs that orphanage on a shoestring," the FSO said. "She never knows where her kids' next meals are coming from. And from what I heard on yesterday's tapes, the handheld you gave Alice is helping a few kids get some sort of education."

"I think I can get a collection from my Marines to support an orphanage," Mary said. "Most of them, the lucky ones, got to spend time in one or three growing up. And I think several of my crew would like to buy themselves new computers. They could donate the old ones to the kids."

Ruth was back up on her feet. "You . . . you . . . rats!" she finally settled for. "You'd bribe that woman to get her to offer up her kids!"

Now Mary was on her feet. "No! I'm not bribing anyone. I'm giving them a chance to make a better Savannah for everyone, and I'm offering them a chance to grab a handhold on it. You've seen those kids. They got no life. No hope for a future. I say give them a fighting chance! I know at their age, I would have jumped at what we're offering them."

Ruth and Mary locked eyes. One, a woman with a mother's fears for her children. The other, just as much a woman but with a different set of hopes and dreams to share with the kids.

It was the third woman who stepped between them. "Ruth, you say this Major Barbara is the only one looking out for these kids. Let's give her a say in what we do. From what you said, if she down-checks Mary's idea, it's dead on arrival anyway."

Next morning's drive started very silently. About the only talking was when Mary assured Ruth the car was bug-free.

The Bear and his cab was parked across from the embassy, but he made no effort to give chase as they left. Mary took them on a twisting and turning route, but no tail developed.

So they went to the river park and enjoyed the view as Mary drove down one side, then crossed at a busy bridge and drove up the river on the other side.

"They're leaving us alone this morning," the Marine finally said.

"They've likely got the Farm staked out real good and don't care where I go otherwise."

"Seems like it. You want to call the Major?"

"She's not a real major. She's in the Salvation Army."

"I know of 'em, ma'am, and if you want my opinion, their captains and major are often a damn sight better than some I've met in the Corps."

Ruth had to chuckle. "Present company and my husband excluded, right?"

"I'm none too sure about Trouble, and I'm never sure about me."

"Spoken like an honest woman. Okay, Mary, why'd you come up with this hairbrain idea to put my kids' heads in the lion's mouth?"

"Ruth, I said what I meant. We need to bust this open before those Earth senators get here. You can't. I can't. If anybody can, it's the kids. Tell me I'm wrong."

Which left Ruth scowling at herself in the window's reflection. "I can't say you're wrong. I just can't be sure you're right."

"As I've learned, ma'am, there ain't no guarantees in life. You pays your money, and you takes your chances."

"But these are kids we're asking to take those chances, Mary."

"Yes, ma'am, but it's these kids' world we're trying to save. It's their future. From where I'm standing, it don't look like much of a future's been dealt them."

Ruth couldn't argue with that. Digging around the ugly underbelly of this planet, she'd found few who had much of a future, and most of those who did didn't deserve it.

"I'll call the Major and set up a meeting."

A half hour later, they were in a small coffee shop a few

blocks from the orphanage. It catered to the Moslem coffee drinkers. It had a large section in back where men sat, smoked from strange contraptions, and chatted as they drank. Behind a thick grill was a small area for women.

In front, there was space for those not of their faith.

Mary ordered coffee for three. What arrived was thick and sweet and served in tiny cups. The waiter left a metal pitcher with a long thin spout for them to refill their cups and departed with a shallow bow.

Major Barbara was not long in arriving. They did not exchange pleasantries for long. Barbara was in a hurry, she said. Mary offered that her Marines were looking for something good to do locally. They'd taken up a collection and had a thousand dinars to give to a good cause and were willing to spend a weekend painting a well-deserving place.

Ruth had suggested Major Barbara's place.

The Major was properly, if a bit tiredly, grateful.

Then Mary raised the prospects of some handheld commlinks for the kids.

And the Major's eyes narrowed.

"Let's go for a walk," she snapped.

Mary paid and followed Ruth and the Major out of the shop. They walked for several blocks before they turned into a vacant lot that showed evidence of the building that had burned down not too long ago.

"Okay, what are you two up to?" Barbara demanded sharply. "I told you before that you will not sell my kids into white slavery. You said you weren't in that trade. Have you changed your mind?"

"Don't talk to me," Ruth said. "This is all her idea," and tossed the ball to Mary.

The Marine quickly introduced herself and her problem. "We know nothing about that drug-research farm. Your kids hang around factories, shops, this town, and learn things. Could they start hanging around the neighborhood with that Farm and learn stuff? I don't know what stuff. Just stuff that might let us break this thing. We need to break it fast, and if we do, we might, just might, break Milassi. I hate to say it, but your kids are our only hope."

Ruth was surprised. The Major didn't snap something like

"go to hell," or "you've got your heads up your asses," or even something more Christian like "that's a lot of bullshit."

Instead, she led them back to the street. Briskly, they walked on for two more blocks before she finally said, "When you offered me that bribe, I almost walked out on you. Now that I know what you're up to, I don't know what to think."

"*We're* not up to it," Ruth said. "*She* is."

"And why aren't you behind this?" the Salvation Army woman asked, turning on Ruth.

"I don't think it's safe for the kids," Ruth stammered.

Major Barbara stomped on. "Nothing is safe for my kids," she muttered to no one. "They can starve to death, and no one will notice. They get sick and die, and no one notices. Some crusher has a bad day and beats them up and leaves them to die in some alley, and nobody notices. Maybe you haven't noticed, but Petrograd is no safe city for kids without a home. Or for those with homes."

"She knows that," Mary said, surprising Ruth by coming to her defense. "She's just not sure that sending them across town into a strange neighborhood isn't taking on more risk than they can handle."

The Major nodded. "That may be a problem. Maybe not. I know a shelter that could take them in at night. Scott has some kids that he maybe could add to your effort. How much money are you willing to fork over?"

"How much can I get away with before somebody notices?" the Marine asked.

"You're not going to paint my place. That would be a dead giveaway. Scott and I might be able to slip a couple of hundred dinars into our budget for a few months without anyone the wiser. How long is this going to take?"

"We can't tell you," Ruth said.

"A secret?" Barbara asked.

"If someone beats you up in a dark alley some night, the less you know, the less they can beat out of you," the Marine said.

Major Barbara frowned. "I guess that's smart. Scott and I will need at least a dozen commlinks. That should let us get our kids connected. The kids will use them at night for school, maybe even during the day if they think they can get away with it. Some of our kids are real smart and hungry to learn. It's a crying shame they have nothing ahead of them but brothels for the girls and day-labor gigs for the boys."

"Is it that bad?" Mary said.

"It's that bad," the Salvation Army woman said. "I'm sorry, Ruth, if you think less of me for putting my kids into this dangerous game you're playing, but right now, they have no life ahead of them. This idea of yours stinks to high heaven, but if it leads to anything, it might give the kids a chance they'll never get anywhere else on this planet."

"Major," Mary said, coming almost to Marine attention, "I work for a guy by the name of Ray Longknife. He married into some money. I swear to you that I will do everything in my power to see that he uses some of it to help your kids get the education they need and the opportunity to make something of themselves."

"Don't make promises you can't keep," the woman of God said. "And we have to see what the kids can get you, first. Okay."

On that, they parted company. The Salvation Army woman headed back to the hungry of her orphanage. Ruth and Mary returned to the safety of the embassy.

TWENTY-THREE

RAY LONGKNIFE LEARNED from Becky Graven what promises his security chief had made for him to keep. He smiled at how free his former enemy was with his checkbook.

Still, when Captain Mary Rodrigo brought the hat around for a donation for "her and Ruth's kids," he dropped several large Wardhaven bills in the kitty. He also sprang for new commlinks for all of Mary's Marine detachment.

He told Mary it was only a down payment on more to come.

There was more to the commlink handoff than just giving the old castoffs to the kids.

The old commlinks disappeared into Becky's secret basement war center for overhaul, update, and modification. Now each had a sensor that picked up the hum of bugs and spy devices. Now the commlinks had their own special channel that not only encrypted the message but allowed it to be squirted line of sight to a like device or transmitted to one and only one station.

The basement.

Oh, and each handheld got its own access to the educational channels. Not only the free ones, but several of the paid channels.

That was Becky's idea. For a hard-hearted FSO, there seemed to be a soft chewy center in there somewhere.

Ray had his own meetings to attend. Those with the Milassi government were a pain, but he showed up. He smiled. Milassi and his henchmen smiled. They all smiled . . . and after each meeting, Ray checked his back to see if there was a knife in it.

His meetings with the local military commanders were even worse. None of them had fought off planet during the Unity War. Their fighting had been domestic, breaking strikes at the factories when the long hours and low pay drove the workers into the streets.

Now, of course, they were all only too happy to wine and dine the "Man Who Killed President Urm." Ray smiled even as his stomach churned.

However, the meetings with the masters of industry and finance left Ray of several minds.

Many factories were run by leftovers from the Unity regime. Somehow, Unity thugs had managed to confiscate a good third of Savannah's industrial base. There were lawsuits now working their way through the courts by the previous owners to get them back, but for now, the thugs and party sycophants still ran the businesses.

Most of their talking ran to what women they were sleeping with or how they'd made money under the table on this deal or that.

Ray ignored them as best he could . . . and washed his hands anytime he had to shake one of theirs.

The other managers fell into two categories. Some were managers of plants owned by major interplanetary corporations. They'd been sent to Savannah to straighten up factories that were operating in the red. They gave Ray some of his more interesting conversations.

Quite a few recognized him as his wife's husband. "You married into the Nuu Enterprises business, didn't you? How does the old man get rim-world workers to work?" did not go over well with Ray.

His initial reply was to snap, "He treats them like human beings." That ended the first two conversations rather abruptly. After that, he limited himself to asking why they were asking. That at least had the virtue of leading to longer talks.

"My work crew don't do anything more than the minimum," one manager said.

Ray offered that the workforce on Wardhaven was much more motivated.

Yet another manager mentioned that during a walk around his plant, he'd come across several of his shop-floor supervisors out behind the main building beating up one of his workers. When he stopped the fight and demanded an explanation, the foremen slunk off leaving him to call the nurse to care for the worker.

"He didn't have anything to say either," the offworlder said, shaking his head. "It might be because his jaw was broken, but even after it healed, he refused to talk. He just went back to his job on the floor."

"What did you do with the supervisors?" Ray asked.

"I tried to fire them."

"Tried?" Ray echoed.

"Yes. It seems I can fire any worker for any reason, but not foremen and midlevel managers. They have an association with a contract that the courts won't break. I can't even think of firing one."

Ray could only raise an eyebrow at that and make a note to find out what was behind it.

The third group Ray felt most at home with. They were owners, many of them the great-grandsons of the men who had started the companies long ago. Unlike their fathers and grandfathers, they were college trained, with ideas of how to run a good company. Most knew the business from the mail room to the plant floor to the front office.

And most were stumped by the structures they inherited of workers harshly split along bitter lines of religion or cultural divisions going back to ancient times on Earth!

"I tried to get committees together to review our work processes. I figured if I included representatives from all the work units, they could come up with ideas they'd have ownership of. At least that was what I learned in my MBA program back on New Eden."

Ray nodded along wisely, wondering how this would end.

"Half my committees only met once. They ended in brawls. Fistfights, for God's sake! I can't even get my people to talk to each other, much less solve problems. How am I going to get anything to change if I can't even get them to talk?"

Neither Ray nor any of those listening had any suggestions.

Clearly, the problems of Savannah went deep, and they were not going to go away with some minor change like driving Milassi off the planet.

Ray did ask Becky about the problem of firing the foremen

and middle managers. She found that interesting and said she'd get back to him. It took her two days to do that.

"You remember that middle-manager-firing problem?" she asked Ray over breakfast in the embassy cafeteria.

"Yes," Ray admitted.

"It seems there is a Fraternal Order of Foremen and Managers on Savannah. No one has to join, but everyone that can does. It costs them ten percent of their pay right off the top, but they get to have this Employment Security Agreement with their business that can't seem to be broken."

"It must be very well written," Ray said.

"And very well defended in court," the FSO quickly added. "All of the money the FOFM raises goes to political activities. Taxes are amazingly low here. Few judges could afford the mansions they live in, but their political action committees are allowed to raise money for their election as well as for their other needs."

"That sounds very corrupt."

"On Savannah, it's not corruption, it's the way life is," the diplomat said.

"I understand there are families that want to take back the businesses that were confiscated during the Unity rule. How are they making out in court?"

"It depends on how well they can pay the judges. And since the leftover Unity types have the businesses and can tap them for donations to the judges' reelection campaigns, you can guess the outcome."

"This place really needs a housecleaning," Ray said.

"And Milassi is doing his level best to see that it won't happen."

"That FOFM group. Are they also buying off Milassi?"

"Half of what they raise goes directly into his bank account."

"Is that enough to pay his bills without the drug money?"

Becky shook her head. "He's got thugs and the Army to pay. It doesn't even come close."

"What other sources of income have you tracked?"

"Have any of your business buddies complained about the cost of their raw materials?"

"Not that I've heard of so far."

"Well, most of the mining, oil, and gas holdings ended up under Unity control. The mines and oil refineries were one of the few places that imported skilled workers. And those workers brought their unions with them. They were the best-paid workers on the planet."

"Were," Ray said, arching an eyebrow.

"That's right, were. Unity offered to break the unions if the mine owners made certain contributions. They did, then cut pay and lengthened the workweek. After all, there was a war on, and under Unity, there was always a war on somewhere. The workers went out on strike. The Army marched in and gunned down anyone who wasn't smart enough to get back to work fast."

"Nice, but how does that lead to present costs?" Ray asked.

"Well, once the unions were broken, Unity started making more demands on the owners. Those that didn't cough up the donations suddenly found their house burning down. And there were few survivors. The courts declared the mines in arrears to some contracts that no one could remember signing. However, since the ink was dry on the signatures, judges found that Unity now owned several mines. When the Unity thugs suggested that other mine owners might want to sell out cheap, it was amazing how quickly the owners did."

"Lie down with dogs, get up with fleas," Ray said.

"A bit of advice they might have wished they'd taken earlier. Anyway, today much of the raw materials for the factories comes from pretty monopolistic sources. The factory owners can either pay up or try to make their products out of thin air."

"Or find their own homes catching fire some night?" Ray added.

"Maybe that, too."

"Any of the previous mine owners trying to reclaim their property?"

The diplomat nodded. "Several of them, but again, the judges aren't moving any too quickly."

"And where does the money go from the mines and refineries?" Ray asked. "Other than to bribing judges."

"Some ends up in Milassi's pockets, but a lot of it seems to go off planet."

"Where?"

Becky shrugged. "We're still chasing that down."

"So Milassi has a police force of thugs and an army to pay and is getting money from the middle managers' security fund and from the extraction sources that Unity controlled. I imagine he's also got some money coming from the Unity-controlled factories."

"Some, but not a lot. Those factories really aren't making much of a profit. Production is down. They need to modernize, but most factories are using obsolete machinery that hasn't been upgraded since it was first built. You can only get so much out of your workers."

"This place is sick," Ray said.

"Yeah. You got any pill you can give it?"

"In my profession, pills are usually 155 mm and delivered from the mouth of a cannon."

"I only wish it were that easy in my line of work," Becky said. "Still, I think there is a critical weakness in the system. If we can bring down that one point, the whole house of cards comes down."

"You having much success on that?"

"Not a lot, yet, but I have high hopes."

With that, Ray left. He'd been invited to observe the annual maneuvers of the Corps of the Capital Guard Divisions. Their headquarters were just outside of town. He'd asked Trouble to come along with him. It was a chance to take the measure of the young Marine officer.

If Becky and her eggheads did find the place to tap this mess and make it all fall apart, Ray would be depending on this man to help him police up the pieces. It would be tragic if the young man wasn't up to the work.

TWENTY-FOUR

MARY TOOK RUTH out the next day. They met Major Barbara and Scott before noon in River Park. It didn't take long to bring Scott up to speed on the problems they faced and their hope to use the street kids to change things.

Briefing done, he and Major Barbara exchanged worried glances. Still, he came on board.

Mary left each an envelope with a hundred dinars. They'd settled on the smaller monthly stipends after the locals explained it wasn't unusual for the orphanage or the shelter to be shaken down by the local cops. Any money lying around or locked in a desk would likely disappear.

"The cops don't get much pay, and it's expected that local business 'donate' to help the cop on the beat. I've told them we're living hand to mouth, but that doesn't cut it with the cops," Scott explained.

Yet another thing Mary didn't like about this place.

The next day, Mary checked out a larger sedan from the motor pool. Once Lek assured her it was bug-free, she and Ruth headed out. Again, the Bear ignored them.

"I think he's just waiting for us to get close to the Farm again," Ruth opined. "If we do, they'll be on us like ticks on a hog."

Mary remembered that a hog was bacon on the hoof. She had no idea what a tick was, but she let it pass. Clearly, this farm girl had a vocabulary different from that of a kid raised in the asteroids.

Once Mary was sure they had not grown a tail, she collected not just Alice Blue Bonnet but a half dozen other kids just at the cusp of becoming women and men.

Like Alice, they were thin to the point of starvation, but with eyes already old that took everything in.

They were the ones who had been working with Alice on learning, or been standing behind them wanting to learn. Now, each drew a commlink. Before they'd gone a block, all the kids squeezed in the backseat had their noses in their new wonder and were soaking up what the handheld offered.

Mouse had wanted to come, but he'd never been separated from his sister, Tiny. And Tiny would not wander too far from Major Barbara's storefront.

Thus Mouse stayed behind with his sister.

Mary wanted to cry for all these kids, handed duties that would break grown men, but she drove a winding route toward the shelter across town.

Ruth insisted they stop for lunch at a collection of lunch wagons. Mary gave each kid a five-dinar note and sent them to order their own lunches. The kids spread out and ended up with sandwiches and burgers, burritos and bentos. But as Mary watched, each of the street kids was required to show the color of their money before their order was taken, and at least two of them were turned away from their first choice when they discovered their money was no good.

There was nothing wrong with the money, but the guy running the lunch wagon didn't like the color of their eyes or the way they combed their hair.

"I told you," Ruth said. "You take these kids outside their own tiny fishbowl, and they don't know where the land mines are."

"But they learn fast," Mary said. "And they'll have Scott's kids to teach them the ropes."

"Brother Scott's kids," Ruth corrected.

"Brother?"

"Yeah. He and the three others working with him are religious."

Mary shook her head. "I didn't see a habit or anything."

"It's kind of rare to find a monk's robe in a bag of discarded clothing," Ruth said. "They wear what they're given and make due as well as they can. If Brother Scott looks thin and sickly, it's because, Major Barbara says, when they're short on food for the kids, he and his associates declare it a fast day for themselves."

"Damn," was all Mary could say.

"Or God bless," Ruth added.

"Yeah. You probably have the better answer," Mary agreed.

The kids came back with their lunches, and the change. They had a hard time believing the grown-ups didn't want the leftover coins and small bills.

It was Alice who solved the problem. "We can save it and make a donation to the place where we sleep tonight." That seemed a good solution to the kids.

It also told Mary that they had already been briefed. They'd not be going back to Major Barbara's anytime soon.

Ruth made the call to the shelter and gave Mary a list of three street corners. They dropped a couple of kids off at each point. There was a skinny kid of their age waiting at each stop. They quickly disappeared down alleys.

Three quick stops, and Mary and Ruth had the car to themselves.

"It's started," Ruth breathed with a sigh.

"How long do we leave them alone?" Mary asked.

"We'll meet Alice at a vacant lot two days from now. She'll bring us up to date with what they're doing. They'll only use the hotline to deliver stuff that needs action fast. For the most part, the kids are on their own."

Mary drove a winding course back to the embassy, wondering just how long two days could be. Then she remembered. When she was a kid, they lasted forever.

TWENTY-FIVE

OLD FATHER JOSEPH enjoyed these afternoon walks. It gave him a chance to work the kinks out of his old bones.

The walk also saw to it that his grandson, David, got home quickly after school.

The young lad had survived his time with the star-striding Colonel Ray Longknife from mankind's home worlds. Still, the priest kept a good eye on the boy.

He enjoyed playing games with his fellows just like he always had, and if Father Joseph wasn't there waiting for him at the schoolhouse gate, he'd play until darkness drove him in like the rest.

Not that the old priest didn't let him play with his friends. A lad needed the lessons his own kind taught him as well as book learning. But he needed book learning, too.

So it happened this fine spring afternoon that the padre and his grandson were walking up the hill to the old parish church when the sun was still well up and the birds sweetly into their song.

The old priest didn't miss a step when he saw what was waiting for him in front of his own church.

Cars there were. Three fine-looking things with the proud seal of the Government of Santa Maria, just as pleasant as could be.

Assuming any good could come of a visit from the lowland lords, may God bless them and keep them far away from here, the old priest prayed.

He tried to mean it.

Now weren't two fine, strapping men in uniforms coming down the hill to meet him.

"And what brings you out on such a fine day as this?" the priest asked.

"We've come for the boy," said the one who strode at the lead and was clearly the commander, not pausing for a fine word at all but coming to the point with the kind of brusqueness that the Protestants of the capital prided themselves on.

"And what might you be wanting with my wee grandson?" the priest said, noticing that the lad had fallen back and was hiding himself in his cassock, something the proud ten-year-old hadn't done for many a year.

Clearly, the wise wee lad had no more use for these bold men than his grandda.

"The colonel himself needs him," the uniformed man said. "Your boy and the other two."

Now the old priest saw the full gathering before the doors of his church. Not only were there more men in the uniform of the bold man before him, but there were also the other two children who, with David, had worked with the colonel to save not only the fine people of the farming country but the whole of Santa Maria, even the lowland Protestants, there being no way for men to understand the holy ways of God's mercy.

The children were there, with tearful elders as well.

The proud men in uniform had made their demands to these others with no more apparent care than they had with him.

The priest fingered his shillelagh. For many years, it had been no better than a walking stick. But in his younger days, before he took to the collar and the Mass, it had been put to many a good use.

Across from him, the proud man in the uniform took this in and his hand came to rest on his own air pistol.

The old priest smiled. His years might not have made him wise, but they had at least made him less of an idjit. He glanced around the gathering crowd. Of course, the old gossip who did such cleaning of the church and his own house as penance for her many sins was right there at the edge.

No doubt she'd have the word of what happened here spread to the six mountain counties before the sun was down.

"Mistress Beth, do you think we could do with a wee spot of tea?" he called out.

"Methinks more like a gallon or two, good priest."

"Then put the kettles on, for I have a mind to see all of us in the parish hall for a fine talk."

The parish hall, unlike the thatch-covered, gray-stone church, was new. Made by the star walkers for their own use, it had been broken down and moved to beside the old church as their thanks for what the fine folks here had done for them during their stay.

The proud ones in their uniforms seemed unsure of this offer of tea, but their leader must not have been dropped on his head as a child. At least not too many times. He recognized that hospitality once offered was not to be turned down.

All of them adjourned to the fine new hall and talked of small things while the kettles boiled. They talked of small things until teacups were filled and passed around, then they talked of any wee thing while it cooled and they drank.

Only after the second cup was cooling for them that asked for one did the old priest finally turn to the pressing matter at hand.

"You say that Colonel Ray Longknife has need of our three bright children again?"

"That was what I was told, and those are my orders," said the proud commander. "Three ships have been sent to bring the children from Santa Maria to the homes of humanity."

"Can you tell an old man why?"

"Isn't the request of a great man like the colonel enough for the likes of you?"

The old priest glanced around at his people, both those teary-eyed and those with more determined looks on their darkening faces. "Some of us would trouble you for more of an explanation before we part with our own flesh and blood."

As it turned out, there was a fuller explanation. The proud one nodded, and a man of his set up one of those magical projectors the star walkers had brought. In two shakes of a lamb's tail, the lights had been turned off and they were watching the colonel himself as he explored among the stars.

And nearly getting himself killed, him and those fine people who followed him.

"That has got to hurt," one of the village men observed as the colonel's helmet and gloves were removed in the vacuum of space. The people of Santa Maria had not had much experience of space since their ancestors came to settle on this God-given and God-blessed orb.

Still, the stories of how space killed had been carried down through the years.

The room cheered as the colonel's sacrifice saved his troops and they, in turn, managed to get him back in his space suit and hurried from the hall that had almost killed them all.

When the lights were back on, the proud one stood. "I am told that the wall he leaned against in that alien space station worked much like the stone that he and your children put their head and hands against during the recent, ah, emergence here on Santa Maria. The colonel has asked that the three children who did that with him be sent to his planet, Wardhaven, where they might go out with their exploration ships and help if they get into any situations like the one you just saw."

"You want my daughter to bare her hands and face to space!" shouted a bold father, jumping to his feet. Beside him, his wife's soft sniffling turned to loud cries of anguish.

Others villagers rose to their feet.

Now the proud uniformed men were up, too, and their hands held their air pistols.

"Now, now, good people," the old priest said, coming slowly to his own old feet. "The colonel did us up fine in our hour of need, he did, that he did. And while some of these lowlanders might have been less than courteous in passing along his, no doubt, gentle and gracious request, we should still entertain it."

"Would you let them do that to your grandson?" the father of the girl demanded.

"I would at least give it some thought. We do owe the colonel a debt. We owe him the courtesy of at least talking about his request like good men and women of the land."

The father looked dubious, but he settled back in his chair. True, it was the edge of his chair from which he clearly meant to leap back up at the first hint that his daughter be sacrificed on any altar.

"Grandda," came from beside the old priest.

"Yes, me bucko."

"I liked the colonel," David said from where he sat. "He was good to us. Us three." Slowly the young boy got to his feet, rising to the full height that his ten years had given him. "He's a brave man, Grandda, and it seems to me that what he did didn't harm him all that much."

"That, me lad, is not something they showed us in the moving picture," the old priest pointed out to the love of his later years.

"I know, Grandda, I saw where it ended. Still, sir, could they maybe make a space suit that would let us touch the stone without going through all that?"

The village smithy was up now. "The young lad has a point. I know I couldn't hammer together anything like a space suit, but still, they can do things we forgot long ago."

"It's not your kid they want to take," the father of the girl growled like a bear defending his own private nest of honey bees.

"May I say something?" came from the back of the room.

The third child, Jon, a bit older lad, stood on a chair so he could be seen and heard. "I lost me ma and da when the monsters came and made some folks walk like people possessed, or so I'm told. The space people protected us kids from all of that. If they want me, I would go."

There was a tremble in the boy's voice that would bring tears to stone eyes.

Two of the uniformed men moved toward the boy, their intent clear.

"Just a moment, my fine men," the old priest said, coming again to his feet. "The child has expressed a fine sentiment, and I applaud him for it, but he is a lad of this village, and we will decide if one so young and inexperienced as he may make such a momentous decision for himself."

Now it was the proud leader of the fine uniformed men who was on his feet. "It seems to me that the lad has spoken well for himself."

A woman now was on her feet. "He is my sister's boy and I'll not see you taking him from here. Not while I have breath to speak. He's all I have left of my darling sister, and I'll not see him hauled off a slave."

Two bold men stood, shillelaghs in hand, blocking the way of the fine, strapping men in uniform.

"People, people, let us keep the peace of the Lord in this his house."

"It's a hall, Father."

"And one built by them Godless spacers," was quickly added.

"But it's our parish hall, next to our fine old church," the old priest put in.

The lowlanders glanced at their leader. At a nod from him, they backed slowly toward their chairs and sat again. Under the stern eye of the priest, the village folk returned to their seats.

The proud man stayed on his feet. "You may talk all you want, but there is a ship in orbit above Santa Maria. It brought a lot of mining gear that we are already putting to use. Metal is pouring from mountains like we have not seen since the survivors landed on this planet. More mining gear will be brought in on the next two ships, gear that will break the Stirling's monopoly on metals for our economy."

"And who's to own all this nice, fine metal?" someone from the back of the room asked.

"Several companies are being set up. Some are registered on Wardhaven, some here. We've passed mining laws that set a tariff on all minerals extracted that will go into the common budget for improvements. Everything is going to change."

"But they want my daughter for all this," the father said, not even rising from his chair.

"Do they want all three of the children on this first ship?" the old priest asked.

"No. They were quite specific on that. One child only on each of the first three ships. They don't want to risk more than one of them on any voyage."

"So space travel ain't so easy as they said, not at all, at all," came again from somewhere in the room.

"Colonel Ray Longknife was straightforward with us all," the padre said for all to hear. "They were lost and needed our help as much as they were helping us. Yes, star walking is not a sure thing, but we on Santa Maria wouldn't be here if it were."

That got the room nodding along with the priest.

In the back of the room, a black figure moved from the door to a chair. Young Father Ian, to be sure, Father Joseph noted. The parish now had two priests. The bishop had said it was to lighten Joseph's load, but the old priest knew the truth of it even if His Lordship the Bishop would not say it to his face.

He was old, and soon he'd be laying down his old bones in the parish graveyard beside his wife's and their infant son and daughter. The years had been hard, and Joseph could not say that he was all that averse to laying down his burdens.

But what of his grandson? David had been left to his care for the five years since his older son and his wife had passed when a sudden storm took the bridge out and them on it. They'd never recovered their bodies, so only a stone remembered them in the yard behind the church.

The young priest was a good man, not one of the city types but a boy from the hills, raised not three villages over. He was fitting in well with the folks of Hazel Dell.

That made up the old priest's mind. He stood, and the room fell silent.

"The brave colonel did not stint in what he gave us, and now he asks for something from us in return. My brave boy, David, has said he's willing to go, and I am inclined to let him walk among the stars and see what they are offering him to see. However, while I trust Colonel Longknife with my own life, I will not trust my grandson's care to anyone that may pass him by," he said, giving the eye to the proud, bold commander of the guards.

"So, I have a mind to go with my grandson and see that he is well taken care of."

That brought on a storm in the hall. Yes, it did indeed.

A good fifteen minutes later, when much had been said that would have to be forgotten, it was generally agreed that yes, Father Ian might be a good priest, but he'd never fill Father Joseph's shoes, but yes, it might be time to let him try his hand at the parish.

Still, Father Joseph would ever be missed, and was it a good idea to let him and his fine young grandson go walking among the stars?

"My mind is made up on this," Father finally said, hugging his grandson and getting a hug right back.

"Thank you, Grandda," David whispered in his ear.

"But what of the others? They are all of them young and in need of someone to stand between them and the likes of these," the mayor said, putting no fine edge on the topic at hand.

"May I say something?" came from a redheaded and freckled young man who'd come early but taken a chair against the wall.

Brennan was a strange one. It had been clear to his elders that they'd never make a farmer of him. He might do something well one moment, then lose everything as his mind wandered off to woolgather. And the village having no sheep, the wool he gathered was always made of clouds and vapor.

So they'd let him try his hand at other trades about the village. He'd proven too light of arm and frame to stand beside the village smith. He had, however, shown a fine hand with a fiddle and harp.

That got him apprenticed to the village singer and harpist. She was amazed at how quickly he learned the songs, and even began memorizing the laws and the exceptions to each one of them. He'd been well on his way to becoming a bard when the spacers came.

And they ruined everything for the young man.

They'd taken him into their employ, and he'd seen much of what they knew of the worlds and what made them turn. He might have left with them, but his old mother was in her final illness. He'd stayed behind at her side.

Father Joseph pointed his hand at the young man, having a strong idea what was about to be said. Brennan did not disappoint.

"I would be willing to stand assist to young Jon, since he has no close family to stand as his young right arm and see that he is well taken care of."

Not if Jon's aunt had any say in the matter. She was quickly on her feet. But Jon moved faster, running to the side of the young troubadour.

"I would go with him to the stars. I've seen them. I want to walk among them," the ten-year-old said. "You have nothing here for me but memories of those I've lost. Please. Let me go."

That seemed to settle the matter for those two.

"But can a youngster like Brennan stand as a protector to anyone so young?" the aunt asked. "Can he even stand as a protector for himself?"

That brought assent to many a throat in the hall.

"You may be right," the young Brennan said, "but I won't be going alone. Father Joseph will be going, and we are going to Colonel Ray Longknife. He's a right strong man, and I can't see all that many willing to stand before his glower. Can you, Father?"

"Not hardly. Not at all, at all," the old priest agreed. "If Brennan can't stand between Jon and ill-usage, then he will know how to get to the colonel, or to me, and I assure you I will get to the colonel through storm, wrack, and ruin."

That seemed to settle it.

The bold uniformed commander said that would fill the first two ships and he could wait for a bit on filling the third. Father Joseph took Brennan and Jon aside, and it was soon decided that those two would go on the first ship.

The old priest was glad of that. It would give him more time to say his good-byes to friends of a lifetime. Brennan and Jon left to pack their few things, and a keg of beer was tapped and many a mug passed around.

The edge came off the bold uniformed commander and his men. Before the second or third mug was raised in toast, they were all singing along with the village troubadour.

"I find I must thank you, old priest," said the proud commander.

"Yes, you must," Father Joseph said, knowing his eyes were sparkling.

"You did take a hot bit of work and cool it. That you did."

"God blesses some works to his end. Why He does not bless others, I have not been blessed to know."

"Well, He blessed you. I, for one, was not at all sure I'd be returning with one of these kids, much less two, maybe three of them. Is that girl Rose as sweet on your David as I think?"

"She's a bit young to be setting her cap for any boy, don't you think?" the old priest said, and made a note that he must go to confession to Father Ian for this bit of a lie. While they might be young, what had transpired between them when they put their heads to the rock seemed to have aged them beyond their years.

"You know these hill folk better than I," the bold commander said. "And I thank you for putting your oar into the waters I troubled. If the folks and their kids had taken off a-running, I doubt I ever could have chased them down in this hill country."

"And maybe it is us that didn't want to have to run, not at all, at all. Have you thought about that?"

"You want to go out to the cold stars?"

"The star walkers were among us longer than they were with you. It's hard to say, but both David and Jon raised their voices to go, and what with all that her folks were carrying on, we never did hear from young Rose, now did we?"

The bold commander took a long pull on his beer. "You may have said more than you know, old priest. You may have said more than I will ever know."

Later that night, before the altar, the old priest would meditate on those words. Just how had it come to pass that at his old age, and David's young years, that they were setting their feet on a path neither one of them could have dreamed of just two years ago?

If the dear Lord was willing, he would have the time to find out.

TWENTY-SIX

RUTH LET MARY drive her out, two days later, to meet Alice Blue Bonnet at a farmer's market. They looked for Alice under her trademark blue bonnet but couldn't find her.

Ruth finally spotted her. Alice was dressed in a black-and-white maid's uniform, though the hem was a bit more above the knee than Ruth would have expected of a maid in a fine house.

"Hurry," Alice said, "I'm here to buy cleaning supplies. I must be quick about it."

"You have a job?" Ruth said, wondering who would have hired the painfully thin young woman.

"Yes, I work at a place frequented by the Farm's technicians and scientists."

The young woman did not meet Ruth or Mary's eyes as she said that. Alarm bells were going off in Ruth's head.

"Who gave you a job?" Mary insisted.

"I am working at a gentlemen's place of leisure," Alice said. "Please, do not tell Major Barbara. It is not what it seems."

"Of course we won't tell Major Barbara," Ruth said, shooting daggers at Mary. The Marine had the good sense to leave the situation to Ruth. "Why do you say it is not what it seems?"

"I'm not one of the working girls, Ruth. I'm a washerwoman. I strip the beds, wash the linens, iron them, and remake the beds. That's *all* I do."

"We understand," Ruth said. "And I'm sure Major Barbara will, too." She kept to herself the fear that if any jaded visitor took a hunger for a painfully thin and young slip of a girl, no doubt the madam would be negotiating a price before he finished the thought.

We've got to get this done, and done quickly.

Alice's "Do you think she will?" would have wrung water from desert rocks.

"We'll make sure she does," Mary said. "Now, about the scientists and techs from the Farm, do they talk much when they come to call?"

"Yes. I also wash glasses at the bar. That gets me extra pay. They talk to the bartender, and he talks to me. I think he likes me," she said, with probably more of a blush than the young girl had experienced in her life.

"Some of the scientists are not happy," she went on quickly. "They say they were offered jobs doing critical research, and instead they find themselves working with this 'shit.' That is what they call it. They are not happy with their bosses."

"Hmm," Mary said. "That's interesting."

"And there are job openings at the Farm," Alice went on as she filled her shopping basket with several boxes of soap detergent. "They need boys to hoe the weeds, spread cow manure, and kill bugs and stuff. It's hard work, but they hire young kids to do it. Three of our boys are in line for jobs."

"That would get them in there," Mary said. "You know I don't know anything about farming, but even to me, that doesn't sound right. Aren't there sprays and stuff for that?"

"Yeah, there are," Ruth said, "but if someone put a herbicide in the sprayer instead of an insecticide, they could wipe out half the crop in an hour."

"Not very trusting, are they?" Mary said.

"Not at all," Ruth said, remembering her own time as a slave on a drug plantation. "Besides, they usually have lots of slave labor growing that shit. They don't need to make sure it's resistant to insecticides or herbicides. They breed it quick for the high they want and get it on the street. Then they develop the next designer drug fast. They don't need any one crop to be very good in the long term."

"Did I tell you I don't like these guys?" the Marine said.

"Several times as I recall."

"We got to do something about this," Mary said.

"Alice, let us know if the boys make it into the Farm. When can we see you next?"

"I have to shop every other day for stuff. We do a lot of

laundry," the young girl said, eyeing her basket and maybe seeing the piles of soiled sheets that lay ahead of her.

Ruth said a prayer that the poor girl wouldn't have to face worse in her future.

Some of the other kids were taking other odd jobs at places around the Farm. They had seen a lot of crushers but managed to stay clear of them. Alice promised to have reports from those kids on where the crushers were and if they moved about or stayed comfortable in their places.

Ruth wished Alice had more to tell her, but it was a start. They would just have to take their time with this.

The drive back to the embassy was quiet as Ruth measured the risks the kids were taking and did not like it at all. Alice must know she was in a helpless situation. Still, the girl had sounded sure of herself—more sure of herself than the street kid had sounded since Ruth first met her.

Apparently, having a chance to change things was putting a bit of pride in her step and hope in her cheeks. Or maybe she just found risky business to her taste.

Back at the embassy, Ruth found that she and Mary were wanted in the basement. Both Becky and Colonel Longknife were waiting for them. Ruth let Mary make the report for them.

The Marine was concise and to the point. Still, the debriefing took close to half an hour.

The diplomat's surprise was evident at the prospects that some of the street kids might actually be hired to work on the Farm. "I wasn't raised on a farm. I don't know much at all about where my food comes from, but don't most farms use gear to do what they want these kids to do?"

"Yes, ma'am," Ruth said. "I did grow up on a farm, and I've seen how these drugs are raised. Fortunately, not with a lash on my back, but close. Too close. You can ask Captain Trouble what that's like." Ruth smiled as she slipped into using her husband's professional handle.

"Still, it seems smart that if you don't want to risk some stupid slave slipping herbicide into your liquid fertilizer, you use the old-fashioned cow stuff. And if you don't want to run any chance of a mix-up of pesticide for herbicide, you have kids you hired cheap hoe down the weeds. I know Trouble got really familiar with the back end of a hoe as well as the front end of a whip."

"And no insecticide?" the colonel asked.

"Some of the drug plants on our plantation had a kind of symbiotic relationship with some bugs. I don't know if it was just to fertilize the flowers or if there was something more to it, but that was what I saw," Ruth said.

"So they use cheap labor here and slave labor there," Becky said.

"But they've got unhappy labor, too," the colonel said, deep in thought.

"You think we can use that against them?" the diplomat asked.

"I'm not sure," the colonel said slowly. "Somehow, we need to contact those unhappy guys. Ruth, did you and Trouble find out how we took down the space station above Riddle?"

"No, sir. We were kind of occupied with other things while you were up there, if you remember."

The colonel laughed. "Yes, I imagine you were. The station was a problem. They had autocannons everywhere, and it looked to be a bloodbath for the Marines. Then my good friend, Trudy Seyd, came up with an absolutely insane idea. Sassy as punch, she waltzed up to the Computer Network shop and offered every man and woman there a pay hike and a five-year contract to work on Wardhaven."

"You're kidding?" Becky said.

The colonel raised his right hand. "I swear. It's the God's honest truth. If we'd sent a squad of Marines in, they'd have been mowed down. One woman walking around like she had good sense got by the auto systems, then she hired away the folks running the guns, and next thing anyone knew, we had the station."

"That's a nice story," Mary said, "but how do we walk up to these guys and get enough time with them to offer them a job? Assuming they'd take it if we offered it to them?"

That stumped the four of them.

They spent the rest of the hour looking at other aspects of the new data. Becky tasked the sensors on the *Patton* in orbit to see if they could trace the trucks full of manure back to their source.

"If we can track them, maybe we could add something to the mix while it's on the road," the colonel said.

"You're getting rather proactive," the diplomat responded.

"Do you have a better idea? Right now, everything is going Milassi's way. I'd like to see how he handles adversity," the colonel said, with a tiger's hungry grin.

TWENTY-SEVEN

MILASSI, OF COURSE, didn't sit on his thumbs waiting for adversity to bite him on the ass.

That night, four Marines who had stepped out for a bite to eat and a bit to drink were accosted by a dozen thugs not three blocks from the embassy. It wasn't a fair fight, but then the thugs didn't intend it to be fair. They had steel pipes and chains. The Marines didn't have much of anything.

Except their training, and being Marines that meant everything.

The corporal who was the senior rank present reported immediately upon their return to barracks. They had skinned knuckles and two black eyes.

The thugs, at least the eight found when the medical detachment arrived at the site of the encounter, were knocked out cold or suffering from broken legs, arms, and other contusions.

Doc and the corpsmen called in the local medical authorities and turned the wreckage over to them without a word said or an observation asked for.

None of the local cops were called in.

But the next morning, there were several dozen cops, billy clubs clearly in evidence, patrolling the embassy's perimeter.

Mary and Trouble were standing at the front gate, observing this new normal, when Colonel Longknife and FSO Graven joined them.

"Ever get the feeling we're under siege?" the colonel asked no one in particular.

"How are we going to get people past that?" Mary asked.

"I'm not sure," Trouble said, "but the next time Ruth and you go out, I want that woman Marine that took out two of the thugs in the backseat with you, and I want half a squad of Marines never more than three blocks from you."

"No problem, sir, but how do we get out?" Mary repeated.

"I think I can solve that," Colonel Ray Longknife said. "Assuming Ms. Graven will allow me the use of her motor pool."

"I can't wait to see how you handle this," the FSO said with a demure grin.

That night, Marines left the embassy in a dozen groups of half-squad strength. None of them were gone for more than an hour, and all returned in good order.

There were, however, a lot of skinned knuckles, several black eyes, and two with broken ribs who hadn't dodged quickly enough where clubs or pipes were concerned.

One Marine had a bad knife wound. He was, of course, one of Mary's boys, from Du's street kids. He'd been off the streets and in the Corps for several years now. Still, it was Dumont and his crew that visited the fellow in sick bay.

And kidded him unmercifully.

Mary was dropping by to check on him just as Du and his buddies were leaving.

"Several of those thugs took knives to our fistfights," Dumont observed.

"Are you surprised after the way we trounced them last night?"

"I shouldn't have been. I won't underestimate these shits again, Mary. Next time we do this, I'll have a sergeant with each team carrying an automatic. If it comes to it, I want someone who can lay down covering fire."

"Pick levelheaded ones, Du. I don't want this escalating any faster than it has to."

"But you don't want any dead Marines, either."

"You're reading me right on that one."

The next morning, there were even more security types stalking around the embassy's wall.

The colonel and Becky stood at the gate, grinning as they began the morning's exercise.

The embassy ambulance, lights flashing and siren blaring, sped up to the gate as the Marines pulled it open. Despite a dozen black uniforms waving their arms for the ambulance to slow down and be inspected, it charged their line.

They leapt aside just in time to avoid having tire marks all over their pretty black uniforms.

Then they were racing for their cars to give chase to the rapidly departing ambulance.

The colonel eyed the developments, then muttered into his commlink.

A second later, a sedan loaded with Marines raced through the gate. The Security forces hadn't yet re-formed their roadblock, so they were hustling to jump into cars and give chase before they had done more than wave at it as it whizzed by.

After a number of pace cars tailed by careening chase cars had begun the morning fun, Colonel Longknife and Captain Trouble counted the police cars across from the gate.

"Getting kind of thin," the colonel said.

"I think the gals can make a run for it now," the captain agreed.

Rather sedately, Mary drove up to the gate. Ruth was riding shotgun and threw Trouble a kiss that his uniform forbade returning. In the back were not one, but two female Marines, though neither would pass muster.

One most definitely.

As they drove out, Mary waved at the taxi driver known as the Bear, and he jumped into this cab to give chase.

However, his chase would have to wait as two large sedans loaded with six Marines each drove out on the bumper of Mary and Ruth's small rental car.

The Bear honked his horn, but had to take last place in the parade now leaving the embassy.

Having done what he set out to do, Colonel Ray Longknife again eyed the thugs in police uniforms who were now closing their ranks and settling in to stare at him. They had few cars left, but it was not cars that worried the colonel.

"We've dissipated their forces with our diversions, sir," Captain Trouble observed.

"Yes, Captain, but we've dissipated the forces at our disposal as well. See to our guard stations, please. We've made our move, now it's their turn."

"Yes, sir," the Marine said, saluting. "But we planned our move. They'll be scrambling to catch up."

"I agree, Captain," Ray Longknife said with a nod, "but

ham-handed reactions by hotheaded fools may not be the problems we want."

"If you say so, sir," the Marine said, and stepped off smartly to see to their first, and only, line of defense.

TWENTY-EIGHT

MARY TOOK A hard right turn and gunned down an alley.
Behind her, one sedan full of Marines hurried on its way, but
the other one slowed down, giving a street stall a wide berth,
but not so wide that the Bear could make it around.

The fake taxi driver rode his horn, but the Marines took
their time letting him get to the alley. By the time he did,
Mary was well on her way, twisting and turning right, then
left, then left and right. She never did catch sight of the Bear
in her rearview.

His demanding, blaring horn fell farther and farther behind.

Once she was sure they had no tail, Mary headed for where
they wanted to go.

"Our escort is four blocks ahead of us," Debbie, the redheaded Marine in the backseat, told Mary. She might have
done major bodily harm to the thugs beating up Ruth, but she
was also a whip with a black box, and had only gotten better
under the bad influence of Lek from Mary's detachment.

"There are two security black-and-reds in the area, Captain, but they don't seem to be doing anything but cruising the
neighborhood. None of them are close to the Marines."

That was good. Mary had a use for those Marines, as well
as what was hidden in the trunk of their sedan.

They drove to the farmers' market and parked several
blocks away. As they approached the market, Mary found out
why Cyn, the blond Marine's, dress was so skimpy.

"We've got one pair of cops at the entrance to the market,"
Debbie said, glancing at her handheld.

Cyn grinned and sashayed forward. "Let me handle them."

"How's she going to handle them?" Ruth asked.

"Best not to ask," Debbie said, "but I think we can count on them not to notice us."

The two cops didn't notice them as they walked into the market. Their eyes were fully occupied trying to look down Cyn's dress.

"Do you think she can handle them?" Ruth asked.

"Cyn tells me that she's been breaking hearts since she got the nice pillows in middle school," Debbie said. "Lord, but I envy her those curves."

Since Mary didn't think Debbie had been all that poorly served in the issuing of lady parts, she assumed the two Marines knew what they were up to. Considering what Mary planned for this evening, she had no right to complain about girls using all that God gave them to leave the boys panting in the dust.

Debbie held back, both to keep an eye on things and to avoid spooking Alice by adding another person to their group.

Alice was waiting for them at the soap stand. "I have to hurry. Tonight there's a big party, and they want everything spick-and-span."

"Will the biologists from the Farm be there?" Ruth asked.

"I think everyone will be there. At least, the girls are all atwitter about things."

"Have you got anything for us?" Ruth asked.

"I have pictures of all of the scientists at the Farm, all fifteen of them," she said, pulling her handheld out of her pocket and pressing a few buttons. "There, now you have them. The last two in the file are the ones I think are happy there. The others aren't.

"The kids also spotted most of the cops on this side of town. Most just walk their street beat. There are some that hang together in groups of four and spend their time in coffee shops or places like mine. I don't know what they do, but here are their usual locations." Again Alice tapped her commlink, and Mary's beeped happily as the new file arrived.

"Likely they're the thugs," Mary observed.

"They are the ones that beat up us kids if we cross their paths. But we're good at running."

"What about jobs at the Farm?" Ruth asked.

"Two boys got hired. One of them told me the manure

always comes from the same farm. Bothell Farms it is. I don't know if that means anything. Now, I've got to get back."

Alice turned to go.

Mary walked along with her for a few steps. "If you see me at the house tonight, don't look at me, and don't look surprised."

"Girls can't come to the party, at least not those that don't work there," Alice said, puzzlement and worry fleeting across her face.

"I may get a job there, just for tonight," Mary said. "That's my worry. You just make sure you don't notice me."

"Yes, ma'am," the young woman said, and increased her pace.

Mary fell behind.

"What was that all about?" Ruth said.

"You, or one of the Marines may get to drive back alone tonight. I'm staying out a bit late."

"What are you up to?" Ruth demanded.

"Nothing you'd approve of," Mary said with a tight smile. "You or that wonderful guy you're married to."

Ruth frowned. "Care to share, girl to girl, or best friend forever to BFF?"

"I'm going to the party tonight. I'm going to talk to the guys who say they want out."

"In bed?"

"If that's the only way I can."

"Mary, I don't think that's a good idea. Did you clear it with anyone back at the embassy?"

"Nope. I suspect it will be easier to get forgiveness tomorrow than get permission today."

"Mary, you're taking a big risk."

"Says the woman that got beat up and nearly killed."

"Well, yes, but I didn't know they'd dare do that."

"And now that you do, would you have done it any differently?"

Ruth scowled. "I really hate drug plantations."

"I really hate Savannah. Now, you get the new information back to the embassy, and I'll get together with the other Marines and see about getting dressed for the party tonight."

Mary and Ruth were still arguing when the four of them

got back to the car. As promised, Cyn had easily wrapped the cops around her little finger, then slipped away before they knew she was leaving.

And, as it turned out, Cyn was no more interested in leaving Mary than she had been about staying with the cops.

"Where's the party?" she asked, then glanced down at what little she was wearing and grinned. "I think I'm dressed just right for this shindig. No?"

"No," Mary said. "I'm going on Lek's elbow. I'm not putting another Marine at risk."

"You on one elbow, me on the other, we'll almost make that old guy look sexy."

How come Trouble never gets this kind of back talk?

Mary's experience of leading Marines was that sometimes she just had to let them do what they were going to do anyway. Maybe it wasn't like that with real Marines, but it was with the mixed bunch that she'd been dealt in the war and been proud to serve with ever since.

Cyn had a point, that two might be better than one, and short of decking her, that was the way it was going to be. Unfortunately, when you let one headstrong girl get away with mutiny, there are others waiting in line.

"I'm staying, too," Debbie announced.

"Lek's only got two elbows for eye candy," Cyn pointed out before Mary got a chance to.

"Yeah," Debbie agreed, "And with you tying up one and the captain here leaning lightly on the other, how's he going to check for bugs and other fine electronic stuff? I'm your back up, Mary, and I'll listen to no arguments from any of you. You need me on the black boxes tonight, and that's where I intend to be."

Mary saw the benefits of it and found herself glad to be surrounded by Marines ready to improvise while she stuck her neck out.

TWENTY-NINE

ONE VERY DISAPPOINTED Marine got stuck with the job of driving Ruth back to the embassy.

The rest started planning their night out once Mary collected Lek and his carful of Marines. Afoot, her team went looking for a place to while away an afternoon while keeping a low profile.

Fortunately, it wasn't long before they picked up a kid who knew just how to do it.

He might have been ten, maybe twelve. It was hard to tell considering how many meals he'd missed. But he spotted them before they spotted him.

At least, he spotted Mary.

"You one of the fine ladies that brung us the learnin' 'puters?" he asked as he passed Mary on the street.

Mary produced a handheld as proof of her answer.

"What you doing on this side of town? I thought you was with Major Barbara?"

"Sometimes I'm there. Sometimes I'm here."

"Well, you better get off of the street, 'cause a bunch of black boots are due to take a walk down these streets, and if you can't say what you're doing walking them, you're in for trouble."

"Can you show us where to go?"

The kid did.

The place he led them to was a pastry shop that specialized in the different breads that the various cultures liked. Some were black and round, others were light and long. They were all represented in the shop, along with soups that only added to the delicious smells.

There were also several kinds of cheeses, many under

glass. Mary suspected that was to avoid mixing their aromas with the rest.

You could also order sandwiches.

The boy ushered the Marines into a back room, where a stooped little old woman took their orders for lunch and just as quickly, served them.

The boy explained they were left-hand types, but they served food for right-handers as well. "They even serve for them head-downer types and beanie-and-shawl ones."

Mary took that to mean that the store was run by Catholics, but was left to wonder how they kept a kosher and halal kitchen at the same time.

The food was delicious and beat anything the embassy cafeteria had served. Lek produced a couple of decks of playing cards, and the eight of them were deep into games when a pair of black-uniform types swaggered into the room.

Mary was proud of her Marines. They didn't miss a play, but kept on laying down and picking up cards, ignoring what passed for police here.

As it turned out, the police ignored them. Mary did see the little old lady leave money on the table near them.

It disappeared, and so did the thugs.

Mary was glad she'd left so generous a tip for lunch.

The card game continued into the afternoon, but for an hour they had to make do without Lek and Debbie. They sauntered off to take the measurements of the bawdy house and found it not only silent of any electronic gear other than the usual screens and players you'd expect at such an establishment, but the streets around it had no surveillance cameras.

"Somebody don't want to be seen enjoying themselves?" Mary asked.

"I'm not surprised. This whole place is kind of light in the electronic stuff," Lek answered. "Not a lot of cameras. I think they like using the old-fashioned ways, busting heads and kicking butts."

Mary couldn't argue with that. From her perspective, it made things easier. Here a blonde distracts, there an old woman coughs up the usual squeeze, and Mary goes her way, doing her best to rip the place's guts out.

She kind of liked that. What did they call it? Poetic justice?

They had supper there, too. The old woman, now aided by a younger and very pretty daughter or granddaughter, helped them choose from the best she had. The Marines paid well, were polite, and left the old woman smiling happily.

No sooner had they finished eating than Mary's handheld beeped. Pictures cascaded down the screen. Someone in the basement had identified by name every one of the scientists at the Farm. The download also provided their professional training and where they got it.

"Impressive," Lek said. He'd gotten the same message.

"So what are they doing here?" Mary asked no one in particular.

"Maybe that will make it easier to get them out of here," Lek offered.

It was that time. When Mary and Lek went to the bathrooms, Mary left an especially large tip.

The old woman seemed puzzled by the largesse, until the two of them emerged dressed for the night and sin.

The old woman had frowned at first at Cyn's getup, but the young woman had been well behaved and seen to it that the Marines behaved themselves, too. Since Cyn was a corporal and most of the boys her junior in rank, it came rather easy.

Now the woman took in Mary's makeup and short electric blue dress with its revealing bodice. She blinked several times, then made a decision.

"I don't know what you are doing. No, I don't."

"Good, Grandmother. Very good," Mary said, putting several hundred more dinars down on the table. "Say nothing of what you have seen here."

The old woman made the money disappear. "What has there been to see?" she asked, and disappeared back into the front of the restaurant.

Mary looked at her Marines. "Okay, troopers, it's time to make this happen. Gunny, keep the troops moving around in groups of two, four if it looks bad. Lek, Cyn, and I will beard the lion in its den. Good luck to us all."

With a hearty if low "Ooo-Rah," the troops moved out to see what the night might bring.

THIRTY

COLONEL RAY LONGKNIFE and Trouble looked over the intel feed Ruth had brought back. It was good, one might even say informative. Still, it burned Ray that Mary had gone bloody rogue.

"Where did that woman come up with this idea that she could charge into a whorehouse and start interrogating any scientist she ran into, flat of her back or otherwise?"

"We did say time was something we didn't have enough of," Trouble pointed out.

"That woman," was all Ray said. Which left him wondering if some wild stunt like this was why he still walked with a bit of a limp. Exactly how had she held that damn rock against him and Wardhaven's best?

"Can we do anything to help her?" Ruth asked, forever the practical one.

"Are any of these wayward scholars in our databases?" Ray asked Becky.

"We're checking on them as you speak," was rewarded moments later by first one then another then all fifteen of their pictures popping up on the large screen in the room. Listed were their degrees, dates of graduation, and alma maters. Some of the best universities in the old fifty planets that humans first colonized were there.

"Ten pharmacological botanists, a chemical engineer, and four gene engineers," Becky summed them up. "One of the botanists and one of the gene engineers wants to stay."

"That or they aren't complaining overmuch," Ray corrected. "Don't assume silence is support for the boss. It may just mean they don't trust the walls not to have ears."

"Yes," Ruth agreed.

"About the source of their manure," Trouble said. "Do we know where that is and if there are any games we can play with the supply?"

Becky was already nodding before Trouble finished. "Captain Umboto hates drug lords more than the average cruiser skipper. She spotted the trucks hauling manure into the Farm and has already backtracked them to here."

Another window opened up on the screen, showing a cattle ranch and feed yard. "There's a nice road into town from there. Plenty of places for some Marines to pass a load of bullshit and add some interesting stuff to the load, don't you think?" the FSO said.

"With pleasure, ma'am," Trouble said, grinning.

"They bring in a load about every other day," the FSO added.

"Then I need to start talking with some of my men about going for a nice drive in the country, sir," Captain Trouble said, turning to Colonel Longknife.

"One word, Captain."

"Yes, sir," the Marine officer said, coming to full attention.

"You have a reputation with drug lords. I doubt that Milassi and his head henchman don't have a file on you. You are grounded, Captain."

"Sir!" was only one word, but it carried a load of disagreement.

"Grounded," the colonel repeated. "You stay in the embassy. I've already got one of my Marine officers prancing around, freelancing her ass into trouble. I won't have both of you hanging out there for Milassi to collect. Besides, I fully expect a move on this embassy sometime soon. I will have you manning the walls when that happens. Am I perfectly clear?"

The Marine deflated. But only a bit. "Yes, sir. I hear you, and I will comply with your order, sir. Though if I may point out, Colonel, you are not in my chain of command, sir."

"Captain Trouble, do I have to have Captain Umboto put her chop on my orders?"

"No, sir, because they are smart orders, and I know it. I just don't like that my wife is sticking her neck out a mile, and I'm stuck here, keeping the home fires burning."

"Or not burning," the colonel said. "I'm glad we understand

each other. Captain, have your fun setting up an intercept for the next load of bullshit from the ranch, but you will delegate the interception."

"Yes, Colonel. Ma'am," he said, turning to the FSO, "how soon until your types have the chemical agents we need to deliver?"

"Later tonight, Captain. Why don't you check our perimeter and establish an assault team for that truck of manure? I can't believe I'm saying that. Things here turn on us doctoring a load of cow manure!"

"That, ma'am, and the weather staying the same," Ruth said. "It's been two weeks since it rained. I know the Farm has irrigation gear, but it's still got to be getting hot and dry."

"Are you thinking what I'm thinking?" the Marine officer said to his wife.

She grinned. "There's nothing like the smell of burning drugs in the morning."

THIRTY-ONE

THE GILDED CAGE proclaimed itself to the world with a neon sign and a well-lit golden birdcage with a stuffed or fake yellow bird inside.

Mary suspected the cage's being there said something about the quality of the education system on this planet.

Lek took his small harem up to the door.

"We don't allow no women of the street in here," a well-muscled bouncer growled.

Lek made money appear in his hand. It disappeared, and they were in.

The place inside was quite an eyeful.

This wasn't the first brothel Mary had seen the inside of. Back on the rock during the war, she'd drawn a liberty, but the Bachelor Officers Quarters at headquarters were full. It had been suggested that she, being a woman, might find the brothel more appealing.

"I mean, they know how to treat a woman right," the civilian at the front desk of the "Q" had stammered.

Mary had, indeed, found that the madam at the brothel, some enterprising type who had landed right behind the lines, knew how to treat a woman willing to pay for a room, a bath, and a pleasant massage.

That evening, she'd discovered what a fine conversationalist Captain Mattim Abeeb could be, and one thing had led to another. Only later had Mary found herself under the man's command. They both did their best not to mention that they knew what the other looked like with their clothes off and had maintained professional boundaries ever since.

Still, Mary had to admit that this whorehouse was much

more splendid than the one for the grimy line beasts in the war.

The wallpaper was a lush crimson and cream. Thick red drapes were held open by golden tassels to reveal screens showing things best left behind closed doors. On the floor was a thick red carpet.

No simple red light to advertise what this place was about.

Lek maneuvered his pair of honeys to a rich mahogany table with only four chairs. The middle-aged madam quickly slipped into the empty one.

"We do not allow street girls in our fine establishment," she said, but it was through a smile that was all money.

Again, Lek made money appear. Again, it disappeared.

"So long as we understand ourselves. You can use room ten. Don't mess it up," the still-smiling woman said as she stood. "And don't expect any free drinks."

"I never drink what I haven't paid for," Lek answered the already retreating bare back. His carefully measured diction came as a surprise to Mary.

"Friendly types," Cyn said.

"Friendly don't pay no bills," Lek said, his language slipping back to the familiar patter of a miner.

"You have surprising skills," Mary said.

"Surprise is my stock-in-trade," he answered.

Since the place had yet to fill up, a bar girl wearing hardly anything quickly appeared at their table for their order. She looked little older than Alice. Lek ordered a scotch for himself, "On very few rocks, if you take my meaning, my dear, and some of the usual for my girls."

Mary found herself drinking a weak fruit punch.

Cyn made a face at it, then sighed. "Right. I'm not here to enjoy myself."

"And we need to keep our wits about us," Mary added softly, one eye on Lek.

"Any day I can't hold a few glasses of good single-malt whiskey as tiny as these, you can toss me out the door."

Speaking of the door, it opened. So far, the place had been rather thinly occupied. Now eight toughs in black uniforms swaggered in. The bar girl quickly took their orders and got her bottom pinched . . . twice.

Their drinks arrived quickly, and not in the tiny glasses Lek was drinking from. Mary didn't notice any money changing hands.

The bar girl didn't hang around for a tip but got pinched twice more.

When the cops are your worst customers, who polices up the others? The question hung there with no answer.

A girl began singing on a small stage. She had a fairly decent voice. She also could dance. Most of her clothes ended up tossed to the customers. Money flew back in kind. The less she wore, the more money landed on stage.

When she was down to next to nothing, she bounced off the stage and circulated among the crowd. More money came her way, though Mary had no idea where it went.

Meanwhile, back onstage, a couple of girls . . . real girls . . . Alice's age at best and in costumes that revealed for all their lack of curves, collected the money on the stage floor and handed it off to the bartender. He folded it into a set of pigeonholes behind the bar. No doubt, the madam and the singer would split it later.

Meanwhile, the singer had attracted the attention of one of the uniformed thugs. He pushed her ahead of him as he headed for the back. Mary spotted the scowl that flitted across her face, but for only a second. A painted-on smile was there in a blink, and the girl went where she was pushed.

Mary was really taking a dislike to this place: the Gilded Cage in particular, Savannah in general.

But she had an advantage over all the other girls in this place tonight. *I can knock heads, kick butt, and change things,* Mary thought and liked the taste of the smile that came to her lips.

Beside her, Lek's face was taking on a decidedly stormy look, with his lips going thin and his eyes getting hard.

"Smile, my friend. You're enjoying yourself with a girl on each arm."

Lek smiled, but it didn't stay.

Cyn leaned over and whispered something in his ear. He laughed at whatever joke she shared.

Unfortunately, his laugh drew attention. One of the thugs glanced their way. He turned back to his friends, but more and more often, his eyes were wandering to their table.

Mary wondered just how high a price she'd have to pay for her seat in this hellhole.

But it wasn't her the thug in uniform was eyeing.

After his friend got back from his time with the singer, they ordered a second round. The next singer managed to hook up with a richly dressed man before she got to their table. The cops were none too happy to be dodged by the lovely redhead whose "carpet" matched the "drapes."

The thugs' grumbling didn't last long as the one who'd been eyeing their table got up and stomped over to them.

In front of them, he hitched up his gun belt. "Old man, you got two, and I got none. You want to share with the friendly arms of the law, don't you?"

"But you wouldn't want to take a man's wife, would you?" Lek said, turning a loving eye on Mary. "Or his mistress," he added, turning a lustful eye on Cyn.

"I'll leave you your wife," the arm of the law growled, "but I do like blondes. And if she's only your mistress, you shouldn't mind sharing."

He put a rough hand on the Marine's arm.

Mary half expected Cyn to rip the guy's arm off. No doubt she could.

Instead, Cyn smiled at Lek and Mary. "I can handle this fine."

She gave Lek a peck on the cheek, which really pissed the guy off, and led him to the rear. "Room ten, right," she called behind her.

"Ten," Mary repeated, her stomach going into free fall. She'd known there was risk to her plan. She just hadn't expected someone else to pay the price.

"Damn," Lek said, taking a long sip from his scotch. "It worked so well in a movie I once saw."

Mary ignored his penitence and took the scotch from Lek's hand and downed what was left in one gulp.

"Down, my girl," Lek said. "She knew the risk when she came with us. She's a big girl. She can handle this."

"But she shouldn't have to," Mary growled.

Their waitress was at Lek's elbow putting down three decent-sized scotches. "He's a bad one. None of the working girls like him," she whispered.

All Mary could do was smile a thank-you for the bad news.

Lek paid the bar girl well and was rewarded with a shy smile. The two Marines waited out the time, both sipping their drinks as lightly as they could.

THIRTY-TWO

IT SEEMED FOREVER, but it was less than ten minutes before Cyn slipped into her chair and downed half of the scotch in front of her.

"Thanks for some medicine," was all she said.

"There's a bruise on your cheek," Mary said.

The girl produced a compact from her purse and began dabbing gently at the dark spot. "A real bastard, that one."

That one strutted back into the parlor, making a show of still hitching up his belt and grinning at Cyn.

She studiously avoided him.

He settled down at his old table, loudly ordered another drink, then ostentatiously fondled the breast of the bar girl when she delivered. Before she could get away, he'd pinched her nipple.

Through it all, the bouncer looked elsewhere.

"Can no one do anything?" Mary found she'd muttered out loud.

"Wait for it," Cyn said, darkly.

The cop lifted his drink in a salute to no one or nothing. Then he chugged it in one quick motion. Done, he laughed derisively.

Then, slowly, the thug's head began to lean more and more to the right. Then his entire body was twisting in that direction. He fell out of his chair and hit the deck with a most satisfying thunk.

He let out a groan, followed a moment later with a choked scream of pain.

Now his friends were standing around him. The bouncer was there, helping him to his feet and aiming him for the door.

"I've called an ambulance," the madam said, all unction and concern.

"If he's been poisoned," one of his buddies threatened.

"Here," the bouncer said, "take the glass with you."

"I assure you, good man," the madam said, hovering, "our drinks are of the finest quality."

One of the cops took the glass and sniffed it. Then he pocketed it.

"There's no poison," Cyn muttered softly.

"No?" Mary said. "You know what ails him?"

"Yep," the scantily clad Marine said. "Something my granny learned from the bad old days, when armies full of rape and pillage still landed on planets."

That was the way it had been, before the Treaty of Hamilton. After that, if a planet lost control of the sky above, it had to surrender. That cut down on the raping and burning. It also left the planet in better shape to pay the huge indemnities that the winner always demanded.

The bankers back on Earth liked it better that way.

Mary eyed the Marine. "And your granny taught you . . . ?"

"Ever heard of acupuncture?"

Lek nodded. "It can be good for what ails you. It takes away the pain without drugs and stuff."

"Yeah, it can do that. But a wise old woman showed Granny how to use it for something else. Put the needles in just right, and, well, as you saw, it does hard things to the muscles of the back. And it hurts."

She took a long pull on her drink. "It hurts like hell."

"Needles, you say. Aren't they usually long and easy to see?" Mary said.

Cyn gave Mary a smile. Not a nice one. Not nice at all. "Or you can use small ones. They go in, and there's nothing to see."

"They'll show up on X-ray," the smart tech said.

"Not if they're plastic," the woman Marine said with the most evil smile Mary had ever seen on a pretty face.

"If they don't lay him on his back, they might work out in a few months. But if he scratches or rolls about . . ." The smile just got more evil.

"Remind me to stay on your good side," Lek said.

"Me too," Mary added.

"I'm a Marine, ma'am. I don't have a good side."

The bouncer and madam were back and talking to the bar girl. She was reduced to tears, but she insisted on her innocence.

"Lek, make sure she gets a very good tip next round of drinks," Mary said.

"I already intended to," was his answer.

"I think the ones we came for are here," Cyn said, her eyes on the door.

Yep, the contingent from the Farm was filing in and taking up tables near the stage. Mary suppressed a frown.

This could make it hard to attract their attention.

It got worse as a flock of girls swooped in to settle at their tables and ask for drinks.

Mary solved her problem by sashaying off to the ladies' room. She didn't stay long, and found that several eyes from the Farm crowd were waiting when she did a rolling saunter back to the table.

One guy couldn't seem to keep his eyes off Mary. That was fine; he was one she wanted to talk to.

She sipped her drink, and made eye contact with him. She even granted him a smile when he raised his glass to her.

Flirting was not something Mary was all that experienced at. Still, she apparently did it right. Before long, the fellow strolled over to their table, sat down, and reached for Mary's hand. She let him have it, and he made pleasant circles in her palm.

Encouraged by the soft moan of pleasure she granted him, he produced a large roll of bills.

"You mind, honey?" Mary asked Lek.

He gave her a sad-eyed look.

"Or do you want to come and watch?" she asked him as she put her hand on the offered roll of cash.

Lek put his arm around Cyn's shoulders. "I guess I'll just have to make due with your kid sister."

Mary took her target by the hand and led him back to room ten. Alice was just finishing up stripping the bed and remaking it. Mary peeled off a large bill and offered it to Alice. The girl bobbed her head, said, "Thank you, ma'am," and hurried out.

One of the sheets in her arms had blood on it.

Mary wiped the thoughts that flooded her mind. Maybe she succeeded.

Her trick was already undoing his trousers. As they fell to the floor, Mary shoved him onto the bed.

Pants down around his ankles, dick waving urgently, he reached for Mary.

Mary settled on the bed next to him . . . and slapped his hands away.

"Dr. Bernardo, we are not here for what you think," she snapped.

"I don't go in for the hard stuff," the young man said, reaching down for his pants.

Mary put a firm hand on his chest and pushed him back down.

"Don't make this take longer than it has to, Doctor. I'm not here to screw you. I'm here to offer you a job. Unless a man who graduated with top honors from the New Eden Agricultural and Pharmacological Institute is happy developing that kind of shit you're wasting your time on."

"How do you know my name and where I graduated?"

"Dr. Bernardo, I know everything I need to know about you. I know that there is a job waiting for you on Wardhaven, developing the next generation of anticancer drugs, and I know it will pay you double what they're paying you here."

The man settled back on the bed, using his hands to cover his naked need, which was rapidly becoming much smaller.

"You can't be serious. And if you are, this is a hell of a place to go head-hunting, if you know what I mean," he said, chuckling at the double meaning of his words.

"You think I'd have better luck if I walked in the front door at the Farm and asked your boss to talk to you?"

Now he scowled. "We'd both end up in trouble if we were lucky and dead otherwise. Which we would be if the boss was having a bad day."

"So we talk here," Mary said flatly.

"You mean it? You can get me a job on Wardhaven in cancer research?"

Mary clearly had his full attention.

"I said it. I mean it. The man behind me can get you the job on the day you land on Wardhaven as well as a nice signing bonus the minute you walk onto the Society cruiser in orbit."

"It's a long way from the Farm to orbit, or haven't you noticed?"

"I noticed, but it's my job to resolve minor inconveniences like those. You want the job?"

"Yes."

"Then get dressed. I'll get a message to you in the next couple of days. Be ready to jump with the clothes on your back. No looking back."

"Nothing I care to look back at," the man said, leveraging himself out of the bed on his own. Mary certainly wasn't about to give him a hand up.

"How will I know the message is from you?" he said, hitching up his pants.

"Because it will come from the last place you'd expect."

He stood. Mary mussed up the bed a bit just in case someone got a glance at it before Alice stripped it.

"By the way, I need to talk to each of your coworkers. Or at least the ones you think will take a job offer like this one. You can skip the ones that might run to the boss. You know any I shouldn't talk to?"

The man sucked on his lower lip. His answer would tell Mary a lot about how much she could trust him.

"Stanley and Kanker are awfully quiet when we get a bitch session going. Still, I've never seen them sucking up to the boss. Truth is, the boss is an idiot who doesn't even wash his hands before entering the labs. His idea of sanitation is rinsing the test tubes in the nearest stream. I don't know how he got this job. Anyway, it's your ass if you talk to them. They might surprise me. Then again, they might surprise you, if you take my meaning right."

"Maybe we let you see if they're willing to take a little walk with you in a couple of days, huh?"

"That might work better."

They returned to the front room. Dr. Bernardo put on a cat-that-ate-the-canary grin as he joined his friends.

"How good's the new girl?" query drew a "See for yourself" response.

One by one, Mary took thirteen of them back to room

ten. One by one, each of them got the surprise of their over-educated and devoid-of-common-sense lives.

None ran screaming from Mary's presence with their pants around their knees and their cocks bobbing in the breeze. All took her up on her offer.

The night was going so very well. Mary was eyeing the door and planning a well-earned and very orderly withdrawal.

Then the bottom fell out.

The big man, Milassi himself, strolled into the party.

THIRTY-THREE

WHEN MARY FIRST walked in, she'd noticed three tables in the corner with RESERVED signs. Well, this was supposed to be a party night. Now those tables filled up with a lot of men Mary didn't recognize.

There was one she couldn't miss.

Milassi had come down with Ray to the car on the first day they landed. Now here he was, bigger than life. All Mary could hope for was that Milassi didn't remember a certain woman in Explorer Corps grays and match her with the gal in the bright blue dress.

Whatever he might or might not remember from that day, he certainly liked what he saw every time he glanced in Mary's direction.

Or was it the blond across from her?

Cyn rose precipitously from her chair. "Excuse me," was all she said as she raced for the ladies' room.

Mary stood, found that Milassi was eyeing her, and flashed him a distracted smile before she followed Cyn into the restroom

There, the young Marine was throwing up.

"What's wrong?" Mary asked as she found a wash rag, dampened it, and put it to her subordinate's forehead.

"I don't know," Cyn said, and heaved up more liquor and older supper. "I thought I was okay with things, but looking at that bastard eyeing me. I just don't see how I could go through that again."

She washed her mouth out. "Besides, I don't have any more needles," she whispered softly to Mary.

Mary glanced around. One of the working women exited

the only occupied stall. She gave Mary and Cyn a knowing smile . . . and left without washing her hands.

Mary made up her mind. "We're leaving as soon as I get ahold of Lek. You go straight out from here."

"No. We've got to go back in there together," Cyn said resolutely.

Mary frowned, but only for a second. The young woman was right. "Okay, we go back to get Lek and beat a slow retreat. But that doesn't mean you have to look gorgeous."

"Ma'am, I always look gorgeous to anything with a swinging dick between his legs."

Mary mussed Cyn's hair. Then she grabbed another washcloth and began cleaning the woman's face of makeup and lip gloss. "No doubt there's gorgeous, but there's also sick and washed-out."

Cyn stared at herself in the mirror, then got the dry heaves again. It was a while before she could weakly say, "Yeah, even my mom wouldn't say I was pretty just now."

A few other girls had passed through the restroom while they'd been busy. They cast them sad looks, but they hurried in and hurried out.

Working girls knew time was money.

Slowly, Mary got Cyn in good enough shape to challenge the parlor, if only long enough to connect with Lek and make their way out.

Still, they didn't move fast enough.

As Mary settled Cyn at the table for the time it took to get them moving out, a dark man appeared at her arm. "President Milassi invites you to his table."

"My friend is too sick to come," Mary said.

"No doubt she is. But it is you the president would like to enjoy time with."

Lek raised an eyebrow at Mary.

"Enjoy time with," was not the kind of thing this thug would say to a Marine officer, so apparently Mary's cover was still holding up.

"You stay here until I get back," Mary told Cyn and Lek.

"It may be quite a while. Maybe they should go," the unctuous man said.

"We'll wait. She'll need a ride," Lek offered.

"I am sure the president can provide her with a ride when they are done," did not sound at all good to Mary. She gave Lek a quick smile and turned to see how much worse the night could get.

Sadly, she had no needles. Then again, she didn't know how to use them.

I must ask Cyn how they work and where to get them, brought a smile to Mary's lips, which was totally misunderstood by the president-for-life as she approached him.

"It is always good to see a smiling face. And a new one, even better," he said.

The man did not rise for a lady, but then, Mary was not playing the role of a lady. Still, she suspected, he didn't rise for *any* woman.

A man vacated the chair next to the president. Mary slipped right into it and quickly found an arm around her shoulder. "Would you like something to drink?"

"Champagne," Mary said.

If I'm going to do this, you're going to pay for it.

A lordly wave of a hand brought a bar girl running. This was a new girl, but she clearly understood the wink that accompanied the president's order. Mary soon found herself daintily sipping from a sparkling drink that had never been touched by fermentation.

Not only was the president-for-life a louse, he was a cheap louse.

"I haven't seen you before," he said, moving closer. His paw was cupping her breast; his thumb stroked her soft flesh.

I wonder if I can throw up like Cyn and claim it's a flu bug.

Instead, Mary smiled. "Every girl has to start sometime," she said with as much mystery as she could muster.

Their chat stayed at that level of banality for several minutes, but it failed to revolt Mary's stomach to the level she needed. She was about to resign herself to having to take this monster to bed when two redheads, identical twins from the looks of them, entered the parlor from the back and made straight for the president's table.

"Steffo! What are you doing?" one said.

"We leave you alone for a minute, and what do you do?" the other said.

"She's not one of the girls we picked out for you."

"Can't I pick out one for myself?" the president-for-life almost whined.

"Who knows where she's been?" the first one said, swatting at Milassi's hand, which was edging Mary's top down to show her nipple.

"Your Excellency, she's already been in back with thirteen other men just this night," the unctuous one said.

"Used goods," one redhead said, making a sour face.

"Not good enough for our Milassi," the other one insisted with a well-oiled smile.

"You need someone fresh. Unspoiled," the other one insisted.

To Mary's horror, she saw Alice being pushed forward by the madam, no stern black-and-white maid's uniform now for the girl, but something that was hardly there.

THIRTY-FOUR

MARY OPENED HER mouth to object, but muscle now stood above her, and a heavy hand rested on her shoulder.

"Do not make a scene," he whispered. "You will be paid well for the distraction you have given His Excellency."

Unarmed, all Mary could do was stay in her seat as the presidential party made its way to the back rooms.

Poor Alice just stood there waiting, eyes wide, pupils dilated so wide Mary could almost fall into them.

The poor child had been drugged.

Mary glanced Lek's way. He had turned in his seat. He saw.

He was also shaking his head. Not much, and it was slow, but the message was clear. *We can do nothing here. Hold it, girl. Hold it.*

Mary held it. She held it by her bleeding fingernails.

She sat in her seat until the presidential party had disappeared in back. Without a word, she took the money she was offered. She stuffed it in her bodice, while tucking her breast back in there as well, as she slowly rejoined Lek and Cyn.

"I need a drink," she said.

"We need to be out of here," he said, and, brooking no argument, stood.

For arm candy, Cyn and Mary must have looked a sight. They left, though the bouncer demanded another bribe to open the door.

Outside, the night was sticky and hot. Lek mumbled something, and they were joined not a block away by Gunny and two Marines.

"Get me to the embassy," Mary demanded.

"No can do, ma'am," Gunny said.

"Why not?" she snapped.

"This kid says it's after curfew. If we try to drive all the way across town, we'll likely be stopped and asked for our papers, ma'am, and we don't have no papers."

Mary scrubbed at her face, trying to wash away the sight of Alice and the president. "I need a drink."

"The kid says we should lay up at the shelter with the brothers and sisters. They'll take care of us."

"Are we putting them at risk?" Lek asked before Mary could.

"He don't think so. I think we ought to give it a try. If it's too risky, they can send us on our way."

Mary nodded. Then she caught sight of the bar girl from that night. She was standing beside a scrawny boy who was doing his best not to stare at how much of her was out there to stare at.

"Why's she here?" Mary asked Gunny.

"She says Alice helped her slip out the back with a load of laundry. She's in some kind of trouble."

"Yeah, most likely, but not as much trouble as Alice is."

"What's wrong?" Gunny asked. He, as well as many of the older Marines, had taken a shine to Alice.

Mary told him the problem.

Then Lek had to put get a tight grip on the old sergeant's arm. "We can't go charging in. The time's not right."

Mary listened to a long string of epithets as Gunny dissected the president and his habits to the fourth generation. The Marine finished with a scowl. "Judgment day is coming, and it can't come soon enough for some."

"Amen," Mary and Lek said.

"Now let's get off the street," Mary added.

It was four blocks to the shelter. They used back alleys because, hard as it was to believe after seeing all the thugs-for-cops at the Gilded Cage, there were still a few walking the streets.

No sooner had Brother Scott opened the back door at their knock than the kid who had led them there was ready to head back.

"I promised Alice that I'd be waiting for her when she got off."

"She may not be getting off anytime soon," Mary said.

"Yeah, I know," the kid said. "I heard what you said. And Alice knew that might happen. She told me so when she got the job. But I promised her that I'd be there for her no matter what, and I will be there. No matter what."

"What happened?" Brother Scott asked, one of the sisters now at his elbow.

Mary watched the faithful lad disappear into the night, then turned to see how the brother and nun would take to the raw unvarnished world outside.

She failed to shock them.

"Yes, Spin told you right," the nun said. "I can only hope that what I told her can help her in a time like this."

"And what did you tell her?" Mary asked.

"That God loves her no matter what evil men may do to her. What else can I tell the girls here? You're a Marine. You've been taught to fight. To kill men who in your eyes need killing. We can hardly train our young woman here to do that, now can we?"

"No," Mary said, "I guess you can't."

"Now, all of you," Brother Scott said, "let's get you bedded down for the night. You'll be wanting to get on your way back to where you belong as soon as the sun's up."

Mary turned to her own. Cyn's teeth had started to chatter during the walk. One of the Marines, a private first class, had put an arm around her, and she'd gotten closer to him as it got worse.

Now the nun put a blanket around the two of them and led them off to a small room with a door that closed. She didn't say a word, but closed them in by themselves.

At Mary's raised eyebrow, Brother Scott said, "We may have taken vows ourselves, but that doesn't mean we expect everyone to live as we do."

"My Marine also got hauled into one of the back rooms and was likely raped by one of those thugs that pass for cops around here," Mary said by way of explanation.

"It's been a bad night for all of you," Brother Scott said as he led Mary into another of the small rooms. The other brother took the rest of the Marines to settle them down on the floor in the large room among street kids who slept on, unaware of what had passed around them.

All except one who woke up whimpering. The nun moved to supply a hug until the girl could fall back asleep.

"Some worse," Mary said. "Some got off easy."

"Did they now?" Brother Scott said, pulling a bottle from a desk drawer and offering it to Mary.

She took a swig.

"Tell me, Brother, how could you let a girl like Alice take a job in a place like that?"

"Is that the best you have to throw at me?" he said, not seeming at all bothered by the sharp accusation buried in Mary's words.

"Maybe I'm just warming up?" she said, then eyed the bottle. "This stuff is strong."

"Raw, too. I know the fellow who runs the still. He drops me off a bit of his white lightning once in a while."

"Whyever for?"

"He was one of my kids until he apprenticed with a moonshiner."

"Another one of your failures, huh?"

"I like to think of him as one of my successes. He's alive, got a wife and a kid, and he's earning enough to keep them off the streets. But then, I might have low expectations, not being a Marine and all that." He took a swig from the bottle.

"So you didn't have any problem letting Alice get a job there?" Mary struck out again.

"Of course I had problems with Alice's job, but how would you have had me keep her from it? She came in here proud as punch. She'd found a way to get information from inside your Farm. Information that, may I point out, all of your fine technology wasn't providing."

But the brother ended up shaking his head sadly. "I knew the risk. She knew the risk, but she thought she could get away with it. What's that old song about the young lady from Niger?"

"Who went for a ride on a tiger," Mary said, reaching for the bottle and taking a good long pull on it. "The tiger ended up wearing her smile and she ended up inside the tiger or something like that."

"I could never make the end of it rhyme either," Brother Scott admitted. "Now, you should get some sleep, and I need to pray. God, but I need to pray," he said. Standing and finding a blanket for Mary, he tossed it her way.

"Where is your God with Alice's being raped tonight?" Mary snapped. She knew it was a foul question, but she was feeling rather distasteful.

The religious man stopped at the door. "I would like to think that my God is there, with Alice, holding her hand as she walks through this valley of death."

"Does thinking that make you feel better for what you did?"

He whirled on Mary. "I did. You did. We all did. No. I will pray for Alice, and I will pray for forgiveness. Both for me and for you. I know I need forgiveness. Do you, Marine?"

Mary hadn't expected that kind of a swing. Her comeback was slow. "I'll forgive myself when that piece of shit is dead."

"And what if you can't kill him? What if the people who hold your leash won't let you?" The brother was showing red at the neck. Clearly, Mary was getting at him, and he was quite able and willing to get at her.

"A painfully good point," Mary admitted.

"I'll pray for both of us and for Alice. And I'll pray for those who are doing this to her. Certainly, there must be some hope for their salvation."

Later, as she rolled up in the offered blanket, Mary found herself reflecting.

Which would be the worst ending for Milassi? A turn of heart that left him feeling all the pain he'd caused? Or a fine pit in hell with plenty of vicious demons roasting his dick over a roaring fire?

Mary decided she wasn't a very nice person. That pit in hell was way ahead in her voting.

THIRTY-FIVE

MARY CAME AWAKE with a start. The back door was opening ever so quietly, but not quietly enough for her to sleep through it tonight.

Keeping the warm blanket around her, Mary went on bare feet into the main hall. There was Brother Scott and the nun, helping Alice and her loyal knight through the door. Mary covered the space to them quickly.

Alice was trembling. Mary shed her warm blanket and wrapped it around the two youngsters.

"Thank you," Alice stammered.

"I'm sorry," Mary said.

"I didn't tell them anything, ma'am. They didn't want anything from me. Any talking, I mean."

"I know," Mary said as softly as she could. This child did not deserve the angry words roiling Mary's gut.

"Can I lie down now?" the slaughtered innocent asked.

"Yes," Brother Scott said. Sister had two blankets in her arms. She threw one around the two kids, and handed the other off to Mary with a "You must be cold."

The two kids moved off toward an empty corner.

"Do you want to give them a room?" Mary asked.

The brother pondered the question for a moment, then shook his head. "They're good kids. Let them hold each other. That will likely be all she can take from him tonight."

Beside him, the sister nodded.

Without a word, both of the religious turned back toward their makeshift chapel, no doubt to thank their God for whatever small gift they and the kids had gotten tonight.

Mary sighed. It came out more a shudder. Alice had lived through the night. She had her best friend to hold her and two blankets to keep her warm. The Marine could think of nothing more she could do for her at the moment.

As Mary made her way back to her sleeping space, she caught Gunny's eye. He was awake, quietly taking it all in with a warrior's eye. In his eyes, she could see the tally count rising higher.

Somebody owed a lot for tonight.

Somebody would pay.

Mary considered that for a moment. The two religious would pray. Gunny would keep the count of all that was owed and hold it tight for a day of reckoning.

That was what Gunnies did so well.

Mary's mouth went to a grim, tight smile. She knew which one was her job and she liked it, thank you very much.

Instead of returning to her tiny room, she settled down next to Gunny. He shared his still-warm blanket with her, and she added her cold one to the floor beneath them.

They said not a word. None was needed. Men would die for the pleasure they had stolen tonight, and the two of them would make sure they did.

The profession of the sword was a hard one. Its discipline and practice could drive a person to death and madness. Certainly, it had driven Mary from it to the easier life of an Explorer Corps guard.

Still, getting payback for things like tonight made it all worthwhile.

Mary promised herself that she'd have her Explorer Corps guards out with the embassy Marines for their morning run. They'd gotten soft.

It was time to get hard again.

Which reminded Mary. She'd have to be careful how she explained tonight to her crew. Half of them had grown up as street kids. They'd all taken a shine to Alice and her kids.

Dumont would have to be told carefully. Like the president-for-life, Dumont had a thing for young girls. Only his thing was to protect them. The last time Du had seen a girl he considered under his protection come to ill use, a lot of scum had died.

Mary would have to make sure that Du understood the scum would die, but not until the time came and those holding their leashes said they died.

194 · Mike Shepherd

Du had a hard time understanding the leash thing.

Sometimes, Mary did, too.

Light showed through the upper windows of the hall. Mary asked Gunny for the time, got her answer, and began rousing her troops. She checked the chapel; the two brothers and nuns were still in there, kneeling in prayer.

Or maybe meditation.

Or maybe a bit of sleep.

Mary didn't bother them. They'd have enough trouble picking up the loose ends of what had happened last night.

Two Marines checked the alley behind the center, found it clear, and all of them headed out. Their cars had not been vandalized.

Two street kids asleep on the hoods likely accounted for that. Gunny tossed them money, and they scampered off.

It was a silent drive back to the embassy.

THIRTY-SIX

MARY REPORTED TO Trouble and the Foreign Service Officer that she'd made contact with thirteen of the scientists and they looked eager to bail on their employer.

"You sure they won't go running to their security types and set a trap for us?" the diplomat asked.

"I don't think so," Mary said. "They looked really interested in a new job. And if they wanted to turn us in, they had their chance last night. President Milassi was there."

"At the bordello?" Trouble actually sounded shocked.

"Not two tables from me," Mary said.

"How'd that go?" Becky asked.

"I got asked to his table," Mary said, and looked away, wishing the conversation hadn't taken this turn.

"What's wrong, Captain? Did something go bad?" Trouble demanded.

"Did Milassi remember you?" the FSO asked.

"No. He made a pass at me," Mary snapped, "but he got redirected at someone new, untouched. It seems I'm old and damaged goods."

"You don't look it to me," Trouble said, gallantly stepping in to bolster Mary's feminine ego.

"Who'd he get redirected to?" the woman FSO officer asked, spotting the potential problem.

"Our mole inside the bordello," Mary said, her voice flat. "Little Alice."

"Damn," Trouble muttered. "The troops aren't going to like that."

"Gunny doesn't," Mary said. "I don't. Lots of those of us who were there really don't like it. Not at all."

The diplomat turned to Trouble. "We aren't going to have a problem with this, are we, Captain Tordon?"

Trouble braced. "No, Ms. Graven, we will not have a problem with this. Will we, Mary?"

Now it was Mary's turn to brace, even if she was still in the little bit of nothing she'd worn last night. "No, ma'am. We know that the best way to get those bastards is to do it by the numbers, and we will do it by the numbers, ma'am."

"Good. I don't want to have any misunderstandings about this," the FSO said. "We're too damn close to getting Milassi's ass where I want it to screw it up because someone couldn't wait. No more rogues. You understand."

For a long moment, the three of them eyed each other. No one flinched. The orders were received, understood, and would be obeyed. There was no doubt of that.

"Sir, if you'll excuse me," Mary said, "I need a shower and a change of clothes. Then I need to talk to my crew."

"By all means, Mary, go get cleaned up."

Mary left. She did get that shower. Afterward, she tossed everything she'd worn the night before into a burn bag.

Back in uniform, she went hunting for the team. She looked up Dumont first. She found him alone in the break room, struggling with paperwork. As she expected, briefing him was a full-time job.

Fortunately, the old street kid was maturing. Thankfully, the break room had one wall with a rubber mat hanging on it. Du slammed his fist into that wall repeatedly as he shouted a long string of language Mary hadn't heard in a while.

"We will get the bastard," Mary repeated.

"You sure as shit better," Dumont spat. Despite the matting, he was waving his hurt hand in the air to shake off some of the self-inflicted pain.

"I want him just as much as you. The captain wants his ass. That diplomat woman running things around here wants his head above her mantelpiece."

"You think there's enough of him to go around?" Dumont asked.

"There will be plenty of little pieces," Mary assured her subordinate.

"Okay, we do it your way," he said, settling down.

Next, Mary called a formation outside. With her team of killers and line beasts standing at parade rest in the break room, she filled them in.

"Some of you are hearing stories about where I and others went last night. There's not a lot that I can tell you about what went down. It's heavy shit, and a lot more shit is coming down. What I can tell you is that yes, Milassi raped Alice Blue Bonnet."

A low growl swept through the ranks.

"He had a choice of me or Alice, and he likes them young and fresh. No one would ever mistake me for either."

That got a soft titter from the ranks.

"I cannot tell you how or when, but I can promise you that we will get Milassi's ass. This is not something to talk about. Don't even mutter it in your beer. But we will have him by the balls before we ship out. This I promise you, so don't screw anything up by doing something out of bounds yourself or spouting off your mouth. Understood?"

"Yes, ma'am," came back at her hard and loud.

"Very good. Dismissed to duties," she ordered. Her sergeant ordered an about-face. The men and women took two steps, then scattered to their jobs, talking softly among themselves.

"Do you think that will hold them?" she asked Dumont.

"For a while," he said, anger still burning in his eyes.

"Yeah, my thoughts exactly," Mary agreed. "I better go talk to the captain about how fast we can separate Milassi from his ass and head."

"Yeah, you do that, old lady," Dumont said, using the comeback the street people had long used for Mary. This time, he had a smile on his face.

"You're getting old yourself, boy," Mary said as she walked away from him.

"All too quickly," was his gentle comeback.

THIRTY-SEVEN

TROUBLE, FOR ONCE, saw it coming.

Mary presented herself most formally, but her words were blunt. "How fast can we take Milassi down? You can have his ass. Becky can have his head. We'll settle for his guts for garters."

"You're in luck. We think we can do it in the next couple of days. Assuming the weather cooperates."

Mary raised a questioning eyebrow, but Trouble dismissed her. He had work to do and would have to choose very carefully who got what duty assignments.

The weather had been hot and unbearable for two weeks, despite repeated promises from the weatherman that the heat spell would break. Regularly, the prognostications were for the high off the coast to break up and let the cool, wet marine air in. Day after day it didn't.

The heat wave blistered on.

At the Farm, the heat wave caused a delay in fertilizing the crop of growing drugs. As Ruth pointed out from her farm experience, they needed to wet down the fertilizer after they laid it. If it rained, they got it wet for free.

If they put down the manure with no rain in the forecast, then they'd have to water the whole thing themselves, and there was a basic flaw in that.

The water pipes to that entire part of town were about six inches too small. It was one of the results of urban sprawl and a growing population. That, and a government that didn't want to spend any more than it had to on infrastructure.

Whatever the causes, the flow of water to that entire end of town was frequently low pressure. Turning on the sprinklers to water twenty hectares worth of drugs would put a major strain on the water supply.

Of course, if Trouble got Ruth the results she wanted, that strain could only be a godsend.

Trouble smiled at the prospects.

As the FSO had suggested, the manure detail was assigned to the embassy Marines. Trouble called in Lieutenant Vu and ordered him to deliver the package himself with a select group of his men and women.

With a grin and a happy salute, Vu left to arrange for them all to take a nice drive in the country.

Maybe even a picnic lunch.

A quick check with the demolition team from the *Patton* showed that they had plenty of what Vu needed to deliver.

That check with the *Patton* also verified that they had the feed lot under surveillance. The delay in shipping manure off to the drug farm and the hot weather had left piles of cow shit drying in the sun. That morning, three large truckloads of the stuff had been loaded up and should have been leaving anytime now.

Trouble left a note for the *Patton* to keep him informed of the fertilizer's progress and made sure he had contract with Vu. Communications would be critical.

Trouble allowed himself a smile and called Ruth to see if she was available for lunch. She allowed that she was, so they collected a lunch from the embassy cafeteria and carried it to the safe room.

"Husband, why are you grinning like the canary that just took a big bite out of the cat?"

"Because I'm serving up revenge both cold and sweet, and I find that it does taste a bit like ice cream."

"And I thought I was hard to understand at times," Ruth said, settling in a chair and taking a bite out of her roast beef sandwich on rye.

Trouble got serious. "I don't know whether to tell you the bad news or the good news first."

Ruth chewed for a bit, swallowed, and said, "Let's start with the bad."

"You were worried about Alice's getting that job in the

bordello," Trouble said, not beating around the bush. At least not much.

"Oh God, no!" Ruth said, then had to grab for her plate before it crashed down onto the floor.

"Yes. Milassi himself came to the place last night, and it seems he likes them young. Really young."

"We should never have let her work there."

"We needed the intel Alice got," Trouble shot back, then added in a softer voice, "And we didn't know Milassi's tastes, and we didn't know he'd go there."

"But . . ." Ruth started but couldn't seem to figure out what to say next.

"Because of Alice's work, Mary was able to make contact with all thirteen of the disaffected scientists at the Farm. They do want out. We think we can get them out tomorrow."

"That's the good news?" Ruth said dubiously, not sounding at all sure the good outweighed the bad.

"Yes. But I think you'll like the distraction we've got planned to help you get them out."

Quickly he filled her in.

"Oh, that's good. That's very good!" she said. "That's my husband the Marine. Blowing shit up and loving it."

"Yeah. And if Becky has it right, taking down the Farm cuts deep into Milassi's revenue stream. Likely, enough to make this place too hot to handle. Way too hot and not at all profitable."

"But will he merely get away, or can we get him?"

"That I don't know," Trouble had to admit. The FSO was not very forthcoming about the next phase of this operation. But then, lacking a crystal ball, Trouble was not at all sure where they were headed.

"I'd really like for you Marines to get your hands on that little shit. No, you Marines are too straight up for the job," Ruth said. "I want dogs. Or pigs. Ever seen a man attacked by feral pigs?"

"Where would we find some feral pigs?" Trouble asked. He didn't think there were any at hand, but from the look in his wife's eyes, it might be worth the effort.

"Or one of those pain collars you wore when the slavers got you. One that you can dial up or down. Let Alice have the controls."

"Honey, the little girl's been raped. Do you think she also needs the burden of being a killer?"

"Likely not," Ruth agreed. "Now me, I would be only too happy to play with the controls."

"You'll have to take turns with Mary. Milassi almost took her into the back room and raped her. Then he got distracted and went off with Alice. I think Mary has survivor's guilt."

"Mary's someone I could share that pain controller with," Ruth said, then shook herself. "When will we know for sure that taking down the Farm is a go?"

"It all depends on the weather. We'll have everything in place by tonight. If it rains, we're in trouble. If things go the way they should, you can meet your scientists for lunch tomorrow."

"I'll need to rent some more cars. The more cars, the better."

"You go do that," Trouble said.

Ruth finished her sandwich quickly. "You think we can get the bastard?" she asked Trouble again.

"Becky wants his head. I want his ass. Mary and her Marines want his guts for garters. Anything you want?"

"If they find a heart anywhere in the guy, I'll take it. But I don't think he has one."

"I don't either," her husband growled.

With that, Ruth went to do her job, and Trouble returned to his.

Communicate. Communicate. Communicate. It was not an easy job to bring all the many parts of a plan together. No doubt this one would not survive contact with the enemy.

Still, until the enemy got its vote, it was Trouble's job to make sure every part fit right in where it belonged.

He sat hunched over a station outside the secure room and checked each of his widely distributed actors. It looked perfect.

As always happens in war, it didn't stay that way.

THIRTY-EIGHT

THE TRUCKS LOADED with manure didn't waste any time on their runs into town. If there was a speed limit, they didn't pay it any attention.

So the Marines passing them to do what needed doing had to drive even faster.

And there was this cop. Apparently, he hadn't made his quota for the day, week, or month.

Did he stop the trucks that were way over the speed limit? Nope.

He stopped the convertible doing the passing.

Trouble let himself cuss a bit, which distracted the intel analysts in the room, so he swallowed his comments and listened in.

"May I see your license and registration?"

"Certainly, Officer. Carol, check and see if there's a registration in the glove compartment. Sorry, Officer, this is a rental. Would the rental contract be enough?"

"May I see it?"

No doubt the rental contract also had several hundred dinars folded into it. At least, Trouble hoped the Marines knew the drill.

Apparently they did, and the money did change hands.

"Yes, it appears everything is in order. I'll let you off with a warning this time. It's nice to drive through the hills, but these roads have a lot more curves than they do on the flat-lands. You hear?"

"Thank you, Officer," was followed by a long pause, then "you shithead," was added when the shithead was well out of earshot.

"Be nice," Trouble said. "He let you off without us having to see if your driver's license would pass muster."

"If you say so, Captain, but now we're way behind the trucks. We had almost delivered all the packets. We still have a few left."

"Leave it be. We were lacing the stuff with two or three times what our experts thought we needed."

"Okay. Can we have our picnic now?"

"Yes," Trouble said.

Trouble watched the cop car on the feed from the *Patton*. He stopped at the next roadside bar and never left it.

So the bribe worked. He didn't hassle the other convertibles on the road. All three manure loads now included a very nice something extra.

The trucks pulled into the Farm just before the close of business. They were parked out behind one of the barns.

Trouble called up his wife.

"We're set. You get the message to Brother Scott to pass along through his boys to the scientists to take an early and long lunch tomorrow."

"And I know just the place," Ruth said. "Thanks, love."

"Thank me when you have the packages here safe in the embassy."

"Chickens and hatching and counting and all that. Yes."

Trouble knew there wouldn't be a lot of sleep tonight. He had one more hard decision to make.

Tomorrow, if a cop stopped a Marine, no amount of bribery would work.

So, what did he authorize his Marines to do?

If they were cuffed and hauled off to jail, they'd likely be beaten to death, and all the Corps would get back was a corpse.

Trouble put his feet up on his desk and watched the bright lights flash on several monitors. Would he let these people kill his unarmed Marines?

Would he arm his Marines and authorize deadly force?

These were the kind of hot potatoes that rightly should be dropped in some senior elephant's lap. However, that had the disadvantage of their having to make a tough call.

A tough call they'd have to admit to making if asked.

There were times when it was wiser to let folks find out what had happened, then react any way they wanted to.

After all, if they wanted to put their oar in Trouble's water, they should have done it earlier.

Right! They hadn't told him not to, so they must mean for him to decide for himself.

There were advantages to being known as Trouble. Certainly, his bosses knew to expect trouble from him.

That matter settled, Trouble put his feet back down on the deck and concentrated on getting all his pieces ready to move in the morning.

THIRTY-NINE

SPIN TROTTED TOWARD the Farm in the dark. He led a dozen other boys from Brother Scott's shelter. Spin was the biggest. Some of the kids headed for the employment line today were pretty scrawny.

It was still very dark. The brothers and sisters had woken them, fed them breakfast, and rushed them off with a blessing.

"You have to be there before three," Brother Scott said as he waved them out the door. Spin was never sure what time it was, but three in the morning seemed awfully early to him.

But this was one day when Spin very much wanted to work. No one would say how or why or what about it, but he had the feeling something special was about to happen. And Spin very much wanted something special to happen.

He liked Alice. He'd waited for her and brought her home that night. It bothered him . . . that night. There were things he wanted to do with Alice. Things he didn't really understand. The idea that those things had left Alice crying and shivering left him torn.

Certainly, if he and Alice did something like he saw the older kids doing, it wouldn't mean she'd cry. Spin wanted to believe that.

And Spin was the one Brother Scott gave the tiny note to.

Spin knew the guy in the white coat that the message needed to get to. What Spin didn't know was what the note said.

Spin didn't read all that well.

Before he met Alice, that didn't bother Spin, but Alice thought everyone should read, and she'd even given Spin some lessons. Anything that let him spend more time with Alice was good, so Spin was doing his best to figure out what all the letters meant.

Now he could real a lot of the street signs. He hadn't figured out how that was better yet, but Alice said it would be, so
he studied them and could even pronounce most of them.

He and the other boys from Brother Scott's got to the
Farm. There weren't a lot of other boys waiting to be hired.
When the boss man came, he quickly counted them off and
let them in through the tall metal gate. There, another guy
with a computer took their thumbprints, asked their names if
they weren't in the computer, and sent them hustling over to
where different hoes and shovels stood.

The shorter boys grabbed hoes.

The bigger boys, like Spin, chose from among the shovels.
If a big kid picked a small shovel, the boss would hand him a
larger one. One big kid who got his hands on the smallest-
sized shovel got shown the door.

It also went the other way around. A kid who chose a
shovel too large for him was handed a smaller one with a
sharp, "We want you working the whole day, not crapping out
on us halfway through the morning."

Spin knew just how large a shovel he could handle. The
boss looked him over and went right on to the next boy.

Today, since it was so dark, they also got handed a headlamp.

"I'm counting these. Don't think you can walk off with it,"
the boss man snarled. "This is our junk, and we look out for
our junk."

Quickly, Spin put on his light. It turned on with a click.
Suddenly, he could see what he was looking at.

Now they were herded around to the trucks. This load of
manure was pretty dry and didn't smell too bad. Spin already
knew how to steer a wheel loader, so he got one out of the barn
and quickly rolled it up to the nearest truck. One of the boss
men had it spew some of its load into Spin's little carrier.

Full, another boss man pointed Spin out into the Farm.
There a boss was waving a chem light. Spin and another boy
from the shelter guided their loads to where that boss was.
Two little boys followed them with hoes.

The boss pointed them at a row of vines growing up a line
of trellises. "Get the manure down between the rows of vines.
Work both sides of the row. Some other team will be tossing
bullshit from the next aisle over. You kids with the hoes,

make sure you got fertilizer all the way up to your half of the row and that it's in among the plants. *Capisce?*"

The hoe boys nodded agreement as they headed down the rows of vines.

"And you shit-tossing guys, get it down the rows, you see, but don't get it on the plants. This is for their roots. It don't do no good on the plants. Got it?"

Spin assured the boss man that he got it.

He'd heard this story before. All of the big boys had heard all this before. They knew what they were supposed to do. Still, the boss men yelled it at them every time they came.

Spin figured the big guys just like to yell at little kids.

And today, Brother Scott had whispered to the bigger boys as they left that it was okay if they got some of the fertilizer on the plants. He didn't say why, but he'd made a special effort to let the boys know cow shit on the plants was not a bad thing today.

Spin wondered why, but he didn't question Brother Scott.

Now, he went to work, tossing the stuff low at first, because his hoe boy was in close. Only when the stuff close in was done and the boy was well back did Spin risk tossing the dry, stinking stuff higher in the air.

There was no wind blowing this early in the morning, but still the dry stuff flew wide as well as far.

If the boss men noticed it, they said nothing. Two had their bottles out, and even the one that was meaner than the rest seemed laid-back in the cool morning air.

They worked on the vines through the dark morning hours. When they emptied the wagon, one of them would take it back for another load. That was the only time the other three got to rest on their shovels or hoes. It was hard work, but at least it was cool. Come the heat of the day, it would not only be stinky work, but thirsty, sweaty work.

The sky was just beginning to show color: gold, reds, and silvers shining off a few thin clouds high in the sky. As they reached the end of the vines, dawn broke.

The boss men collected the headbands with lights and went off to turn them in. No doubt there would be a careful check of the numbers handed out and the numbers coming back. The bosses shouted for the boys to keep working, to go on to a low-bushes section and start on them.

The boys tossed out what was left in their wagons. At some carts, the bigger bullied the smaller to take the wagon back for a refill. Spin did a quick round of rock, paper, scissors with his buddy from the shelter, just as the brothers and sisters had taught them.

Spin got to rest on his shovel while his friend joined a long line of wagons going back for a load. The smaller boys finished spreading what had been tossed their way, then rested, too.

Spin didn't let his hoe boys rest too long. They had to move to the bushes, and it was best to get there early so you could pick your own row. Some of the bushes were more bushy than others. It was easier on the hoe boys if they got one of the scrawny ones.

Today, Spin picked a row that was more average. He wanted to have plenty of chances to toss shit on the bushes. He didn't know what would come of it, but if Brother Scott said to do it, he'd do almost anything he asked.

One hoe boy complained, but Spin reminded him who was the biggest and had the larger fists. Spin didn't think *everything* could be settled with rock, paper, scissors.

The wagon came back, and they started tossing the stinky stuff. With the sun up, it was already getting hot.

A bit later, the scientist that Spin had the message for came out to look things over. He told some of the boys to lay it on heavier, others to be spread it around more.

Apparently, all grown-ups liked to tell kids they were doing something wrong.

He eyed Spin for a moment but didn't tell him to do anything different.

He had turned to go when Spin took a big load of cow shit and tossed it so that half the load ended up on the back of the guy's pants and shoes.

"What are you doing, kid?" the guy demanded, and slugged out at Spin.

"I'm sorry, I'm sorry," Spin cried, but the message for the man was between his fingers and as his fist hit Spin's hand, the bit of paper slipped from one to the other.

"I ought to," the man said, but he didn't finish what he ought to do. Instead, he stomped away. "I got to change my clothes," was the last Spin heard from him.

One of the half-drunk bosses stumbled up to Spin. "You foul up again today, and you're out of here with no pay."

"Please, sir, I won't foul up, sir," Spin swore. He wasn't sure that he shouldn't foul up. The message was delivered. Should he bolt for home to let Brother Scott know?

But the point was to work today, and things were supposed to get interesting in a bit. Spin really wanted to see what was coming.

Also, the smaller boys didn't know that anything was up. Spin didn't know what was coming down, but it might be dangerous, and the little guys might need help getting out of here.

Spin kept slinging the fertilizer and doing it with care. A lot landed on the plants, but not enough to draw any reaction. The day got hotter.

It was thirsty work, and some of the smaller kids shouted that they were dizzy.

The boss men shouted for them to keep on working, but someone must have decided it was really hot work.

Last summer, so the story went, a kid had died, and it caused some trouble.

Today, apparently, the Farm didn't want the trouble that came with a dead kid.

A dozen girls came out well before noon, lugging water jugs between them. They put them on the ground, filled tin cups, and took them to the boys.

Alice was one of the girls this morning.

She offered Spin a tin cup to drink from.

"What are you doing here?" Spin demanded as he slurped the offered water.

"I want to see what happens. Be careful of that water. You don't want to get any of it on the cow shit."

"Why not?"

"You just don't want to. Sister said to tell you. She didn't say why. Just be careful."

Beside them, one of the hoe boys spilled a bit. It hit the ground and began to sizzle and smoke. Alice stomped on it and kept her booted foot on it until it quit whatever it was doing.

"Drink it," she snapped. "Don't spill it. If you do, step on it."

She took her foot off the . . . whatever. It smoked gently, but didn't do anything else.

One of the bosses came up. "What's that smell?" he demanded.

"What smell?" Spin said. "I can't smell nothing but shit."

"Get back to work. You had your drink. If you're not working by the time I count three, all five of you will be out of here."

The crew turned to, and Alice slipped away.

Which left Spin time to think.

He didn't usually do a lot of thinking, but what he'd seen was strange. He'd spilled plenty of water on cow manure. It never caught fire. Had it really caught fire?

He found himself doubting what he'd seen.

But Alice had seen it. She'd put her foot down on it. Was this the something that had been hinted at? As soon as they got all the fertilizer down, the boss men would turn on the water sprinklers.

If all this cow shit acted like the stuff Alice stepped on . . . ?

Spin smiled as he tossed another load of manure high through the bushes.

FORTY

TROUBLE INFORMED THE duty officer at spook central in the basement that he intended to use their spaces to brief his city detachments before today's op. The boss intelligence man seemed to understand exactly what Trouble intended . . . and not a bit more.

Thirty minutes later, the man dropped by Trouble's borrowed station. "You can have the space for your folks, Captain. The station chief, Ms. Graven, and the colonel regret that they won't be here to see your folks off. They're at some sort of big show at the Presidential Palace. Something about visitors coming in before the senators arrive from Earth."

"I hadn't heard about anything," Trouble said, and set his workstation to show him the palace. "Yep, they got bleachers and a reviewing stand up in front of the place."

"Reviewing stand," the spook said. "Wonder what they intend to review?"

"Oh, shit," Trouble said, and started following the wide boulevard back the way it came. There, strung out along River Road, was a mile or so of tanks. Also included were armored infantry fighting vehicles that had their tops removed so the men with guns riding in them could stand up and be intimidating.

Tube, rocket, and antiaircraft artillery were also parked, ready to roll up the end.

"Is that going to be a problem?" the chief duty spook asked.

"Only if we run into them," Trouble said as he tapped his commlink. "Mary, get a hold of Dumont and see me in the basement."

He tapped again. "Honey, I think I'm looking at something you might want to see. I'm in the basement."

Another tap, and he was talking to Lieutenant Vu. "Shag your ass down here. Someone is causing us a whole lot of trouble."

The duty spook backed away and went to check with his people. He was back in a minute. "The tanks rolled in about three o'clock this morning and have been hunkered down by the river ever since."

"Thanks. I must have napped through something I should have noticed."

"You were here all yesterday and through the night, Captain. You may be a Marine, but you're also human."

"Not permitted in the Corps. It says so right there in the officer's manual. Human. Not allowed."

The spook shook his head and stepped away as Mary, Ruth, Dumont, and Vu hurried in. Trouble quickly briefed them on this new twist to their situation.

For a long minute, they just stood around the screen and took in what they saw.

"If they're going to pass in review of the Presidential Palace, they'll be going away from where we are," Mary finally observed.

"But they'll be cutting down the number of bridges we can use to get back to the embassy," Ruth said. "We'll only have three instead of five."

"So our options to razzle-dazzle any pursuit will be cut down," Lieutenant Vu said, laying the conclusion out for all to see.

"I was kind of hoping with the distraction you have planned," Ruth said, "that all the attention would be going that way, not looking at what was coming our way."

"But will Milassi want to distract his visitors from the heavy metal he has parading down in front of them?" Mary said. "Likely, the tanks will keep on rolling and the president-for-life will keep on taking the salutes."

"That fire is going to cost him a nice chunk of change," Trouble said. "I think he'll be very interested in what is going on across town. Even if he doesn't have tanks rolling that way, he'll have a lot of police and fire-department personnel hot-footing it for there."

"Fire department, yes," Ruth said. "Police?"

"Whenever anything happens, Milassi sends in the police," the chief duty spook put in. He'd been quietly listening. Now he offered his intel take.

"So, how long will it take them to notice that their favorite eggheads didn't come back from lunch?" Ruth asked. "What with a fire going on?"

"Maybe fifteen minutes to an hour," Trouble mused.

"So we get them back to the embassy in an hour, max," Mary said.

"Assuming the bridges aren't blocked by traffic or just on general principle," the spook said. "Rational behavior has been in pretty short supply since I got here."

"So what do we do if the bridges are blocked?" Ruth asked. "Lay up somewhere?"

"Not a good idea," Mary said before Trouble had to say the same. "Once they know the cats are out of the bag, they'll tear this place apart. Both to find the scientists and to collect the heads of the arsonists."

Mary shook her head. "No, we've got to get them out of here. And, folks, I don't mean to be a party pooper, but looking at all that rolling heavy metal, suddenly I'm not so sure that bringing them to the embassy is all that smart an idea. Do you really think a diplomatic mission will get any kind of respect if Milassi takes it in his head to run a dozen tanks through it?"

"Now that you mention it," the spook said, "it's not something I'd take bets on."

"So," Trouble said slowly, not at all happy to see his plan unravel, but unable to find fault in Mary's logic. "We need to get them not only out of the Farm but off the planet."

That idea hung in the air for a long moment. Then heads began to nod.

"Only how?" the spook asked.

"Good question," Trouble said, a grin coming out to play on his lips. "Fortunately, I just happen to know one Navy captain who really hates drugs. They killed her sister's kid, and she's had a thing against them ever since. Mr. Spook, can you get me a secure line to the *Patton* overhead?"

"My pleasure," he said, and waved at one of his crew.

She did something to her board and waved back. "You're patched through to the *Patton*, boss."

Only a moment later and they heard, "Captain Umboto here."

"Skipper, we got a problem."

"That you, Trouble? Of course you have a problem."

That drew smiles around the room.

"This time it's a rather big one, Skipper. We are about to hire away thirteen guys who are helping grow next year's designer drugs."

"Ooh, I like this problem," came back at them.

"Our problem is that we need to get them well out of reach of the local president-for-life."

"And the good ship *Patton* just happened to come to mind, right?" the skipper said.

"You are our first choice," Trouble admitted.

"And your only hope," she added.

"Kind of."

"So, how do we make this happen?" the cruiser captain asked.

"There are several lakes in the foothills up above the city here."

"And you think I can drop a shuttle in one?" she said before Trouble could ask.

"Kind of. It's either that or we haul them over to the embassy. We're thinking the embassy might not get all the respect it's supposed to."

"No doubt," the skipper said. "Now, this may surprise you, but with me having you dirtside, I've had spare time on my hands, seeing how I didn't have to clean up any of your messes. I have also been studying where I might put down a Navy landing party should the need arise. You see that nice Bear Lake?"

"The one fifteen miles out of town?" Ruth said.

"That very same. Nice deep lake. Several good boat landings where I might run a shuttle up on the beach. There's a second option, Clear Lake, but it's shallow, and I'm not so sure about the beaches."

"We'll go for Bear Lake," Trouble said. "There are three roads into it. That might turn out nice."

"Then Bear Lake it is," the skipper said. "When do you want us? We need at least ninety minutes of warning. This station is in a low orbit, and we only pass over your neck of the woods every hour and a half."

"We'll let you know right after lunch," Trouble said. "Trouble out."

"*Patton* out," Umboto signaled.

"Now," Trouble said, "we may have moved the goal post, but that doesn't mean we want them to know it. Ruth and Mary, you take out the rented cars and retrieve the packages. Dumont and Vu, you take out the embassy's rigs and run interference for the packages and distractions. Vu, your personnel in particular will make as much noise as you can, attract as much police attention as you can, and point it all back toward the embassy."

Vu grinned. "The old goal has become a diversion and we keep them chasing after us until they discover we don't have anything they want. I like that."

"But how will the cops take to finding no one but Marines in the rigs?" Ruth asked, worry clear on her face.

"We've been running them ragged with our daily meanderings," Trouble said. "It will take them a while to realize the stakes in the game have gone from penny-ante stuff to the real thing. Hopefully by then, Vu's Marines will be back home, and your packages will be on their way to the *Patton*. Even Milassi's thugs can't get them there."

"But you'll still be here," the chief duty spook observed dryly.

"I can only hope those thugs do try coming over our walls," Dumont said, his smile feral and hungry. "I'd like to see those shits try the kind of games they been playing with unarmed civilians on my line beasts. Let them see who wins then."

Trouble remembered that Mary's troops were civilians drafted into the Corps, given minimal training, then sent out to kill or be killed. Her survivors were the ones that got the killing part down real good. Though himself sworn to the profession of the sword, the look on Du's face still sent shivers down Trouble's spine.

If those thugs knew what was good for them, they'd stay clear of that man.

Of course, being thugs, they wouldn't.

Trouble glanced at Mary. She nodded almost imperceptibly. Message received, and she would act on it when she had time.

If she ever had time.

"All right, crew. We'll start spitting cars out of here at ten hundred. Let's have a formation at oh nine hundred here in the basement, so we can say what we mean and mean what we say. Any questions?"

As usual, there were none. The Marines departed to prepare their teams.

Ruth stayed behind. "Do those tanks worry you?" she asked.

"You know that little car you drive?" he said.

"Yes."

"One of those tanks could drive right over it and not even notice the bump."

She stroked the tense muscles of his back as she studied the screen. "Yes, I imagine they could. But my little car can turn down an alley that would bring one of those things to a halt."

"Don't bet on it, my dear. If Milassi is really screaming on net, those things will plow through your alley right behind you."

"You may be right, Marine and husband, but it's bound to slow them down, and those alleys won't slow me down one bit."

"No," he agreed. "Not even a little bit." Then he turned to her. "You will be careful. How many kids do you want?"

"I'm down to three," Ruth said, with a bit of a blush. "Maybe we can fit in a fourth."

"Then you take care of the mother of my kids that can't be more than a gleam in my eye."

"Keep your eyes gleaming," she said, as she went up on tiptoes and gave him a kiss right in the middle of spook central.

Then, without a glance back, she turned and left. She had a job to do today, and for the rest of the day, she would be all job.

Trouble smiled at the woman as she left and gently rubbed

his lip, tasting again the kiss she'd planted in defiance of God, the regs, and everything.

What a woman.

He turned back to the board. He too had a job to do today.

FORTY-ONE

RUTH WAS BACK in the basement at nine o'clock her time—0900 hours to her husband's time tick. She was doing her best to adapt to Marine life.

Today, all the Marines were dressed in civvies like her. With their high-and-tight haircuts, hard muscles, and ramrod backs, only a blind man could mistake them for anything but Marines.

Well, a blind man or a civilian who never thought about those things.

Even in civilian clothes, they were forming up in ranks, filling the open space in the middle of the intel analysts' basement. Their own officers stood in front of the trigger pullers. All were facing toward her husband.

"Today, a dark sun sets. And while the mission may sound simple," Trouble said, "its execution may be anything but. It's unlikely, but you may be sharing the road with tanks today."

Ruth glanced over the ranks as her husband did, checking for the Marines' reactions. She saw none. Apparently, their officers had warned them.

"Some of you will be briefed in how to extract our packages and deliver them to someplace safe. Others of you will be doing a bang-up job of distracting anyone out to stop the main objective. All of you will be contributing to bringing Milassi down. Down hard."

That got a solid, if low "Ooo-Rah" from the troops.

"Those of you who will be involved with the packages will stay behind when dismissed. Those of you who will be otherwise deployed will take your orders from Lieutenant Vu. Many of you will get a nice drive around town. Some may even get out in the country. All will draw a box lunch from the cafeteria. Likely, there will be little time to stop for lunch."

Trouble paused, then said the words that usually ended such a Marine briefing. "Any questions?"

"Yes, sir," came like a shot from Mary, captain of her own detachment. Her lieutenant, Dumont was raising his hand, so, likely Mary chose to speak up so she could stay ahead of him. Ruth was none too sure how she felt about the young lieutenant, but with Mary talking, he dropped his hand to his side.

"Yes, Captain," Trouble said.

"Are we weapons loose today, sir?"

Like so many conversations Ruth had heard among the Marines, those few words held a whole lot of meaning.

Her husband took a deep breath before he turned to Ruth. "Honey, would you please record this?"

"Yes, love. Recorder on," Ruth said. She'd heard Trouble joke with his fellow Marine officers about career-ending decisions. They'd even seriously debated whether they would like to have their career-ending decision on tape, where there was no question about it at their courts-martial, or not taped so they might wiggle out.

Trouble had always said, "If I'm talking, you can damn well record it. If I say it I mean it, and I'll stand by it."

Ruth prepared to record his words so there could be no mistake what he said.

"All personnel going outside the wire today will be issued sidearms," Trouble said smartly. The room fell so quiet you could hear a pin drop.

"Sergeants will issue M-6s to the best sharpshooter in each vehicle. They will also issue six light antitank rockets to each vehicle."

Now the room really was quiet. Even the spooks at their intel stations along the walls were not breathing.

"Under normal conditions, I would tell you that if a police officer stops you, you should go with them, and we will get you out of the hoosegow later." Captain Trouble's face took on a scowl Ruth had never seen the likes of as he turned toward her.

"We have seen what these thugs with badges do to defenseless people."

Ruth found that every eye among the troops had swung to look at her. Her knees went weak with all the attention, but she strove to stay at attention, as good as any of them, as she withstood their gazes.

"Come sundown tonight, I want no dead Marines. Do you hear me?"

"Sir. Yes, sir," roared back at their captain.

"I would personally prefer that there are *no* dead bodies on the ground, come sundown. I would take that as a personal kindness, seeing how I will no doubt be buried in paperwork if there are."

That drew nervous laughs from some in the ranks, hard smiles from the NCOs and officers.

"Whatever happens, however, always be guided by my first preference. No dead Marines."

That drew a solid "Ooo-Rah" from the crew and, Ruth discovered, from herself as well.

"Now, folks, if there are no more questions, let's go out and add another proud page to the Corps' history."

No one voiced a question. Lieutenant Vu departed with his detachment. Ruth drew close to the map screen and began making her own assignments.

"We have thirteen small rental cars for thirteen packages. That leaves room for a driver and two Marines riding shotgun in each cars."

"What if the last two jokers show up?" Mary asked. "Do we take them or leave them?"

Ruth winced. She had not given any thought to that. "No. We leave no scientist behind."

She considered the problem for a moment. "Mary, would you drive a sedan today that can carry two? I'll drive one as well. It will be harder to drive up an alley. However, if we get the long rifles out, there will be more room, and we won't be jostling sharpshooters' elbows."

Mary frowned. "I can do that."

Mary and Ruth would go to the pickup restaurant and collect the scientists. They would take them out into the parking lot to be snatched up by their rides, then follow along behind the rest in their own sedans.

"We don't want to take the same road. A convoy this long would be bound to draw attention."

Ruth and Mary stood by while the other drivers picked different side streets and distributed them among the eleven small rental cars. The drivers studied their routes. A spook brought enough hard-copy maps of Petrograd for each car to have one, but no marks were made on them. Each driver and their backup memorized their route and studied the other routes.

Each expected to have to deviate from their planned routes, but no one wanted to get so off their street that they ended up on someone else's.

They were good teams, and most of them had plenty of experience driving this crazy city's streets, thanks to the game of hide-and-seek they'd been playing for the last several weeks.

Done, there was another "Ooo-Rah," and the teams went their way. Ruth paused for another kiss from her husband. "You be careful in here," she told him.

"Right, I might get a very nasty paper cut," he growled into her ear as she hugged him.

Gunny turned out to be riding shotgun with Ruth.

"Shouldn't you be riding herd on some green kid?" she asked him as he took the passenger's front seat. He'd just come from his own double, or maybe triple check with the motor pool that their sedan was bug-free.

"Ma'am, all the green kids are staying inside the wire with your husband. But he made it clear before I got out of his sight that if you aren't tucked nicely into bed beside him tonight, I should apply for a job with the local sewer department."

"He wouldn't do that," Ruth said.

Gunny didn't look persuaded.

"My husband is not that kind of man," she insisted.

"He's a Marine officer, ma'am. Even Gunnies fear them when they get that look in their eyes."

Ruth decided silence was the only way to win this conversation. The backseat had hardly any room taken up by the woman Marine who had done such a fine job of breaking bones when Ruth was last rescued.

"Good to see you again, Debbie. I hope this goes quieter than the last time we rode together."

"No doubt it will. Gunny, I got a weapon bag with my M-6 in it and a dozen antitank rocket grenades. It's got pretty flower stickers on it. Can I keep it in back or do you want it in the trunk?"

"Gunner's choice," Gunny said.

In the rearview, Ruth caught Debbie's smile before she settled her bag in the footwell in front of her.

Ruth distinctly remembered her husband authorizing a half dozen rockets. Not a dozen. But then, he'd often said Marines became hard of hearing when he tried to restrict their weapons load outs.

The first car, an embassy rig, moved out of the gate at a sedate pace. A police car took off trailing it. A second black car got a tail as well. When a rental went out next, there was a tail. One after another, cars drove out of the embassy lot, and after each, a police car sped along behind.

"I'm guessing with the big parade scheduled for today," Gunny muttered, "they ain't taking any chances with us spoiling things."

"Then this may get interesting, trying to lose a tail with a rig this wide," Ruth said. Still, she might need the extra room. None of those overpaid farm engineers looked like they'd skipped any meals since taking on their jobs here.

Mary headed out ahead of her. Then it was Ruth's turn.

As luck would have it, there was still a cop car left to tail Ruth as she left the empty embassy motor pool.

She turned right the first chance she got, away from the Presidential Palace and its parade. She led her tail up that way as far as she could go and still catch the last bridge to cross the Anna River. Through it all, the black police car behind her kept her sedate pace.

Once on the other side of the river, Ruth hopped an expressway and headed out of town. The cop stayed with her for the first couple of turnoffs, then took the fifth one and headed back into town.

Ruth used the seventh exit to make her own turnaround. She half expected the cop to be waiting for her, but he was long gone.

Keeping a careful eye on her rear for any regrown tail, she

TO DO OR DIE · 223

made her way, in a very roundabout way, to Momma's Best Burgers.

She was there ahead of Mary.

"I'll stay in the car with the bag," Debbie said, sprawling out in the backseat and settling in for what some might take for a nap.

Gunny took the parking lot in with a studied eye, found it carried acceptable risks, and joined Ruth heading for the front door.

Inside, they took a table in the back and ordered the signature special. The burgers were greasy, and the fries were stale. The lettuce was wilted and what passed for tomatoes had to be seen to be believed.

"There are some things I will not miss when we see this place in the rearview mirror," Gunny muttered as he gingerly essayed a bite.

Five minutes later, Mary arrived with her own sergeant. They took a table a couple down from Ruth and assiduously did not look at them more than once.

It was getting on toward noon when the packages began wandering in in groups of three or four. They looked furtively around. Anyone not blind would know they were up to something and very likely all coconspirators.

Ruth did her best not to look their way, and they, after being ignored ten or twenty times, learned to do the same.

More burgers were ordered and delivered.

Ruth glanced at her watch.

The problem with this kind of operation was that it depended on someone else to start it. She watched, and waited, trying not to glance out the window too many times.

As it turned out, she didn't need to be looking out the window when it started. It was pretty spectacular. You couldn't avoid noticing it.

FORTY-TWO

SPIN TOSSED THE last shovel of cow shit and returned his shovel to the rack.

He'd brought the last load of manure off the truck, and they'd tossed it with more enthusiasm than the heat of the day deserved. They'd earned their pay: three dinars for the big boys, two for the small ones, and one for the water girls.

Now, all of them crowded toward the gate to collect their coins.

Alice hung back at the end, so Spin did too. The paymaster, as usual, took his time doling out the money they'd earned, as if it came from his own pocket. Or as if he enjoyed making them fidget all the more for what they'd earned with their own sweat.

Spin had just gotten to the head of the line when one of the bosses shouted to the others to turn on the water.

Spin's pay dropped into his palm just as it all started to happen.

"Look!" Alice shouted, apparently not at all interested in her money.

Spin spun around and looked.

As usual, the boss men were turning on all the water spigots at the same time. Brother Scott said that wasn't too smart, since if they watered only one area at a time, they wouldn't make such a big hit on the water tanks, but no, as usual, they were turning all the sprinklers on at once, so they could get it over with and get out of the sun.

What with them having spread twice the manure, Spin figured the water problem would be even worse. But it wasn't bad yet.

All the sprinklers were on and flowing at full blast.

As the water hit the ground, there were bright white flashes. Maybe the bosses were too hungover or just not paying any attention, but the water kept coming and the flashes just kept getting bigger.

Then the manure began catching fire.

Spin had once seen a manure pile burn. It had been delivered on a hot day and just left where it was dumped. It lay in the sun for a couple of days and it kind of started burning. It stank to high heaven as it burned, but it burned.

Now, all the spread-out manure was sparkling with these white explosions and burning. Somehow, the water only made it worse.

"What burns when water hits it?" Spin asked Alice.

"I dunno," she said. The pay man was looking, his mouth falling open slowly as he did. He slapped a copper dinar in Alice's hand and stood there gawking. He took a couple of steps toward the burning plants but stopped. Then he backed up, as if to start running, but then he paused and stepped forward again. He did it several times.

He couldn't seem to decide what to do next.

The boss guys were shouting at each other. The senior guy was insisting they turn up the water, but it was up as far as it would go.

No, it was already starting to run down. The spray from the sprinklers was reaching less and less manure, and where it no longer reached, the fire was really catching on.

The plant leaves were dry to start with, some even showing brown. Now they flared up and burned. Some floated on the hot wind for a bit and landed among the plants that hadn't been fertilized.

The fire spread.

Someone somewhere else must have decided they needed help, because a siren began to wail. It was soon joined by more sirens, all coming closer.

Spin pulled at Alice's elbow. "We don't want to be here when the people get here."

"I know, I know," Alice said. But even with Spin pulling her through the Farm's gate, she walked backward, eyes bright with what she saw.

"Take that, Milassi. You take that," she whispered.

FORTY-THREE

RUTH LOOKED OUT the window and smiled at what she saw.

Dense brown smoke roiled up from the Farm. She could just make out the white sparkles as magnesium flared when water kissed it.

The diversion was up and running.

The scientists stood and stared out the window. All their mouths hung open or flapped, depending on their personal bent.

Dr. Bernardo looked back at Mary and turned pale.

Ruth tossed a couple of bills on the table and stood up. Gunny followed her out. Mary did the same.

Walking through the gawking scientists, she whispered. "Pay your bills and join us in the parking lot. Move fast. Your rides won't be here forever."

A few of the guys in white smocks quickly dropped money on the table for their meals and followed. Others were last seen arguing among themselves.

Ruth had put out a call to her posse when she first spotted the fire. A blue sports car pulled into the parking lot. She opened the back door and shoved a scientist into the empty seat before he could say a word.

She did the same for the next two cars that drove through the lot like race cars making an unavoidable pit stop.

Then Dr. Bernardo got to her elbow.

"What have you done?" he demanded.

"Set up a diversion," Ruth said, and tried to shove him into the latest car to pause in front of her.

He refused to be shoved.

So Mary shoved the next guy in line and Ruth stepped aside to argue with an overeducated dolt.

"Did you think this was going to be easy?" she snapped as a police car, siren blaring, raced by, a bright red fire engine close on its bumper. "We've got their attention where we want it. Now you can leave."

One of the nice things about this parking lot was its back entrance. Now that the street out front was full of wailing emergency-response vehicles, the Marines were pulling in through the back road and leaving the same way.

"But what about my work?" Dr. Bernardo cried. "It's ruined!"

That brought Mary's head around even as she shoved a guy in the next car. Ruth didn't care for violence, but she had to throttle an urge to slug the scientist. Maybe she should leave him behind to look after his work and explain this little setback to his employer.

"And this work would be better off distributed around human space and pumped into the veins of people too stupid to know better?"

The good doctor's self-absorption did have some limits. He frowned in thought for a few moments. "Yes. Yes. You may have a point there."

"My employer thinks so. Now, are you going?"

Ruth got ready to shove him in the next car, but she missed her chance as a new fellow, lab coat flying, raced into the parking lot.

"Dr. Bernardo. Doctor Bernardo. I thought I'd find you here," the man shouted, then, out of breath, halted a few meters away to rest his hands on his knees as he gasped for air.

A second man was not far behind. What he shouted had Mary reaching for her automatic. Reaching, but not quite pulling it out.

"What have you done? What is going on? Why are our fields burning even as we water them?"

"You're the chemist," Bernardo shouted back. "You tell me."

The man turned back to the Farm and frowned. Gunny started moving toward him with purpose.

"The initial sparkles that ignited the fire were bright white. Magnesium. Did someone mix magnesium in with the fertilizer?"

"Enough, mister, you're coming with us," Gunny told him.

"I think we better go with them, wherever they're going," the first newcomer said, now having caught his breath. "Do you want to talk to the boss when all this gets out? Even if we can convince him we had nothing to do with this, he'll still skin us alive."

All four of the scientists still in the parking lot shivered. Apparently, he was not speaking metaphorically.

"Can we go?" the last man there asked.

"Mary, you take those two idiots," Ruth said, shoving two the Marine's way.

"I'll take these two fools," Ruth finished, pulling Bernardo and the last to arrive toward her car.

"We're already gone," Mary said, and, grabbing an elbow of each, towed them toward her sedan.

Ruth shoved them in the backseat with Debbie. They immediately began insisting that they each got a window seat. The Marine settled at least half of the argument by hauling out her M-6 and pulling back purposefully on the arming bolt.

Dr. Bernardo insisted he should ride up front but grew quickly silent when Gunny drew his automatic.

"What have we fallen in with?" the new fellow whined.

"Marines," Gunny growled.

"If you want the double pay, shut up, sit still, and don't cause us any trouble," Ruth ordered.

"Double pay!" Suddenly, the new fellow was all ears.

"On Wardhaven," Dr. Bernardo added.

The backseat grew suddenly hushed.

Two police cars drove in the front entrance just as Ruth pulled carefully into the side street's sparse traffic.

The cops parked and got out, apparently more intent on coffee than the fire.

Or the people who set it.

Ruth drove at the speed limit as she put distance between herself and the cops.

FORTY-FOUR

COLONEL RAY LONGKNIFE was bored. If he never saw another tank, infantry assault vehicle, or gun carriage in his life, it would be too soon.

Around him, minor civilian officials looked at them with pride mixed with terror. As an old infantry officer, Ray looked at them as targets. From the looks of most of them, they'd be easy kills.

Not all, but most.

For a nickel, he'd leave.

His commlink buzzed, as did Becky's next to him. They both took the excuse to pull their commlinks out and purposefully withdraw from the crowd. That involved leaving the reviewing stand and ducking out the back.

As far as Ray was concerned, it just got better and better.

"Longknife here," was matched with a simple "Graven."

"I'm glad I caught both of you," came in Captain Tordon's voice. "The packages have been collected. Everything is going smoothly, but I can't say how long that will last."

Ray tried not to smile. The Marine was talking like an experienced combat officer.

"Thank you for the call," Graven said.

"If you should choose to come back to the embassy, I can have some extra Marines meet your limo," said a lot without saying anything at all.

Ray eyed the diplomat. Her nod toward where the limos were parked was almost, but not quite, imperceptible.

So was his nod of agreement. Away from the rumble of tanks, Ray could just pick up the noise of distant sirens. Apparently, the distraction was going very well.

He did not look around to search for smoke. He'd learned long ago not to gawk.

He and the Foreign Service Officer turned to leave.

And found themselves facing Milassi himself.

The big man wasn't so big up close, but he was large enough, with his two ever-present bodyguards, to block their way.

"Leaving so soon," was not a question.

"Once you've seen one tank, you've seen them all," Ray said, lightly.

"But we have so many for you to see," was a growled threat.

"And if I see that same tank again from the 4th Armored Brigade with its laser range finder hanging by a thread . . ." was intentionally left vague.

When the president-for-life didn't react, Ray went on. "What is it, the fourth time you've rolled the same tanks by the reviewing stand?"

Milassi shrugged. "I should have known I couldn't fool a real war hero. Even after I had the unit's license plates painted over."

"That was my first tell you were playing games," Ray said. "But the black horses were still on the side of each tank. The 4th Brigade's black horses—2nd Brigade is the white horses. Rampant lions for the 12th Infantry, and death's-heads for the 20th."

"It was a shame to obliterate all that lovely artwork," Milassi said with a shrug.

"Well, if you'll excuse me, we really must be going," Ms. Graven said, and made to step around the strongman.

He stepped in front of her.

"I am not your enemy," he said with a softness that did not belie the threat.

"I don't see you as one," the professional diplomat answered, diplomatically.

Ray tried to go around his other side, but the man side-stepped in front of him. "I'm only trying to make a living. We can't all marry into money, can we now?"

Ray reminded himself that he was a diplomat today. There was no need to honestly discuss this man's predilections and depredations. Indeed, there was no time to discuss anything.

If Ruth and Mary had the scientists moving away from this man's clutches and toward Wardhaven, the game was afoot, and there was a definite advantage to Ray's side for him to stay free and not end up this man's hostage.

"I hope you may find as much happiness with your wife as I find with mine," Ray said. "And as soon as I've had a quick meeting with the senators, I'll be on my way back home."

"That will be nice," Milassi said with a grin that had no joy in it. "To be home with your wife before the baby comes."

"Yes," Ray said, letting himself smile with all the joy the thought brought him.

Happy smile to vicious smile, they faced each other for a long moment. Then the big man stepped aside, and Ray and Becky began a casual stroll to their waiting limo.

Off to the west, there was definitely something burning. Gray smoke rose in the hot, dry air before leveling out several thousand feet high and dissipating into a haze.

"You know, we may have outthought ourselves, accepting this invitation," Ray said, allowing himself to speed up his walk.

"After seeing that man and his tanks, I think you may be right. Can we get around that long line of vehicles?"

"It depends on how far they're going before they loop around and come back to see us again. I'd say two, maybe three blocks. We can get around that."

The limo's motor was already running as they approached it. Ray held the back door open for Becky. She got in, then scooted across the seat so he could get in right after her.

"George, to the embassy, and make haste without looking like it."

"Yes, ma'am," he said, and they were moving before either one of them could belt in.

Trouble didn't breathe until the limo pulled out of the Presidential Palace and began to wind its way around the circular parade route.

Of course, if he was able to follow the limo's squawker, then anyone could.

Not all of his Marines were on the other side of town close to Ruth.

"Lieutenant Vu, your diplomat and my colonel are leaving the palace in a marked limo. Could you rendezvous with them about five blocks out?" Trouble said, and sent him the intercept coordinates.

"Got them. Be there in two minutes."

"I'll have two more rigs meet you there or close by."

"What do you want? Do we escort them in?" Vu asked.

"I don't think that would be such a good idea. Abandon the limo and switch them to your rigs."

"Take the driver, too?"

"Would you want to be driving a traceable vehicle today?"

"Good point, Skipper. Secure all the people. Material is expendable."

"You got that."

"I have the limo in sight."

"I'll advise the colonel. Trouble out."

Trouble switched his commlink's connection. "Colonel, I have a new ride approaching you from your front. Black SUV. Full of Marines in civvies. Lieutenant Vu in command. I strongly recommend that you park the limo and return to the embassy with the Marines."

Colonel Ray Longknife frowned at this latest communication.

"Either Trouble is becoming a worried old lady in long skirts, or things are getting more risky than we thought."

"After your little talk with Milassi," Becky said, "you still think this is not a risk?"

"I just don't think he's willing to start shooting people with our reputations and connections."

"I do," the diplomat said.

That settled it for Ray. When civilians with diplomatic immunity started to worry, it was time to expand the safety margins of the operation.

"Driver, pull over. We'll be changing rides."

"George, you come, too," Becky said.

The driver didn't argue but pulled over to the curb and locked the car as soon as they were all out.

The Marine rig was large. It needed to be to hold the four Marines and three others who piled in. They turned at the end of the block, but as Ray looked back, three police cars were racing up to the limo, lights flashing but silent.

The Marine rig picked up two more of its kind at the next corner. As they made another turn, Ray heard a loud explosion.

"What was that?" he asked.

"I don't know," Lieutenant Vu said, "but there's smoke behind us."

Through the back window, Ray could see oily black smoke rising from where his last ride most likely was.

"Why blow up an empty limo?" George asked.

"Because it was empty, and that was the only way Milassi could send a message," Ray said as he tapped his commlink.

"Captain Tordon, this is Colonel Ray Longknife. I am issuing this order as senior officer present. You have weapons release. I repeat, you have weapons release. Please advise all Society of Humanity armed forces on this planet that they are to defend themselves if they conclude that they are at risk."

"Understood, sir. I will issue the order."

Ray turned to face forward. "Milassi sent his message. Now I've sent mine."

"Speaking for all the Marines dirtside, sir, may I say thank you," Lieutenant Vu said.

"God help us all," the Foreign Service Officer said.

"This is Captain Tordon, Society of Humanity Marine Corps, Colonel Ray Longknife has ordered weapons release," Trouble said, then added the minor limit the colonel had made to the rules of engagement. If some poor young corporals found themselves in a hot spot, now they didn't have to worry about covering their asses.

It was nice when the local elephant was an old line beast.

* * *

"Sergeant," Cyn said, fingering her M-6, "that cop who's been tailing us for the last mile is not hanging back."

"I saw," Sergeant Daly said. "Hold on, and you can take the safety off that toy of yours, gal."

Cyn grinned, flipped the safety, and pulled back the arming bolt. She was loaded for bear.

And the Bear was coming for them, no question about that. The cop was closing fast, and now a hand with a pistol emerged from the passenger side. Cyn heard six shots, but nothing hit the car.

"The idiot is firing wide," the sergeant said as he floored the sedan and headed for the bridge back to the embassy.

That really seemed to bug their pursuer. He sped up; someone in the backseat hung out the window. This one had a machine pistol in hand.

"Lots of fire coming our way," Cyn announced.

The sergeant glanced into his rearview. "End this race before someone gets hurt."

"Yes, sir," Cyn said with a happy grin.

She did not sight her M-6 at the man, or even at the driver. No, the radiator was a much larger and steadier target than any of them.

Her first round punched a hole in the rear window. The three rounds that quickly followed punched holes in the trailing car just where she intended.

The radiator started spewing scorching water and coolant. The gunner, who had yet to get a round off, suddenly dropped his gun and grabbed for his eyes as boiling steam washed over him.

The situation back there must have gotten confusing. The car wavered right, then left, then took a hard right turn, slammed through the bridge rail, and sailed very nicely out over the river before vanishing from view.

"Very good, Corporal. Very good."

"Why thank you, Sarge. That *was* pretty good, if I do say so myself."

"Let me check in with the skipper," the sergeant said.

A minute later he said. "Captain says well done. If we

want to come in, we can. Or we can stay out. Your call, Corporal."

"I don't feel a need to go back to the embassy, Sarge. Do you need a change of underwear?"

"Not on your life, Marine."

"Then let's keep trawling for trolls."

FORTY-FIVE

RUTH LISTENED TO voices on the net. They did not chatter. Marines were too professional to chatter.

What she heard sent chills up her spine.

Milassi was going to war with the embassy.

No doubt, he thought he had good cause. Alice reported through Brother Scott that not only had the half of the crop they'd targeted gone up in smoke, but the fire had spread to the rest of the fields. There were lots of fire trucks at the Farm now.

But none had much water, and most of the firemen were standing around watching the dope burn.

No wonder Milassi had torched the embassy limo in his rage.

Ruth heard sirens blaring off in the distance. Different sirens from different directions. Some to her right. Some to her left. Some behind her.

But it was the ones in front of her that worried her the most.

The sirens would light off, frequently followed by long bursts of automatic weapons fire. Gunny could identify them by the sound.

"Some cop's machine pistol," he'd growl.

"That's an M-6," he would say as single shots or short bursts responded.

That usually ended the conversation. A few shots, and the sirens would go quiet. If it was close, Ruth might hear the echoes of a crash.

Usually, she didn't.

The cops were losing the high-speed chases.

So, of course, they changed the game.

"Ruth, there's a roadblock about a mile ahead of you," Trouble advised her.

She immediately took a left.

They were edging toward the suburbs now. The streets were wider. The buildings here were brick row houses. Some had flowerpots in the upper windows. Some had lawns.

Ruth had gone three blocks when a cop stepped out from behind a tree. He was in the middle of the road in the blink of an eye. One hand on his holster, the other pointing at her and waving her down.

Ruth considered slamming it into reverse, but Gunny said, "Go ahead and stop. Edge over to my side."

As Ruth did, Gunny rolled his window down.

"Is there a problem, Officer?" he called, head half-out the window.

The man glanced at their license plates, then at his wrist unit, checking their plate against a list. He did the check but didn't tap his wrist to send in a report.

That might be promising.

Or not.

He drew his weapon as he approached Gunny's open window.

"You are wanted for questioning. You will have to come with me," the officer said.

Ruth withdrew several hundred dinar notes from her pocket and passed them over to Gunny. He laid them on the windowsill.

"I am afraid that today I cannot be bought off," the cop said sadly.

"I figured as much," Gunny said.

"Now, out of the car," came with a wave of the pistol.

Gunny groaned as he made to get out, suddenly an old man with old bones.

But the door slammed open like the strike of a snake. The top of it took the cop on the chin, knocking him back. His gun flew one way as he went down hard on his ass.

"You earned your pay today, sir," Gunny said, tucking the money in the cop's boot. "Now let's get out of here," he said, closing the door.

Ruth was off before it clicked shut.

"Mind telling me what that was all about?" Debbie asked from the backseat. She had her M-6 out, but with no order from Gunny, she'd played it as cool as he.

From the smell of it, at least one of the scientists needed a change of underwear.

"Alice mentioned that some of the street cops weren't too bad. Maybe not good by our standards, but not too bad for locals. How could anyone be in a corrupt system like this and not smell of it? Anyway, when he didn't call us in, I figured there was a good chance his heart really wasn't in what he had to do today. As it seems, it wasn't."

"I wish you'd told me that, Gunny," Debbie said.

"I wish I'd had time to," Gunny admitted.

Ruth had turned at several corners, putting distance between her and the down cop, when sirens lit up close by.

"Honey," Trouble said on net, "that roadblock just cleared, but I'm afraid all the cops are moving in your direction."

"So I hear," Ruth allowed.

"I've got several Marine rigs headed your way. I see you meeting them in about six blocks." He gave her the coordinates, and she drove for them.

"Is this going to be a shoot-out at the OK Corral?" Gunny asked.

"It kind of looks it," Trouble said. "Milassi's guys are starting to get desperate."

"How's our ride coming?" Ruth asked.

"It's headed in. Izzy's flying one of them."

"Oh, Lord," Ruth said. "We're all in trouble."

Captain Umboto flew shuttles the way she lived: fast and wild. Considering the smell from the backseat, Ruth chose to keep that thought to herself.

"Can we make the pickup?" Ruth asked. "Is it my imagination, or are there a whole lot of police ahead of us?"

"That's what it's looking like to me, too, dear."

"Can you see some options ahead of us?"

"Wait one," her husband said.

FORTY-SIX

TROUBLE SAW ON his board what Ruth had intuitively concluded from her place on the ground. Milassi was concentrating his forces on the northeast side of town.

There, the roads led to the foothills and Bear Lake.

But the police weren't the only problem. A battalion of tanks had turned out of the line of elephants parading past Milassi.

A roadblock centered on a huge armored monster would have true authority.

It was time to change the game.

First, he advised Captain Umboto of what she faced and of the need to move the goal post.

"No problem, Trouble. I kind of expect trouble when I'm dealing with you."

Next, he called up several Marine rigs he had in the area and ordered them to meet up with Ruth. Then he backed them up with more. Just about everyone not returning with the colonel to the embassy was headed for the north side of town.

No need to be coy now.

Then he ordered the rentals to head off to the northwest, careful-like.

Quickly, the pieces came together. The only question was how much of a mess there would be when it was all done?

"Oh, this is going to be fun," Sergeant Daly said as he got their orders.

"What's up, Sarge?" Cyn asked from the backseat.

"You'll be so glad we didn't head back to the barn when you hear this, lovely."

"You 'lovely' me, and this better be good."

"We're riding interference for Ruth and Mary."

"I got no problem with that. Unless . . ." Cyn thought about the big, shit-eating grin the sarge was sporting. "What do you mean by 'interference'?"

"Head-to-head with these big black meanies."

Now Cyn had a grin of her own. She checked her magazine; she'd only used a dozen rounds or so. Still, she popped out the old one and slapped in a new ninety-round mag.

Alongside, Sarge picked up another SUV, this one with four Marines. The two of them drove down the road, Sarge in the right lane, the other one facing oncoming traffic.

There wasn't any traffic. Then they rounded a curve, and there was.

Lots of it.

The green sedan that Ruth had been standing by earlier in the day was leading a whole gang of black cars, their lights flashing.

Strange, their sirens were off.

The Marine rig next to them fell back, leaving plenty of room for the sedan to zoom by.

Then it pulled back into oncoming traffic and drove side by side with Sarge.

Suddenly, there were all kinds of sirens.

"How's this gonna work?" Cyn asked, checking her seat belt. It was tight.

"Their choice," Sarge said with a laugh. "I got all the road I need."

The cops took in this game of chicken.

And chickened out.

Black cars hit the curbs going sixty miles an hour as they fled from the charging Marine rigs.

One flipped. Another smashed into a house. A third hit a small, struggling tree and kept right on going into a lamppost. A fire hydrant stopped another in a gush of spouting water.

One car tried to brake but ended up sideways. Sarge braked and went right. The other Marine rig went left as they bounced over the curbs.

There were advantages to going a sedate thirty miles an hour.

Now, police cars were slamming into the backs of the cars ahead of them.

"I think we should get out of here," Sarge said, coming to a crossroad. He took a hard right. The other Marine went left.

Cyn turned in her seat to see what happened.

Two cars tried to make the turn but failed and slid into the houses on either side. The next two cars smashed into them. So did the third.

Only the fourth and fifth cars back managed to slow down, miss the mess, and tiptoe their way through the wreckage. Now, with lights and sirens blaring, they raced to catch up with Sarge or took off after the other rig.

"Cyn, take out their radiators."

"You bet, Sarge."

The way the day was going, Cyn didn't feel that she had to be chased for too long before she feared for her life.

Those are the rules of engagement, aren't they?

Three shots, and the first car fell out, spewing steam.

The second car had a good driver. He swerved from left to right, then back again.

Cyn didn't want to waste ammo. She also didn't want to have stray rounds wandering around this otherwise-nice neighborhood.

She waited.

The fellow had a bad habit of hanging out at the end of a swerve for a second before he turned back in. Cyn timed her shot carefully. As he reached the end of one swerve, she squeezed off three quick rounds.

His radiator gushed steam as he fell behind.

"When this mess is over, Sarge, we got to go into business for ourselves, importing radiators. I bet you there will be quite a market for new coolers. What do you think?"

"You just might have a deal there, gal. A real good deal. Let me report in, and we'll see what's happening.

Trouble looked upon what he had done and saw it was good.

Damn good!

Milassi had to be running out of cop cars. Or at least cop cars on the north side of town. Both Ruth and Mary had shed their tails. Ruth's following had self-destructed most spectacularly. That Cyn was quite a gunner as well as a looker.

Trouble had been worried about putting her out there today after what happened to her last week. Still, the Marine was aiming for the material, not the men, and she was doing a very good job of taking them all out.

The door to the spook den opened, and Trouble soon found he had both Colonel Ray Longknife and FSO Becky Graven at his elbow. Without taking his eyes from his developing board, he briefed them on what was happening. He borrowed a screen from the chief duty spook to rerun the take from the smashup of Ruth's tail.

"Outstanding," the colonel said.

"Not shabby at all," the diplomat said.

"Hard-core," Trouble said.

"I take it that all of you are quite happy, in your own way," the spook watch officer said.

"I think we said that," the colonel agreed.

"You haven't actually shot anyone?" the diplomat asked.

"Not one, ma'am. They're falling all over themselves like some kind of comedy routine. But so far, so good," Trouble admitted.

"Don't expect it to stay that way," the colonel said, rubbing his knee.

"We've got tanks moving across the bridge," the spook said, and Trouble's screen lit up to show fifty big armored mammoths ponderously rolling across the main bridge between the Presidential Palace and the north side of town.

"What does Milassi think he can use them for?" the diplomat asked.

"I have no idea," Trouble said, "but I suspect I'll find out soon enough."

FORTY-SEVEN

RUTH WEAVED HER way, block by block, through houses that sometimes had yards between them. Rear alleys still offered her a dodge if she needed one. Other roads were flanked by row houses packed in tight.

Whatever the neighborhood, Ruth zigged and zagged down roads and alleyways, careful to keep her speed down so she could turn at the first hint of trouble.

Here and there, cops would catch sight of her for a while, give chase, and lose her as she twisted from street to alley to street.

It was almost as if the cops didn't want to catch her.

"Honey, I think we have a problem," didn't sound at all nice from her husband.

"What kind of problem?" sounded like a dumb question, but she couldn't think of a better one, what with her mind on her driving.

"There are tanks headed out the main expressways."

"Tanks!" Ruth said, the same time as everyone else in the car.

"Yeah, tanks, Gunny. You know, those big heavy metal targets you like to shoot."

"Yeah, Skipper, but I don't have any heavy antitank rounds today," Gunny pointed out, somewhat unnecessarily.

"I know, Gunny."

"But they were in town, at the Presidential Palace, right?" Ruth pointed out.

"They were, but they're headed out your way using the two expressways."

"How fast can those things go?" Ruth asked.

"They're doing about forty, fifty kilometers an hour," Trouble answered, pain in his voice.

"They can't do that," Gunny snapped. "They'll throw a tread."

"Yep, you're right, Gunny. Four, no, make that five, have thrown treads and dropped out. There are still forty-five or so headed your way."

In the backseat, Debbie muttered something nasty.

"Honey," Ruth said, "if Milassi has those tanks start throwing their weight around, it's going to get real messy out here. Civilian casualties and stuff like that."

"Those tanks were hauled in for parade duty," Gunny remarked. "Would you give some tank driver a full weapons load to drive by the dictator?"

"Good point," Trouble told Gunny. "Still, he's got them moving out to intercept you. Maybe they've just got their weight and horsepower. Maybe they've got more."

"They got any infantry with them?" Gunny asked.

"None so far," Trouble answered.

"Well, thank God for minor favors," Gunny kind of prayed.

"What's Milassi's problem?" Ruth asked no one in particular. "We burned his dope. He has no seed crop to sell. What's he after?"

"Your head. Our ass. Their skin. Your guess is as good as anyone else's," her husband answered softly on net.

"It's not like we can go back and undo what we've done. We've won," Ruth pointed out, knowing it didn't matter.

"He's lost, but we can still lose too," came from a new voice online. "This is Colonel Ray Longknife. Let's be grateful for what we have. Whoever is calling the shots thinks tanks alone are mean enough to squish you. I think you can teach him a lesson. I understand that your gunners have some light antitank rockets."

"Yes, sir," Gunny said, maybe sitting up even more ramrod straight if that was possible.

"They aren't the best rounds for poking holes in heavy tanks, but the seal between hull and turret is a weak spot, as are the rear and sides of the tanks. If you can hit a road wheel or the struts supporting it, you can stop it in its tracks. Oh, there is one other weak spot. I came across it in a history book I read from way back in the bloody twentieth."

The colonel paused before going on. "They claimed that someone ricocheted a round off the deck and into the thin underbelly of one of those monsters. I can't claim to have tried that one, but it's in the history book."

"Was it a kinetic round, sir?" Gunny asked. "Or a fused explosive like we're firing?"

"I don't know, Gunny," Colonel Ray Longknife answered. "You'll have to try it and find out."

"Let me get this straight," came from Mary on net. "You're suggesting we take on these tanks?"

"What I'm saying is that Milassi is willing to kill a lot of his people to get at you and your packages. I suspect that we'll be pressured to surrender to save him from sacrificing his innocent civilians. Given that choice, if the tankers are willing to play Milassi's game, all we can do is kill tanks to save ourselves and the innocent," the colonel said.

"Anyone see another way around this?" Trouble asked.

"Nobody joins the Corps for a bed of roses," Gunny growled.

"Ooo-Rah," answered him on net.

"I'll start vectoring Marine rigs in on the package carriers. We'll try to get two of them running interference for each of you," Trouble said.

In the backseat, Debbie pulled the first of her antitank rockets from her bag and settled it in its place under the barrel of her rifle. It gave back a satisfying click.

"Lord, for what they are about to receive, may they be truly grateful," came almost with reverence.

What Ruth heard next was not at all reverent.

"Shit, that son of a bitch."

Trouble didn't normally talk like that.

"What's the matter, love?"

"Honey, there are tanks coming at you from every direction, and Milassi picked now to show us what he has. That SOB can jam our remotes, and he just did. Dear, you got tanks all around you, and, right now, I can't see a thing."

Now it was Ruth's turn to say some unladylike things that her mother would not approve of.

FORTY-EIGHT

ONE OF THOSE tanks picked that particular moment to turn onto the street directly in front of Ruth.

So Ruth slammed on the brakes and backed up the few meters it took her to dodge into the alley she had just passed.

She got out of that street a split second before she would have been blown out. The wind from the 122 mm round was powerful enough as it went by to give her sedan a decided shove.

The roar from its explosion as it blew out the front of the house at the corner of the alley was deafening.

Ruth gunned the sedan, and they took off.

"Next corner, stop and let me out," Debbie said.

Next corner had a Marine sedan waiting for them. A young Marine was already dismounted.

Cyn waved jauntily as Ruth passed. The Marine sedan fell in behind Ruth, clearly intent that the tank got at her over his dead body.

Ruth shivered but kept driving. She was just turning into another street when the tank turned up the alley.

Cyn edged her head around the concrete-block garage she was hiding behind.

The tank driver was sloppy as he made the turn. He took out the side of the building. Then again, his gunner's fire had taken out the front of it.

Out the back door, a woman with two small kids fled. One of the kids had blood running down her arm.

That kind of shit would not go down on Cyn's watch. She

brought up her M-6, adjusted the sights for an antitank rocket, and pulled the trigger.

The rocket headed down the alley like a bat out of hell. It took the tank right between the big ugly turret with the long phallic gun barrel and the tank's body.

Its explosion hardly marred the paint job.

"Damn," Cyn cursed as she loaded her next round.

"Anyone listening on net, I just tried a shot at between the turret and the hull of the tank, and it didn't work all that well. Now I'll try to bounce a rocket under the damn thing."

The gun's roar was truly deafening this close-up, but the round went long, blowing up the building behind Cyn.

She refused to cringe from all the debris flying around her. That was what body armor was for. She aimed her second rocket and fired.

It hit the deck right in front of the tank, then skittered beneath it to explode behind it.

A two-by-four took Cyn in the back as the wreckage from the house settled to the deck. She shrugged off the pain as she loaded her third round.

Cyn could feel the ground rumbling through her boots. She wouldn't get another shot. For a second she considered waiting until the tank passed her, but she shook that idea off. This bastard would likely drive *through* the garage to get at her rather than risk giving her a shot at its vulnerable side.

She stepped out from her cover, aimed the round at the deck just under the shadow of the tank's too-damn-close bow, and fired.

The rocket hit the deck—and bounced.

It hit the soft underbelly of the tank—and exploded.

For a moment longer, the tank rumbled forward. The main gun was coming down. Down until it was aimed right between Cyn's eyes.

Then there was a second explosion, this one bigger than the first. Now flames poured out the bottom of the tank. Smoke curled from several hatches.

Cyn ran for it.

Then the whole tank blew, and Cyn found herself flying

down the alley. She hit hard, but rolled rather nicely, she thought, her rifle still cradled in her arms.

Behind her, there were more explosions but they seemed aimed at the sky where the turret was hanging incongruously in midair.

It flipped several times before beginning its fall back to earth.

Cyn was glad that the wayward turret elected to fall on the side away from her. At the moment, she was feeling the pain and not at all ready to run.

Considering that other chunks of flaming tank were falling from the sky not that far from her, Cyn pried herself from the deck and began hobbling off, putting distance between her and her recent target.

The woman with the two kids came up, and with the woman on one side, the not-bleeding daughter on the other, they helped Cyn remove herself from harm.

"Folks on net, this is Cyn," she happily announced. "Scratch one tank. Comments on tank killing. Maybe I did it wrong, but that shot for the seal between the turret and the hull didn't scratch the paint. The first shot at bouncing one under the tank didn't do any better. My second shot was too damn close, but it hit the deck a bit more ahead of the tank, bounced nicely, and that tank is burning rather cheerily, thank you very much."

She paused to catch her breath before going on. "This idea of standing up front and personal with a tank sucks. I'd suggest you make like a little mouse and let it roll up next to you and then slip the rocket into the side armor. I was dumb but lucky the first time. I'll be smarter the next time."

"Thanks for the experience report, Corporal," Captain Tordon said on net. "Well done. Very well done again today. Sergeant Daly, can you pick up your wayward corporal?"

"Already headed that way, sir."

"Oh, Skipper, I got help from a mother and her two daughters after I killed that tank. One of her kids was hurt by the tank before I killed it. Would you mind if we took time out from this fine sport of tank hunting to get them to a hospital?"

"I think you've earned a break," Captain Trouble said on

net. "I would suggest that you drop her off outside the hospital. We aren't exactly loved by the local management today."

"Good suggestion, Skipper," Sergeant Daly said. "Will do."

Cyn spotted her ride coming up the alley toward them. She managed a weak wave.

She was glad she'd killed her dragon, but she wasn't all that sure she had another kill in her. She hoped Ruth had picked up a couple of more Marine escorts and could afford to let her and this kind woman lick their wounds for a bit.

FORTY-NINE

RUTH TWISTED AND turned, was spotted by tanks, and lost them only to be spotted by others, or a cop car, or both.

Most of the tanks didn't fire at her. Gunny thought that only the platoon and company commanders had carried ammo to the parade. None seemed to have ready machine-gun ammo.

Ah, who can fathom the thinking of a despot who wants to live forever?

Ruth dodged and, when necessary, the Marines escorting her took out a cop car.

Debbie fumed in the backseat that she was missing all the fun.

The two scientists regularly pleaded to be left on any street corner.

They actually thought they could just go back to their old jobs and all would be forgiven. At times, Ruth was sorely tempted to let them have their way.

Still, she kept the rear doors locked and drove despite their whining.

Tanks were getting thick on the ground. Ruth lost first one escort as it paused to distract a beast, then her second.

She was alone when a tank pulled onto the road in front of her.

"Turn here," Gunny shouted. He'd been studying the map more and more intently. Ruth hooked a hard left.

"Stop the first chance you get," he said.

It wasn't much of a stop. Little more than an unloading zone, but Ruth pulled in.

"Debbie, hand me your rifle and rockets," Gunny told the Marine who had been grumbling about missing all the fun.

"Gunny!" was her response.

"Marine, I've spent my entire career practicing how to take one of those beasts down. Are you going to deprive me of my one chance to actually bag one?"

With a few well-chosen words, the Marine passed her rifle and duffel bag to the front seat.

"Besides, if Ruth opened one rear door to let you out, those bozos would bolt out the other."

The aforementioned bozos said nothing. One had been working the door handle, trying to do just that, but failed. Now he sighed.

"Drive around the block," Gunny ordered. "If this works like I intend, you can pick me up when you drive by a flaming tank."

"Good luck," Ruth said, but her car was moving as soon as he closed the door.

Gunny Smith didn't watch the woman drive off. He could hear the rumble of the tank. He had work to do.

As the aerial photo showed, a garage stood in front of him. He covered the few paces to the back door, then had to kick it in.

It was your usual empty garage. The front wooden door on the right was half-open; the one on the left was closed. Gunny shrugged. *You take the fight you're handed.*

It was strange. He could feel the ground tremble under the pounding tank treads. That was not in the sims. He'd tell them to add that to the training device.

Other than that, he felt just like he had during a hundred practice sessions.

Even to the point where the first rocket refused to attach to the launcher on the M-6. He prayed the problem was with the rocket and not the launcher.

Some nice infantry god listened to his prayer.

The second rocket slid right into place with a reassuring click.

The M-6's computer connected with the rocket's tiny brain, and the red light came up bright on the rear of the blast deflector. He had a hot round.

And not a second too soon. The tank ground its way into view through the half-open front door.

Gunny took the approved stance, his back to the open back door, and squeezed off the rocket. He aimed for the sweet spot between the first and second road wheels, just as he shouted to give his ears a chance to survive the coming over-pressure wave.

The rocket shot off right as he pulled the trigger and whooshed to exactly where he aimed.

The explosion shattered the track, and the tank came to a halt as it rolled off its treads.

"You ain't going nowhere," Gunny said with a grin.

Unfortunately, the side armor had held the rocket's explosion out. The tank wasn't going anywhere, but it was a wounded beast with a whole lot of rage still inside.

The turret swung around. The gun slammed into the garage's wall, shaking the place to the rafters. The turret swung back out to get a stronger head of steam for the next swing, one that Gunny doubted the worn wooden shed could take.

Automatically, he'd reloaded. He fired again, shouting again as the rocket launched. He aimed for the same spot.

The tank shook this time, and the turret locked up where it was. Gunny could hear the servos struggling to move the turret, but, though the tank armor still held, the tank's hull was now out of true.

Gunny loaded a third rocket and fired it almost without thought.

The rocket hit again where he'd aimed the other two.

The explosion seemed smaller this time. For a second, he feared he had a dud. He was already rummaging in Debbie's duffel for the next rocket when the full impact of the hit began to eat the guts out of the tank.

There was a second explosion, then a third. Gunny began to backpedal through the back door. The tank now gaped, a large hole in its side. Through the hole, he could see fire.

He could also see the driver trying to pull himself from the tank, but he'd forgotten to unplug his headphones, and it hung him up for just the second it took for the next explosion to catapult him up, legless, from his vehicle.

Gunny quit sightseeing, turned, and took off running. He

was running past a solid brick building when the tank began to explode in earnest.

He turned the corner, to find a familiar-looking sedan waiting for him, door open and motor running.

He leapt inside and pulled the door shut as they gunned away from the curve.

"Didn't I tell you to drive around the block?" he growled as he pulled his seat belt on.

"Do you honestly think I could drive past that thing?" Ruth said, nodding toward the exploding fire behind them.

"Hmm, maybe I should have thought that through more."

"We're fine," Debbie said, though the scientists she shared the backseat with disagreed. "How'd it go, and can I have my rifle back?"

"Straight by the book," Gunny said. "Even to the point where the first rocket I loaded refused to arm," he said, passing said rifle to the demanding woman Marine.

"It wouldn't dare be any other way for you, Gunny," Debbie said with a laugh.

Ruth gunned the car up to sixty. A cop car started to get in her way, but it took one look at her, or maybe at the rising smoke behind her, and turned away.

FIFTY

CYN WAS FINALLY coming down from a wild adrenaline high. They'd dropped off the woman and her kids at the foot of the emergency entrance to the hospital. The unhurt girl had waved good-bye as her mother hurried the injured girl up the driveway.

"You think we can head back to the embassy?" Cyn asked.

"I think we've earned our pay today," Sergeant Daly allowed.

Then Cyn spotted the tanks.

"Go around the block again, Sarge," she ordered her superior. "Not a left, a right."

"Did you see something?"

"Maybe I did. Maybe I didn't."

The sergeant went around the block.

As they drove up the cross street, they could both see it plain as day. Two blocks up, at least two tanks were parked. The crews were out and doing something.

Sarge pulled the car over and, without a word, they dismounted. Cyn had her rifle, and she counted out three rockets left. Others had joked about taking more than the skipper authorized. Cyn had followed his orders.

She wouldn't make that mistake again.

Sarge was already peering around the corner. When he glanced back, he had a dark look on his face.

"They're transferring ammo from one tank to the other three."

Cyn nodded. Most of the tanks had only threatened to run you down, not that having a sixty-ton tank roll over your sedan wouldn't flatten you. Some platoon leader had gotten smart and was distributing the ammo wealth.

The sergeant reported their findings on net. Two more rigs were dispatched to support them, but they'd be a while arriving.

Sarge drew his automatic and signaled Cyn to cover him.

He trotted forward, weapon low, and disappeared into a doorway.

Cyn studied the tankers. They were all busy hauling up rounds from one tank and passing them across, bucket-brigade style before handing them up to another.

Cyn took the scene in and began forming a plan.

When Sarge signaled for her to advance past him, she slung her rifle low, unthreatened her silhouette, and, wishing she had on full battle armor, strode like a good civilian up the narrow alleyway to a loading zone.

She didn't see anything to add to her situation assessment. She signaled Sarge to move forward and across the street. He walked slowly until he ducked into the doorway across from her.

It wasn't going to get any better than this.

Cyn pulled back the arming handle on her M-6, checked that the safety was off, and leveled her weapon at the busy tankers. Across the way, the sarge stared at them over the sights of his automatic.

He nodded. Once. Twice. As he brought it down the third time, Cyn gently squeezed off a round aimed at the guy about to hand off the shell he'd just lifted from inside the tank.

She hit him square in the chest. He stood there for a second, shell tumbling from his hand, staring at the fountain of blood gushing from his chest—then crumpled.

Cyn was already aiming for the next guy. He got a bullet in the back instead of the 122 mm shell he'd been reaching for.

Cyn skipped one, but went for the guy next to him. He was turning to hand off a shell. She put a bullet in his back, which spun him around as the live round fell from his hands.

Sarge was firing more and hitting less. It was a bit long for a hand gun. Still, no one was thinking of moving ammunition anymore. Everyone was hitting the dirt or scrambling to put a tank between them and the source of the incoming.

Cyn figured they had a minute, maybe less, before one of the 122 mm shells was aimed at her head.

She fit her first rocket and aimed it at the round that had come to a rolling halt on the tank.

She fired it just right, but the rocket only nipped the shell and sent it spinning off the tank even as the antitank rocket only scorched the monster.

Cyn loaded the next round and aimed it at the shell on the deck. She was about to pull the trigger when she realized she didn't have a red light.

She gently resettled the rocket in place, but it refused to click.

Swearing to herself, Cyn pulled her last round from her bag. Carefully, she sighted it for the deck a few centimeters this side of the shell on the deck. Muttering if not a prayer, then a petition not to screw up, she pulled the trigger.

The rocket flew hot and straight, hitting the deck just a bit short of the target shell and then skittering forward to impact right on the shell's fuse.

Rocket, shell, and everything close by blew with all the force God authorized.

Screams came from scorched lungs. The two nearest tanks caught fire.

Then another shell contributed to the excitement.

A man ran screaming, his clothes on fire. Sarge, across the way, put a bullet in him. He fell, still screaming. Sarge's second round blew out his brains and gave him peace.

Cyn looked at her bad round and decided it wasn't doing any good where it was. With a shout, she threw it overhand at the mess. It landed on its nose and added another explosion to the flames.

Another tank, however, was grinding forward, its turret coming out of train and swinging around at Cyn.

She made a quick dash across the street to join Sarge. "We got a tank rolling."

"There's always one that doesn't get the word. You think it has a round up the spout?"

"It's acting like it does."

Sarge looked up the alley to the next street. There were also several back doors into the houses and stores.

Sarge risked a glance around the corner. "Yep, that tank's pushing one we fried out of the way. Maybe it's time for us to boogie."

But before they could turn to run, there was an explosion,

followed quickly by another. Sarge peeked around the corner again and laughed.

"The Marines have landed, and the tanks are roasting."

Cyn allowed herself another peek. The tank that had been shoving one out of the way was now going nowhere. It burned with the rest.

There was a roar as a fourth tank fired up its engines, but that was quickly followed by several rockets going off in quick succession.

"I wonder if they'll try that stunt again?" Sarge asked no one in particular. "Me, I always figured tank guys for the type never to get out from behind all that metal when bullets were flying. What you want to bet me that any more ammo transfers take place a long ways from here?"

"No way I'll take that bet," Cyn said, and when the call came on net to pack it in and head out, she and Sarge did just that.

FIFTY-ONE

RUTH FOLLOWED THE chatter on net. And yes, the Marines were chattering in their elation. They could not only dodge tanks and take them down when they were chased, but they'd gone hunting tanks and burned them where they stood.

The Marines were happy.

And Ruth was starting to feel almost as happy. Despite the grousing from the backseat, they were out of town and headed toward Clear Lake. She would have loved to have her husband give her a report on where the cops and tanks were, but her own eyes were telling her that they were not around her.

Now that they were out of town, there were only two roads they could drive. Ruth began to catch sight of more and more of her rentals. There were a few big SUVs with Marines in them, but mostly it was just the small cars with one scientist each.

Maybe the cars with only one bozo had it better. The two in Ruth's backseat were now arguing whose fault it was that they were in this mess.

But when Debbie asked if she could just shoot them, Gunny refused permission.

Sad to say, that only silenced the pair for a few moments. Soon, they were back to bickering.

Ruth heard the sonic booms before she saw the contrails from the two shuttles. Now she had to decide what to do next. There was no question that the fifteen scientists had to go up to the *Patton*.

The question was, who else should take the easy ride out?

Once the scientists were out of reach, even Milassi would have to admit there was little he could do about it. Ruth herself, however, was only too well-known. As much as she hated the idea of leaving Trouble alone dirtside, she should think about staying well out of reach of the local cops for a while until things worked their way out down here.

So, as Ruth watched the shuttles settle into Clear Lake with a spray of white and steam, she knew she'd have to take the ride up. As the cars collected at the landing, and Marines spread out to secure a perimeter, Ruth went looking for Mary.

"How's your day gone?" she asked.

"So-so. Seen a few tanks. Blew a few up. You know, the usual day at the office," the Marine officer said through an exhausted grin.

Ruth found herself wondering if she looked that bad and decided she probably did.

"I'm going to ride the shuttle up and stay a few days on the *Patton* until things settle down. Milassi knows me and would likely do his best to take this out of my hide."

Now the Marine scowled. "Milassi knows me all too up close and personal."

Ruth nodded. "I was kind of thinking that."

Mary looked around at the Marines going about their duties with little supervision from their sergeants and officers. "I hate to look like I'm bugging out on my troops."

"I could tell Trouble, that in my professional capacity as an officer of the Alcohol, Drug, and Explosives Enforcement Agency I think you should take some time as far from Milassi's clutches as possible."

When Mary's scowl got even deeper, Ruth quickly added, "In my advisory capacity, I assure you. Or I could go to Izzy herself and have her make it an order."

"I'm not in her chain of command," Mary quickly pointed out.

"You want me to go to your colonel? What's his name?"

"Ray Longknife. You do fight dirty," Mary said through a scowl.

"I like to keep my friends alive," Ruth said.

Mary tapped her commlink. "Trouble, is Colonel Ray Longknife there?"

"At my elbow," Trouble answered.

"And paying very close attention, even if there isn't a lot to watch," came in the colonel's voice.

"Mrs. Tordon, the Alcohol, Drug, Explosives and general

pain in the neck Agent, has pointed out that I made the acquaintance of president-for-life-or-much-shorter face-to-face. She thinks I ought to spend some quality time back on the *Second Chance* while things sort themselves out down here."

"I was about to make the same suggestion or order it if necessary," the colonel said.

"I figured as much. I hate it when people are right and I don't want to hear it," Mary said.

"Well, you get yourself on one of the *Patton*'s shuttles all by your lonesome, and you won't have to listen to us being right."

"Mary over, out, and off this planet," she grumbled.

That settled, Ruth went looking for her two former passengers. She found them still arguing.

"Captain Izzy Umboto is flying one of those shuttles," Ruth pointed out. "She doesn't stand for any shit. So, whichever one of you has got the smelly pants, you get your sorry ass down into that cold lake water and clean yourself up. Otherwise, you can expect her to have you strip naked before you board her clean shuttle."

Shamefaced, both of them stepped gingerly into the lake and began cleaning themselves up.

Ruth began to think this might end with no more nail-biting, but as the shuttles approached the landing, word came down from the lookouts on the ridge above the lake.

"We got a platoon of tanks coming up the road."

Mary quickly asked on net, "Trouble, how do you want to do this?"

"Do they have infantry with them?" came back just as quick.

"That's a negative, Skipper. They haven't learned a thing."

"You got to love them when they're dumb," Trouble said with a bit of a chuckle. "My photos show brush along the road approach to the ridge above the lake."

"That's what I saw on the drive in," Mary agreed.

"May I suggest that you deploy a dozen Marines with anti-tank rockets to meet those tanks halfway? Spread the troops out in the brush before the tanks get there. If they want a fight, they can have it with us on their flanks. We'll eat their lunch."

Mary quickly ordered Lieutenant Dumont and Gunny to

select a dozen troops, assure that they had plenty of rockets, and get them down the road pronto. That done, she turned to the shuttles and began getting everything organized to get fifteen scientists on board.

FIFTY-TWO

CYN FIGURED SHE had a right to head back to the embassy for a cold one, but somehow, she and Sarge ended up at the lake with the rest. She expected it would be a cakewalk the rest of the day. With luck, she might actually get to cool off with a swim in the lake.

The day had sure been hot enough.

The shuttle was already down, and she was wondering if the guys would keep their underwear on . . . and if they didn't, would she? . . . when someone reported more tanks incoming.

She'd shot herself dry. She had the right to wave someone else off and wish them good hunting.

She'd done her duty; it was time for someone else to take a turn in the barrel.

But when Gunny waved her over, she went. And when he stripped rockets off others and loaded them in her duffel, she didn't say a word.

He assigned Debbie to work with her. Perchance to shoot more dragons.

They piled into two SUVs, all fourteen who'd been chosen, and barreled down the road until tanks came into view over a low hill. The lead rig with that Lieutenant Dumont from Mary's team just kept on driving.

Gunny let out a low whistle but kept his rig right on the lieutenant's tail.

They couldn't have been more than five klicks from the tanks when the lead rig slammed on its brakes and came to a screeching halt sideways across the road.

Gunny ordered their driver to block the rest of the road. As soon as they halted, he shouted, "Out! Out! Deploy! Take cover, and keep those safeties on until they fire or we order it."

Cyn and Debbie were out of the rig and running. Several of the troops went to ground fast, but Cyn kept running, and Debbie followed.

Once they were deep enough in the brush that it provided cover, Cyn started edging forward. She wanted to be within four hundred yards of the tanks with a solid shot at their thinner side armor.

"How many tanks did you get today?" Debbie whispered.

"Two or three," Cyn said, trying to sound humble, but she was grinning and not doing humble at all well.

"Damn. I hope I get a shot at one of those bastards."

"You can have mine."

"You'll let me take the first shot?"

Cyn considered that and knew very well what the answer was. "Not likely, but there are five of them and only two of us. What's that, a target-rich environment?"

"I think that's what The Book calls it."

They were a good two hundred meters from the road, and about six hundred forward of where the officers' rigs sat. Gunny had gone to ground, but the lieutenant from Mary's detachment stood in front of his rig, rifle slung but with an antitank rocket already loaded.

"What's that guy doing?" Debbie wondered out loud.

"Putting his marker down. This far you may go, and no farther."

"He want to be the first to die?"

"Either that, or he's letting them know he don't scare easy." Cyn had found where she wanted to go to ground and did, behind several thick bits of brush that offered her good cover, small protection, but a good fire lane to the road.

The tanks lumbered up, shaking the air with their power. But they quit rumbling a good klick back from where the lieutenant stood.

The lead turret opened, and an officer stuck his head cautiously above the hatch. He looked around and seemed pained that he could see so little.

"You there," he shouted. "You're blocking the road."

"It sure looks like I am," the lieutenant answered.

"Make way for the 2nd Brigade."

"You look more like a platoon to me."

"I am the commander of the 2nd Armored Brigade. Get out of my way."

"And I am a lieutenant in the Society of Humanity Marine Corps and we kicked your butts in the war. Quit bothering me."

"You did not kick our butts. We never deployed."

That was a mistake.

"I know *you* didn't. I *did* deploy."

"You are not making sense. Are you drunk?"

"Nope. I've drunk no beer today. Only tank driver's blood."

That put the tank driver in his place. He looked around a bit. His glance swept past where Cyn was lurking but it didn't stop. As she expected, he saw nothing.

What kind of dumb-ass tank jockey tools around town with no infantry?

"I'll tell you one last time," he finally shouted. "Get out of my way, or I will push your puny vehicles out of my way."

"That would not be wise," was all the lieutenant said.

Cyn was content for them to keep up this pissing contest for as long as they wanted. All she had to do was close her eyes, and she could hear again the screams of dying men. Smell the stink of burning flesh.

She kept her eyes open.

Behind her, a roar began, then grew almost earsplitting. She glanced up. Two darts climbing fast into the cloudless blue sky. What the tankers had come for was on those space-bound ships.

Did that proud brigade commander know his goose had flown?

Or would it have to be cooked as well?

Apparently he knew when the game was up. He followed the shuttles with his eyes for a long moment, then dropped back into his tank and swung the hatch closed with a clank.

A moment later, the tanks did a neutral steer about-face in place. It made a mess of the road, but tankers didn't ever seem to worry much about that.

In a moment, the tanks were headed back the way they had come. The lieutenant waited until they were all over the hill before he signaled his troops in. After receiving orders from the skipper, they mounted up and cautiously followed the tanks back into town.

The beer that night in the embassy cafeteria was on Colonel Ray Longknife. Cyn couldn't remember tasting any that good in her life.

FIFTY-THREE

MARY FELL ASLEEP on the shuttle ride up; she was that tired.

They docked on the *Patton* rather than the space station to make sure there was no interference with the scientists. Mary quickly paid her respects to Captain Umboto and was granted permission to head for the *Second Chance* and her bunk.

Gladly, she went.

Maybe it was because she was so tired, or maybe it was because she'd shoved tanks around today and was just pure out of shove. Later, Mary would try to explain what she did that afternoon on the station, but she was never fully satisfied with any of her answers.

Anyway, a ship had just docked on High Petrograd and was unloading a stream of passengers. She paused to let them pass, leaning against a handy stanchion, and almost fell asleep listening to her breathing.

Suddenly, she was wide-awake and glaring.

There was a bigwig. So big that someone from Milassi's own entourage was there, guiding the man in uniform.

Mary remembered that henchman. He was the one who had paid her not to go to the back room with the big man.

But it was the other guy who held her glower.

He wore the uniform of a full admiral. Only it wasn't quite right for the Society of Humanity Navy. The color of his blues was a tad too bright, and the stripes of his rank were in a twisted weave rather than the straight lines of regular Navy.

Rather than a five-pointed star, his stripes ended in a starburst.

Mary used her commlink to snap a picture. Then snapped several more.

What is Admiral Whitebred doing here, of all places? she demanded of nothing, and got no answer.

Whitebred had been cashiered from the Society Navy for ordering the *Sheffield*, now the *Second Chance*, to relativity bomb Wardhaven back to the Stone Age, killing a billion humans in the process.

Mary had played her own small part in seeing that it didn't happen. Whitebred had been whisked away shortly after to face a court-martial.

Mary had fond hopes of never seeing him again.

Now, her thoughts came quickly. Nothing good could come of the failed butcher of Wardhaven showing up on the arm of one of Milassi's henchmen. As soon as the parade of disembarking passengers slowed down, Mary made a beeline for the *Second Chance* and Captain Abeeb.

"We got company," she said, shoving her pictures under his nose.

"Him! In uniform again!" was Abeeb's first answer.

"A full admiral, if those stripes mean anything. But the uniform is all wrong," Mary pointed out.

"Computer," Captain Abeeb said. "Capture Mary's picture. Analyze the uniform. What Navy is that?"

"The color of the blues uniform and the weaving of the rank stripes appear to be appropriate for the Savannah Navy. However, no one in that Navy rose above the rank of captain in the recent war. President-for-life Milassi has been photographed wearing a Navy admiral's uniform with the stripes of a full admiral."

"Savannah Navy! Savannah doesn't have a Navy," Mary almost spat. "What kind of game is Milassi running?"

"Or Whitebred," Captain Abeeb mused. "Wearing the same rank as Milassi. Whatever game either one of them thinks he's playing, it predates the predicament you dropped in both their laps today."

Captain Abeeb chuckled at the thought and shared a wide grin, showing his white teeth off against his ebony complexion. "Computer, connect me to Colonel Ray Longknife. He will want to know that the man who almost slaughtered his planet just arrived here and wears a uniform once more."

The computer made the connection. Captain Umboto of

the *Patton* was added, and Mary quickly brought them all up-to-date on what she'd just seen.

"Savannah Navy? They can't have their own Navy anymore," was Umboto's immediate input. "We're all just one big happy family in the Society of Humanity. Those local navies and armies are supposed to be vanishing away."

"I'm still a colonel in the Wardhaven Army," Colonel Ray Longknife pointed out. "Though I thought we were frozen in ranks and status."

"Want to bet Whitebred's rank was backdated to before they locked everyone in?" Mary said, making a sour face.

"What matters today is his employer or employers, as the case may be," Captain Abeeb pointed out. "Just exactly who was giving him an extra paycheck when he ordered my ship to pound Wardhaven has never been identified. It leaves me to wonder if Milassi knows exactly who he has hired."

"Yes," Colonel Ray Longknife said. "I'm pretty sure Whitebred left the software in the *Second Chance* that caused the bad jump that almost killed us. We will definitely keep an eye out for him down here. Abeeb, you might want to have someone hang around the station A deck. No telling what else we might see."

"I'll do that," Captain Abeeb said.

But as it turned out, he couldn't.

A couple of dozen thugs showed up at the gangplank of both the *Patton* and the *Second Chance*. They made it clear to anyone who tried to leave that it wasn't going to happen.

A few minutes later, the power from the station cut off, then communications went down. Water and sewer were the last to be cut off, but they were.

The two cruisers were totally isolated.

Captain Umboto reported this by radio to Colonel Ray Longknife just before jamming cut even that line of communications.

FIFTY-FOUR

"WE'RE UNDER SIEGE," Colonel Longknife told Captain Trouble and FSO Graven at the same time. "Double the guard and close the gate."

The night passed quietly, but by morning, the local employees couldn't make it to work through the ring of cops around the embassy. Midmorning, the power was cut as well as the landlines.

The ambassador insisted on being driven to Savannah's foreign ministry to demand services be restored, and quickly.

His limo was halted within a block of the embassy. Rough men in civilian clothes dragged him and his driver from their car and began beating them.

Gunny saw it from the front gate and sounded the alarm. Trouble was out of the basement in a flash and personally led the rescue party. The attackers fled before the relief column got to the ambassador, but the long walk back one block to the embassy saw them surrounded by a second mob that closed in while those in the back hurled rocks.

More Marines arrived. These, under Gunny, were in armor and had fixed bayonets. The surly crowd gave way.

The ambassador was unconscious when they got him to sick bay.

"Can we rush him to the nearest hospital?" FSO Graven asked Colonel Ray Longknife. She was now the *chargé d'affaires.*

"Do you think he'd get any farther headed for a hospital than he got headed for the ministry?"

She shook her head, and the ambassador stayed under the care of the embassy doctor in sick bay.

The crowd outside got noisier. Thugs with badges fell back

to the other side of the street and seemed more intent on watching the show than doing anything about it.

Colonel Ray Longknife suggested Trouble deploy his troops in full battle gear.

The embassy Marines had no such equipment, but Trouble's and Mary's detachments had come fully equipped for battle . . . even if that hadn't been considered a part of the plan.

Now the embassy Marines fell back from the fence as Marines in full battle rattle, bayonets fixed, took their places in the line.

The crowd took one look at them and fell silent. A lot of them seemed to suddenly remember it was suppertime and left.

"No doubt they'll be back later tonight, very well lubricated," Trouble told the colonel.

"No doubt."

They did come back, with rocks to throw. But that didn't work out as well as they thought it would. Several of the embassy Marines had recently acquired sling shots with a goodly supply of ball bearings.

Trouble deployed them on the embassy's roof, under Lieutenant Dumont, who had some recent experience with unruly crowds.

Someone threw a rock. A Marine returned fire with a ball bearing.

The mob might be drunk, but its individual members seemed educable. If someone near you threw something, someone near you stopped a fast, hard object.

And that someone might be you.

The mob thinned out a whole lot faster than the folks who had hired it expected.

Come midnight, it was even possible for a kid to make it in across the fence.

He looked in bad shape, but he insisted the Marines take him to "Momma Ruth" before they care for him.

Trouble came immediately.

He knelt beside the child. "Ruth is my wife. She's safe on a cruiser in orbit."

"That's good that she's safe," the boy said. "Major Barbara says that I should warn you. They burned out her place."

"Is she okay?" Trouble asked.

"Yes. Us kids got warnings from some of the people in the neighborhood that the crushers were coming. Major Barbara got everyone out before they got there. They ripped the place apart, then burned it. But we was lucky. Brother Scott got it worse."

"What happened there?" Trouble asked, afraid for what he'd hear.

"They didn't get warned. They beat them up real bad. They did horrible things to the nuns, Major Barbara says, but we don't know it all. Then they burned them down, too."

Trouble had been getting reports from the lookouts on the roof that there were a lot of fires burning in the city, but no sound of sirens or visuals of fire engines racing to do their duty.

Apparently, Milassi's idea of duty was getting very narrow.

Trouble sent the kid to sick bay before returning to his place in the basement. Colonel Ray Longknife hadn't left the command center since he got back from Milassi's parade.

Trouble quickly brought Ray up to speed.

"Milassi has gone crazy," Ray said. "He's lashing out at anything he can, but it's not going to do him any good. The dope crop is burned, and his employer can't be happy about that."

"How long before someone delivers that message?" the FSO asked.

"I don't know," Ray admitted. "But I have to wonder about this Admiral Whitebred. Did Milassi hire him for some job, or was he sent here by Milassi's boss to do something?"

"It can't be a response to us burning the drugs," Becky pointed out. "That just happened."

"Yes, but how will that play into this?" Ray asked no one in particular.

"We're bound to find out."

"Of course, what we find could be a howling mob coming over our fence," Trouble said.

"Captain, may I suggest that you prepare for that while we prepare for other alternatives," said Colonel Ray Longknife.

Trouble went to check his guards. He arranged for half his troops to get at least four hours' sleep.

No doubt, tomorrow would be another long day full of creative leadership challenges.

FIFTY-FIVE

WHEN WORD CAME, it was from a surprising source for Savannah.

The noon news reported that President-for-Life Steffo Milassi had chosen now to take a vacation. While he was gone, war hero Admiral Horatio Whitebred would exercise executive powers.

Shortly after that announcement, the jamming of radio communications between the embassy and the cruisers switched off. As it turned out, the *Second Chance* had patched themselves into the station's security cameras. They had full color coverage of Milassi as he arrived with his large entourage and was trundled around A deck to the liner that had just brought in Whitebred.

The ship wasn't due to seal air locks until the following day, although the *Second Chance* intercepted several demands from the great man that they depart immediately.

That was mighty inconsiderate of him, seeing that throughout most of the day, shuttles were docking, and more of his henchmen were themselves making the journey across A deck to what looked more and more like the last ship out under the Milassi administration.

The liner departed on schedule, apparently stuffed to the gills with loot and looters.

Izzy was heard to darkly mutter about the need for the *Patton* to have some target practice, but the liner got away without any of the justice, poetic or otherwise, that it so dearly deserved.

That left Savannah to pick up the pieces of his ten-year Reich.

Old habits die hard, though, and the State Security Special

Police were just as heavy-handed with their brutality as they had ever been.

Ms. Becky Graven, by right of her being the *chargé d'affaires*, demanded to see the admiral. He met with her, but at a place of his choosing.

That place was the burned-out experimental drug farm.

There he gave her a cock-and-bull story that the plants were part of a pharmacological effort to get a new cure for cancer, heart disease, and the common cold.

"I will personally see to it that the criminals who did this are prosecuted to the full extent of the law and that what few plants survived are propagated with care."

He didn't seem to be all that concerned that the planet around him was going to hell in a handbasket.

Becky returned fuming and used words that weren't at all diplomatic.

Colonel Ray Longknife turned to Trouble. "Then it seems that it's up to us to do what we can to restore peace and order to this member of the Society of Humanity before the arrival of the senators. Becky, when are they due here?"

"Tomorrow originally," she said, "but we've got more time. It seems the senators were delayed on New Amsterdam. They've got some very entertaining, ah, entertainment the senators felt they needed to closely examine, if you know what I mean."

"Did Milassi have anything to do with New Amsterdam ending up on their agenda?" Ray asked.

"He may have. Who knows? But one of my contacts says that Milassi did ask them to delay a bit. That message went out right after the fire at the farm and before Whitebred arrived."

"And, no doubt, they were happy to accommodate him."

"So I'm told," Becky said.

"For now, we have as much of a free hand as we may choose to take," Colonel Ray Longknife said with a tight grin. "Becky, can you get some interplanetary messages sent?"

"I think I can. What do you have in mind?"

"One of the toughest bunch of infantry that I ever had the misfortune to be on the wrong side of in a war was the light infantry from Lorna Do. Their roots go back to Scotland on Old Earth, as does their fondness for the kilt. Ladies from

Hell, they call themselves, and I'm not one to gainsay them. Can you get off a message, as an official of the Society of Humanity, asking Lorna Do for the use of several of their battalions for peacekeeping purposes here on Savannah?"

"That usually requires authorization from way above my pay grade," Becky said.

"If we're going to keep this place from tearing itself apart, we need to move fast. All of us need to ratchet up our games to way above what they pay us," Ray said.

Becky ran her tongue along her teeth for a moment. "Hell, I didn't really want to do this job until I retired. Colonel Ray Longknife, you will have your request out just as fast as I can get to the comm center. What Lorna Do will do with the request is anybody's guess."

"And that may well depend on what I say in my message to another old broken-down warhorse."

They left together to get their messages off.

That night, Colonel Ray Longknife stood on the embassy roof and watched as more fires broke out throughout the city. Which of them were set by thugs with badges and which were to settle age-old feuds was impossible to say from this distance.

What was clear was that if someone didn't stop it, there might not be much of a city here in a week or two.

Trouble joined him on the roof.

"You getting a breath of air?" the colonel asked.

"It was a bit thick down in the basement."

"No doubt we must ask Becky for permission to air the place out."

"Do you think we could do it tomorrow without getting a boatload of bugs?" the Marine said.

Ray made a face. "Nope. This place must be thick with the things."

"But we haven't had any more jamming since the liner pulled out. Could the guy running Milassi's electronic gear have bugged out, too?"

Ray shrugged. "Toward the last, they were leaving with not much more than the shirts on their backs. We'll have to wait a few days and see."

Trouble made a point of surveying the horizon. There

were at least a dozen fires standing out in the night. "If we wait too long, there might not be anything to see."

"Yes, there is that. Captain, I would like to talk to you about a mission for tomorrow."

"What kind?" Trouble asked, with a big grin he failed to suppress.

Ray suspected that the Marine was desperate to get outside these walls. He weighed the risks versus benefits and found it good.

"It will involve getting up early tomorrow morning, but I think you'll love the idea."

"Getting up early, enjoying the morning air. I'm already loving it."

"Then let me tell you what I have in mind."

Trouble's grin grew wider and wider.

FIFTY-SIX

THE MORNING WAS getting hot early, but at least Trouble's Marines had shade on their side of the street. Though the thugs were hunkered down, lying about the veranda of their headquarters, the sun was streaming in low and heating up where they sat.

And they were drinking—lots.

Though they were officially State Security Special Police, they were universally known as crushers or black boots. And as such, they were hated.

None of the police here were any great shakes, but these guys were the worst.

So Colonel Ray Longknife suggested that Trouble and his Marines take them off the streets.

It had started early in the morning, though it need not have. Trouble and his Marines from the *Patton* arrived outside their headquarters at first light to find Savannah's best sleeping it off. He secured the gates to the parking lot with chains, locks, and just in case someone was slow to get the message, some nice explosives to back up the lock.

Trouble had stationed Gunny on that side of the building with a platoon and orders to see that no police car left.

About nine, Gunny reported that someone insisted on raising the gate. There had been a small explosion after that, and the Marines had provided quick transport to the nearest hospital.

The initial report was that the hand would have to come off.

Trouble's demolition expert had frowned at that. "A finger, likely, but the whole hand, sir? We didn't use that much explosives."

"Maybe the level of care has something to do with the guy needing it," Trouble said.

The demolition man nodded. "Likely he hasn't been using that hand for all that much good. No doubt the doc doesn't think he'll miss it that much."

"Kind of what I was thinking," Trouble said. If they couldn't get a legal system in place quickly to resolve these age-old festering problems, there would be a lot of rough justice like this, and not all of it would only cost a hand.

Trouble was prevented from further reflection when one of the inhabitants of the headquarters in front of him stumbled out onto the veranda and shouted, "What da ya think you're doing here?"

Trouble came to a loose attention and kind of saluted. "I am Captain Tordon of the Society of Humanity Marine Corps, and I have orders to keep your people off the streets today."

The guy shouted for Trouble to do something he loved to have Ruth do, but could hardly do himself. It came out slurred, no doubt from the night before. To confirm Trouble's opinion, the guy shouting the question reached behind him and waved his hand.

Someone put a bottle in it, and he drank long and hard before shouting, "We're the Special Police. No one stands in our way."

"We stand here, and we stand in your way."

"You can't."

"We can indeed," Trouble said, doing his best to keep a grin off his face. Maybe he succeeded. "My superiors have ordered us into peacekeeping mode under the charter of the Society of Humanity. Savannah, recently being in arms against the Society and now being surrendered to the same, has been determined to be suffering from civil disorder. You, sir, and your so-called police have been identified as a major cause of civil disorder. You may not leave your headquarters today."

"And who's gonna stop us?" was delayed by another long swig on the bottle

"We will, sir," Trouble said, simply.

"We'll see about that," he shouted, and went back inside.

Over the next hour, more and more Special Police in

various stages of inebriation and disheveled dress settled down on the chairs across from the Marines. They flaunted their machine pistols for all the Marines to see.

Across the street, Marines stood with their backs to the wall of the brick building behind them and kept their hands off their triggers.

It went that way as the sun rose higher in the sky. The heat of the day came in with hammers, and more bottles got emptied on the veranda.

"How's it look in back?" Trouble asked Gunny.

"Every half hour or so someone comes out to take a look at us and make sure we're still here. I wave friendly-like, and they scowl and stomp back into their headquarters. How's it look at your end, sir?"

"About the same, only less friendly. A lot of drinking going on."

"That's not good."

"I didn't expect today to be good for them," Trouble said, darkly.

"See you, sir, when this is over."

A half hour later, Trouble's commlink sounded.

"Trouble here," he said.

"Colonel Ray Longknife here. We just fielded a call from someone who said he was Milassi's personal secretary. I pointed out that Milassi's personal office was no longer in this system, and he corrected to say that he was Admiral Whitebred's personal secretary. The guy was slow, but able to adjust. He ordered us to withdraw you. I refused to do so. He said Whitebred would personally call me back. That was fifteen minutes ago, and I've heard nothing."

"I doubt you will."

"So do I; however, I think your situation is about to reach the boiling point."

"So do I, sir. Now, if you'll excuse me, I think I hear the teapot whistling."

"Good luck, Captain."

"The same to you, Colonel. Trouble out."

Now he walked down the line of his troops. "Hold it tight, but you may rest your fingers on the trigger. Safety off. Expect trouble anytime now."

He was answered by soft "Ooo-Rahs" and clenched fists.

Across the street, a phone rang. The guy Trouble had tagged for the boss man answered it on the second ring. From the looks of it, he didn't much like the answer he got. He slammed the receiver down and glanced around.

His men met his eyes. Trouble considered them way too bleary, but they weren't Marines and never would be.

The boss man nodded.

As one, the men rose from their chairs, brought their machine pistols up, and opened fire.

As one, the Marines brought their M-6s up to their shoulders, got a solid sight picture on a gunner, and squeezed off a round.

Behind Trouble, bullets pocked the red bricks, sending dust flying.

Across from him, thug after thug took a bullet to the chest or stomach. Some went down, screaming. Others became enraged and fired even as they fell.

Single shots rang out from the Marines, dropping those who had survived the first volley. Then more single shots took those that were still firing even as they withered on the ground.

The last machine pistols fell silent. Two shots later, the M-6s did the same.

"Medic," came from down the line.

"It's just a flesh wound," a woman Marine snapped back. "I've bled more from my period. I don't need no medic. I can handle it myself."

"Have a medic look at it," Trouble shouted, and turned to the carnage across from him. He tapped his commlink. "Memorial Hospital, please."

A second later, a pleasant voice allowed that he had reached, "Memorial Hospital. How may we help you?"

"This is Captain Tordon of the Society of Humanity Marines. We are on peacekeeping duty here. There has been an incident at the headquarters of the State Security Special Police. There are many special police down and bleeding from gunshot wounds."

"How many of them, sir?"

"All of them, I think," Trouble said.

"That sounds wonderful. Now don't you worry about them one bit, sir. We'll have our ambulances around to collect them real soon now." She paused. "Oops, they've all just left for lunch, sir, but they'll get right on it as soon as they get back. You did say all of them, didn't you, sir?"

Trouble noted that no one had come out of the building once the firing stopped.

"Yep, it looks like all of them to me."

"Well, you just mosey on sir, and we'll be around real soon."

Trouble had put the hospital on speaker for the last bit of their conversation. Two medics listened, then cast each other worried glances as they also took in the carnage across the street.

Clearly, they were torn between their duty to those in pain and their duty to those these people had put in pain. If the locals took off for lunch when they heard they were needed to care for this bunch of bullies, should the Marines be any more concerned?

As if to settle the matter, one of the wounded worked his way up on an elbow and tried to raise his machine pistol. Three Marines added more rounds to his wounds, at least one to the head.

Thus ended the last stand of the Special Police.

"Mount up, Marines," Trouble ordered. The medics went where he ordered. With several walking backward to make sure no one else tried a final shot, the Marines headed for their rides home.

"Gunny, it's over on this side. You got any action on yours?"

"Not a damn thing, sir. How'd it go?"

"Cyn got a flesh wound that she doesn't think was all that much, but I'll have a medic look at it before we roll."

"What about the Special Police?"

"I've reported their situation to the nearest hospital. Memorial reports that they'll have someone right over, once they finish the lunch they all bolted for right after the call came in."

"So it's that way, huh? Ah, sir, are you leaving all those weapons lying around unsecured?"

Trouble frowned. That was a problem. But one of the street

kids was standing there beside the road as the Marines marched by.

"Hey, kid."

"Yes, sir."

"We'll pay five hundred dinars for any of those guns brought to the embassy this afternoon."

"Five hundred dinars!"

"You bet."

The kid suddenly had a half dozen pals coming out of the woodwork. They lit out for the headquarters.

As the Marines loaded up, there would be an occasional shot from where they'd come. No doubt, someone didn't want to part with his weapon.

Trouble made sure to give Cyn a hand, though he had to be careful. That woman did not want any special help even when he ordered a medic to look at her.

"Skipper, since you insist on staying underfoot," she said as the medic cared for her wound, "can you explain to me why all of them are dead or headed that way, and I'm the only unlucky sod that's shed a drop of good blood this day?"

"Likely or not, you used up all your luck yesterday," he said, kind of dodging the question he knew she meant.

"And glad I am to have used it yesterday. Those damn tanks could have blown a hole in me or flattened me and never even noticed I was there. But, Captain, you know what I mean. They had all those machine pistols blasting away and I'm standing there feeling the brick and mortar flying all around me and I squeeze off one shot, pick a new target and squeeze off a second, and next thing I know, I've shot three of them, and there's no one standing. I've got this little sting, and all the rest of these lunkheads are standing around gawking at me 'cause I'm the only one bleeding. What happened?"

Pinned, Trouble gave the only answer he could. "You ever fired your M-6 on full auto?"

"No, sir. Gunny on the range said it was a damn waste of money, and if we needed to go full rock and roll, we were already dead anyway, so he wasn't going to teach us any bad habits."

"Corporal, you have my permission, next time you're at the range, to empty a magazine at full auto. Just don't do it any time when we're short of ammo or you need to qualify."

"Sir?"

"You go full auto, and you're going to spray the area with lead, but you're not going to hit anything you're aiming at."

"You're sure of that, sir? I am a Marine and sharpshooter qualified." Clearly she was, but she sure wasn't sure of what he'd just told her.

"Corporal, not you, not Gunny, not many can hit the bull at full auto. You may put one in the bull of the next target over, but none of your own. Not a chance."

"So I didn't have anything to worry about from the drunk goon right across from me? It was more the guy down the way, huh."

"Exactly, Corporal. But we put them all down real fast. They never had a chance."

She glanced over her shoulder. "You got that right, sir."

Trouble ordered the mount up and move out. They headed back to the embassy. That evening, they'd get their nightly ration of two beers.

FIFTY-SEVEN

COLONEL RAY LONGKNIFE was happy with that day's work. The estimate was that there had been a hundred machine pistols on the veranda of the headquarters of the State Security Special Police and maybe four hundred more in the armory under lock and key.

He paid for 473 of them that afternoon. Several kids walked in with four of the things slung over their stooped shoulders.

The Marine guards at the gate took special care to safety the weapons and unload them after the first one showed up at the desk fully loaded and ready to rock and roll.

There were no incidents requiring medics, however.

That night, there were no new fires.

The next morning, answers began to arrive to the messages Colonel Ray Longknife had sent out. Colonel Stewart was only too happy to have his 4th Highlanders ordered to take ship for Savannah. With any luck, their lead elements would arrive in a week. The full battalion would be on the ground by the end of the month.

Lorna Do promised to flow more units to Savannah right behind the 4th.

That would get Ray some good men. Now he needed money.

Buying up nearly five hundred machine pistols to get them off the street had about emptied his wallet. If he was to do more than watch things develop, he needed money, and for that, his father-in-law, Ernie Nuu, came through when he needed him.

"The attached letter of credit," Ernie's message said, "is to establish a fund to improve conditions on Savannah. It's not to be invested. It's a donation. Spend it how you see fit. I'll argue with the tax folks later. But it will help me if you kept some records."

Ray would need the money; the city was a mess. Even without the goons roaming it, or maybe just without the worst of the goons, it took Ray a full day to arrange his council of war.

Next morning, Major Barbara showed up, along with Brother Scott. He had to be rolled into the embassy conference room in a primitive wheelchair. Alice did the pushing, and as soon as she had him at the table, she began to step back toward the door.

"You're not going anywhere," Ruth told the timid soul. "This meeting is about the future of Savannah, and you of all people deserve a seat at the table."

Unsure, Alice glanced around but saw only assurance that she belonged here. Still, she settled very uncomfortably into a chair at the large table and seemed intent on swallowing her tongue.

Ray had all his critical Marine staff present: Trouble, Mary, and Dumont. The last looked only slightly more comfortable than Alice to be at the grown-ups' table.

Ruth had come down from the *Patton* on the same shuttle as Mary. She took her place with solid intent. It would take explosives to get her out of here.

Becky Graven had her own staff: a junior diplomat and two of her spook watch chiefs. They were just getting coffee and settling into their seats at the table when one of Becky's spooks brought in a message flimsy.

"This is interesting," she said, and instantly had everyone's attention. "A freighter that just entered the system reported to High Petrograd Control that the liner that passed through the jump just before it, had hardly started accelerating out before it exploded."

"Exploded?" Ray snapped.

"Hold it. There's more," Becky said, hand raised for silence. "The second officer of the freighter was a Navy officer in the war. He says the explosion looked like the liner lost its reactor's containment field. The freighter waited for an hour, but there were no signals from survival pods. We can only assume that all were lost."

"Was that the liner that Milassi was taking for his 'vacation'?" Ruth asked.

"The very same," the spook said. "We checked. The only ship that's used that jump for the last forty-eight hours was the *Witch of Endor*. If a ship blew up, she's the only one in line for that honor."

Colonel Ray Longknife scowled. "Folks, I damn near got killed by some software glitch left in the *Sheffield* computer. That Whitebred fellow was hauled off it in cuffs, and the next jump it attempted went all wrong. Now, Whitebred gets off a ship, and it blows itself to bits after its next jump. Mary, do you think this is just a coincidence?"

"Once, maybe, colonel. But twice around that damned Whitebred, and I'm thinking enemy action."

"Yeah," Ray said, and turned to Becky. "How good are your computer wizards?"

"We like to think of them as damn good," the FSO said.

"Can they protect our embassy system from invasion?"

"Yes, sir," both of the spooks at the table said.

"Can you crack into the city and planet's system and make sure it's not sabotaged?"

That gave the two head spooks pause. "Can we get back to you on that?"

"In ten minutes," Ray said.

They excused themselves. The message carrier had gotten a five-foot head start and added two feet to it before they got out the door.

"You really think this Whitebred fellow is that dangerous?" Becky asked.

"No," Ray said. "He's nothing but a puppet, but the company he keeps is damn deadly. Also, whoever it is who employs him is too large a question mark for my tastes. He almost wiped out all life on my planet. If he had succeeded, the Unity War would still be going and us or them would be wiping out a planet every week until there was nothing left. No, the man is nothing, but for his next paycheck, he can be as deadly as any rattlesnake."

"Not an easy problem to deal with," Becky said.

"And he's been dropped in our lap."

"There is an upside," came in a whisper.

Every head turned to Alice.

"Milassi will not be coming back from his vacation," she said, her eyes wide, her smile pure venom.

"That is for sure," Ruth said. "And he took a whole hell of a lot of his people with him," she quickly added.

"Straight to hell," Mary said, also sporting the tight smile of a cobra.

"Remind me to stay on you ladies' good sides," Trouble said.

One of the spooks returned. He settled at the table and took a sip of his cold coffee before clearing his throat.

"We are now running a series of checks on the planetary system. We have, of late, been monitoring it rather closely. It seems that we weren't keeping a close enough eye on it. There have been several viruses inserted into the system in the last twenty-four hours."

He paused for only a moment. "What we found before I came back here was not good. Several of them are clearly malware of destructive intent. We are putting in place security measures that will let us close them down should they be activated, but we don't really want to tip our hands before we have to."

He shrugged. "If the hacker knows we've been in there, he might do something that we couldn't spot. Just how good is this person?"

Now it was Ray's turn to shrug. "We thought he was just the instigator, inserting something he was provided. There's nothing in his background that says he's anything but a vanilla business guy."

"Who else came with him to Savannah?" Becky asked.

Eyes went up around the table.

"We'll check the manifest of the *Witch of Endor*," the spook said, and trotted out the door again.

"I find it troubling that your spook is not using the net to pass along my question," Ray said.

"I find it reassuring, myself," Becky said. "Why risk a breach when it's just downstairs?"

Ray thought about that and found it satisfactory. "Shall we get on with the meeting we all came here for? What's happening around town?"

"I had planned to let my intelligence people present their own information," Becky said, "since they did such a good job of gathering and correlating it, but since the colonel here has them chasing vapor tails, I'll give their report for them."

She paused, to take a breath and glance at a flimsy.

"One of the interesting tidbits they uncovered concerns your Admiral Whitebred. Yesterday, he filed to run for president. We thought that strange. Now it seems that he knew something about President Milassi's travel plans that neither we nor he knew."

"You can say that again," Mary said.

"Who else is in the running to be our new president?" Ray asked.

"I was about to come to that. A Mr. Alberto Eliade has tossed his hat in the ring, along with Professor Romali's expected protest bid. There are others, but they have very little name recognition on the streets."

"And these do?" Ruth said. "I've never heard of them."

"I have," Major Barbara said, entering the conversation. "The professor has made a name for himself by being a thorn in Milassi's side. As much of a thorn as you can be and not have a mysterious accident. The Eliade family have been industrialist giants since the early days of settlement. They always landed on their feet no matter which way the wind blew."

"I'm not sure whether you praised them or damned them," Ray said.

"She's said what there is to say," Brother Scott said, through unmoving lips. "Appear to be any kind of a threat to Milassi and you die, sadly, sorrowfully, but you die. What kind of survivors do you expect us to have? All you have to do is look around this table, and the truth should be clear. If you caused the big man any trouble, he caused you more. To survive, you caused very little trouble."

"Has either of you thought of running for president?" Ruth asked.

"Don't make me laugh," Brother Scott snorted, then clutched at the bindings to his broken ribs.

"Be labeled a pawn of the offworlders, and you won't get two votes," Major Barbara explained.

"How will that play for Whitebred then?" Ray asked.

"He inherits Milassi's machine," the Salvation Army officer said. "It will deliver the necessary votes. And if it can't, the voting machines will report that they *have* delivered the votes. You don't expect an honest election here, do you? There hasn't been one since, I don't know, Landing Day."

Alice nodded. Brother Scott coughed painfully.

Colonel Ray Longknife drummed his fingers softly on the table. "So we need to make people believe that they can have an honest vote, then make sure we deliver an honest count."

"That's a tall order," Becky said.

"But he is the man who killed President Urm," Mary said. "It was in all the media."

Ray groaned. Mary and the rest of the crew of the *Second Chance* were in on that little joke, but very few other people knew the truth. Eyes around the table turned to him with hope, or in the case of Becky, puzzlement.

"Exactly how did you do that?" she asked softly.

"Get back to me later," he whispered. For the rest, he said, "It seems to me that bringing in peacekeeping troops from off planet give us a chance to show the folks here that the rest of humanity cares what happens here and will stand by them if they take a chance and vote for whom they want."

"That sounds nice," Dumont said, interrupting, "but how do we do it and who do we do it for? Which one of these guys is gonna be better for Alice here, or are they both going to be just as bad as Whitebred? I killed a good man once for that bastard. I don't much care for the idea of his being top dog here."

The room fell silent as Dumont's words sunk in. All of them. Like the true story of President Urm's demise, Ray knew the truth about Dumont. Few others did.

Becky Graven finally broke the silence. "As I see it, our first order of business is to make sure both of the not-Whitebred candidates stay alive. After that, we can decide who's the better of the two, and maybe help them get their message out. Colonel, how do you suggest we keep them from getting suddenly dead?"

"That's a good question," Ray said. "I don't think it would help either of their chances to be seen with a platoon of Society Marines tagging along behind them."

"But without that platoon," Mary pointed out, "their chances of surviving until after the votes are counted, assuming anyone bothers to count them, are pretty slim."

"Trust us to make sure the votes are counted," one of the spooks said, rejoining the meeting. "As for keeping the candidates alive and getting their message out, that's a hard one and outside my job description."

Ray eyed Mary and Dumont. Neither one of them had haircuts that would pass muster from a good Gunnery Sergeant. "Mary, how about you, Dumont, and that computer wizard of yours, what's his name?"

"Lek, sir," Mary provided.

"How about the three of you visit our two candidates today and do a security check for them? Maybe some of your exploration guards could ditch their uniforms and see about doing bodyguard duty for them, assuming they want protection."

Mary and Dumont both sprouted grins. "Don't mind if we do, sir," Mary said for both of them.

"We still need to take the measure of these two," the diplomat said.

"I think Brother Scott and I should pay them a visit," said Major Barbara. "Maybe at the same time your Mary does. We can at least get some idea of where they stand."

"Could I come too?" came timidly from Alice. "They both have kids about my age. I'd kind of like to talk to them. See what they're like. I don't know, maybe knowing something about how they treat their kids and what their kids are like would tell us . . ." Alice ran out of words.

But she didn't stop talking for lack of encouragement. Both Major Barbara and Brother Scott were nodding along, smiling. So were Mary and Dumont.

"Kids say a lot about a man," Ray said, wincing inside at being so far from his own impending fatherhood. "Alice, you've got yourself a job. I'll look forward to your report."

If anything, the poor girl seemed to grow smaller under the pressure of universal approval. "Can I tell you my report?" she asked. "I don't write so good."

"Alice, you write fine," Major Barbara said, but then hastened to add as panic spread across the young woman's face, "But yes, you can tell us all about your visits with the kids."

"Thank you," came in barely a whisper.

"You're going to need to come up with some idea to help the candidates get their messages out," the spook added after a pause for Alice to recover. "We're monitoring the public media, and it's flooded with your Mr. Whitebred's smiling face and all his promises. Not sure exactly what he's promising, but he's promising that tomorrow the sun will rise, and it will be warm."

Ray and Becky exchanged looks.

"We'll have to think about that," Becky said.

"Tell me. Who owns the media around here?" Ray asked, fearing the answer.

"The government pretty much controls the net," the intelligence analyst said. "There are a few independent sources, but they only survive because they didn't upset Milassi."

"And what are the chances they'll be willing to upset Whitebred?" Mary asked.

"Today, slim to nil," the spook replied.

"We'll need to change that by the end of the week, at the latest," Ruth said with a smile that brooked no disagreement.

On that note, the meeting broke up.

FIFTY-EIGHT

MARY ARRANGED A visit to Professor Romali's home early that afternoon. They had a late-dinner invitation to Mr. Eliade's estate.

She chose three armored SUVs from the embassy motor pool and filled them with nine of her former Marines. The older half of them had spent most of their lives as asteroid miners, and the younger half were street kids like Dumont. None would be mistaken for hard-core Marines once they donned civvies.

With body armor underneath.

Automatics were issued to all, with discreet holsters. Long guns and antitank weapons went into the back, easily accessible, but not in anyone's face.

Major Barbara went into one rig, Brother Scott the next. Mary and Dumont led, with Lek eyeballing his black boxes. They got to the professor's home with no alarms. Mary liked that.

The professor's home was on a tree-lined lane one block from the university. It was a pleasant brick two-story, with ivy growing up the north wall. Students and professor types walked and rode bikes up and down the street.

Mary had seen places like this in vids, but she'd never actually been to one. Considering what she'd seen so far of Petrograd, she wondered if somehow her SUV had made a jump and deposited them on another planet.

"Wow, this is my kind of street," Dumont whispered to Mary. "I bet their trash cans are fat pickings."

"Shut it down, Marine," Mary said softly, through tight lips. "You're a lieutenant in the Society of Humanity Marine

Corps. You eat off linen in the ship's wardroom. Neither you nor I will gawk. Read me?"

"Loud and clear, old lady, Captain, ma'am," he said, but he had his game face on as he headed down the line to supervise the establishment of a secure perimeter. There were four steps between the curb and the professor's front door. Alice helped Brother Scott out of the rig, then held him up with one of his arms over her shoulder. His other arm was over Major Barbara's. With halting steps, they made it toward the door.

A dog began barking. It must have been a greeting because the professor, his wife, and two teenage children were at the door, and soon helping Brother Scott, as if five people made it easier than two.

Lek slipped in the house easily with everyone's attention focused on Brother Scott and was back at the door with an "all safe" signal for Mary as the others worked their way up the final two steps. Fortunately, the front parlor was their goal, so once they were in the house, they hadn't far to go.

The wife dismissed herself and the kids to get something for their visitors to drink. Somehow, Alice managed to attach herself to the son and daughter as they retreated with their mother to the kitchen. The wife returned quickly with tea and biscuits for their guests, then joined her husband on a couch.

What Mary would have bet was the Father Chair had been given to Brother Scott. Mary joined Major Barbara on the couch facing the professor. Lek and Dumont found portions of the wall not covered with paintings—the wife painted—or certificates and pictures of the professor with colleagues or students.

It took only a few questions from Major Barbara before the professor launched into a long list of what was wrong with Savannah and what he would do to change them. Mary liked what she heard but noticed that, like the mice who voted to bell the cat in the ancient cautionary tale, the professor was long on bells but kind of short on specifics as to how the bell got around the cat's neck.

Then again, it had been a long time since anyone on Savannah had had a chance to make anything happen.

The professor did admit that he could not do all of this

294 • Mike Shepherd

himself. He had begun a series of meetings with academics, as well as people from finance and industry, to see what they could do in a new administration. He was even able to name names. A few, he admitted, were bureaucrats from the present administration.

"The people who run the waterworks or the solid-waste-treatment plant were hired for their skills, not their political résumés."

Mary liked that practical twist.

Still, she had to wonder, how much did the professor believe in what he was saying and how much of it was language he spouted because it sounded good? Lek was watching the numbers on one of his rarely used black boxes. With any luck, he'd have an opinion on what the candidate actually believed and what was held a mite bit loosely.

He ended his sales spiel by asking Major Barbara and Brother Scott to endorse him. They skillfully dodged the issue, pointing out that they'd be talking to Mr. Eliade that evening, and they'd like to withhold judgment until after that.

"Are you meeting with Mr. Whitebred?" he asked.

"He hasn't returned our call," Major Barbara said.

Which came as a surprise to Mary. Had these two actually asked to talk to the new strongman?

"Would you please tell me if he does? I've called him about arranging a three-way debate, but I haven't heard back from either of the others."

"Is that how you intend to get your message out?" Brother Scott asked.

That produced a worried frown from the professor. His wife rested a supportive hand on his knee.

"I've contacted everyone I know in the media. Right now, none of them can even offer me a price sheet for time on their channel. They're booked solid by Whitebred. It looks like I'll have to take it personally to the people, but how do I even get the message out that I'll be holding a rally? Some of the students are offering to distribute handbills, but there are parts of town none of them dare go," he said with an expressive shrug.

"Maybe we can look into other options," Major Barbara said, standing.

The withdrawal was no easier, although this time Alice had the son help her with Brother Scott, leaving the adults more time to talk. The professor seemed talked out, but the wife stepped in.

She was very troubled by the children abandoned to live on the street. "But I don't think the kids are the real problem. Why do so many husbands die on the job? Why do so many wives die? What is wrong with our society that so very many children have no place to go but the streets?"

Mary liked that question. She made a note to ask the smart people back at the embassy if they had any answers. Mary had a lot of questions, but she put them off until she was back at the embassy, down in the basement . . . and debugged.

Lek reported they'd only picked up two bugs.

"How come even the college area has spy bugs drifting around?" Mary asked no one in particular as she settled down at the conference table in the embassy.

"Maybe it's not just the college, but the home of a presidential candidate," Becky said. One of her spooks, the one who'd debugged them, nodded agreement.

Before the major or brother could start talking, Mary stepped in. "Lek, were you running your voice-stress analyzer at the professor's place?"

"Guilty as charged," the old computer mage agreed.

"And you found?" Mary gave him a lead when he didn't go on.

"He believes in what he's saying, I'll give him that much. He's not at all sure how he's going to make it happen, but what he says is true and what he hopes for he sincerely wants to do."

Colonel Ray Longknife turned to Major Barbara. "What do you think of what he had to say?"

"I liked what I heard," she said slowly.

"I liked that he's already talking to people who can help him make it happen," Brother Scott added. "He strikes me as a bit more practical than some professors I've met."

"I liked what his wife said about taking better care of parents to keep us kids off the street," Alice said.

Mary had no idea how the young woman had ended up on the street. She hadn't dared to ask. Now Alice provided the answer.

296 · Mike Shepherd

"My father died when a crane toppled and killed him. Mom took sick, us not allowed to use the company clinic after that, and she died, too." She hung her head. "I tried to take care of my baby brother, but he died before we'd been on the street a year. It's hard on the streets."

"Kids your age belong in school," Ruth said, as softly as she could.

"The professor's kids are in a school at the university," Alice said in answer to Ruth. "They like it. They go to school with a lot of other professors' kids. His daughter's in a competitive piano program. Her dad comes to all her recitals. He even changes some of his speaking engagements to fit her into his schedule."

"How does she feel about his running for president? That may mess up his getting to recitals," the colonel asked.

"She knows that. She was kind of leaning toward putting her playing on hold for a few months so she could campaign with him. Maybe play before all the political talking gets started. She really thinks he'd make a good president." Alice paused. "Though she admits that she's not all that sure what kind of dad a president can be. She said she thinks he'll still make time for her and her brother."

"What's her brother think?" Becky, the diplomat, asked.

"He's not so sure. I think he and his dad have it a bit harder, getting together. His sister says that's just because they're two bulls in the same field, whatever that means."

"I've been there," Ray admitted with a tight scowl. "My old man and I were never happier than when he was on one planet, and I was on another."

The meeting got rather quiet.

"So," Becky said, "do you agree with his kids that he'd make a good president, Alice?"

"They're not stuck-up. The boy asked me where I went to school. I told him it was on the net. He gave me his password so I could drop in on some of his classes." The young woman suddenly got flustered. "I don't know, maybe I'll watch them. Not say anything."

Mary wondered if going to net school here had the same stigma it did where she came from but didn't ask.

"So," Mary said, "how do so many kids like Alice end up on the street when their folks die?"

That brought the roar of silence from those around the table. Major Barbara finally answered.

"There are no safety laws for workers. You get hurt a little bit, and the plant infirmary patches you up. You get too sick to work, and you get laid off. Maybe until you get well or maybe permanently. Your family can use the infirmary when it's not busy with workers."

"No health care?" Ray said.

"There is, if you can afford it, but most can't," Brother Scott said. "There was some talk in the war about expanding the hospitals to support war casualties, but nothing came of it. There was also talk about the number of lost-hour accidents, but again, the war ended before anyone got serious about it. Besides, how do you build a medical infrastructure when you're fighting a war?"

"How do you build one when you aren't?" Ruth asked.

No one had an answer.

"Well, we'll meet back here after you talk to Mr. Eliade," Becky said, and rose, ending the meeting.

"Did you leave anyone behind to protect the professor from an 'accident'?" Trouble asked.

"No, it didn't get covered in the conversation," Mary admitted. "I figured it would come up later if we decided to back him. By the way, he will need help distributing flyers about his rallies."

"To people who can hardly read," Major Barbara said, standing behind them.

"Is it that bad? After all, they're running major industrial plants," Mary said.

"They do the same thing, time after time," Brother Scott put in. "In a more developed economy, they'd all be replaced by robots."

"They were producing a load of warships and munitions in the war," Trouble pointed out.

"And they were running three shifts," Major Barbara said. "It was full employment. Now they're down to one shift a day, and things are dog-eat-dog in the hiring line again."

"And what will it be for the poor fellow who gets elected president?" Ray asked, joining the conversation.

"If the people got decent wages," Major Barbara said, "they could buy the quality of life they deserve. A consumer economy could get this place out of this postwar depression, but the workers need decent pay to be consumers."

"Mary," Trouble said, "get Dumont and a couple of your former Marines back over to the professor's house. Tell them to keep an eye on the place from a distance. Until we ask him, we don't want to be too obvious, but we also don't want him firebombed tonight.

"I'll get right on it, sir," Mary said, and went to correct her mistake from the afternoon.

FIFTY-NINE

MARY HAD A bit of a problem. Dumont wanted to attend the dinner at Mr. Eliade's residence. However, he'd spent a lot of time staring around the professor's house. No doubt his eyes would have bugged right out of his head at the Eliade family mansion. Mary sent him to stake out the professor's house. As expected, the Eliade place was expensive, and it was huge, with more space than Mary figured a family could ever fill up.

Of course, the man had help.

A butler stood at the door as they drove up the circular driveway. When he saw their difficulty getting Brother Scott out of the rig and into his wheelchair, he summoned two more strapping men to assist them. They made easy progress with the wheelchair. Although it was five steps up to the door, there was a handicapped access ramp to the right of the porch.

One of the junior butlers took over wheeling Brother Scott when Alice had trouble dealing with the incline. The look she gave the help, and her surroundings, said it must be nice to have money like that.

However, with a shrug, the street urchin followed them into the foyer.

The meeting was supposed to be arranged around dinner, but an elegantly dressed Madame Eliade explained that her husband had been delayed at the office and offered aperitifs in the library.

Mary let Major Barbara take the lead, and they soon found themselves seated around a roaring fire, juggling small drinks and even smaller hors d'oeuvre plates in a room large enough to bunk down a battalion, even if you kept in all the bookshelves and cabinets for rare books and art objects.

No youths were in evidence, so Alice ended up tagging along with her elders. She balked at the alcoholic drinks and asked for cold lemonade.

From the look on Alice's face when she sipped her drink, Mary would have bet good Wardhaven dollars that the kid had never tasted fresh-squeezed lemons.

Madame Eliade proved herself an expert on extending light conversation long after anyone else would have let painful silence reign. Still, it must have been a relief when her husband finally arrived nearly an hour late.

"You must excuse me. I was unavoidably delayed at the office. I was discussing with several of my friends and donors just what we can do about this damnable hold that Whitebred has on the news outlets. We may just have to buy our own channel. There is one that is deep in debt, and we're looking into buying up its short-term bonds. That might solve its problem and ours."

"You assume," Major Barbara said, "that Whitebred does not know of its debt problem and will not get there before you."

Mr. Eliade, whose butler was helping him shrug out of his coat at that moment, paused, coat half-off. He finished, dismissed his man, then took a chair. His wife offered him a cigar and lit it expertly. He blew several puffs before eyeing them.

"Strange. None of us even considered that a possibility, but now that you mention it, he will, no doubt, drive up the bidding."

"And the bidding may not only depend on monetary issues," Brother Scott said, waving a hand at his chair. Not all the bandages were off his face yet.

The industrialist frowned for a long moment. "You don't honestly think . . . You don't mean to say that you're . . ." Again, the thought died unspoken.

Mary expected the two locals to launch into a blunt indictment of the previous administration's crimes. Instead, they sat quiet.

On second thought, it would be a waste of time to describe color to a blind man.

The silence grew long and began to bend and twist. Before

it reached pretzel proportions, the industrialist cleared his throat.

"One hears rumors," he admitted.

More silence.

Finally, the man mashed out his cigar and leaned forward. "Has it been that bad downtown?"

"I was raped by Milassi," Alice whispered. "I had a job stripping beds and washing linens in a bordello. Then his girlfriends noticed me, and I found myself as the spice in a game the three of them played." She swallowed hard.

Mary stood up from her chair and went to sit next to Alice. She held her hand as the girl studied the carpet.

"I got off easy," Brother Scott said. "They just burned down my hostel for street children and beat me to a pulp. His thugs raped our nuns. Major Barbara, here, got warned just in time to get her street kids out of her homeless shelter. It still got burned down. So, yes, sir. Things have been bad downtown."

The man relaxed back into his chair and studied each of them, one by one. "And your story," he said to Mary.

"I'm a Marine, sir. I burned Milassi's drug farm and got his scientists off planet. Some of my associates blew up a few of his tanks in the process. Infantry like blowing up tanks. I'm just here to keep you alive if you ask for our protection. We'll also try to keep the professor in one piece."

"Has he asked for protection?"

"No, sir. At the moment, we are trying to decide if it's worth our while to keep either of you alive or should we just give the planet over to Milassi's handpicked successor."

The wife looked shocked, but the businessman nodded.

"Which of us, me or the professor, will you back to win?"

"I am authorized to say neither," Mary said. "We will attempt to keep the playing field as level as we can. Who wins is up to the people of Savannah. Isn't that the way it's supposed to be in a democracy, sir?"

"I don't know," he said with a chuckle. "I've never lived in one." He raised an eyebrow to his wife. "I'd like to live in one, wouldn't you dear?"

"No, love. Not if it will cost me your life."

"We went over this before I announced."

The wife, tears in her eyes, turned to Mary. "Can you protect him? Keep him from what happened to him," she said, nodding to Brother Scott.

"I will try, ma'am. As I learned in the war, there are no guarantees."

The wife fled the room in tears.

"Sir," Major Barbara asked, "are you in the race?"

He paused to think. In the background, Mary found herself listening to a clock tick away the seconds. Finally, the man sucked in a deep breath. "I am in it. This planet needs a chance, and if it's not me, who will it be?"

"The professor?" Brother Scott said.

"That old dreamer. He's never met a payroll. He's full of ideas, but show me one thing he's ever finished . . . besides a class or a book," he hastily added.

"He has ideas," Major Barbara said.

"If I need a minister of navel gazing, he'll be first on my list," the industrialist snorted.

And began to lay out his own agenda. He wanted change, just like the professor did, but his was more centered on what he and his friends had obviously been talking about before he came home. Change was needed, but it must be slow. Labor unrest would not be allowed. Order, respect for law, and the sanctity of property must come first.

Of course, democracy was the goal, but for now, voting should be limited to only those who could show a serious commitment to the welfare of this planet. "A man must have twenty thousand dinars' worth of property or real estate. Forty thousand for a man and wife."

"And if the husband only has twenty?" Major Barbara asked.

"He votes."

"And if it was money she brought into the marriage?" Major Barbara shot back.

The industrialist had no snap reply. Instead he sat back and thought for a good five seconds. "That is a good question. I had not thought about the wife being the one who brought wealth into the family."

"A widow or the only child of her parents might well be the one with the money," Major Barbara pointed out.

"Clearly, we need to think more on this," Mr. Eliade allowed.

He mulled that thought for a while, then went on. "Our foreign police will, no doubt, be established from Earth. Fortunately, we owe no debts to Earth banks, so that is not at issue."

"What about the young?" Alice asked. "Those who have supported the change movement at the risk of their lives?"

That clearly stopped the man in his tracks. "Aren't children in school?" he finally said. "I know mine are."

"Where are they now?" Alice asked.

"Doing their homework. They always eat an early supper since I may have to work late. I try to see them for a few minutes each evening, or at least tuck them into bed."

"Well, some of us kids risked our lives to burn down Milassi's drug plantation," Alice said.

The businessman's eyes grew wide. "So that really was arson, not an accident? I'd heard both."

"Yesterday, after the shoot-out at the Special Police barracks," Mary said quickly, not sure how the conversation would go if that arson claim got too much air, "it was kids who brought in the weapons. We paid them a bounty to keep the guns off the street, but they risked going through the headquarters looking for guns."

Again, the man seemed more poleaxed than informed.

"Some of us thought we heard shooting, but it was over so quickly."

"We Marines prefer our firefights short and deadly," Mary said.

After a pause for the industrialist to absorb that, their conversation went on for quite a while longer. Frequently, when he talked of government, he spoke more of management than governing. Mary wondered if she was the only one who spotted that. Doubtless, she was not the only one who found that troubling.

There was no call to dinner. When they rose to leave, the wife and two children, both boys, were lined up in the foyer to shake their hands as they left.

"That was interesting," Mary said, joining Major Barbara and Brother Scott in the middle SUV.

"Yes. 'Interesting' is a good word," the Salvation Army minister allowed.

"Now we know what the monied interests want and the dreamers think," Brother Scott said. "May God help us all."

Mary heard it as a prayer.

SIXTY

THE COLONEL WAS waiting at the embassy door. "How'd it go?"

"We'll tell you in a moment, sir," Mary said, and led the way to the basement. They found they'd picked up a better class of bugs, and more of them, but between Becky's spooks and Lek, they were soon clean and ready to talk.

They let Major Barbara run down the facts from the interview. No surprise, the wealthy industrialist was very concerned about maintaining the present conditions he and his friends enjoyed, and he viewed governance as just a case of good management.

"I don't think his 'good management' has much to do with the health and welfare of most workers or kids," Alice said.

"So," Ray said when they were finished, "we've got a dreamer and a manager, neither of which have any idea what it's like to govern a planet."

"Is that any surprise?" Brother Scott said. "If anyone did look like competition for Milassi, they ended up like me, or worse."

"And out of this, somehow, this planet is supposed to now govern itself," Becky said.

"Well, Whitebred is only too willing to take that problem off their hands," Mary said, giving her sarcasm full run.

"Did you ask Mr. Eliade if he wanted protection?" Trouble asked.

"This time I did," Mary said. "He has his own security guards and doesn't see any reason to increase his protection. No doubt, if he does, he'll buy it."

"He better be careful who he gets. More than one king has been shot in the back by his own guard," Ray said.

306 · Mike Shepherd

"So, Eliade is on his own. What about the professor?" the diplomat said.

"He, at least, is talking to a diverse group," Major Barbara said.

"He's got a problem getting people to know him," Alice said, slowly. "We kids could distribute flyers around the factory gates and the lunch wagons. If he's going to give talks, we could help people know when and where."

"Mary," Ray said, "tomorrow, when you check back with the professor about protection, take Alice with you. I think she has a good idea."

"Will, do, Colonel."

"Make that General," Becky said, with a diplomatic smile.

"General?" echoed around the table.

"Since we have three battalions of light infantry coming from Lorna Do and Pitts Hope, it seems that someone at Society of Humanity headquarters thought there ought to be a general to coordinate them all. Despite the freeze on local armed-forces promotions, I now find myself a brigadier general in the Society of Humanity Army. Fancy that."

"Will there be a wetting-down party, Brigadier General, sir? I'm always willing to swill someone else's booze," Mary said through a big grin.

"Maybe after the election. Until then, I want you clear-eyed and sober."

With that, the meeting broke up.

Next day, things got busy. The leading elements of the 4th Highlanders landed and were barracked in a run-down hotel two blocks from the embassy.

Mary had her little talk with the professor. He wasn't nearly as shocked that he might be a target of violence as the businessman was. "Some of my students have been worked over by the Special Police. I thought they'd been put out of business?"

"They have, but Milassi had all kind of thugs on his employment roster. We only got the most visible."

He accepted the protection. He also accepted Alice's idea and hired her on the spot to be his youth coordinator. He had scheduled his first rally for Friday evening and was wondering how he'd get the word out. The net was still closed to him.

When Mary left, he was deep in conversation with Alice and his campaign manager, a woman who'd been a business manager for a small company until it was closed down in the war. She, and a history student doing his doctoral dissertation on the History of Democratic Elections, seemed very happy to have some legs for their ideas, even if the legs were short and many illiterate.

Since the professor didn't want to look like the "off-planet candidate," Mary picked her most-long-haired Explorer Corps types to hang out with the campaign and her stealthiest types to handle night-guard duty around the professor's house.

For the first week, things were kind of easy.

The handouts and flyers went out on Wednesday, and the kids had them hanging from every wooden lamppost in the industrial part of the city by noon. There were also kids outside the plants at shift change, even the midnight shift.

There were a lot of crude jokes about "thanks for the toilet paper," but when the professor went on stage at the city outdoor amphitheater, it was standing room only.

That was a nice start, but it didn't end well. A fight broke out between one group and another, maybe it was right-handers and left-handers, maybe it was an old family feud. There was no way of telling, and no way of figuring out who sparked it, but with a fight raging at the left of the stage, it was impossible for the professor to finish his speech.

He and his idealistic campaign staff were pretty down afterward, but Mary promised to have her own security team roaming the crowd at his next big rally. Alice suggested that he show up at the plant doors at shift change to shake hands and let the folks get to know him personally.

The professor cringed at the thought, but his doctoral candidate quickly pulled up some research that said that was the way it was done in the old days before all the media. Mary arranged for him to have some scruffy-looking guys hanging with him, and they got the professor off to bed.

Next day, the professor was outside plants for the morning shift change, and he managed to hit three plants during the staggered lunch breaks. He talked to middle managers in restaurants during their coffee breaks and ended the day covering the afternoon shift change.

Mary personally took an ugly knife away from some guy with no plant pass. He was slipping up behind the professor with no great skill. She hustled him away from the line and frisked him. He had a wad of new bills, but no ID. She relieved him of his pay, since he hadn't earned it, broke his wrist, and sent him on his way to report back to those who hired him.

She didn't bother the professor with that, but she did pass the word to the security details. Next time, no doubt, White-bred would hire someone with better skills.

That set the template for most of the days that week. The professor shook a lot of hands, shared some really bad food with people who ate the likes of it every day of their lives, and talked about making Savannah a better place for them and their kids.

The dreaming side of the campaign-management team offered a bit of advice. "We campaign in poetry. We govern in prose."

Mary was none too sure anyone else on her team understood the difference between poetry and prose. Dumont admitted not knowing either one. After Mary explained the difference between words that were vague, loaded, and pretty versus words that were exact, limited, and hard, he nodded.

"Well, that explains why what we think we're getting from a politician and what we get are so different."

The professor overheard that. "I'm telling people what I want to do. Hope to do. What I'll be able to actually do will be something else entirely. I know it. Politics, governance, is the art of the possible, not the ideal. At least that's what I'm reading in these books. Now, Milassi, he had everything his own way, and look what that got for the rest of us. I don't want to be the next Milassi. I'm not sure what I *will* be, but him. No way."

Mary redoubled her efforts to see that the guy lived long enough to find out.

SIXTY-ONE

BUT IT WASN'T the professor Mary needed to look out for.

Friday's rally did not end in a fight. Several got started, but Marines moved in quickly and ended them before they could grow into brawls. Better, the Marines collected the brawlers and found that most had recently gotten a major payday.

Under questioning, they admitted to being hired to start a fight.

"Who hired you?" elicited only vague descriptions with no names attached.

"At least tonight we dodged the bullet," Mary muttered to herself as the crowd streamed out of the amphitheater. Someone had set up a booth to sell T-shirts and was having quite a night.

Maybe the professor was catching on.

Somebody must have thought so.

Later that evening, Mary got a call.

"You know that guy that's the professor's assistant campaign manager?" Dumont started with.

"Yeah, the one that drops a quote every five minutes."

"He just got beat up on his way home from the rally. I got a team responding to his commlink. A medic and others."

"I'll meet you there," Mary said, giving up on getting to bed early.

The young fellow had been beaten up badly and both his wrists broken.

Send a message, get one back.

They got him to the university hospital, where they did their best to reduce his pain as they worked on him.

"Those wrists are never going to be as good as they were," the doc admitted to Mary.

That didn't surprise her. But what did surprise her was the first visitor to arrive at the hospital. The police commissioner, despite the late hour, showed up to ask about the fellow.

The doc gave him the same story she'd given Mary. Then the commissioner turned to Mary. "I'm tired of all these beatings happening on my watch. I'd like to stop them but don't know how."

"Are you really willing to give it a try?" Lek asked.

"Yes."

"Even if you do make an arrest," Mary said, "do you have a judge who will hand down a conviction?"

"Yes. I have one, maybe three that are listening to the professor, to Alberto, and would like to see Savannah the way they see it."

"Well," Lek said, "I just might be able to give you the guys who did this to that young fellow."

"How?" both Mary and the commissioner asked.

"I don't know if you know it, Commissioner, but Savannah is crawling with bugs. Every time we go out of the embassy, we get all buggy. I run a jammer just to be on the safe side, myself. When we go back to the embassy, we debug ourselves. Now at first, we just squished the bugs, but the more we got, the more I thought, why not put them to work for me? I've been subverting the little darlings, turning them to the bright side, if you will, and that young fellow was bugged. I have the video of his beating."

"You do?" Mary said.

"Can we see it?" the commissioner asked.

Lek ran it. The images of those beating up the man appeared in the air in front of them.

"That's the Bear," Mary said, pointing out one hefty fellow standing well back and out of the way of thrown punches. "I know him from his chasing Ruth and me. He beat up the wife of one of our Marine officers."

"But he's not beating up this fellow," the commissioner pointed out.

"No doubt he paid for it," Lek said.

"I don't doubt you. I can convict the fellows throwing the punches but not him, unless one of these three turns on him."

"Do you know them?" Mary asked.

"They are known to me and mine," the commissioner said, punching his own commlink. "Can I have a copy of that video?"

Lek sent it to him.

The police moved quickly after that. Lek and Mary were in court the next day. The judge refused bail for the three thugs and sent them on their way to the local jail.

Unfortunately, none of them lived long enough to talk to the prosecutors about a deal to roll on the Bear. Two were shanked in the shower, the other in the exercise yard.

The commissioner was not happy. "I knew we had bad cops. I didn't know we had bad prison guards. I'll take better care of the next ones we catch."

"No doubt it will be harder for someone to hire the next batch, what with the retirement plan they gave these last three," Mary said.

"No doubt," the commissioner agreed, then went on. "Could you get me an introduction to your commander, General Longknife? Those infantry troops arriving. What plans does he have for them?"

So Mary introduced the commissioner to General Ray Longknife and the two of them soon expanded their meeting to include Colonel Stewart of the 4th Highlanders. By the next day, Highlanders were joining cops walking the beat, one for one, two for two, and the level of violent crimes began to plummet.

Part of that might have been the rumor that got around that surveillance bugs were now working for the cops and even dark, out-of-the-way corners might be covered in living color.

A few days after that, the price of airtime on the net dropped a lot. The professor still had his rallies, but he needed bigger venues. Working-class people now rubbed elbows with people from the suburbs who no longer feared coming downtown at night.

Things only got more peaceful as the 1st Battalion, Pitts Hope Grenadiers joined the local police walking their beat. And the quality of the policing improved.

It's hard to be a dishonest cop when you've got a kid in a kilt carrying a slung rifle walking the beat beside you.

As the election drew close, it turned out the senators from Earth would arrive two days before it and would be there for it. While Trouble went with General Longknife to meet with the two battalion colonels, it was Mary who somehow got stuck with the job of setting up a watch list to have soldiers or Marines cover all the voting sites.

Then Whitebred did something stupid that could have decided the election for him but didn't.

SIXTY-TWO

MARY WAS DONE with her rounds for the night. She and Lek had visited most of the professor's campaign headquarters. Before Mary chose to call it a night, she decided to make one last check at the professor's house.

"We got problems," Lek said, when they were still three blocks away.

"What kind of problems?" Mary said.

"Someone is jamming the cameras I got around the place. The guard should have turned out immediately. Unless their take has been suborned and they're watching something patched into their feed."

Mary put her foot down, and they covered the last few blocks like teenagers with a death wish.

The outside of the professor's home looked no different. The pair of Highlanders posted on the street did not look alarmed.

At least they didn't until Mary drove like a madwoman into the driveway and came to a squealing stop.

Having made as much noise as she intended to, she signaled the Highlanders to go around the far side of the house, while she and Lek covered the near side.

It was hard to tell with ivy covering the walls, but they looked clear.

It was in the back that they found the broken window to the rear door.

The house was dark, and stayed that way when Mary tried to turn on the lights. The jammer killed a call for backup, and the landline was dead when Lek tried it.

The house was silent, except for some muted noise coming

from the basement. Mary signaled one Highlander to head upstairs and rouse the residents. She, Lek, and the other Highlander, guns at the ready, headed downstairs.

There, by the light of a single hand lamp, two men were emptying cans of a volatile-smelling liquid while the third, the Bear, jiggered the fuse box.

Before Mary could shout "halt," one of them spotted Mary and tossed his gas can at her, splattering her with the stuff. With his other hand, he went for his gun.

"This is a gas bomb, don't shoot, you idiot," Mary shouted.

"I ain't dying in no jail," the other man yelled as he tossed his now-empty can in Mary's general direction and also went for his gun. Even the Bear turned from the fuse box as he went for his automatic.

Mary put three rounds into the Bear's chest. His own shots went into the basement's concrete floor. Sparks flew.

Or maybe it was one of the other arsonists. Both of them were falling from Lek and the Highlander's fire. Their own fire went wild, adding to the ignition sources.

The basement exploded.

Mary found her arm on fire from the splattered gas. She dropped her weapon and began beating at the flames as she backed up the stairs. She turned to run, preferring to risk fanning her own flames to facing what was happening in the basement.

At the top of the stairs, Mary ordered the other Highlander to help his buddy. That Highlander was down from the second floor, two kids limping along beside him.

"They've been drugged. I got the kids. You get the parents."

"Go with him, Lek," Mary ordered as she headed out the back door.

Around front, Mary found a fire truck. Its crew went about their business with intent.

"Anyone in there?" the engine chief shouted.

"Two parents upstairs. I've sent men to help them out. Three arsonists may still be in the basement. That's where the fire started."

The engine chief shouted orders in his radio, and two pairs of firefighters led their hoses around the back of the house. A moment later, water began to flow.

At that moment, Lek and the Highlander brought the professor and his wife out the front door to collapse on the grass beside their kids. The teary reunion drew almost as much water as the pumper was putting out.

A rescue team joined the collection of red fire gear in front of the house, and Mary made her way there. They took one look at her burned arm and went to work covering it with healing gel. That cut into some of the pain starting to flood Mary.

Weak in the knees, she settled on the back bumper of the rescue unit and watched the house. It looked like they might succeed in containing the fire in the basement.

"Fancy meeting you here," came in a familiar voice.

Mary looked up. "Hi, Commissioner. I might say the same thing. What brings you out of your bed this late at night?"

"A neighbor saw lights in the professor's basement and tried to call out. Strange, their commlink was jammed, but their old landline worked just fine. They called the police station. Their captain called me. Said this likely had 'political' all over it."

"Very likely," Mary agreed, then took in the mob following the commissioner. "Who called the newsies?"

"I did," he said. "You're not the only one who wants a different Savannah."

Mary started to shiver. The commissioner located a blanket and wrapped it around her.

"Thanks," Mary said through chattering teeth.

"Can you tell me what happened?"

"We were just checking things out before hitting the rack and didn't like the jamming any more than the next guy. We found the Bear and two henchmen getting ready to set the fire. Dumb fools, they chose to shoot it out in the middle of a gas bomb. I got some splashed on me. Likely you'll find the three arsonists in the basement. Very likely they'll have bullet holes in them. You want my gun or something?"

"You're Marine, or something. Talk to your own chain of command. I'll accept this as a preliminary report pending our own investigation."

He paused and eyed the house, where the fire seemed to be going out. "But thanks for doing my job for me."

"It's a hard job," Mary said, as an ambulance pulled up. The medic put a needle in her arm, and she found herself very sleepy. She hardly noticed as they laid her out on a gurney.

SIXTY-THREE

WHEN MARY WOKE up the next morning, she found herself flat on her back in a burn unit, facing a parade of visitors.

The doc was encouraging. "Not too much of your body was involved, and you got it out fast. We'll need to do some skin grafts, but I've already extracted some, and they are growing nicely."

"Is that why my butt hurts?"

"Did you have some other preferred donation site?"

Mary left it at a smarting rump.

Trouble was next; Ruth came along.

"Thanks for getting that shit that beat me up," Ruth said.

"My pleasure," Mary admitted, "but don't tell anyone, or I might go from hero to perp in two easy steps."

"We won't," Trouble agreed. "For someone who doesn't like being in uniform, you're sure collecting a pile of medals. I've got my clerk writing you up for a couple."

"You can donate them to Alice and the other kids. Those are your real heroes. And they don't get paid for it."

"Ray's setting up some scholarship money for them from the funds his father-in-law sent."

"I hope he can," Mary breathed, and found herself tired.

When she woke up the next time, the professor, his wife, and their kids were waiting patiently at her bedside. "Thank you for saving our lives," he said.

"Thank you for saving all of us," his wife said.

"That's just part of my job," Mary said. "I much prefer saving lives to that other thing I sometimes have to do."

"Well, you sure did it for us," the son piped in.

The daughter handed Mary a vase of flowers. "I cut them myself," she said.

"So the house didn't burn to the ground," Mary said.

"Not even the books in my study on the ground floor," the professor said.

"How is this playing on the net?" Mary had to ask. "I saw a lot of reporters and cameras there last night."

"They gave my husband marvelous coverage," his wife gushed.

"And I got a call from Mr. Eliade about an hour ago. He wants to close down his campaign and back me. I'm sure there will be some horse trading after the election, but Admiral Whitebred will only be facing a single name against him on the ballot. That has got to help."

"The fool really outdid himself this time, didn't he?" Mary whispered.

"It appears so."

Mary was once again tired, but it felt very good to fall back to sleep this time. Being a hero didn't matter much to an old space miner. Making a better world for some kids. Now, that mattered a lot to her.

The next day, she felt better. The doctor released her to light duty, and when she got back to the embassy, she got a cheer from just about every Marine who wasn't on duty or couldn't sneak away for a second.

That was nice, but Trouble confined her to the embassy until she got released to full duty. Thus, she missed out on the final fiasco that Whitebred came up with to wreck the election.

SIXTY-FOUR

GENERAL RAY LONGKNIFE liked it when plans came together—even if it wasn't really much of a plan, and he didn't have a lot to do with it.

You had to love it when a scumbag like Whitebred overreached and made his fate even less pleasant. The go at the professor and his family made all the news, and the discovery of the burned bodies in his basement cinched the deal.

The police commissioner traced the Bear back to both Milassi and Whitebred, and the news ran with it. The one thing that he and Becky feared, that the two decent guys might split the votes enough for Whitebred to sneak out a first-place finish, vanished when the industrialist withdrew.

Ray Longknife had a wide grin on his face as the final days of the campaign wound down.

Then Whitebred made his last desperate gamble.

How Whitebred got his arsonists into the warehouse where the voting machines were stored never did come out, but midnight, two days before the vote, the warehouse was on fire. The fire was caught fast. There were guards from the 4th Highlanders on duty, and they smelled the smoke even if the detectors had been disabled.

The fire department was quick to answer the alarm.

As was the police commissioner.

He had an arson investigation going before the fire department had the fire out.

General Ray Longknife found himself shaking his head at the whole thing. It wasn't like this was Whitebred's only way to handle the voting machines. The spooks, working with Lek, had spotted plenty of back doors and extra software in the computers.

Understandably, Savannah did not have a boatload of voting machines lying around waiting for the next election. The only election anyone remembered had been almost six years back. Still, computers from all over town had been collected at the warehouse and loaded with software that would turn them into voting machines.

From the looks of their software, these machines would have counted every vote as one for Whitebred.

Becky's spooks had plans to change that at the last minute, but they'd been lying low, not wanting to scare Whitebred into making it any harder on them than it had to be.

So why burn the machines?

"That's just plain crazy," the Foreign Service Officer said.

"Becky, you have to understand what pressure does to people," General Ray Longknife said. "They panic. When people panic, they do stupid things, like mess with their sure thing. Whitebred panicked, did his last stupid thing, and you can only guess how the voters will react to their voting machines' burning. Will they blame the contender?" Ray grinned. "Or will they blame the folks responsible for maintaining the security of the voting machines? I know how I'll bet."

General Ray Longknife would have won his bet.

The professor won with over 60 percent of the vote. He even won the miners from up-country and the farmers.

Becky had been worried about them since all the professor's rallies had been in town, and Whitebred owned the media feed to the hinterland. Still, the report of the fire at the professor's house and the fire at the voting-machine warehouse went out to the entire planet.

And had its impact.

It also didn't hurt that on election day, there were peacekeepers at every voting site, and the senators from Earth drove around, observing the election.

And when someone threw the switch to activate all the software bombs left in the unburned computers, Becky's spooks were there to throw their own switch and cancel the software before it could do anything to the count.

Very interesting, that.

What was a surprise was Whitbread's next move.

He left the next day for the space station. There, he did not book himself a suite on the liner that brought in the senators. Instead, he settled into a suite at the Hilton next to the station's shipyard. Lots of coded traffic flowed between his rooms and the yard, but no one on the *Second Chance* could read it.

He might have skipped the liner, but he was just about the only one from the old regime who did.

There followed a second run of rats leaving a sinking ship, or at least a ship that had made a hard U-turn. Many of those leaving were wanted for various crimes under the color of law. Quite a few people in the incoming administration wanted to put out arrest warrants for them, but the system collapsed.

Too many of the judges had booked passage for themselves.

There were some left, but their courts were quickly overloaded. The courts ground slow, and justice delayed turned out too often to be justice evaded by flight.

The professor didn't want to continue Milassi's practice of naming his own judges. Instead, he tried to arrange a parliament to name replacements.

He recalled the last one that Milassi suppressed some ten years back. However, many of its members had died, left, or recently fled their crimes. What remained did not amount to a quorum.

Savannah began a second round of elections, this time for members of a new parliament.

SIXTY-FIVE

GENERAL RAY LONGKNIFE left the locals to this new round of politicking. He had business of his own. The senators from Earth wanted to talk to him.

They invited him to a special reception.

Just him and them.

It turned out all they really wanted was to have their pictures taken shaking the hand of the man who killed President Urm of Unity and saved them the cost of a long, bloody war.

Ray tried to explain to the first one he talked to that it hadn't happened the way it was being reported in the media. The senator made it clear that he didn't care how it actually happened; the media version was fine by him. What he wanted was to have his picture taken shaking the hand of the man who killed President Urm.

After a second failure at getting the truth out, General Ray Longknife switched gears.

"The star map I discovered on Santa Maria could be a problem."

"How so?" the leader of the Senate's committee on business and commerce asked.

"I'm concerned that in the rush to find easy planets to colonize, we may discover something that doesn't like us and is bigger and badder than we are."

"Surely you jest, General," said the senator who headed the subcommittee for the Navy's budget.

"I don't know. I don't know if we are alone in this galaxy or if we have company. Do you really want to find out that we aren't and that we are the second-nastiest thing here?"

"You military men are so predictable. Give you a vista to enjoy, and all you see is a battleground. We, however, see potential, don't we, Senator?"

"Potential and profits, my good man."

"Could we at least set limits on how far afield we search?" Ray suggested. "We should also establish a system for tracking scout ships that go out. That way, we'll know if some fail to come back."

"No, my good man, that won't work at all. This is free enterprise at its best. I don't want to tell George here that I'm sending a probe out to this bunch of stars. He might rush a probe out there just ahead of me. No, General, this is best left to business. We know how to do that."

Ray tried different senators that evening, and got the feeling very quickly that they all knew of his ideas before he'd talked to the second bunch.

And they all intended to do nothing about any of his suggestions.

Kill President Urm. Good.

Limit exploration. Never!

That night, he shared a beer in the embassy cafeteria with Captain Tordon.

"Trouble, you're a good man," Ray Longknife said after he'd quickly downed two beers and ordered a third.

"Huh?" the Marine said. "When a general starts talking nice to a captain, only trouble can come of it."

"Well, trouble may come of this day, but it won't be from what you and I talk about. It will be what those damn politicians don't want to talk about."

"And that is?" the captain said, clearly willing to lend the general an ear.

Ray rose to the bait and bent the good captain's ear at great length. "Yes, I believe in the Explorer Corps. Hell, I'm getting it funded from a damn tightfisted Wardhaven legislature, but if we let every Tom, Dick, and Harriet go blundering around the jump points, God only knows what we'll run into. It's just plain stupid to bite off more than we can chew before we've grown into the space we've got."

"Stupid but profitable," Trouble pointed out.

"Dumb and deadly," Ray said, ordering a fourth beer.

"If I may point out, General, we haven't stumbled upon any evidence that there's anyone out there. Other than the jump points, I mean."

"But we *do* have the jump points and the three species that built them," Ray said, pointing at Trouble with his beer bottle. The local brew here came in long-necked bottles. Ray liked that.

"You didn't happen to come upon anything about other aliens when you had your head against that stone, did you?"

Ray thought for a moment. Maybe more. It couldn't be the beer, or the scotch the senators had provided him with at their reception. Damn fine scotch it was, too.

"No, I can't think of anything. But the rock just seemed to be a map. How long has it been since you saw an ordnance map with 'Here there be dragons,' I ask you?"

"I don't recall ever having seen one, sir."

"I am not going to say, 'Back in my day we had 'em.' No, I'm not going to give you that joke to tell on me. I'm not that much older than you."

"No, sir, but I think you've had a lot more to drink today than I have."

Ray nodded. "I likely have, Trouble. I likely have. But you want to know something, Trouble?"

"Likely not, but you're going to tell me anyway."

"I'm scared. I'm really scared. The kind of scared that raises the hair on the back of your neck even before you know what you have to be scared of.

"Oh, and I want another beer."

"Sir, the hairs on the back of my neck tell me that you don't need another beer. You need to find your bed before you do anything you'll regret in the morning."

"Captain, are you giving your general an order?"

"Only a suggestion, sir," Trouble said, and left his second beer only half-finished as he helped Ray from his chair and down the hall and across the embassy's yard to the VIP quarters.

Ray remembered the Marine's helping him out of his clothes and even tucking him into bed.

"Thanks, soldier," Ray thought he said, as he curled up with his pillow.

"You're welcome, trooper," he remembered hearing. And maybe even, "God help us if you're scared about the right thing."

SIXTY-SIX

TROUBLE WAS GLAD he sent himself off to bed right after putting the general down, because two hours later—his comm-link said 0100 exactly—he got a call from the duty desk.

"I don't know if I should bother you, sir, but we've got a donnybrook going downtown. Some guys from the divisions in the Capital Corps came to town and got drunk. Now they're swinging at anything that isn't wearing the same color uniform they are: Marines, Highlanders, Grenadiers. Everybody."

"Thanks for calling, Sergeant. I'll be there in five," Trouble said, rolling out of bed.

"Anything wrong?" a groggy Ruth asked.

"Not likely. Just some local soldiers blowing off steam on anyone who wears a peacekeeper's uniform. I better go down there. No doubt some officer will be in here before dawn to get his drunks back."

"Be careful," Ruth said, sitting up in bed. Her nighty did a very poor job of covering her breasts.

"With you to come home to, love, I will be the best of careful."

"You do that."

In undress greens, Trouble gave his wife a kiss that prom-ised he'd be careful, and trotted for the duty desk. Gunny was there ahead of him.

"Several streets downtown are now fully involved in the brawl," Gunny reported. "We allowed a large leave party. It seemed like the worst was over, and we could relax, sir."

"A good call," Trouble said. "Apparently, someone else thought the same."

"Yeah," Gunny growled.

The duty driver had a gun truck, minus the gun, waiting for them at the embassy front door. They headed downtown.

At exactly 0122, the night was lit by a flash, followed by a loud boom.

"What was that?" the driver said.

"I think we'd better find out," Trouble said, spotting a brightly lit fire. "Head for that."

"Yes, sir."

At 0124, there was another explosion followed by a fire not all that far from the first.

"I think we got a problem," Gunny muttered.

Trouble hit his commlink. "Duty desk, turn out the troops. Full battle kit. More orders to follow." He tapped off. "Corporal, does this rig have a gun locker?"

"Under your seats, sir. Combination is forty-one, thirty-eight, forty-one. My old lady's measurements."

Trouble stood, while Gunny opened the gun locker and issued rifles to himself and the corporal. He handed a holstered automatic to his captain. They settled back down in their seats and watched the night light up. A layer of low-hanging clouds had moved in. Unfortunately, it was more smog than a portent of rain to cool the place off.

Two fires reflected brightly from the low scud, giving the city a hellish glow.

Sirens added sound to the visuals.

The driver slowed down as they approached the center of town. There were still several drunken fights going on along the street they drove. Trouble ignored them.

The flaming building at the end of the street, surrounded by a traffic circle, held his eyes.

"Isn't that the Justice Building?" Gunny asked.

"That it is," Trouble said.

A police officer halted them before they got too close. Ordering the driver to stay put, Trouble and Gunny dismounted and talked their way past the police line.

As they got closer, Trouble spotted the police commissioner's car. He only had to ask twice for directions to find the man watching the fire burn.

"Morning, Commissioner," Trouble said.

"Morning, Trouble. What brings you to my little bonfire?"

"Same thing that brings you, sir. I thought we'd posted guards at all your municipal buildings?"

"You had. I had. Have you heard about the brawl the soldiers of the 1st Corps threw tonight?"

"Yep, that's what got me up."

"I understand the beat cops had to holler for help. The Highlanders called out the guard, as you say, and we pulled in reinforcements from all over town."

"Including the building guards," Trouble provided.

"Yep."

"That boom I saw and heard on the way in here," Trouble began, "sure seemed familiar. Kind of like military-grade explosives."

"I didn't actually see either explosion," the commissioner admitted. "I'll take your word for it. By the way, if you have any experts on what a military-grade bomb looks like after it does its boom thing, I'd be grateful for the help."

Trouble made a call, and more people got roused from their beauty sleep.

More fire equipment arrived and went to work, but the building was fully involved and burning furiously.

The fire commissioner joined the police commissioner. He agreed, in his professional capacity, that this fire had a major accelerant behind it.

"Can this poor stranger ask what I'm watching burn?" Trouble ventured.

"The easy answer is the Justice Department," the police commissioner said. "Think all the courts and their records, as well as the records of all investigations into any and everything we've done or had reported by someone in hope of justice for the last ten years."

"So if a poor woman got raped by someone or ones," Trouble offered, "all records of that investigation are now going up in smoke."

"Yes. Everything. Likely even the reports made by the station cops. All our records were centrally located. For efficiency." The commissioner's reply had a bitter twist to it.

Trouble looked around and spotted a second fire's glow off to their left. "Can I ask what else is burning?"

This time it was the fire commissioner who answered. "The Interior Ministry Building. Strange that," he added after a pregnant pause. "There were always rumors that Milassi had his good friend at the Interior Ministry run a snitch operation. You want to know which of your neighbors is reporting on you, you'd likely go to the Interior Ministry. Not last month, I admit, but next week, under a new administration, those records just might be available."

"I take it that that's not likely after tonight."

"Not very," both locals growled at the same time.

Trouble turned around. Up the street, a large contingent of Highlanders was breaking up a fight. There was a bus filling with drunken brawlers, many of them hanging out the windows and filling the gutter with vomit.

"I was planning on just turning those troops over to their officers when they asked for them. Professional courtesy and all," Trouble said.

"I'd prefer that you didn't," the police commissioner said.

Trouble didn't respond directly, just raised a questioning eyebrow.

"We may have a major problem with our Army," the police commissioner said.

"And that blasted dam," the fire commissioner added.

"I have this uneasy feeling that there's something about the lay of the land here that I wasn't briefed on."

"Can you set us up with a meeting with your boss types? Not at the embassy. They better come in the back door at my office. I'll try to get the professor in, too. He better know what we know."

"Pick a time. I'll have them there," Trouble said, confident a captain could order a hungover general and a chief of missions to march to his drum.

Once he told them the little tidbits that had been dropped in his lap, he doubted wild horses could keep them away.

SIXTY-SEVEN

TROUBLE FOUND THE meeting was set for 1000 hours next morning. He led General Ray Longknife, Becky Graven, Mary, and Lek in the back door of the police commissioner's office building. A secretary met them and hurried them up a back staircase. It seemed important that few saw them.

The offworlders did their part. Lek's bug buster worked overtime on their entire approach march.

The police commissioner seemed surprised to be shushed in his own conference room, but his eyes grew wide as Lek first identified, then destroyed a dozen bugs. Included was one on the room's projector and commlink.

When Lek finished, the fire commissioner asked if he'd mind dropping by his office. Lek promised he would, then found a seat by the door and settled down to meditate on his black box.

No one suggested he leave.

The police commissioner had given over the head of the table to the professor, now president elect, pending a swearing in that had yet to be scheduled. Since Savannah's record for swearing in new chief executives was kind of sparse, there was no set date in their law.

Trouble hoped it would be real soon.

The police commissioner stood and spoke without preamble. "We have a problem. The fire commissioner and I have known we had a potential problem for some time. After last night, it's clear that it is a real one. The Army," he said, with finality.

"What kind of an Army did Milassi pay for?" Trouble asked. He was junior here, and likely the least informed, but it might help if they were all singing from the same page.

"The 1st Corps at Camp Milassi is the only major force on this planet," the police commissioner said. "It has an armored division and a mechanized infantry division. But that is only part of our problem."

"I would have thought," General Ray Longknife said, "that a pair of heavy divisions would be enough of a problem."

"There is the dam," the fire commissioner said. "The Anna River is dammed about thirty klicks upstream from Petrograd. And only fifteen klicks from the camp. The Army regularly patrols the reservoir. Good training, I was told."

"And the problem is?" Becky Graven said.

"If they opened the slush gates and emptied the reservoir, this city could be washed away.

"That's one way of canceling the results of an election," Trouble said dryly. "Cancel the voters."

"The word we have is that the commanders of the 1st Corps are considering marching their tanks into town and declaring for Whitebred. He's in touch with them from his safe perch in the station above. He wants them to roll in and take over. Civilians are not much good against tanks."

"Light infantry is," Trouble said, grinning wide.

"Yes, there is that," the police commissioner said. "If Milassi had still been here, we figured he'd have rolled the Army into town a week before the election and had a tank at every voting station. Instead, Milassi's dead, and you're here, and your Marines gave the Army a black eye. Then came voting time, and there was a peacekeeper at every polling station."

"I think matters got away from Whitebred," the fireman said.

"So why this sudden interest in making sure I don't get sworn in?" the future president, maybe, said.

The head cop looked pained. "For most problems, Milassi had the Special Police, damn them to hell. They pretty much raped, stole, and killed to their hearts' content and Milassi's courts protected them. Now they're facing a higher judgment, and what they did here is well past accounting for. However, the Army was on call whenever extra heads needed breaking. And things done while the Army was in town on Milassi's business were wrong but didn't make it into court. Reports were written up if someone complained, but they went nowhere."

"Nowhere, but up in smoke last night," the fireman said, taking up the story. "That's why both the Justice Building *and* the Interior Ministry had to burn. Oh, and they were burned to the ground. Burned and blown up we can now officially say."

"So you have no records?" Becky said.

"But that doesn't mean that we have no witnesses," the police commissioner said.

And heads nodded around the table.

"So suddenly, the scum that did the bidding of those in power are fearing for their necks," General Ray Longknife said. "Those not having a bed on the liner out of here are suddenly very interested in who is appointing judges and controlling the courts."

"That's it in a nutshell. They could roll in here and take over, but your Marines made that option look less an easy bet than last month. Or they could just open the dam and flood everything down here. Then they'd have no one to stop them from driving in and picking up what few pieces are left."

"It wouldn't be much," the fire commissioner said, "but they'd be king of all they surveyed."

"Better to rule in hell than face a judge in heaven," Trouble misquoted Milton.

"Precisely."

Trouble's commlink buzzed. He glanced at it. "Excuse me, folks, but I left Gunny at the city jail with all those soldiers puking their guts out. What with stuff happening to that jail's inmates, I figured a few of us should keep an eye on our fellow troopers."

"Good idea," General Ray Longknife said through a knowing grin.

Trouble listened for a long minute, then reported to General Longknife. "Gunny is facing down a major from the 3rd Motorized Rifles Brigade demanding the release of his soldiers. Anyone want to bet that if we let them go home to sober up, we'll next see them over the sights of their infantry fighting vehicles?"

"No bet, Captain," the general said, standing. "Captain, I'd be grateful if you would tell the major that his people will have to stay a while until we get a full accounting of any property damaged or civilians assaulted. I'm assuming our Marines, Highlanders, and Grenadiers gave as good as they got."

"Better, sir. I don't think these guys pay all that attention to their PT or hand-to-hand training."

"Not a good reflection on their officer," General Ray Longknife said. "Now, Mr. President, since there is, at present, no formal and recognized government on Savannah, I will consult with the commanders of my peacekeepers about what we will do about this problem."

"Should I be sworn in immediately?" the professor asked.

"I'd prefer that you didn't, sir," General Ray Longknife said. "There may be some blood on the ground before the evening is done, and I think it would be better if it was only on the hands of offworlders, not people who have to stay here and live together."

"That sounds ominous," the professor said.

"Yes, but I expect that it will be mainly for those out there in the cantonment."

Trouble stood. He measured General Ray Longknife and liked what he saw. The man had his game face on: hard, firm, unbending. Their stance was the same. Trouble was glad the man was on his side. He'd hate to face this man from across a battlefield.

They exited the building the way they had come. Trouble took one of the embassy's SUVs to the jail. He refused the major's insistent demands to have his men turned over to his custody. He did invite the major to tour the facilities with him to assure that his men were being well cared for.

Five minutes in the stink of their drunken filth, and the major cut short his inspection and left.

Trouble relieved Gunny and the others on jail duty, after making it clear to the prison superintendent that those were soldiers, not civilians, and that he and his guards would answer to the Marines for any harm that came to them. That included harm from other prisoners or from anyone else that dropped in and took a disliking to a trooper.

"There will be courts to settle up any claims against these men."

Trouble doubted anyone had ever expressed quite that level of concern for prisoners, and certainly that level of personal payback.

The superintendent assured Trouble the soldiers would be well cared for. And kept behind bars.

Trouble and Gunny headed back to the embassy. On the way there, they passed Highlanders headed out of town toward the 1st Corps' camp.

"General Longknife doesn't waste any time, does he, Skipper?" Gunny observed.

"You got to like that in a man. You see to getting the troops mounted up and ready to go. Issue all the antitank rockets we got. I'll go see what the elephants are screaming about."

Gunny grinned, saluted, and went to do Trouble's bidding.

Trouble squared his shoulders . . . and marched for another damn meeting.

SIXTY-EIGHT

THE MEETING WAS in full swing and heavily attended by the time Trouble arrived.

It was in the basement, surrounded by the intel analysts at their stations. Once in a while, one spook would bring a report to the duty chief at the table, who'd pass it along to Becky, then General Ray Longknife.

The table in front of them now showed an orbital image of Camp Milassi. As Trouble found an empty chair, the image was updated. A column of tanks, some fifty strong, were rolling out of the camp. No infantry went with them.

"These guys really don't learn, do they?" Trouble said. "Tanks without infantry to protect them are dead meat."

Across the table from him, the general nodded in agreement. "Colonel Wallace, will your company from the 2nd Highlanders be in place to stop them?"

"With an hour to spare," the colonel said, his Scottish brogue thick enough you'd need a dirk to cut it. "But if you don't mind a wee bit, I'll be getting another company up the road to back them up."

"Good idea," General Ray Longknife said.

"Where is their infantry?" Trouble asked.

"Going into defensive mode," Ray said, and the map zoomed in on a mountain between the camp and the city. "Apparently someone thinks digging his infantry in on Black Mountain, backed up with artillery, will hold the camp. Then he can use tank runs into town to terrorize the locals."

"Those tanks are no going to town," Colonel Wallace promised.

"But there's more where they came from," the general said, "and if we don't do something about them, sooner or later someone is going to read *Modern Combat for Dummies* and figure out that tanks need infantry as much as infantry need tanks. Present company excepted," he got out quickly before the scowls of the light infantrymen around the table got too deep.

"I'll just leave this thing to you gentlemen," the FSO said. "Until a couple of days ago, I never would have expected infantry to take out tanks, but I, at least, can learn when you rub my face in it."

"Tanks and infantry work together in a game of paper, rock, and scissors," General Ray Longknife told the diplomat. "What would kill infantry, the tanks kill. What would kill tanks, the infantry kill. Long-range artillery, now that's a problem."

"There are a whole lot of guns in that camp," Colonel Stewart said.

"What's the forecast for tonight?"

The duty lead spook snapped his fingers, and an update was delivered five seconds later. "It seems that those high clouds last night did portend a change. There is a chain of thunderstorms headed this way. By late evening, we should be treated to thunder, lightning, rain, hail, and torrential downpours."

Becky shivered. "A good night to stay home," then paused as she took in the looks of the light infantrymen around the table.

"Or to go dancing," Colonel Stewart said. He turned to Trouble. "You Marines up to a bit of a ball?"

"We'll fill up your dance card, you lovely Ladies from Hell."

The Highland colonel frowned. "We'll see who's leading when the night is done."

"No doubt," Trouble said, grinning, "we'll be leading together, and pity the poor ones who need to hitch a ride to a good fight."

The colonel slapped the Marine captain on the back. "Good man. Good man."

"I'm not sure I can spare any more good men for you," General Ray Longknife said. "Wallace, I want your battalion to form a blocking force to keep the tanks both in camp and out of the rear of the 4th and the Marines."

"What about me?" Colonel DeGrasse of the 1st Grenadiers asked.

"I hate to say it, Gus, but we've got to keep your men in town to back up the cops. Things may get wild tonight."

"May I mount up a company of reserves, sir, just in case they get in trouble out in the boondocks?"

"You may, Colonel, but don't count on motor transport. Captain Trouble, does Izzy have an electromagnetic pulse emitter on board the *Patton*?"

"I believe she may have an EMP in the bottom of her lingerie drawer."

"Good. Ask her to send it down," Ray said, and Trouble hit his commlink.

"Oh, and find out if it's dialable and just how far we can dial it back."

Trouble did as he was bid. "The EMP emitter is on its way down. It cannot be dialed back to less than thirty klicks."

Ray opened up the table to a wider view: city, camp, mountain, dam. He asked for a thirty-klick radius over the camp. It included Black Mountain as well as the dam. He directed it to center the circle over Black Mountain. It still covered the camp and the dam.

"I think we're going to turn the lights off here in town," he muttered. "Is there any other power plant for the city?"

The chief spook expanded the map. "There is the Milassi fusion plant thirty klicks downriver."

"Is everything named for that nutcase?" Trouble asked.

"Pretty much. What he didn't build himself, he had renamed after he took power," Becky said.

"If we set off the EMP and close down all the electronic gear at the dam, will that put it out of harm's way until we get troops up there?" Ray asked.

The spook was shaking his head even before Ray finished. He flipped through his reader, then slid it across to the general. "They've got manual backup, just in case the place starts to flood and blows out the electronic controls. Even with no electricity, they can flood the city."

"And we'll have turned off all the lights and warning sirens," Ray said slowly. "Ruth."

"Yes, General."

"You ready for a drive in the country?"

"Who do I get for company this time?"

Trouble had noticed his wife was at the table. He'd assumed she was just there as one of the gang. He scowled as she set herself up for a night just as bad as his.

She grinned across the table. He could almost hear, "What's good for Captain Gander is great for Mrs. Goose."

"You have a problem, Captain?" the general said.

"No, sir. Yes, sir. Does it matter, sir. Wife, Mary is on light duty. Sending her off on this might keep her from demanding to go dancing with our lady friends here. I'd suggest Cyn as well. She's good at killing tanks, and Deb is mad that she hasn't killed one yet. That's assuming tanks come your way, woman."

"You make sure they don't," Ruth said, flipping her hair at him.

"I've got my wife home and pregnant, or, no doubt, she'd want in on the fun, too," General Ray Longknife said. "Okay, Ruth, you and your team had best be on your way. You've got a ways to go to get to that dam, and you don't need to hear what we're about to cover."

Ruth took the dismissal with good grace, and even threw her husband a kiss as she left the meeting.

General Ray Longknife smiled at Trouble's discomfort in this professional gathering and leaned over the map. "As I see it, there are three sets of trenches being dug on Black Mountain . . ."

SIXTY-NINE

RUTH DROVE UP to the small truck stop. The dam-control building was off to her right. Above her, black and roiling clouds swept in, obliterating the sunset and bringing dark early.

Two farm-to-market trucks, one with a load of potatoes, the other with complaining chickens, were parked close to the stop. Right in front stood a green gun truck, complete with machine gun aimed toward the sky.

"Damn recruits," Cyn spat. "They'll get water down the barrel of that gun, and there will be hell to pay when they try to use it."

"Let us thank God for His gifts," Mary said.

Ruth took a deep breath, checked the lay of her automatic in the small of her back, and entered the store.

To the left was a small shop, sparsely supplied with snacks and recordings to make the drive go easier. To the right were tables and a counter. Two civilians, no doubt the drivers, huddled at the counter. One table held four men in uniform.

One of the soldiers took in the four women and grinned. "I got a warm place for you to sit, girlie," he said, slapping his lap.

The other soldiers laughed as Ruth and her associates studiously ignored him and chose their own table . . . well away from the troopers.

But in easy automatic range.

A middle-aged woman in tight slacks and an even tighter shirt appeared with menus. Ruth and her girls made it easy by ordering four identical hamburgers and fries with colas. The waitress looked out the window as thunder shook the building.

"Looks like rain." She turned to the drivers. "You going to want to bed down for the night here?"

"And deliver those chickens all soaked?"

"Maybe the lightning will cook a few for us," the joke of a trooper suggested.

Both drivers tossed money on the counter and took their leave.

"You two want me to fill up your thermoses for you?" the waitress asked.

They allowed that that would be nice and paused in their leaving.

Ruth suspected they'd be a lot longer leaving than they planned.

The lights went out.

Ruth stood in the dim light of fading day and stepped out of the line of fire of the other three. They'd been issued Colt-Pfizer's best sleepy darts. Three pops almost in unison, and the three closest soldiers went down.

Ruth got the last one as he tried to bring his rifle to bear.

"You'll pardon us, folks," Mary said, swinging her automatic around to cover the three civilians. Four; the cook had come from the kitchen.

"We don't got any power. None at all," he said, not seeing the automatics covering him.

"This will go easier on all of you if you'll just lie down on your backs," Ruth said.

"You're gonna kill us all?" the waitress said. "Just like in the movies?"

"None of you will be any the worse for the experience, come morning," Ruth said. "Now, we can put you to sleep where you are, and you'll have bruises from where you hit the floor, or you can lie down gentle-like, and we'll put you to sleep nice and easy."

"Any of you have heart problems?" Mary asked, coming up beside Ruth.

All shook their heads. The two drivers settled down on the floor, meek-like. The waitress and cook didn't sound at all happy, but they went down. Mary put two shots into the first driver's arm.

"That didn't hurt," he said, then his eyes rolled up, and his head lolled over.

The next driver looked pretty relaxed as they put him to

sleep. The waitress had her eyes scrunched up and a big breath held in, ready for the pain. Her breath left her in a gentle sigh.

The cook looked ready to come off the floor if the waitress so much as moaned, but with her sleeping nicely beside him, he relaxed and took his shots easily.

"That went better than I'd expected," Mary said.

"It went like I was hoping," Ruth said, as they headed for their sedan. The rain was just starting.

"Pretty much what I was hoping, too," Mary said, "just not expecting it to go down that smoothly. You know what I mean."

"No battle plan survives contact with the enemy," Cyn said, pulling an M-6 from the trunk and checking it out. The others drew their rifles and, holding them slung down so they wouldn't show in their silhouette, began the long stroll to the dam-control building.

"I wonder how Trouble's doing," Ruth whispered to any listening gods.

SEVENTY

TROUBLE AND HIS Marines were busy pulling sixteen 155 mm guns forward. Thank heavens they were just wheeled guns, not armored, track-laying monsters. Highland infantry were pulling the caissons. There was no question that the original location of the guns had been registered and sent back to the 1st Corps' own guns, who now had them sighted in and ready to suppress.

But that was before the EMP took a thousand years off the available technology.

If the other side's cannon cockers were able to figure out how to fire their guns manually, they'd be pounding mud a good thousand meters behind the new gun line General Ray Longknife was setting up.

Even with rain falling in his eyes, Trouble had to like this part of the plan.

They waste their ammo pounding mud to soup while our gun bunnies pound their poor bloody infantry to a pulp. Nice.

The heavy rain held off until they almost had the guns in their new positions. Since they'd known to expect the EMP, the gunners had done some serious planning on that assumption.

The Marines weren't too wet and muddy by the time the guns were in place, but it began to hail just as a few desultory rounds landed where the guns had been. Apparently, the jokers dug in on the high ground ahead of them hadn't thought that, even if their radios and landlines were dead, they could still run a messenger back to the guns about how things had changed in front of them.

"Stay dumb," Trouble muttered to any gods listening.

Their sixteen 155 mm's were all the light infantry battalions had brought with them. They weren't much, but they would have to do. Trouble left Lieutenants Vu and Dumont to get the 147 Marines organized to assault the first line of trenches and went to the Artillery CP for a final time check.

Commlinks weren't going to give anyone a time tick tonight. The professor had scrounged up a half dozen treasured antique windup watches. When he'd delivered them to General Ray Longknife, he'd had the good sense not to tell men who were facing death and destruction not to break the family treasures.

So, of course, Ray had.

Major Drummond of the 2nd Highlanders was the chief cannon cocker for the evening's pleasantries. Colonel Stewart had all three of his company commanders in for a final word and time check. Trouble was not pleased to discover his large silver watch, complete with chain and fob, had lost two minutes in the last six hours. Others also had to adjust their archaic timepieces.

No one questioned that the major's time was right.

The gun-bunny major glanced outside the tent he'd set up with paper maps and tables. "It should be full dark by 2030 hours, what with this cloud cover. We'll start the bombardment at 2015 and lift it from the first trench line at 2045. We plan to hit the second line hard at 2215 and lift it at 2230 sharp. We'll hit the third trench after that, and we'll need word from you when to lift our fire."

"I've got my grandfather's Very pistol," Colonel Stewart said, patting an oversize holster at his side. "I'll fire a white flare and a red flare. You cease fire on the red one."

"That we will, Colonel. Any more questions?"

Since all questions had been answered as well as they could for now, there were none raised.

Colonel Stewart chose to speak the final benediction. "The poet said of another stiff situation, 'Ours not to reason why, ours but to do and die.' Well, gentlemen, we know the reason why and it's ours to do and theirs to die," he said with a nod toward the unseen mountain.

The Highland officers gave a cheer. Trouble gave a "Ooo-Rah."

"Good luck, Trouble," Colonel Stewart said, offering the Marine his hand. "We'll see you at the top."

"That you will, sir, waving down at the rest of you," Trouble said, shaking the offered hand firmly.

"In a pig's eye, you bloody jarhead."

"Don't trip on your skirts." Since all four officers were, indeed, kilted, Trouble smiled broadly as he said it.

With more good-natured jabs at the other's poor choice of uniformed service, they went their separate ways.

Trouble returned to find his troops spread out, dug in and huddled under rain gear. Thick clouds brought gusty, chilled winds and deepening dark but indecision as to what they wanted to do: rain, downpour, sleet, or hail.

In response to the occasional lightning, there was sporadic fire from spooked recruits on the mountain.

Marines hunkered low. Random fire could kill you just as dead as a well-aimed round.

Half an hour before the guns were due to start, Trouble ordered his Marines out of their holes. They began a slow, low walk forward. Sergeants moved up and down the line, whispering for troopers to keep quiet, keep low, and keep five or more paces between them and the next trigger puller.

When lightning lit them up, they froze in place without an order given.

They were a bit over a klick from the hostiles' first line of resistance when the guns opened up right on time, or only fifteen seconds after Trouble's watch said they should. He took the beginning of the shoot for a time check and adjusted his watch accordingly.

After a brief pause to adjust themselves to the noise and flash of artillery landing damn near in their lap, sergeants got the troops moving again.

Trouble had picked a rock about two hundred meters from the trench line where he'd call a halt. Getting that close to an active bombardment's maelstrom was risky.

But letting the enemy have time to recover from the shock of the guns would be more deadly.

Trouble got to his phase line a good five minutes before the bombardment was due to raise its main interest to the second line. Along the line, troops settled into the mud, lying as low as physics allowed.

Here and there, grenades came out, both rifle grenades and

hand-thrown ones. With any luck, the grenades would confuse the green troops above and leave them still groping for the bottom of their trench thinking the shells were still coming.

As to how the more experienced soldiers above them would take matters, Trouble would leave that to fate.

Down the line, a call for a medic went up. Someone had been hit, by a shell fragment or rock; it didn't much matter. They were bleeding, and the fight hadn't started.

His borrowed watch said it was time. There was one final crash of shells, then a silence that was deafening.

"Troops up! Grenades fire!" Trouble shouted, and the soft pop of launched grenades was followed by explosions along the line ahead of them. Not as loud as the ones before, but loud enough.

The troopers were up. Ray had ordered them to silence, but from his left came the shout of a Highland charge in full rush. Now his Marines took up the shout and, with bayonets flashing in the lightning, they rushed for the parapets.

Here and there, a head popped up. A rifle came up. Automatic fire began to cut the night's silence. Along Trouble's line, sharpshooters paused in their rush to do what they were best at. With all modern aids stripped away, they'd fire two quick shots.

Heads above them slumped down into the mud.

The Marines were now at the trench line. It was actually a collection of hastily dug ditches. Some were deeper than others. Some were longer than the next. Here men stood up, hands in the air. Other soldiers still groveled in the mud at the bottom of the hole, too shocked by the bombardment to do anything.

A few fought, but not many, and those did not fight for long.

Before Trouble had a chance to fire a single shot, he was ordering his lieutenants and sergeants to organize the prisoners for withdrawal. The few walking-wounded Marines led them back.

None of the Marines had been hit so bad they couldn't walk.

There was one incident where a hardcase type thought he could overpower the wounded woman marching him and ten others off the hill.

He died, and the man behind him as well. The other prisoners took that in and raised their hands higher.

With the hostiles out of the trenches, Trouble surveyed his situation.

Certainly, the other side's gun bunnies knew where their own trench line was. Trouble ordered his Marines forward to rocks two or three hundred meters forward of the trench. To his left, he saw kilts doing the same.

He carefully counted the minutes. About thirty of them went by before a shitload of artillery, that was a technical cannon-cocker term a gunner had once told Trouble, began to fall on the abandoned first trench.

Content with the night's work thus far, Trouble found himself wondering how Ruth's evening was going.

SEVENTY-ONE

RUTH WAS SURPRISED to find the control building empty. There was not a single person in the operations room. Still, it was good to be out of the rain.

Strange, not a single light was visible in the complex. Apparently none of the men who worked here figured their emergency lights would go off-line. And hand torches, too. She pulled a candle from her pack and lit it.

"Shall we sit here a spell?" Mary asked. "The manual release for the spillway is over here, and it hasn't been tripped." She pointed at a dozen man-tall levers ranked along the rear of the room.

"You really have to put your back into it," Debbie put in. "There's tackle over there." Chains, lever bars, and pulleys hung on the back wall.

Ruth went to the window, which gave a good view of the entire dam complex. By the next lightning bolt, she spotted a clump of people running in the rain toward the control center.

"We got company coming," she announced.

"You leave a light in the window, and they're bound to see it and take it for an invite," Mary drawled softly.

The Marines did a quick weapons check and prepared to be hospitable. That involved slipping into the shadowy corners and keeping quiet as a dozen men entered the room and gathered around the candle.

"I didn't do that," one man said. "Did any of you?"

That drew a generally negative reply.

"I lit the candle," Ruth said, stepping toward the light.

"Who the hell are you, lady?" the first speaker said. Apparently the tall, thin, balding fellow was the boss.

"I'm your new superboss in charge of operations," Ruth

said. "And since there won't be any operations, it should be easy on all of us." She presented her automatic for their notice, but kept it aimed at the overhead.

The boss man stepped closer. "You want to tell me just what is going on here?"

"You've been hit by an EMP," Ruth said simply.

"I told you all it was an electromagnetic pulse," one of the men behind him said.

"Yes, Ralph, you said it was, now shut up," the boss man said over his shoulder. "Okay, lady, you hit us with a nasty thingy. Why?"

"I didn't hit you with the EMP. You got caught in the thing. No offense intended."

"Well, lady, when you put me in the dark and much of Savannah most likely, I do take offense." He took a step closer to Ruth.

Before he could take a second step, three Marines stepped out of the shadows, rifles slapping down hard on their hands.

That concentrated his, and his work crew's, attention.

Several raised their hands.

"No offense intended," the boss man said, as he stepped back and slowly raised his own hands.

"We have no bone to pick with you," Ruth said. "However, as we speak, quite a few bones are being picked around Camp Milassi. Our job here is to make sure the sluice gates are not opened."

"Cripes lady," the boss man said, "it's bad enough that you damn near fried our gear. But if you opened those gates, we'd lose our head of water. We're just about as down as we can get this summer. We wouldn't get back to electrical production until late autumn."

"I don't want to open your gates. I'm here to keep the Army from doing it."

Even in the dim light, Ruth could see realization dawning on the man's face. "We got Army guards around the complex."

"Yep, I know. Four of them. They're sleeping nicely over at the truck stop. Are there any more?"

"Not until shift change at midnight," one of the others provided.

"And unless they get a new battery, that's not going to happen," Mary put in.

"So you got just us on your hands," the boss man said. "And, lady, I'm just as interested in keeping things the way they are as you seem to be."

"Any fans of Milassi standing around behind you?" Mary asked, her rifle roving over them.

"Nope," "Not me," and "Hated the guy" provided the answers.

Strange how a living strongman has lots of friends. A dead strongman, not so much.

"So," Ruth said, "why don't you settle your men down against that wall, and we'll hold this opposite wall, and maybe you can get some sleep, or tell stories. What did happen when that EMP hit you?"

"Christ, everything went crazy, but Ralph there pulled the circuits. Put us in the dark."

"And got cussed out something to hurt my feelings for a month," Ralph added.

"But we saved the turbines and instruments."

Ruth found herself a comfortable swivel chair and settled in to keep an eye on the men inside and the storm outside. She could only hope Trouble's job was going as well.

SEVENTY-TWO

TROUBLE HOPED RUTH was having an easier night of it.

It was hailing again, big things the size of baseballs that bounced when they landed and hurt when they hit. His troops were huddling under their ponchos, keeping a cautious eye on what lay ahead of them.

The trenches up above were obscured. Mother Nature provided sleet and hail. The cannon cockers contributed shells that slung mud and rocks into the air.

The 1st Corps gun bunnies had called it quits for a while, the weather being what it was. No more rounds buried themselves in the mud of the first trench line. Their communications and control or gun liners must not be all that good.

Several shorts had landed among Trouble's troops.

Not all the ponchos covered shivering Marines.

Trouble ducked under his poncho and snapped an antique lighter until it sparked and lit the gasoline it was burning. He'd timed it pretty good. Fifteen minutes until the bombardment lifted on the second trench line. He flipped off the lighter, pulled his head out of his poncho, and waited a bit for his night vision to recover.

It was a slow process. The lightning flashes didn't help. He spotted Gunny and made a time hack at his wrist. Gunny began working his way down the line, rousing Marines for the next rush.

When Trouble stood and gave the signal, the troops moved out at a hunched-over walk.

The next lightning flash showed Highlanders on his left flank frozen in place, just like his Marines.

Good light infantry.

The second trench line was less of a line, more a collection of fighting holes and just plain old rocks in the right place. The artillery pounded the ground ahead, its flashes competing with the lightning to ruin a man's night vision. The cold rain froze a man's hands on his weapon. Here and there, troops removed their bayonets and sheathed them, the easier to get at them if it came to close hand-to-hand in cramped quarters.

The artillery fire ended, but the rain, if possible, got worse. Sleet and hail mingled together. The night was dark as a witch's hindquarters as the troops struggled forward, slipping and sliding in the mud.

From above them, fire started. Sporadic at first, then it grew.

"Fire grenades!" Trouble shouted.

Grenades arched out toward gun muzzles. Some guns fell silent. Others were joined by more desperate men, intent on living through this night and not as someone's prisoners.

"I think the higher up we go, the harder cases we'll be facing," Gunny shouted.

"If you were in charge of this bunch, wouldn't you put the innocent cannon fodder in front?" Trouble answered, and began to fire his automatic at any flash in the night up ahead.

They shot at what they saw, either in flashes of lightning or flashes of muzzles. Other times, they stumbled blindly into a fighting hole or a slit trench. Some of the hostiles rose, hands over their heads. Other came at them, knives in hand.

People fought. People died. Often those who deserved to.

But not always.

Trouble shot a man as he rose, bloody knife in hand from stabbing a Marine in the back.

"Medic," Trouble shouted. Then had to shout it again.

The medics were doing a lot of business in the mud and rain that night.

Another Marine did what she could to staunch the inky blood flowing from the man's back.

Trouble went on deeper into the nightmare.

Here a hostile huddled in a fighting hole that had been missed, rising just enough to shoot Marines in the back who missed him in the dark and passed him by.

A sergeant coming up late caught him the second time he

tried that stunt and put three rounds in the back of his head. Then the sergeant hollered for a medic.

He needed two. He got one.

From that hole, another half dozen rose to surrender. The Marines moved on, leaving one of their own to guard the docile. But one of them was more desperate than cowed. A grenade came at the Marine, exploding in her face. Some of the surrendered took metal fragments, too, but the one who tossed it now took off running.

Trouble turned at the sound of the grenade to his rear. A lightning flash showed a horrible scene, but it also let him get off a snap shot of at the one running from it.

He crumpled into the mud and slid into a hole. Trouble dropped back, to put two more rounds into that one's head and call a medic for the Marine.

One of the captured ones, a young kid, was already doing what he could for her. Likely, she'd never see again. Trouble rustled up a medic and a wounded Marine. One took over the care of her. The other made sure there were no more surprises from this bunch.

Naked and shivering in the cold, they walked off the mountain ahead of the wounded Marine.

Trouble attached himself to a squad clearing out one serious trench system in the second line. The corporal ahead of him rounded a corner—and was jumped by a guy with a knife who had hidden out in a shallow hole dug into the side of the trench. Covered with mud, he was invisible in the night until he moved.

The two rolled in water and mud at the bottom of the trench. The Marine ditched his rifle and pulled his bayonet. Trouble tried to get a shot at the attacker, but had to give it up.

With both covered in mud, he was none too sure which was which.

The Marine finally slipped his bayonet up under the man's chin, then drove it deep. The attacker collapsed atop the trooper.

Trouble pulled the body off.

"Thanks, sir."

"I tried to shoot him, but I wasn't sure which of you was which."

"No, problem, sir," the corporal said, searching the muck and mud for his rifle. "There were times there I wasn't sure which I was."

That was the way of the second line. A hundred separate, desperate battles, fought with knives and fists as much as with guns and grenades. When the butcher's bill was settled up, there were more Marines down than at the first line—and fewer prisoners.

"Something tells me the next one is gonna be a bitch," Gunny said.

"So let's get us moved out of this target and settled in for what rest we can get," Trouble said. Vu was one of those being carried down the mountain. Dumont was the only lieutenant Trouble had left. They and the sergeants moved Marines up the mountain a good two hundred meters before letting them go to ground.

The artillery barrage began crashing in behind them almost thirty minutes later, to the second.

Nice I can count on something from 1st Corps, Trouble thought.

Then again, with him getting all this action, there must be little left for Ruth.

At least he wanted to think that.

SEVENTY-THREE

CAPTAIN MARY RODRIGO stared into the dark up the road to Camp Milassi. Lightning would flash, and she'd see the same thing she'd seen before.

Then came a lightning flash, and there might have been something different.

A second lightning flash definitely showed something different. A short column of men moved slow, hunched over against the hail and sleet, but they were moving toward the dam.

"We got company coming," Mary said to those huddled in the chill of the dam's operations center.

"Had we better douse the candle?" Ruth asked.

"I think they've already seen our little light in the darkness," Mary said, "and, if you don't mind being a target, it might focus their simple minds on a place to go."

Ruth made a face, but she stopped her walk toward the candle.

"Everybody down," Mary said, getting her own head below the level of the windows used to observe the dam and its environs from the command center. Most of the dam's evening shift were already sitting on the floor, along with Mary's two Marines: Cyn and Debbie.

They made a final check of their M-6s and weapons load and, keeping low, trotted to Mary's side. One at a time, they put their heads up to observe the approach to the dam from the Army camp off in the hills to the west of them.

One or two lightning flashes later, and they ducked down beside Mary.

"Looks like a bit of a firefight. I make them to be about twenty," Cyn said.

hers. Hopefully, he wouldn't get buck fever and start shooting before she wanted.

The rain came down in sheets and pillowcases. The troublemakers took their time arriving. But Mary had guessed right. The light did draw them.

They came down the approach road, deployed in loose bunches of twos and threes. No Marine sergeant would allow that kind of messing around. If Mary read them right, most were senior sergeants with a couple of captains thrown in. There might have been a major, but no one seemed in charge.

Mary guessed they didn't expect trouble.

Stupid them.

The other Marines let them get well into the kill zone before Mary took her first shot.

It was not like shooting fish in a barrel. The yard was a whole lot bigger than a barrel, and these fish shot back.

Some shot too damn well.

Mary used the concrete barriers for cover, but never shot from the same place twice. Shoot off two rounds, duck, scoot down the way. Pop up, choose a target. Shoot. Then repeat.

Still, she got nicked in the ear. Way too close for comfort.

Mary let it bleed and kept up her fire.

The shoot-out seemed to last forever.

Mother Nature lit them up once in a while with lightning and pounded them with sleet and rain. Mary gave up on gently pulling the trigger; her fingers were too frozen. She yanked the unfelt trigger. The rifle fired when it wanted to and not before.

Some dude did try to use the guardhouse for a hangout. He got a big surprise. Debbie might have overdone it. It blew out in all directions. One sheet of metal wall sliced another guy in half.

These really were hardcases. Their sins must be horrible and plentiful, to keep up the fight so they could wash away Petrograd and tens of thousands of women and children.

Mary and her Marines dropped them one by one by one, but they just kept coming, even after being hit, in some cases hit two or three times.

Mary's hit took down two as they charged the command center, but another two made it into the building.

The candle upstairs in the operations center went out as the door slammed behind them.

Mary slung her rifle and slid down the ladder rungs as fast as she ever had in the mines. She trotted carefully for the command center.

Not carefully enough. A "dead" body rose up and aimed her way. Behind her, an automatic spoke three, four times, and the body did die sincerely this time.

Mary turned. A rather pale Ralph was holding his pistol with both hands, just like she'd taught him, still aimed at the fallen enemy.

"Thanks," Mary said, and raced for the door.

She need not have hurried. Above her, as she yanked open the door, an automatic barked. Machine pistols replied on full auto, but that didn't last very long.

Mary sprinted up the stairs. At the top she found two dead, sodden bodies, machine pistols close at hand. Ruth was relighting the candle.

"Your shoulder's bleeding," Mary said.

"Yeah, I guess one of them got me," Ruth said, as matter-of-fact as any Marine.

Mary went to slap a bandage on the wound as Ruth gently settled to the deck.

"Dear God, don't let anyone shoot Trouble," Mary heard Ruth pray before she passed out cold and fell over.

SEVENTY-FOUR

TROUBLE WAS GLAD to be in one piece, but other than that, there wasn't a whole lot to be glad about this miserable morning.

It was cold, muddy, and wet in all of Mother Nature's variety. It had actually snowed for five minutes, causing a few Marines to break into song about a white Christmas.

A few artillery shorts put an end to that levity.

Artillery put an end to way too much. Maybe someone on the other side of the hill was getting smarter, or maybe the tubes were drooping, but more shells fell short of the second trench line and into the bit of ground where Trouble had spread out his Marines to wait between the second and final trench lines.

And friendly artillery wasn't doing as good a job of keeping the heads down up above. More and more fire came from there. To Trouble, it didn't seem like his friendly artillery was any less heavy. Maybe it was as Gunny was wont to say: "The really big scumbags who thought they could stay safe in the third line are now finding out different."

Everything pointed to the next fight being unshirted hell.

In all the hammering noise of the battlefield, a new pop drew Trouble's attention to where the Highlanders had their command post. A rocket arched up into the rain.

The colonel was signaling the artillery to pour it on for fifteen minutes, then check fire for the infantry to finish the fight.

A lightning bolt took the rocket in midair before it could blossom. If it exploded, it was lost on Trouble.

And likely lost on the forward artillery observer.

Trouble waited for the next flare. He waited a long time.

It didn't come.

Scowling at the luck, Trouble retrieved a rifle from beside a poncho that now served as a body bag, checked its load, pocketed two extra magazines, and began to make his way toward the Highlanders' CP.

He took a few near misses and shot a few rounds back for the favor. He arrived at the CP just as a young woman was taking off at a run for the rear.

"She's my last messenger," Colonel Stewart muttered. "Three guys didn't make it."

"She'll make it," the color sergeant at his elbow said. "She's the fastest runner in the battalion."

She ran like a gazelle; fast, steady on her feet, through mud, into shell holes and up again. Shots followed her, but she forced them to take deflection shots, zigging and zagging to throw them off.

"Smart girl," the color sergeant whispered.

But an artillery shell doesn't care how smart you are. It just swats you down with no mercy, and a shell caught her in midstride as she leapt out of the second-line trenches.

"Damn," came from all hands in the CP.

"What's wrong with the Very pistol?" Trouble asked.

The colonel pointed the antique at the sky and pulled the trigger. There was a click and nothing else.

Trouble shrugged at the fates. "I'll take the message."

"You got a command to lead, sir," the color sergeant said. "I'm up next."

"You got your thirty years in, McPherson," the colonel said. "Your approved retirement papers are in your pocket."

"And likely too wet to read, Colonel. I'm the one to go. If an old sweat like me can't get there, then no one can."

"You've used up all your luck, Color Sergeant," the colonel said.

"So I'll use guile, sir," and the sergeant ditched most of his gear before starting out at a low crouch. He walked at first, then dropped into shell holes just as the automatic weapons from the trench line above began to chatter.

Around Trouble, kilted men laid down cover fire. A man with a knee mortar popped off rounds. Trouble joined in the volleys.

Now the color sergeant was crawling and slithering from

shell hole to shell hole, just a bit of moving mud almost impossible to tell from the rest. He tumbled into a section of the second trench line and crawled out of it a good ten feet to the left of where he went in.

Random shells flew close, but he ran at a crouch. Rifle fire and machine guns reached for him, but he slipped away from them untouched.

Trouble spent part of his time providing cover fire and the other part glancing over his shoulder and half cheering, half praying him on.

The color sergeant was almost to the first trench line when a long shell hit behind him and blew him into the air.

He crumpled into the mud and just lay there. From the trenches above, fire picked up, reaching out for the fallen Highlander. Trouble turned and quickly emptied his magazine at any muzzle blasts that sparked before him.

"He's got him," drew Trouble's attention back to the color sergeant.

A trooper, muddy bandage covering the crown of his head and one eye, had crawled from a shell hole and latched onto the sergeant. Together, they slipped and slid back to that hole. Trouble only started breathing again when the two disappeared into what safety that muddy hole offered.

"We'll need another runner," the colonel said with a sigh.

"Maybe not, sir," Trouble said.

The soldier who'd saved the sergeant was up, out of the hole, dragging himself through the mud, sliding and slipping toward the first trenches. He rolled into one, disappeared for what seemed like forever before pulling himself up, and again crawled and slid down the mountain.

Above them, a mortar gave vent to the 1st Corps' rage, reaching out, falling first long, then short, then left, then right of the trooper. He slipped into a shell hole as the next round landed right behind him. Three more rounds hit in rapid succession, then the mortar fell silent.

And the trooper was on his feet, stumbling forward, slipping but getting back up to fumble his way some more. He found a friendly bit of mud, sat on his rump, and slid a good twenty feet downhill as the mortar again tried to reach for him but missed.

Then two Highlanders were helping support the man and hurrying him from the battle's hell.

Trouble stumbled and slid his own way back to his company. "Get ready for the last push," he told Gunny, and The Word went down the line.

Ahead of them, the artillery maelstrom grew worse, if that was possible. Marines edged forward. They'd done this before. They knew the risks that came from holding back and the chances of friendly fire if they didn't.

Most Marines drew close to their own fire, their bellies as low as the mud and muck would allow.

Then the firestorm ended with deafening quiet. "Grenadiers, lay it on them!" Trouble shouted.

Grenades arched up to the trenches. The grenadiers reloaded and fired again. That was good because heads and guns were coming up along the parapet.

Mother Nature seemed to pause, herself intent on the freezing, muddy tableau. The rain held back, though the lightning continued to provide strobe lighting to the night's tragedies.

Marines ran for the trenches, pausing a moment to add their own suppressing fire, dropping one target above them before dashing on.

This time, there were no boots huddling at the bottom of the trench. Men fought, and men died. They died blown to a pulp by grenades. They died as a bullet to the face blew their brains into the back of their helmet. They died as they fought hand-to-hand with knives or were held down in the muddy water to drown.

Men fought, and men died. It wasn't always the better man who lived. Luck played a fickle role in the freezing dark.

But skill and training were not to be ignored. Marines and Highlanders fought to save a buddy.

Few of the hostiles seemed to care about anyone but themselves.

Defeated, they turned from their acquaintances and fled. Marines and Highlanders shot them down. Or tried. Too often, armored backs held the rounds at bay.

But the force of hits knocked people off their feet to sprawl facedown in the mud.

So Marines shot them again until they gave up and rolled over, filthy hands in the air.

Some did make their escape, bringing the news of defeat to those below.

Four companies of trained Marines and Highlanders had defeated three brigades of Savannah's best infantry. At least they'd defeated as many of the three brigades as were not in the drunk tank and were willing to dig themselves in and try their hand at stopping the just wrath of a vengeful people.

In the end, some fled, some surrendered, some wounded begged for aid, and others pulled a grenade, pistol, or knife and ended their own lives. The Marines held back until the locals could sort themselves out, then carefully took those willing to be prisoners into custody.

As if nature finally had had enough, the storm blew itself out, and a quarter moon cast dim light on the slaughter field. Trouble chose his better surviving troops to dig in on the side of the hill facing Camp Milassi but was content to rest there.

The Highlanders did the same. With their companies reduced to little more than reinforced platoons, there wasn't a lot of choice in the matter.

The gun bunnies struggled up the hill, stringing landline that had been carefully kept out of the reach of the EMP blast, and then settled into holes, ready to call in artillery on Camp Milassi and its occupants.

Trouble cast a worried eye toward the dam but could see nothing.

Good or bad, news will come when it comes, he reminded himself, and made the rounds of his troops.

Dawn would bring its own set of problems.

Or not, as it proved.

Come sunrise, there was little activity in the camp. Tanks and infantry fighting vehicles were parked where they'd been before the pulse, but other than them, there wasn't much to see.

"What all is that?" Gunny asked Trouble, pointing at litter strewn about the camp.

The Marine officer focused his binoculars on the camp and laughed. "Gunny, thems is uniforms. Uniforms, shed, no doubt, by people who think it's better to be seen running in your skivvies than in uniform."

"Do tell, sir. Do tell."

Trouble meandered over to the 4th Highlanders' CP. "When do you plan to stroll into that camp?"

"Someone has to do it sooner or later," Colonel Stewart said with no suggestion which he'd chosen.

"I'm ready when you are," Trouble allowed.

"Latest rumor I've caught is that the 2nd Highlanders have been awarded the honor of cleaning out that rats' den. Don't you miss the company of a good radio? Anyway, until I hear different, we can catch our breath up here."

Trouble returned to his much-reduced company and kept overwatch as the 2nd Highlanders' trucks delivered them to a thousand meters from the camp. The kilted laddies dismounted, fixed bayonets, and cautiously approached the camp in skirmish lines.

Fire was light. Most of it involved despondent men who had delayed their final leave-taking. A few chose suicide by light infantry. To show yourself under arms was a quick death sentence. Some men did straggle in, having reconsidered that it might be safer to surrender to soldiers than be caught by civilians.

The sun brought back the heat of the last few weeks. With all the mud and water, Black Mountain was soon a steaming swamp stinking of shit and death. The exhausted troops were grateful when Trouble ordered them to pack it in and head down the mountain.

They went down the same side they'd fought up. That joined them with the others who had been released earlier to treat the wounded and retrieve the dead.

At the foot of the mountain there was a line of ambulances from Petrograd, ready to rush any wounded off to local care. A fire-department helicopter even waited, rotors spinning slowly, to take those who warranted true speed.

"Kind of nice to see folks care about us," Gunny observed.

"Yeah, nice," Trouble said, catching eye of a line of ponchos, a good two dozen long, giving decent privacy to Marines who would never be rushed again.

Just as Trouble was getting back to the gun line, a gun truck with 2nd Highlander markings drove up.

Ruth shot from it into his muddy arms.

"You're alive. You're alive," she shouted, and mumbled as she covered his muddy face with kisses.

When he managed to come up for air, he used it to ask, "What's wrong with your arm?"

She made a dismissive face. "I got hit by a ricochet from a bastard I'd already killed," she said.

"You got hit!"

"It's not bad. You'd say it was just a flesh wound."

"And I'd be lying through my teeth."

Ruth giggled. "I'll remind you of that next time you get banged up."

"Woman, what am I going to do with you?"

"I'd love to have a baby," she said, eyes gleaming.

"We'll have to do something about that when there's not so much of a crowd around," Trouble said to laughter from all his troops in listening range.

SEVENTY-FIVE

ALL GENERAL RAY Longknife wanted to do was head for the door, for home and his wife and her growing belly. But you don't walk out on a place like Savannah that easily.

There was a new president to swear in.

The president asked for an inauguration parade that sure looked more like a victory parade for the peacekeepers than any inauguration Ray had ever seen.

And the new president insisted General Ray Longknife share the place of honor in the reviewing stand with him.

The parade went off without a hitch. It included, along with those marching, a lot of walking wounded and other troopers in worse shape riding in cars and waving whatever they had that wasn't bandaged.

At the head of the parade was a convertible with two soldiers: Color Sergeant McPherson and newly promoted Sergeant Halverson. They sported what had to be the ugliest medal in human history, the wine-colored ribbon and dull gunmetal gray of the Victoria Cross.

Another thing Lorna Do had borrowed, some said ripped off, from Old Earth.

The people turned out to cheer and, for once, or maybe as a start, there were no brawls between the different nationalities that made up Savannah's diverse and divisive population.

The professor took pains to mention that to General Ray Longknife. "I think you've helped us pull together. To see ourselves as one, not many. To turn us into a melting pot instead of piles of slag to be thrown at each other."

"I hope so."

Shanghaied himself onto the reviewing stand, Ray insisted that Ruth Tordon stand at his left hand. She and her Marines at the dam had stood solid and turned what could have been months of soggy cleanup into a wonderful day of celebration.

Ray was none too sure, but it looked like the Marines under her husband, Trouble, rendered their honors a bit early for the president but perfect for his wife.

Ah, to be young and in love. Which reminded Ray that he still qualified for both, assuming his pregnant wife had not given up on him.

He'd sent her an apologetic note and a full report of what he'd accomplished here. He was still waiting for an answer.

The embassy had orders to bring any message for him from Wardhaven right to him. Still, he was surprised to see Becky approach him with a flimsy.

And the alarmed look on her face.

"Is it my wife?"

"No, Ray, no. Rita's fine. It's that request you made for those kids from Santa Maria to come to Wardhaven. The second ship, the one with a kid named David and his grandfather, a priest. Their ship is overdue and presumed lost."

"How could that happen?" Ray demanded.

"Rita doesn't know. They sent a ship backtracking along the flight path to Santa Maria. All the way to Santa Maria. No ship. No wreckage. It's just vanished.

"That's impossible. Something's wrong."

"But what?" the diplomat asked.

Whatever it was, General Ray Longknife would get to the bottom of it.

SEVENTY-SIX

FATHER JOSEPH KNEW something was wrong. He just could not figure out how and why.

The skipper had insisted to all the passengers that there was no money to be made shipping cargo to Santa Maria and deadheading home with a few passengers. So he would make his money by doing a few side trips along the way.

There was a fortune to be had if he discovered a single Earth-type planet.

So, the trip back was taking sixteen jumps instead of eight.

David loved it. He got to see more stars and a whole lot of different planets.

They were making their eighth jump when matters went horribly wrong.

David had his eyes glued to the forward screen in the lounge. Joseph was reading his prayer book. Both were strapped into chairs that were snapped down solid to the deck so the zero gee would cause them as few problems as possible as they went softly through the jump.

"What's that?" David asked.

Joseph looked up from his prayers.

There was a ship right under their nose.

"Grandda, I've been studying the new ships they make," David said, "and none of them look like that."

Joseph had to agree. The ship was a huge ball with what looked like four engine nacelles equally spaced around the circumference.

Humans always put their engines in the rear.

If there was any doubt as to the surprise here, the strange ship disappeared when the *Prosperous Goose* flipped ship as it would need to if the skipper wanted to go back through the jump he's just come out of.

Suddenly, there was a loud racket, and the pressure in Joseph's ears went wrong.

"Hull breach aft," the PA system announced. "Hull breach aft."

The ship continued its flip all the way around, giving them another look at the strange ship. They got several looks at it as their ship continued to flip over and over again.

They also got a good look at what was going on across space from them. Several launches drew away from the other ship. They had people strapped to their outside.

Only the people weren't exactly people. Father Joseph tried to count the arms and legs of those strapped to the launches. He kept getting too many.

One flip, it looked like six. The next, eight. The next flip also came up eight.

"Grandda," David piped up, "those people have too many arms and legs. Eight I think."

"Yes, they may," Joseph agreed like a good grandda should.

"And there's something strange about their hands, Grandda."

"Come, David," his grandfather said. It wouldn't do to explain to a twelve-year-old that the strange people with too many arms and legs also appeared to be carrying weapons.

No sooner were they out of their seats and drifting toward the door than the PA system blared again. "All passengers report to the mess deck. All hands report to the mess deck. Chief Master at Arms report to the weapons locker. All hands with weapons experience report to the weapons locker."

"Oh dear," Father Joseph said, and aimed himself up the main spindle toward command country and away from the mess deck. Normally, a priest and preteen would have been stopped well short of the weapons locker, but normal was long gone.

He spotted the captain as he entered the security area, and shoved himself off on a collision course for him.

"Father, what the hell are you doing here?" the captain demanded as the priest hit the center of his back.

"Keeping you from a horrible mistake. Have you counted the number of aliens headed for us?"

"No, and who told you they were aliens?" was a weak comeback.

"My grandson and I were watching them approach when you announced your impending folly. You are outnumbered, and very likely outgunned. If you resort to force, we will lose, and very likely all die for your folly."

"I will not have a passenger, certainly not a priest, lecturing me," the captain said, but his words were hollow of the usual arrogance of one in his position.

Around him, sailors were looking at their weapons with a lot less enthusiasm.

"How many of these aliens did you count?" the second officer asked.

"There were a dozen launches headed our way, each with six to eight aliens hanging on the outside and likely more inside," the priest reported.

"Oh shit," came from several of the dozen men crowded around the weapons locker.

The second officer twisted in place to face the captain. "Skipper, he may be a sky pilot, but he can count. We're outnumbered on a ship that's not going anywhere. Do we really want to piss them off?"

The captain whirled on Father Joseph, something he could only do because he rested a restraining hand on the weapons locker. "Be it on your head, priest," he spat, but he seemed relieved to have the decision made and his hands washed of it.

"Chief Master at Arms, collect the guns and put them just inside the main hatch, then everyone muster on the mess deck," the captain ordered, and was quickly obeyed.

Father Joseph followed three sailors with the twelve rifles and six revolvers down the main spindle and this time pushed himself off on the mess deck.

All hands were mustering in the officer's wardroom, which also passed for the passenger lounge. Someone had broken out the spirits, and several of the passengers and crew were already well oiled.

The skipper announced that they were about to be boarded by creatures unknown, and they would not resist.

One passenger, a large, loud man, demanded a gun so he could fight "if the rest of you are yellow cowards."

Three women tearfully begged him not to endanger all of them.

It didn't matter. The captain had made the call. No one would offer resistance.

That done, more people adjourned to the bar, intent on drinking up the ship's full supply of spirits.

Several gathered around Father Joseph and joined him in prayer.

They were still praying when two creatures in gray space suits drifted up the spindle. They paused to study the passengers and crew, keeping them covered with something they treated like a weapon. They talked, but with their helmets on, the sound was very muffled.

A few moments later, one in a gold-colored space suit arrived. He had a human rifle in his hand. In a moment, one in a green suit joined him. That one held a box with all kinds of figures dancing upon it. He, too, said something, then doffed his helmet.

Father Joseph would bet the first words out of his mouth were "Thank God, the air didn't kill me," or the equivalent.

The gold suit eyed the helmetless one for a long minute, which might count for even longer since he had four eyes and was able to almost see around to behind him. Then he took his helmet off, too.

And immediately said something. He seemed to grow angry when no answer was forthcoming.

With a fast act of contrition, Father Joseph pushed himself off from David and drifted toward the aliens. He held up one finger. "One." A second finger. "Two." And went from there to five.

The alien showed no reaction. Then he held up his hand. It looked like he had two opposing thumbs and only two fingers in between them. He held up one thumb. "Ow." A finger. "Due." A second finger. "Fin." And the second thumb. "Tin."

Clearly, language was not going to come easy.

The gold-suited one eyed Father Joseph for a moment longer, then said something to the one in green. He produced a rope and began tying the priest's wrist. Quickly, he added David to the line, then the captain, then more. Before he was done, one of the grays took the line and began hauling them down the spindle.

"They move through zero gee as if they were born to it," Father Joseph said.

"Who knows, maybe they are," the skipper said.

And got cuffed on the mouth for it by a gray suit they were passing.

"Don't talk," Father Joseph whispered to his grandson.

The youth nodded back.

The priest closed his eyes and allowed himself to be tugged along.

Dear God, what door have you opened to me now?

Father Joseph tried to make it a prayer . . . and not a cry of despair.

Her Imperial Highness the Grand Duchess Victoria Maria Teresa Inez Smythe-Peterwald, daughter of wealth and power, was raised to do little except be attractive and marry well. Then everything changed—her brother, her father's favorite and the heir apparent, was killed in battle by Lieutenant Kris Longknife, daughter of the Peterwalds' longtime enemies. Vicky vowed revenge, but her skill set was more suitable for seduction than assassination, and she failed. Angry and disappointed, her father decided she needed military training and forced her to join the Navy.

Now Ensign Vicky Peterwald is part of a whole new world, where use of her ample charms will not lead to advancement. But her father is the Emperor, and what he wants he gets. What he wants is for Vicky to learn to be efficiently ruthless and deadly.

Though the lessons are hard learned, Vicky masters them—with help from an unexpected source: Kris Longknife.

ABOUT THE AUTHOR

Mike grew up Navy. It taught him early about change and the chain of command. He's worked as a bartender and cabdriver, personnel advisor and labor negotiator. Now retired from building databases about the endangered critters of the Pacific Northwest, he's having a lot of fun reading and writing.

Mike lives in Vancouver, Washington, with his wife, Ellen, and close to his daughter and grandchildren. He enjoys reading, writing, dreaming, watching grandchildren for story ideas, and upgrading his computer—all are never-ending.

He's hard at work on the first of three Iteeche War novels as well as the next books in the universe of the Jump Points: *Kris Longknife: Tenacious* and *Vicky Peterwald: Target*.

You can learn more about Mike and all his books at his website mikeshepherd.org, e-mail him at Mike_Shepherd@ comcast.net, or follow Kris Longknife on Facebook.

FROM
MIKE MOSCOE

Author of the national bestselling
Kris Longknife series as MIKE SHEPHERD

THEY ALSO
SERVE

- A Jump Universe Novel -

Colonel Ray Longknife and Marine Captain Mary Rodrigo
were once enemies in an interstellar war. Now they're working
together to keep the peace.

When a bad space jump flings their starship thousands of
light-years away from home, they make an amazing discovery:
a planet inhabited by the descendants of a ship's crew—lost
three hundred years earlier.

Longknife is eager to welcome the population back into
the fold of humanity. But Rodrigo is suspicious. She senses
that something is wrong under the planet's veneer of peace and
prosperity. And she's right....

PRAISE FOR *THE FIRST CASUALTY*

"A lot of fun."

—Jack McDevitt, Nebula Award–winning author

"Good escapist fare."

—*Locus*

mikemoscoe.com
penguin.com

An original military science fiction novella from
MIKE SHEPHERD

KRIS LONGKNIFE: Welcome Home / Go Away

A Penguin Group Special from Ace

Kris Longknife is back home from her galactic adventures, but her entire Fleet of Discovery has been annihilated. And the alien race that she fought has now declared war on humanity. Some people think Kris is to blame, and it may take more than the efforts of her war-hero great-grandfather to save her from the wrath of the angry—and frightened—citizens of her home planet!

• • •

Praise for the Kris Longknife series

"A rousing space opera that has extremely entertaining characters."   —*Night Owl Reviews*

"Kris can kick, shoot, and punch her way out of any dangerous situation, and she can do it while wearing stilettos and a tight cocktail dress."   —*Sci Fi Weekly*

Only available as an e-book!
Download it today!

facebook.com/AceRocBooks
mikeshepherd.org
penguin.com

M1140T1013